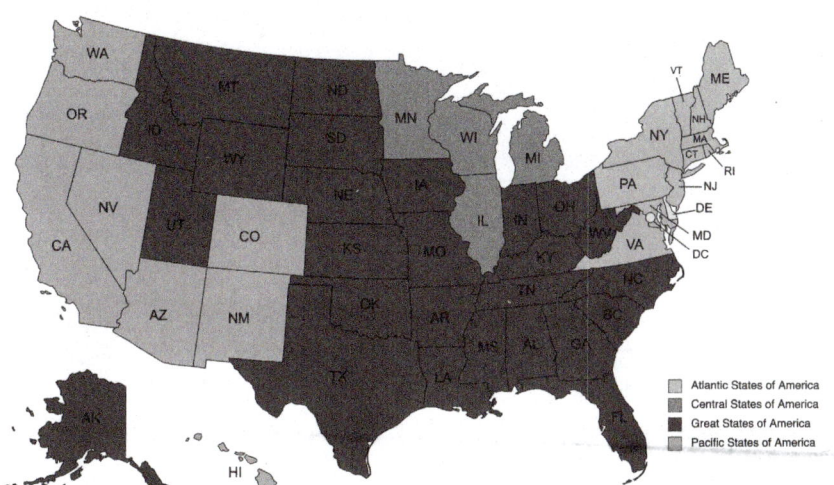

Map of the Former United States of America, 2026

MINE!

A Novel of The Trump

GEORGE MERLIS

JAAND Books

Copyright © 2022 George Merlis

All rights reserved

The characters and events portrayed in this book are fictitious. Any similarity to real persons, living or dead, is coincidental -- despite the familiar names of some characters -- and not intended by the author.

No part of this book may be reproduced, or stored in a retrieval system, or transmitted in any form or by any means, electronic, mechanical, photocopying, recording, or otherwise, without express written permission of the publisher.

Cover design by: George Merlis

This book is dedicated to Sue Merlis, to our children, Jimmy and Andy Merlis, and to their children (in birth order): Jasper, Zeke, Vanessa, Ollie, Coco, Fiona and Quintin.

I hope none of you ever finds yourself living in a country even vaguely resembling the dystopia of the Great States of America.

THE TRUMP

The lapsed monk, Stepan Arkadyevich Oblonsky, said: "Q is the name of the missing gospels. You see, the Gospels of Matthew, Mark, and Luke were written well after the death of the Savior. So, they were writing about what they had not witnessed. Mark was written first and has the least amount of material, so the others must have had another source: and that source — the missing gospel — is called Q."

He continued: "The concept of The Christ — not the name, Jesus Christ, but the title — The Christ, is based on the Old Testament concept of the Messiah. That Old Testament Messiah, or The Christ, is the one who will lead the Hebrews to redemption. In the New Testament, The Christ is the physical manifestation of God; He is God's son and physical manifestation all in one body. So Q, who is named for the missing gospel, can preach that The Trump is personification of God's will; the Lord's orders for humankind physically manifested."

Sofia Ivanova Pushkina took the fact that a bolt of lightning had not torn through the window and struck Oblonsky dead as a sure sign there was no God. She stopped listening to his theological droning. She did, however, like the idea of The Trump as the embodiment of God's will. Q could use that.

ACKNOWLEDGEMENTS

My thanks to James Madison, author of the Constitution of the United States and to the 39 of the 55 delegates to the Philadelphia Convention who signed the document.

You guys nailed it; except for the slavery stuff and for depriving women full citizenship. But rest easy in your graves; subsequent generations took care of those items.

My thanks, also, to the late Professor Wallace E. Davies of the University of Pennsylvania, and to the many historians whose books made history come alive for me. Thanks, too, to the memoirists, biographers and autobiographers whose work continues to inform and inspire.

A special thank you to my wife, Sue Merlis whose support, inspiration, spelling prowess, grammatical exactitude and editing skills kept the following 80,000 words from turning into a tower of babel.

PROLOGUE

Want to know something? Everything is mine. You know, everything. – Donald J. Trump

The Playground, Forest Hills, Queens, New York City, United States Of America, August, 1947

Toes turned out, legs bowed, the toddler half-fell, half-walked forward.

"Careful, Honeyboy," his mother called. "Be careful. Don't go too fast." He toddled faster.

Honeyboy had long, wild reddish-blond hair, fine as corn silk. The humid breeze lifted and whipped it into a frenzied dance.

He was plump, even for a toddler. The heat and the exertion of stumbling forward had turned his ruddy complexion stopsign red. Sweat flowed down his brow and into his eyes, stinging them.

He staggered forward another two steps, teetering dangerously, then fell back, his butt made contact with the playground cement, the landing softened some by his freshly-filled diaper. He felt no discomfort on that score; only the sweltering New York heat and humidity annoyed him.

Honeyboy's stare was fixed on a big, yellow metal Tonka dump truck, nearly one-third his size and likely half his weight. The Holy Grail of toys, was two, maybe staggers away. He studied it. He wanted it. He would take it. It would be his.

He was oblivious to the stream of teething spittle running down his chin and onto his cotton shirt; he was conscious only of the Tonka truck. He rocked back and forth and with elaborate effort regained his footing. Another step. Then his mother spotted the target.

"Honeyboy, that's someone else's truck. It's not your toy. We have to ask if we can play with it."

She looked around: eight, maybe nine toddlers, nearly a dozen three- to four-year-olds; it was impossible to identify the truck's owner, she would have to wait until he made himself known after Honeyboy took possession of it. There were sure to be tears.

MINE!

"Honeyboy, let's go on the swings."

He heard the words but recognized only "Honeyboy." He ignored the summons.

He reached the truck and began pushing it toward the recessed sand box where other toddlers were playing. They were concentrating intensely, picking up sand with their hands or with toy shovels and spilling it back in small piles.

He was three staggers from the sandbox when his mother swooped him up. He brought the truck up with him until its full weight forced him to open his tiny fat fingers. As it fell, he screamed, "M-M-MINE!" It was his first word other than Moma and Dada.

The truck crashed to the ground. Noisily. He looked down at it, then at the sandbox and the other toddlers playing in it. Then back down to the truck. He opened his mouth wide and let out a high-pitched wail: "MIIIIIINE!" followed by, "Waaaaaaiiiiiiiii!" Eighty decibels; painful to anyone close by — that is to say, his mother. She could not believe such small lungs could make such a sustained loud sound.

A second scream, even louder, ninety-five decibels: "WAIIIIIIIIIIIIIII!"

Everyone — toddlers, kids, parents, nannies, dogs on leashes, squirrels in the trees, crows in the sky — turned. All eyes were on him. Him! A third one: "WAAAAAAAAAAEEEEEEEEEEIIIIII!" One hundred and eight decibels. Long and loud. Painful; even his ears hurt. No one turned away; they stared at him, transfixed by a sound and volume totally new to them.

The center of wide-eyed attention, Honeyboy launched the next phase of his show: tears and a succession of loud wails, sobs, screams. He erupted; a volcanic tantrum. Tears did not roll so much as fly down his cheeks. The cries came steadily, with barely a breath between them. Drool covered his chin. Snot jetted from his nose. He struggled to catch enough breath to power the next burst. Arms and legs flailed in anger. Repeatedly, he kicked his mother; so she set him down on his feet. He threw himself to the ground, rolled over on his back, paused for a nanosecond to draw a huge breath and then started all over again.

Other toddlers began to cry. A couple of them stood up in the sandbox and looked around for their mommies or nannies. Desperate at not seeing them immediately they melted into tantrums of their own. The screaming and sobbing was contagious. Some of the older kids, the three- and four-year-olds, began to cry, too. Mothers and nannies rushed around the playground and into the sandbox to rescue their frantic kids. It was a cacophony of frustration, fear, anger — crying, screaming, wailing, all of it high-pitched. Some toddlers were pounding the sand, causing little puffs of ejecta to fly up and hit their faces, which only fed their hysteria. Little cheeks were turning red with inarticulate frustration. Even the three- and four-year-olds were having trouble finding words. There was a universal chorus of screaming.

Honeyboy silently surveyed the turmoil he had started; the Tonka truck forgotten. Who needed a yellow truck when you had this?

"We're getting out of here. We're going home," his mother said. She swept him up.

He did not understand the words, but understood her intent. He switched his tantrum on once more.

Chaos! His mother put him down. He saw the Tonka truck and remembered how it had all started. He put the toy back on its wheels and pushed it into the sandbox full of screaming toddlers. The wheels sank into the sand and the truck stopped short of striking the nearest clot of children.

CHAPTER ONE

I am your voice. I alone can fix it. I will restore law and order. — Donald J. Trump

The Basement, Mar-A-Lago, Palm Beach Florida, Great States Of America, August, 2026

Stately, plump Donald Trump stalked down the basement hallway bearing the iPhone on which he had been thumbing a series of truculent denunciations, dire threats and whining complaints of, to and about a variety of individuals, foes and realities. He had unleashed his customary morning blizzard of digital grievance; the only commonalities of the snowflakes in that storm were the abundant misspellings, errant CAPITALIZATIONS and pervasive mendacity.

He stood in the doorway, wearing only black socks, a billowing opaque plastic operating room cap and a prissy-blue paper examining gown untied at the back. His habitual twelve-degree forward tilt made the gown billow out, hiding his obesity while exposing his flabby white buttocks to anyone following him. His garb was silly but he knew he was a giant among pigmies, an ocean liner amid rowboats, a skyscraper towering over hovels. His self-regard convinced him he was handsome and appealing despite the omission thus far today of the fifty-minute grooming regime that rendered him camera-ready when in public. Others might consider him pale and sickly now; he didn't see it that way. In the mirror this morning he had seen an image of health, wealth, power and intelligence.

A brass plaque on the door in front of him read:

> "On August 8, 2020, a team of 50-heavily armed FBI agents in full combat dress raided my beautiful home, Mar-a-Lago and planted evidence in this storeroom as part of a Democrat Deep State plot to incriminate me. — Donald J. Trump, 45th President of the United States of America."

Gotta update that plaque; not just 45th President of US; first President of the Great States of America. I'm GSA's George fucking Washington!

Soon his likeness would be on the country's money and stamps. There was no need to abide by the United States' outmoded rule that only deceased leaders be so honored; GSA could use the British example: the reigning head of state's portrait adorning currency, coinage and postage. A fine branding opportunity; a multiple-times-a-day reminder of who's the boss.

MINE!

He stepped into the room that had once contained 47 banker boxes haphazardly stuffed with official United States documents, well over 100 of which were classified as Confidential, Secret, Top Secret or Top Secret Compartmented. It remained an aggressively utilitarian space: white walls, institutional fluorescent lighting, grey vinyl flooring, no pictures on the walls, no adornment whatsoever. Its sole unique feature was a machine: the Vaian Linear Accelerator; not just any Vaian Linear Accelerator; *his* Vaian Linear Accelerator.

A million bucks, that thing. An accelerator. You think of accelerator, I think of the gas pedal in a car, not that thing. A million-dollar accelerator. Another four hundred and fifty thousand to renovate the room, build that control room. Radiation shielding in the walls, the ceiling. Weighs 17,000 pounds. What's that? Fifty-nine, sixty bucks a pound? My fucking money, too.

His personal money had not paid for the accelerator and the room renovation, the project had been written off as a campaign expense, but Trump saw no distinction between his political war chest and his personal bank accounts. He had been reluctant to pay for the medical gear with campaign funds until Chief of Staff Stephen Miller convinced him that if government money covered the costs, there was a danger his diagnosis would leak to the media.

His glanced at the big glass window to the control room.

Control room, they call it. Me, I call this a fishbowl. One guy sits there, looks through a big glass window to see what he's doing. That's a fishbowl, not a control room. Four hundred and fifty thousand. And a linoleum floor. You never saw linoleum in a Trump building. Ugly. A million for the machine, four hundred and fifty thousand to ruin a perfectly good storeroom on top of the million. For that kind of money, it should look good. Do the walls in a different color — a white with a little pink in it; makes everybody look healthier. Too late now; I'm not spending another buck to fix it. Who sees it, anyway?

Two of his bodyguards — WRMs — followed him into the room. The acronym stood for Well-Regulated Militia, but without a vowel to guide pronunciation, everyone followed the presidential example and called them WORMs. Unlike the Secret Service bodyguards back in the United States, with their cheap suits, white shirts and narrow ties, WORMs wore uniforms: black fatigues, black berets, black jump boots, black ballistic vests, black fingerless gloves. On their shoulders was the only color they sported, round bright yellow patches embroidered with crossed black assault rifles above the letters: WRM and the words, in capital letters: PRAESIDIS FIDES ABSOLUTUS — Absolute Loyalty to the President.

The technician, a dark-complexioned man in his mid-forties wearing a long white lab coat, came out of the control room. One of the WORMs watched him warily; the other WORM stood behind the president, facing into the hallway, ignoring the bare presidential ass. Both WORMs had their

XM-5s slung across their chests, both had their fingers on the trigger guards of the weapons.

Fucking trigger-happy WORMs. Don't like that. Never liked that. A sneeze away from shooting off their foot. Worse, my foot. They were told not to do that. Why do they have to do that, keep their fingers up by the trigger? All four years in the U.S., I never saw a Secret Service schmuck draw a weapon much less put his finger near the trigger. These guys, these WORMs, they got their fingers on top of the trigger all the time. What happened in Tulsa; that should have ended their trigger-happy shit.

What happened in Tulsa was, to use Trump's term for it, a clusterfuck of the first magnitude. The traveling vice presidential WORM team, 100 men and two women strong, was bringing VP Tucker Carlson to the BOK Center for a rally. A WORM, stationed at the far end of the parking lot — well away from the VP and his immediate protectors — saw a feral dog. Or maybe it was a coyote. He made a split-second decision to take it out and fired a hastily-aimed single round at the creature. The entire WORM team reacted as if they had been fired on. Everyone began shooting and kept shooting until their ammo clips were empty. Some of them went through a second clip and a few closest to the vice president went through three clips. No one pulled the vice president to the ground and covered him with their own body. They did not form a flying wedge to get him into the interior of the building or back to his armored SUV; they were too busy shooting 30-round clips at imagined assailants. After enough of them ran out of ammo, they clustered around Carlson and rushed him to the SUV, which roared off to the airport without the rest of his protective motorcade. The vice-presidential SUV hit four parked cars on the way to the airport, but Carlson was delivered safely to his plane, which blasted down the runway the instant the hatch shut behind him. He had taken his seat, but not fastened his seat belt when the wheels left the ground. Half the members of his immediate protective detail were left on the tarmac, inhaling jet fumes.

The Oklahoma State Bureau of Investigation found 3,244 brass shell casings, a lot of shattered glass, 89 damaged cars, five demolished trash bins, and eight damaged light posts. No humans were killed or injured except for the nine WORMs who got first-degree burns to their fingers when they touched the overheated barrels of their rifles. Even the dog — or coyote — was unharmed. Physically. There was no way of knowing what effect dodging 3,244 rounds of ammunition had on its psyche.

A subsequent Congressional hearing found the WORMs had responded to a distant sniper who took a single shot at the vice president, missed and immediately fled. That was the story introduced to the world by Tucker Carlson, himself, in an hour-long, primetime return to his alma mater, Fox News. The special report won stunning acclaim from his faithful viewers who had been missing his nightly hour of bitching and moaning. The ratings were so high, Fox re-ran the program five times in different dayparts. The best part: Fox got Carlson back on the air without having to pay him; it was all profit.

Congress appropriated nine million dollars to give the WORMs a six-week training course before letting them get close to the president or vice president. During the six weeks, the Palm Beach city police and the Palm Beach County Sheriff's Department provided protection to Trump and Carlson. The cops and deputies were professional, courteous and caused no incidents, unlike the WORMs, who had a history of frequent arrests for off-duty DUI, brawling and vandalism infractions.

Two days of that WORM training was mandated and named by the president himself: "Trigger Respect." Trump had attended a military prep school as a teen and claimed to be more familiar with weaponry than any soldier, militia member, WORM or hunter. Although he had not hefted or pointed any weapons more serious than his right index finger for close to 70 years, he was right about the WORMs' distressing habit of always keeping their fingers on the trigger guards of their assault rifles; an especially grievous habit since they also always had a round in the chamber and had their safeties clicked off. Trigger Respect was designed to teach the WORMs to keep their fingers off the trigger guards unless they were in a threatening situation. It was hard to break the habits they had learned back in the 20-teens and early 2020s when they were a rabble of Proud Boys, Oath Keepers and Three Percenters, so most of them constantly backslid on Trigger Respect.

The best thing to come of the Tulsa debacle: it gave Trump a reason to bar Carlson from doing any more rallies; he was just too good a performer at them; he reminded Trump of Trump. "The Vice President is clearly a target of Antifa fanatics and for his own protection, we have mutually decided to keep his public appearances to a minimum," said a statement attributed to both men. Carlson saw it for the first time when it was reported by his former Fox News colleagues.

The other good thing that emerged: it gave Donald Trump something else to complain about. A world-class grievance monger, little pleased him more than loudly bitching. He did that now, poking a pudgy digit at the WORM's weapon.

"You wanna take your finger off of the trigger, WORM?"

"Sorry, sir." The WORM moved the offending finger.

Great! The WORM had given him another grievance to complain about: "Excellency, son! Not sir. It's 'sorry, Excellency!'"

"Sorry, Excellency."

Don't like that asshole's attitude. He should be guarding Melania or the kids or the fucking chief of staff. Finger on the trigger guard. Calling me sir. Fuck sir. It's Excellency.

Excellency! Before the inauguration, Trump had picked the honorific. John Adams, the first United States vice president — Washington's vice president — had wanted the president to be called "your executive majesty" or "your mightiness." Washington was having none of that; he selected "Mr. President" as the proper way to address the head of state. To Trump, Washington was too modest for his own good and — more importantly — for the good of his presidential successors, especially his 44th successor. For his new country, Trump rejected "Mr. President" and dictated "Excellency."

"You know who is a mister," Trump demanded of his staff, "The first guy teacher you had in grade school, the first man teacher. The owner of the grocery story. Those are misters. A president isn't a mister; a mister is a poor science teacher putz in a bad suit. 'Excellency,' that's a title for a president, 'Excellency!' What kind of branding is 'mister?' Crap branding is what it is. 'Excellency,' now that's branding. It's a value: *excellent*. You say 'mister' to me and I see the grocer or a faggot sixth grade algebra teacher. You say 'Excellency' and I see a leader. I see a *brand*. An excellent brand."

He was thereafter called "Your Excellency" or "Excellency." Except when people slipped and called him "Mr. President" or "sir."

"Excellency," the technician said, gesturing toward the step stool alongside the accelerator's couch. Trump didn't need the step stool because the technician had lowered the couch as far as it could go. He simply sat on it and swiveled on his butt to get his legs up on the couch.

"Now, if you would lie on your back with you head….."

"My fourth time, fella. I know how to do it. You don't gotta repeat it each time."

"Yes, Excellency."

"Where you from, anyway?" Trump asked.

"Orlando, originally, Excellency," the technician said.

Orlando? Not what I meant. I meant what are you? Indian or something? An Arab? Maybe he was Iranian. Latino? Who the fuck knows? It's gotta be okay if he gets this close to me, no matter where he comes from. Someone vetted the fucker. I hope.

Flat on his back, he closed his eyes. "Let's get this over with. I got phone calls to make and negotiating to do." The technician pushed a button and the couch lifted into position.

"If you need to stop, just say so, Excellency. I'll be able to hear you, there's a microphone on the gantry."

"I know, I know? Think I don't know? I know."

MINE!

Course I know. You say it every time; this is the fourth time. What am I? Stupid? Orlando thinks I'm stupid? Well, he's got another think coming, Orlando.

"I'll be right outside the door, Excellency" the "sir" WORM said. "And Falk will be in the control room with….." He did not need to say more.

With Orlando, the foreign tech. Falk would be in the fishbowl standing behind that guy. In that case, I don't give a shit he has his finger on the trigger guard. Fact, it'd be better he had his finger there. Let this Persian prick — if that's what he is — know he better not screw around. Where do they find them, these Orlandos? These medical techs? Can't tell me there aren't any competent Americans, real Americans, can work this gizmo. Americans probably designed it. Built it. Americans can work it. Where the hell are they, Americans that can work it?

The lead-lined door swung shut and he was alone for the first time since he rolled out of bed at 10 in the morning after a fitful night of half-sleep, quarter-sleep and no sleep. Alone with his thoughts.

Fuck you, prostate! Least no one knows. This clown, Orlando, a couple of doctors. A few WORMs, of course. They know I'm getting treated, but not what for. NDAs all around. And the doctors, they got no future this gets out, no future. Except the inside of a DLO detention cell.

His thought train was derailed by a crackling speaker mounted near the ceiling: "Starting in ten seconds, excellency."

Click, click, buzz, buzzz, buzzzzz.

Loud, but not that loud. Annoying, though. You look at that machine; that tower; the size of the thing, you expect a lot more noise. Like an MRI. Isn't that bad, the accelerator. And it doesn't last 20, 30 minutes. Not in a tunnel with your belly nearly touching the top of it. You'd think they could figure out a quieter way to do it. Guy comes up with that should get a Noble prize.

Trump often made that mistake; he assumed it was a prize awarded for noble achievement, rather than a prize named after Alfred Nobel.

What about my noble prize? Noble peace prize. Where was that? They give it to fucking Obama before he does anything, then he fucks up everything he touches. Do they take it back; say they made a mistake. No way. Me? They gave me squat. Nada. Bupkis. Nothing. No one deserved a Noble prize more than me. Did a lot more for peace, too. More than HUSSEIN Obama. No wars when Trump was president. No new wars, anyways. Give it to Obama and not to Trump. Sure they do. That's just racist, is what it is. Give it to the colored guy, but not the white guy.

"Just a few more minutes, your excellency," Orlando's voice was crackly over the speaker.

"Yeah, sure. I know."

A few more minutes, then fatigue, brain fog, pissing every five minutes, headache, bellyache, nausea. And a full day of being president.

◆ ◆ ◆

Whenever you see the words "sources say" in the fake news media, and they don't mention names, it is very possible that those sources don't exist but are made up by fake news writers. — Donald J. Trump

British Broadcasting Corporation Office, Palm Beach Business Center, West Palm Beach, Florida, Great States Of America

By BBC standards, Walter Cholmondeley – not yet 40 and with only ten years of broadcast reporting experience — was a noob, a novice, a rookie. Despite his inexperience, his bosses in London made him chief of the Great States of America bureau. They were motivated by impishness; they knew that every American he encountered would suffer multiple verbal pratfalls trying to pronounce his surname, forcing him to come to their rescue with, "It's Chumley."

The powers-that-were at Broadcasting House could only imagine the mischief they created, but every time Cholmondeley filed a report, they were reminded of their prank. And he filed a lot of reports; Walter Cholmondeley was one of the most productive journalists on the BBC's 250-person correspondent roster.

As a staff member in the Washington Bureau in the old United States, he had supplied blow-by-blow coverage of the disastrous 2024 election, the murderous rioting that followed it, the cratering of the nation, the formation of the four republics, and the drafting and adoption of the GSA constitution.

Six months ago, passport, BBC identification card and GSA work visa in hand, Cholmondeley presented himself at the presidential media office, impeccable in an off-the-peg suit that fit so well it looked bespoke.

The gaffers back in London would have been pleased; by noon, no fewer than four functionaries had stumbled over his name. Even Cholmondeley was amused.

Having more-or-less mastered his name, the press room staffers issued him a Class B credential which afforded him admission to the viewing room for press briefings but banned him from the briefing room, where he might ask a question.

Like other Class B journalists, he watched what they called The Morning Follies on a big screen TV, as the favored Class A credential holders got to toss questions at the Mar-a-Lago communications staff.

Class B was, all-in-all, a select company of some of the world's most illustrious outlets. In addition to the BBC, there were The Toronto Globe and Mail, CBC, Le Figero, Der Spiegel. Also relegated to Class B were North American outlets like The New York Times, The Washington Post, The Boston Globe, The Chicago Tribune, The Los Angeles Times, NBC, CBS, ABC. It was accepted as fact that CNN was Class B only because there was no Class C; Trump's long-running feud with the cable network had not abated despite CNN's hiring spree of conservative-leaning anchors, reporters and commentators that began in '22.

Class A credentials went only to the friendlies: Brietbart, InfoWars, the Christian Broadcasting Network, Steve Bannon's War Room, OANN, Newsmax and, despite Trump's on-again-off again feuds with the family patriarch, all outlets owned by the Murdochs. A few chosen foreign outlets enjoyed Class A credentials as well: The Times of London, The Sun — which were Murdoch properties, after all — as well as outlets controlled by friendly regimes: Putin's Tass and Pravda and Orbán's Magyar Jelen.

*

Cholmondeley had a boyish appeal; he reminded some of the young Hugh Grant in "Four Weddings and a Funeral," although he was better dressed. He appeared approachable; people cozied up to him and told him things. Despite his Class B credential, he'd broken some good stories. Until now, his proudest achievement was revealing an irony: despite Trump repeatedly labeling climate change a "hoax," the GSA had contracted to build a $3.5 billion seawall to protect Mar-a-Lago from the rising Atlantic Ocean.

Van DeLoon Engineering, a Dutch firm that was said to specialize in building dykes in its native Holland, had the contract. While the story won him plaudits from Broadcasting House, Cholmondeley had missed a big piece of it: there was no Van DeLoon Engineering; it was a shell corporation headquartered in a mail drop in Panama City, Panama and was wholly owned by Trump Enterprises. Had he dug deeper, he would have learned that Trump Enterprises tried to create a joint venture with the venerable Dutch engineering firm Van Oord, but that company refused to go along with the family slush fund appended to the project's budget. So Trump Enterprises poached several Van Oord engineers and created Van DeLoon. Unhappily for Mar-a-Lago, the poached engineers specialized in drainage, not seawall construction. Real seawall engineers would have told Cholmondeley that by mid-century the basement of the club-cum-government-office would be flooded to its ceiling and the first floor would have two-to-three inches of water intrusion every day at high tide.

Now, Cholmondeley had a bigger story; he had all of it, and he had it alone. It was the biggest story of his career. He began organizing the script the way he always did; silently reciting the opening lines of Rudyard Kipling's "I Keep Six Honest Serving-Men:

"I keep six honest serving-men

(They taught me all I knew);

Their names are What and Why and When

And How and Where and Who."

On a legal pad he re-ordered the old imperialist's serving-men to suit the story:

> Who: DJT, Pres. GSA
>
> What: Prost canc, progno poor, no to surg., rad treat
>
> How: Ndle biop
>
> When: 4, 5 mos. ago, decline biop '24
>
> Where: M-A-L (biopsy + treat, special, custom rm)

He wrote the story. Rewrote it. Rewrote the rewrite. He made a few tweaks to the rewrite of the rewrite. Then he read it silently from his laptop. Like a semiliterate, he moved his lips while he read; a trick of the trade to insure there were no words or phrases that would trip him up when he read it aloud. He timed his reading; London wanted four minutes. His reading came in at 4:40. He knew when he read it into the microphone it would be longer, likely more than five minutes. Let them deal with it at Broadcasting House.

He plugged the microphone into the laptop's USB port, opened the recording application and leaned forward so his mouth was exactly six inches away from the mic.

"Trump Prostate story, take one. In five.... four... three ... two....." He left the "one" unspoken, expanded his diaphragm to draw in a deep breath and then let the air flow, producing a deep, resonant, plummy, authoritative BBC radio voice; a voice speaking gold-standard British English. English English. Perfectly pronounced, regionally indistinguishable English. English, as they were fond of saying at the BBC, as God meant it to sound and likely as He, Himself, spoke it:

"BBC News have learned that Donald J. Trump, President of the Great States of America, has advanced metastatic prostate cancer. Mr. Trump's prognosis is considered poor.

"Five separate reliable sources close to or in the administration have told BBC that Mr. Trump was diagnosed between three and five months ago. According to these sources, Mr. Trump refused surgical removal of his prostate gland — the course of treatment recommended by his doctors at the time.

"According to two of the sources, Mr. Trump declined the surgery because it would have required a general anesthetic and that, in turn, would have required Mr. Trump to temporarily pass the duties of the presidency to his vice president, the former broadcaster, Tucker Carlson.

Mr. Trump has insisted that his diagnosis be kept confidential. It is unknown if Mr. Carlson has been informed of the president's illness.

"Three of BBC's sources said the president has been receiving radiation therapy in a medical suite clandestinely installed in the basement of Mar-a-Lago.

"Maintaining the secrecy surrounding Mr. Trump's diagnosis, treatment and prognosis is considered remarkable because Mar-a-Lago continues to operate as a private membership club in addition to serving as the Great States' executive mansion and executive office centre.

"As a club and a catering venue available for weddings and other events, Mar-a-Lago sees a steady flow of people in and out of the building, most of whom are not subject to security vetting nor to the administration's rigorous non-disclosure agreements.

"BBC's sources say Mr. Trump was warned that his PSA was unacceptably high in 2024, during the last presidential campaign in the United States. An Elevated PSA, or prostate specific antigen, is an early-warning sign of prostate cancer. At the time Mr. Trump declined to undergo a biopsy and continued campaigning.

"Several months ago, blood tests revealed his PSA was even higher, sources tell BBC. Mr. Trump relented at that time, samples were taken using a so-called needle biopsy. Those samples yielded the cancer diagnosis. Further testing, the sources tell BBC, revealed Mr. Trump's cancer has spread from his prostate to his bones.

"The Mar-a-Lago press office denied that Mr. Trump had any form of cancer but declined to further discuss his health. The media office also insisted BBC name its sources. BBC has declined to do so.

"Three sources told BBC Mr. Trump has designated Eric Frederick Trump, his son, as the successor to complete his six-year term should he die in office. Eric Trump is the youngest son from the first of the elder Mr. Trump's three marriages.

"Eric Trump is 40 and has no government experience. He has been managing Trump Enterprises, the real estate, media, manufacturing and financial services conglomerate owned by the Trump family. In selecting Eric, Donald Trump skipped over his two older adult children, Donald Trump Jr.

and Ivanka Trump. Our sources could not say definitively why Mr. Trump selected Eric, but they speculated it might be because the president continued to be displeased that Donald Junior and Ivanka submitted to interviews with the Congressional Committee investigating the January 6 insurrection.

"Eric Trump is being referred to within the highest administration circles as the president-select, although no such title exists in either the Great States of America's constitution or in its laws.

"President Trump has the power to change that situation because the constitution gives him the authority to create laws and have them take effect once they are ratified by a simple majority of the nation's single-chamber congress. Mr. Trump has not yet submitted a new law of succession. BBC's sources said he did not want to do that because he wants to keep his medical condition secret for as long as possible.

"In bypassing his elected vice president, Mr. Carlson, President Trump appears intent on creating a governing dynasty.

"Family dynasties are not unheard of in North America. The United States of America had two instances of father/son presidencies. John Adams and his son John Quincy Adams were the second and fifth presidents and George Herbert Walker Bush and George Walker Bush were the

41st and 43rd presidents. The difference, between the Adams and Bush presidencies and the possible presidency of Eric Trump, is that those United States presidents were elected by voters, while the younger Mr. Trump — if or when he assumes the presidency — will have been selected by his father.

"This is Walter Cholmondeley reporting from Palm Beach, Florida, GSA."

Cholmondeley played it back and timed it; five minutes 45 seconds. He looked over the script for trims. If they cut from the bottom, it would work, although he was fond of the bit about earlier dynastic presidents having been elected rather than selected; a nice touch, but expendable. If they wanted to shorten it, let them do it in London; he filed what he had recorded.

Five minutes after he sent the file the London radio news desk phoned. "What's your source, Mate?" No hellos, no attaboys, nothing but a gruff challenge in an East London accent; one of those street-smart journalists whose voice will never be heard on BBC because his accent betrayed his origin.

Cholmondeley said, "Sources. It's in the story; sources. There are three for the political stuff, two for most of the medical, three for some of the medical. I don't want to name them. The line might not be secure. The sources are in positions to know. You *do* know, people tell me things. They see me as trustworthy and tell me things."

"You would have made a fine priest," East London said.

"Not really. Not much of a believer. I think you need that to be a priest."

"Not always, mate. I've known a few choice ones in my time, priests. Okay, they wanted it shorter, but I'm going to fight with them about it. I think it's fine at this length and maybe should be a bit longer. This is big. And we have it exclusively?"

"Yes, *I* have it exclusively." Cholmondeley awarded himself the credit; it was his story.

"The United States becoming an autocracy," East London said. "A patrilineal autocracy."

"Not the United States. The Great States of America. Nothing united about it, as you well know," Cholmondeley said.

"I'm going to recommend six minutes," East London said. "You have stuff you can add?"

"Yes, I've got more. A lot more. I can add quite a bit about Eric. Personality angle, lack of experience. Running a family business that appears to be profiting from GSA government contracts. The Trump Organization fraud charges in New York in the past."

At that moment, the door to the office burst open and four men charged in. They wore black balaclavas, black bulletproof vests and black fatigues. They had assault rifles at the ready, fingers on the triggers. Not the trigger guards, but the actual triggers.

"Yer unner arrest," one of them bellowed.

Cholmondeley heard East London shouting over the phone: "What the hell's going on?" Before he could answer, one of the intruders grabbed the receiver out of his hand, dropped it on the floor and hit it with the butt of his XM5. The round in the chamber went off, sending a lead slug through the soundproof ceiling. The slug impacted the cement above the soundproofing, flattened and dropped to the carpet, missing the phone assassin's head by an inch.

"Shit, that wasn't supposed to happen."

While the phone killer examined his rifle to see why it fired, the other three intruders zip tied Cholmondeley's hands behind his back, pulled a black hood over his head and roughly hustled him out of the office. The hood smelled of someone else's vomit. Cholmondeley gagged.

"Move it, Chumply!" Someone nudged him forward with the butt of his rifle. "Move it!"

MINE!

◆ ◆ ◆

Real power is — I don't even want to use the word — fear. —Donald J. Trump

Executive Office Suite, Mar-A-Lago, Palm Beach, Florida, Great States Of America

It is an apocryphal canard that Stephen Miller's antipathy toward Latinos was a direct result of Rosarita Gonzalez laughing at him when he invited her to the junior prom at Santa Monica High School. She did not laugh at him. Probably because he did not invite her to the prom. The foundation of Miller's bigotry was less cause and effect than that; he was born prejudiced.

True, Rosarita's older brother, the formidable Mario — who at 15 had already developed the heft and awesome authority of a Toltec warrior statue — had snatched Stephen's sneakers, tied the laces together and tossed them up onto a telephone line where they dangled, decaying, for the next five years. Bad enough he lost a pair of Nikes. Even worse, Mario had stranded them on a phone line Stephen could see out the window of his bedroom, so they haunted him through the end of middle and through all of high school. Stephen dreaded the formidable Mario. Rosarita, on the other hand, was an object of enduring lust, after she accidentally displayed her still-developing eighth-grader's breasts to to him by bending over to retrieve something from her backpack in Mrs. Cohen's homeroom. Miller missed her nipples because he blinked, but he had no trouble convincing himself he had seen them.

While Mario's bullying and Rosarita's inadvertent cock-teasing were not the sources of his ethnic hostility; they affirmed and buttressed his instinctive bigotry. He was born a white supremacist, an uncomfortable predilection for a Jew.

Miller lived a fundamental irony: his fellow haters hated him. Early in his high school years, his mother admonished: "The people who hate the coloreds and the Hispanics hate Jews, too."

It fell on deaf ears.

His grandmother went further, citing unproven and unlikely genetics: "A Jew can't hate."

His unspoken response was, Oh, yeah, gramma, watch me.

Miller's instinctive bigotry had taken him far in MAGA politics. He had worked for Jefferson Beauregard Sessions III, whose first two names — homages to the president and a war hero of the Confederacy — told you everything you needed to know about him. Miller was an unlikely choice to be a top aide to the diminutive politician and not-so-closeted racist senator from Alabama, but there he was, communications director, crafting racist dog-whistles that Sessions gleefully blew.

At Sessions' recommendation, Trump hired Miller to write speeches. Miller crafted Trump's dark and threatening inaugural address. He also wrote most of Trump's most flagrant and inflammatory anti-immigrant, anti-Muslim, anti-Latino speeches.

In the GSA, he had leveraged his antipathy toward minorities — save his own — to become the president's chief of staff. GSA was a new country, tailored to the likes of Miller who believed in the principal that all men are not created equal and only some are endowed by their creator with the unalienable rights of life, liberty and the pursuit of happiness.

Miller's intercom buzzed. "The Proprietor," his secretary said. Miller picked up.

"Murdoch here," The voice was unmistakable, nasal, reedy with a heavy Aussie accent that only got stronger the longer he lived in North America. "He's not in the office yet? Taking his time this morning, isn't he?"

The Proprietor knew Trump was not in the 45/1 office; he would not be calling Miller if he had reached the president. Trump had not picked up Murdoch's call because the president was in the basement being bombarded with radiation at the moment.

Miller was accustomed to being the second choice on the call list of Trump advisors, cronies, lawyers and family members. He was adept at covering for the president, whose office attendance in the GSA was even more casual than it had been in the White House. Miller covered now with, "I don't expect he will be in for another hour or so because he's meeting with the Secretary at the Department of Defense right now. At the DOD."

Even as Miller pulled that lie out of thin air, he realized it was a really stupid cover story; it raised questions and was easily exposed. Murdoch had reporters at the GSA Department of Defense and at Mar-a-Lago and a phone call to each of them would have revealed the lie. Miller worried his falsehood might arouse The Proprietor's slumbering internal journalist. At 95, Murdoch still fancied himself a newshound. He might smell a story; something going on that was so important the president had to meet face-to-face at the Defense Department with Mike Flynn, the retired general, convicted felon and mad zealot who was now the GSA's Secretary of Defense.

This was Flynn's second rodeo in Trump's service. In 2017, Flynn had served Trump as a National Security Advisor for 22 days before being forced out for lying to the vice president, which was not a crime, and to the FBI, which was a felony. Charged with that crime, Flynn pleaded guilty, then changed his plea to not guilty and was convicted. Trump pardoned him in 2020. That sordid history — not to mention his services as an unregistered agent for Turkey, Saudi Arabia and the Russian Federation while on the payroll of the Trump election campaign — ought to have rendered him unsuitable for government service. In the old United States and in the other three republics, acceptance of a pardon was a tacit admission of guilt. But that sort of formal legalese cut no ice with the president of the Great States of America, who prized loyalty from his staff above honesty, competence and mental stability.

Would The Proprietor ask why the president was meeting in private with Flynn at the DOD? Would he have his minions try to run down the story behind the meeting? No. Fortunately for Miller, The Proprietor's dislike of the unstable Flynn overcame his journalism instincts and instead of asking about the fictional meeting, Murdoch thundered: "Why is that guy in the cabinet? I told Trump not to have anything to do with Flynn. He's a mad man and he should have his car keys taken away from him, not be given a department to run, much less one that has anything to do with men at arms."

"No serious arms," Miller said.

The GSA military consisted of the National Guard units of its constituent states and the slapdash, skimpily trained WRM corps, whose leadership, drawn from the top echelon of competing white supremacist militias, could not stop bickering long enough to accomplish anything meaningful.

"Thank God for that," Murdoch said. "Imagine him with a nuclear button on his desk."

Although he, himself, was a Trump zealot, Miller recognized that Flynn had passed over into cult territory. The secretary of defense was a full-throated QAnon conspiracy adherent. Like Murdoch, Miller was thankful that the nuclear arsenal assembled by the old United States was beyond Flynn's reach. The nukes, like the former United States Army, Navy, Air Force and Space Force, remained under joint control of all four republics and was commanded by the professional staff at ATO — The American Treaty Organization — which was headquartered near Denver in the Pacific States of America.

Miller suspected The Proprietor did not know the depth of Flynn's descent into madness; he probably did not know that the walls of Flynn's office were covered with maps marked with arrows showing invasion paths into Arizona from Utah, into Colorado from Nebraska and Kansas, into New Mexico from Texas and into Nevada from Idaho and Utah. In addition to adorning his walls with the maps, he had them the iPad he carried everywhere so he could show them to any and every one he encountered. Flynn would explain, "Once we take those, we consolidate our forces in Arizona and go after California. All I need is eight brigades, to include armor."

He did not have eight brigades and he had scant armor, all of it last-generation National Guard equipment.

"Don't much like that Flynn," The Proprietor said. "Don't like him at all."

"Yes, Mr. Murdoch."

"How's that pretty wife of yours doing," Murdoch asked.

Good, he was thinking Page Six of the NY Post now, not Page One of the Wall Street Journal. The old man's journalism instinct was definitely small c catholic.

"She's fine, sir. Taking care of little Mackenzie. I'll send her your regards."

Miller imagined Murdoch wanted Katie to pose in a tight sweater or low-cut blouse for his tabloid rags.

"Well, when you see The Boss, tell him I wanna talk. Okay? Bye." The Proprietor hung up.

Miller was stumped: what the hell was that all about? The old man asked for no favors, offered no advice. He expressed his distaste for Flynn, but that was only because Miller's inept lie brought Flynn into the conversation. So why did Murdoch call? Had he heard rumors of the cancer? Was he playing reporter and trying to nail the scoop himself? If so, it never came up in the call.

That wasn't it. Murdoch just wanted to schmooze; wanted to let Trump know he was paying attention and Trump needed to reciprocate and attend to The Proprietor's political agenda.

After he hung up the phone, Murdoch jotted on a Post-it: "TELL TRUMP FIRE FLYNN," and added three exclamation points. Why did Trump tolerate that man? It was difficult enough turning his media outlets into Trump's Völkischer Beobachter. Why did Trump have to make it more difficult by staffing his administration with lunatics?

*

Miller's iPhone chimed; a text message: "BBC reporting on prez 'condition.' Have arrested BBC reporter. Taking to basement Trump International."

"Oh, shit!" Miller was up and out the door.

◆ ◆ ◆

When you guys put somebody in the car and you're protecting their head... I said, you can take your hand away, okay -- Donald J. Trump

Trump International Golf Club, West Palm Beach, Florida, Great States Of America

Someone, two someones — four grabbing hands — roughly yanked Walter Cholmondeley out of the back seat of the SUV. It was a long step down to the ground and he landed unsteadily. The two men, much taller and heftier than he, steadied him. Despite the stale vomit smell of the hood, Cholmondeley could make out the scents of his guards. The one on his left smelled strongly of cheap aftershave or cologne. The one on his right just smelled; a toxic miasma of bodily emissions, the least objectionable of which was sweat.

"All yours," said someone behind him and the SUV drove away.

"This way, Chambly," growled Right, the stinky one. They guided him through the oppressive heat by his shoulders and elbows. There were five or six paces across a macadam driveway.

"Step up," Left said, applying a bit of uplift to the elbow he was gripping. "Just one step."

Cholmondeley's toe struck the top of the riser and he fell forward. Left pulled to keep him upright, Right shoved him forward, adding to his momentum. Cholmondeley would have put out his hands to break his fall, but they were flexcuffed behind him. He fell, chest-forward, onto concrete, his right knee landing first. It hurt like hell; he felt blood trickling down his shin. They pulled him to his feet and charged through a door into air conditioning so aggressive his teeth began chattering.

"Let's take the elevator," Left said.

"Or we could just throw him down the stairs," Right said.

They took the elevator. It went down to what must have been a basement hallway where there was no air conditioning. The atmosphere was close, hot and thick with humidity. Left and Right guided him a dozen steps forward. The floor was slippery so he placed his feet carefully. They took him into a room, cut the plastic flex cuffs and sat him on a chair. The vomit-y hood was pulled off. He closed his eyes against the brightness. Head down, he opened his eyes a slit and peeked. A small, ugly room. Grey-painted cinderblock walls. Acoustic ceiling tiles. A beat-up grey metal desk in front of him. A basement storeroom repurposed as a detention/interrogation room? The floor was bare concrete and had significant puddles in its many low spots. Where had the water come from? Clogged drain? Backed-up bathtub? Clogged toilet? Waterboarding interrogation subjects? He willed himself not to shudder; his will failed. This was scary; he was helpless. He had not signed on for this.

Right and Left were across the desk, standing in front of him, their sturdy legs at parade rest; they were too far away to smell them and differentiate which was which.

Like the four who'd seized him in his studio, Right and Left were wearing black balaclavas, black fatigues and black ballistic vests. He searched for name tags or organization insignia, but there were none. Across their chests they'd slung MX-5s, assault rifles that were more sophisticated weapons than most ATO troops or any state National Guardsmen carried. WORMs, Cholmondeley knew, carried MX-5s; his captors were likely WORMs.

One of them — Right, he decided — had his hand on the pistol grip and his forefinger on the trigger guard. Left — if that's who it was —- was not touching his weapon. Good cop, bad cop?

Struggling to affect calm, Cholmondeley said, "You *do* know, that I'm a representative of the BBC, a British subject and that my corporation will report this to the Foreign Office and there will be serious repercussions?"

"Shut the fuck up and speak when you're spoken to," said the one who wasn't fondling his weapon. Was it going to be bad cop, worse cop?

The door behind him opened, then shut. A soft voice said, "You can go now." Right and Left nodded and walked around behind him. "Nice meeting you, Chumpley," one of them said.

He turned his head, but the newcomer was directly behind him and he could catch only a hint of him in his peripheral vision.

"Mr. Cholmondeley of the British Broadcasting Corporation," the newcomer said, pronouncing the name correctly on first try.

"And you would be?"

"Not important or relevant. What is important are the names of the five sources that you relied on for that fake news story you filed just now: the one about the president's health. The one you will be rescinding and apologizing for."

"I'll say nothing until I know to whom I'm speaking. Or at very least what agency you represent."

"No position to make demands, are you, Mr. Cholmondeley? But demand away, if that's what you want. Waste your time and my time." He said Cholmondeley correctly again, as if to indicate that it wasn't just a fluke that he had gotten it right the first time.

Cholmondeley forced himself to sound firm, unafraid: "My story's not fake news, and you know it, whoever you are. My sources were solid. They were and will remain anonymous."

"So you say now."

"Are you going to torture me? Waterboard me?" His fear showed with that, his voice less steady than he wished it to be.

"Oh? The water on the floor?" A forced laugh; then: "That's not from waterboarding. That's brackish water.

Salt water from the ocean leaking into groundwater and contaminating it. Works its way up through the floor. The ocean level's rising, as you know. Global warming. High tide comes and we get water here in the basement. Have for years now. Gets worse every year."

"So climate change and rising ocean levels? True? Not a hoax?"

"Please. You know better. You broke the story about the Mar-a-Lago dyke. You know that we know it's real. The hoax thing; that's for the base. They need to hear that. We know better."

"May I quote you."

"No. First of all you don't know who I am, do you? You can't even call me a source, can you? You have no idea if I'm with the administration or some free-lancer. I could be a white supremacist terrorist. Or an Antifa terrorist. Or an environmental terrorist. Or even an Islamofascist. There'll be no story coming out of this encounter, Mr. Cholmondeley. Do we understand each other?"

Cholmondeley said nothing. "Here is what I need from you: the names of the five sources in your incorrect story about the president's health. And you'll call London and tell the news desk your sources misled you and Mr. Trump is in fine health. That he's the healthiest president we've had in a long time. Maybe the healthiest ever."

Cholmondeley tried a scoffing laugh; it didn't come out the way he intended. He used his words instead: "I won't do that, and you know you can't hold me here against my will. It's kidnapping."

"I can hold you in detention, I am doing just that, and I will continue to detain you. You are aware that we make the laws. You said so yourself in the report you filed." Some paper rustled behind him, and the voice continued, reading from a transcript of his report: "President Trump has the power to change that situation because the constitution gives him the authority to create laws and have them take effect once they are ratified by a simple majority of the nation's single-chamber congress." The papers rustled again. "That part is correct; the president can dictate a law and you know this Congress will ratify it for him, so if we wanted to pass a law that says journalists could be detained for filing false stories, we can do it."

"We? Not doing a very good job of hiding your affiliation," Cholmondeley said. "Would you care to walk around the table and let me see who I'm talking to?"

"No. I'm not going to do that."

"I'm not getting out of here, am I" Cholmondeley said.

"Don't worry. You're getting out. Just cooperate. We're not violent people. Nothing untoward will happen to you."

"It already has. You snatched me out of my office, pulled a vomity hood over my head, held me in restraint, threw me down on a concrete step and intimidated me with armed thugs. How it that nothing untoward?"

"Some of our people take literally what the president says when he's joking. They need to take him seriously, not literally. The manhandling? It happens. I don't think it has to happen again. I just need those sources' names."

"My office; you people bugged my office?"

"We make it a practice to read or hear the news early. Before it's published or broadcast. It helps us with refutations to fake news stories, like yours."

Several foreign journalists told Cholmondeley they suspected their offices, phones and radio circuits were bugged because the Mar-a-Lago press operation was ready with rebuttals almost instantly after they filed a story.

"Okay: My sources were Eric Trump, Ivanka Trump, Jared Kushner, Donald Trump, Jr. and Tiffany Trump. I did not get a chance to interview Barron Trump."

"Unfunny. I need the real five names."

"What you need, quite frankly, is to release me. I will file kidnapping charges and the British government will create a major diplomatic incident, if I am not released."

"The British government answers to our ally, Mr. Murdoch," the voice said. "And I was talking to Mr. Murdoch, on the phone just a couple of minutes ago. He's very cooperative with our administration. You know that. There will be no diplomatic incident. Even without Murdoch, your PM, Mr. Johnson, and our president are close and cooperative friends. As you know, Johnson has no love for the BBC, after what you did to him the last time he was PM. And where are you going file those kidnapping charges? The State of Florida? Governor Gaetz won't be interested. The GSA federal government? Do you think for a minute AG Powell's going to investigate, much less prosecute?" He paused. "I'm leaving now; let's give you a few minutes to think about your decision."

Presidential chief of staff Stephen Miller left the room; Cholmondeley never saw him. He did see Right and Left re-enter immediately. They must have been waiting in the hall because they were back in front of him before he heard the door slam shut. One of them, Right? Left? — they were two far away for his olfactory nerves to distinguish which was which — had slung his assault rifle in back and was slapping an ugly black leather cosh into his open palm.

"Now, do you know what that drain in the floor is for?"

"Drainage?"

"Don't get funny with us, mister...." he said.

"Your mate who was in here with me told me groundwater rises into the basement; it's for that, not waterboarding."

"Oh, yeah? You really wanna take that chance?"

Slap. Slap. Slap. SLAP! He hit his palm so hard he must have winced under his balaclava.

◆ ◆ ◆

I've said if Ivanka weren't my daughter, perhaps I'd be dating her. — Donald J. Trump

Casa Clase Alta, Miami, Florida, Great States Of America

The hostage video had been her undoing.

Not that she had been a hostage when she made it, but the image and her demeanor looked like the poorly produced videos made under duress by terrorists' frightened captives. Ivanka had been frightened and was her own hostage when her testimony was recorded by the January Sixth Committee. She was a captive of conflicting emotions: her trepidatious admiration for Daddy, her abundant self-regard and her coincidental concerns for the health, wealth and safety of her husband and their children.

Caught in the bright light, her eyes darting to and fro, her emotionless voice low and gurgling with vocal fry, she sealed her doom with Daddy in that voluntary Zoom interview. Recorded months earlier, the first portion of the video aired in prime time on June 9, 2022. Ivanka was seated in front of grey/white marble tiles; she wore a pale blue blazer and white blouse; her lipstick was a shiny pale pink; her eye makeup excessive. A video clip of the former attorney general of the United States, Bill Barr, had just been played. Barr slumped in his chair, a large, amorphous presence — Jabba the Hutt after a visit to Brooks Brothers. Long considered Trump's stooge, Barr debunked the former president's repeated and obsessive claims of 2020 election fraud, calling them "nonsense" and, retreating even further from legalese, "bullshit." And then the Ivanka video played: "I respect Attorney General Barr. I accepted what he was saying."

That was it; the straw that broke the camel's back. She had been on the precipice's edge after decamping Washington with her family and moving to Miami before Daddy's presidency ran out the clock. Trump pushed her off after 20 million Americans saw the hostage video. He banished his own daughter the same way he had fired countless aides: via social media, where the whole world could share his victim's humiliation. On Truth, his struggling version of Twitter, Trump wrote: "Ivanka Trump was not involved in looking at, or studying, Election results. She had long since checked out and was, in my opinion only trying to be respectful to Bill Barr and his position as Attorney General (he sucked!)." As Trump kiss-offs went it was mild stuff. Certainly nothing that would inspire any of his fanatics to go gunning for her.

But there would be no more publicly expressed incest fantasies. Ivanka had committed the worst of sins; she had been disloyal. Down she tumbled, taking her husband, Jared Kushner, with her. They were sent to Coventry, exiled to Siberia, deported to Elba, put out on an ice floe, banished from court. Shut out. Excluded. Banned. Ousted. The fawning daughter who for four long, arduous, plague-filled years had played Goneril — the eye-batting flatterer — to Trump's Lear, had been recast by her enraged father as Cordelia — the daughter spurned for telling the truth.

Javanka was the scornful jumble of their names all Washington had adopted in 2017 — a protest against the blatant nepotism that had turned two aspiring New York socialite dilettantes into policy-influencing insiders. Javanka were now Miami outsiders with no influence.

Trump, himself, followed their retreat to Florida on January 20, 2021, leaving Washington immediately before the beginning of inauguration ceremonies for his successor, Joe Biden. The timing was critical: if Biden had not yet been sworn in to replace him, Trump was still president and the blue-liveried Boeing 747 in which he was flying was Air Force One. As soon as his successor finished the oath of office, it became just another airplane. An additional incentive to skipping Biden's inauguration: he would not be seen on TV as that most contemptible of creatures, a *loser*!

The geographic proximity of the Javanka mansion in Miami to Mar-a-Lago in Palm Beach seemed to offer the possibility of reconciliation. But Javanka might as well have been on Mars as far as Trump was concerned. There were no paternal visits, little outreach and only an occasional perfunctory phone call on birthdays. That was the situation *before* the prime-time betrayal aired, when their only crime was bailing from the White House before Daddy retreated to Florida. The brief video clip moved them from mere personae non grata to enemies.

"She has long since checked out" resonated in Javanka's 14,000-square-foot beachfront home, Casa Clase Alta, where the family had self-exiled. Those words were ominous. And after the election of 2024, the words were no longer a threat; they were a fact. The Kushners were, indeed, "checked out." Checked out of the Trump orbit, out of favor, out of influence, out of the perfunctory phone calls. The silence from Palm Beach chilled the hot Florida air. And the silence was not just from Trump and Trumpworld. Javanka checked out of most human interactions. They had long-ago burned all their old New York contacts, eager suck-ups when Javanka was a rich couple with an 8,000 square foot apartment who occasionally donated noteworthy amounts to someone's pet charity. New York backs turned on them when they joined Daddy's administration. The new acquaintances they had made in

Washington were fair weather friends interested only in power or proximity to power. The out-of-favor daughter and son-in-law of an ex-President had no power and Trump's cold shoulder made sure they had no proximity, either. For the Trump cultists, the hostage video justified, if not mandated, abandoning Javanka. The only people who remained in regular contact were the half dozen Jared cronies on the payroll of his Saudi-financed hedge fund, where they were busying themselves making two billion petrodollars disappear at a rate that could be replicated only by burning cash in a fireplace.

As bad as that was, it got worse: Three weeks earlier, the Javanka clan's punishment went from banishment to imprisonment. They were put under house arrest; more accurately, mansion arrest. Staff members were free to come and go, but the family was locked down and locked in. Around the clock, black-uniformed WORMs, assault rifles slung across their chests and holstered Glocks on their hips, kept everyone whose last name was Kushner in the house or on the grounds. Even the kids' activities were curtailed; 15-year-old Arabella, had to quit ballet lessons, 13-year-old Joey dropped out of Hebrew lessons only weeks after his promising performance at his bar mitzvah and 10-year-old Theo went stir crazy, breaking his toys and fighting with his brother constantly. In addition to the cook, two maids, gardener, tutors and rabbi who were free to visit, the family applied for and was granted permission to add a child psychologist who worked with the kids individually and in group sessions.

When Cholmondeley's BBC radio report aired in the UK and globally over the BBC World Service, other news outlets tried to follow up on the story. Ivanka's phone — which had an unlisted number — began ringing several times an hour as enterprising reporters managed to get her number and call for confirmation or comment. She stopped answering after the eighth call. She turned off the phone after the eleventh.

Now, she was FaceTiming her older and younger brothers, Junior and Eric. Junior had also been banished for giving a three-hour interview to the January Sixth Committee, even though none of what he had said in deposition had earned him prime time exposure. Eric was the only one of Trump's first three children still in communication with Daddy. He had to be; he managed Trump Enterprises.

Junior had relocated to a $10 million home in Jupiter, Florida, closer to Mar-a-Lago than Miami. Junior's enhanced proximity merely added to the frustration. He was living just down the road from his father/namesake, but, as with Javanka, he might as well have been on Mars.

Eric continued to live in New York, commuting to Florida when necessary. He had taken over his father's 11,000-square-foot apartment on the top three floors of Trump Tower on Fifth Avenue. He joined the FaceTime call from his office in the apartment.

There wasn't a lot of meat on Eric Trump's frame, so he looked even taller than his actual six-foot-five-inches. Unlike many tall men, he had no self-conscious slouch; he stood tall and straight. Eric's confident posture belied a mind filled with insecurity and self-doubt. In dollar terms, his net worth was $500 million — "halfway to wealth," according to Daddy. In self-esteem terms, he had no net worth. Quieter than Junior, less a social animal than Ivanka, Eric avoided media attention and quietly attended to the business of making money, lots of money; although never enough for Daddy. Trump Senior's vocabulary did not include the word "enough."

Cholmondeley's story included information that Eric, not Vice President Carlson, would be the successor to the 45/1 Office. That put Eric where he least wanted to be: the focal point of political and media attention.

Eric hated it. To his father, any media coverage was good coverage; to Eric, it was the reverse, all coverage was bad coverage. His parents had gone through a vicious divorce when he was only eight years old; one that provided constant front-page fodder for tabloid newspapers. At the time, he did not know exactly what was going on, but seeing the family name on front pages several times a week was mortifying.

Two years earlier, when he was only six, he and his siblings had been the involuntary audience for an operatic confrontation between his mother, Ivana, and Daddy's then-mistress and future wife, Marla Maples. It was during a family ski vacation in Aspen, and his memory of that event was flawed. But he had read accounts: How Daddy brought Marla along on the vacation and stashed her in a convenient hotel. How Marla had approached all of them in a restaurant. How Marla said to Ivana, "I love your husband. Do you?" How that precipitated a shouting match.

He remembered what followed: the women screaming at each other, but he did not remember what they screamed. He remembered his mother's red face and tears. He remembered the frightened weeping of his 13-year-old brother and his 11-year-old sister. He thought he remembered Daddy, wide-eyed and silent — unembarrassed — watching the spectacle. Was Daddy awe-struck? Pleased? Concerned? Proud? Eric didn't know.

He remembered one thing more: only Junior reached out to reassure him. It was the most traumatic event of his life; it still haunted him. He had never discussed it with anyone; not his siblings, not his wife, not his late mother, not even his psychoanalyst. And certainly not Daddy.

On Ivanka's iPhone, Eric looked calm and orderly. He used his office for Zoom meetings, so it was well-lit, and he wore a headset with a microphone. Junior, on the other hand, looked puffy and exhausted. His hair, usually heavily gelled and slicked straight back, was a mess, strands going every which way. His beard was greyer; he really needed to shave that off. His lighting was crappy, and the sound was scratchy; he couldn't be bothered to use his earbuds and made do with the speakerphone. Ivanka was fully made up and groomed, having spent nearly half an hour in a chair with one of the housekeepers who was a retired TV hair and makeup artist. She was wearing a white sleeveless blouse. Eric and Junior couldn't see what else she had on, but they knew it was fresh from the cleaners, crisp and stylish.

Ivanka spoke first, "You talk to him, Eric. What do you know? Is it true? How long have you known?"

"Yes. It's true. It's…. It's bad. Very bad."

"And you knew when?" Junior demanded.

"For a little while."

Ivanka said, "A little while? What's that? Since yesterday or since last week? What's a little while?"

"A little while, okay. A couple of months," Eric said.

Junior exploded: "You little shit! You know Daddy's got cancer and maybe dying, and you know it a couple of months and you don't say anything to us?"

"Sorry."

"Sorry doesn't cut it, Eric," Ivanka said,

"Why didn't you open a mouth; and tell us?"

"Daddy. He made me promise. He made me promise not to say anything, even to you. They didn't want it leaking. *He* didn't want it leaking."

"You think we'd leak it? *He* thought we'd leak it?" Ivanka demanded. "Who the hell would we leak it to?"

"You can't trust your brother and sister? Junior asked.

"And you're going to be president if he dies? Is that it?" Ivanka said. "So you didn't say anything so you could be president?"

"No! That's not it. I don't want to be president. I never asked for this."

Junior looked and sounded angry, "Did you tell *him* that? Did you say that to *him*? Tell him, not us. How the hell can they do that, anyway? Does anybody know? Isn't there a vice-presdent and a line of succession? A constitution?"

"They have a way. It's something to do with, I don't know, the president proposing laws. Something like that," Eric said. "He told me, but I don't think I understood. I'm not sure he understands how it can be done, but they said it could be done."

"So you don't want to be president, but you didn't tell Daddy?" Ivanka said.

"I'd call that pretty convenient, wouldn't you?" Junior said.

Eric protested, "Isn't it too late now? It's out there."

"You watch; they're going to call it fake news. They're going to do everything they can to knock it down," Ivanka said. "But it *is* true? Right, Eric, he's got cancer?"

"He's getting chemo or radiation," Eric said. "I forget which. Maybe both. I don't know. They say it could help. I don't know."

Junior said, "You're the only one who does know and you're saying, 'I don't know?'"

Ivanka was more interested in the line of succession. She said, "Eric, you need to tell him, tell Daddy. Tell him you don't want it. Tell him to talk to me. He hasn't talked to be in...."

Junior cut her off, "Why you, sis? You're volunteering to be President-Select? Is that what you're getting at?"

"What? You think it should be you?" Ivanka said.

"I should be the one. I should be the president-select," Junior said. "I'm the one made the speeches. Did all the rallies. I'm the surrogate. I'm the one the base loves. I wrote the books, didn't I?"

There were two books, "Triggered: How the Left Thrives on Hate and Wants to Silence Us" and "Liberal Privilege: Joe Biden and The Democrats' Defense of the Indefensible." The volumes bore Junior's name as author, and he had actually read both manuscripts and suggested some changes to the writers before they were published. The books were currently available in some conservative bookstores as remainders for $3.69 each or $5.50 for both.

"If I'm the President-Select, I could be the first woman president in the Americas."

"And the first Jewish president, which is why it won't happen," Eric said. "The base would never stand for that.

"I agree," Eric said. "Daddy's base won't accept that. They won't ever go for…. y'know. A woman, either. So I think Don is right. It should be him."

"Try. Talk to him," Junior said

"I'm not on board," Ivanka said.

"Sis, it just ain't gonna happen," Junior said. "Not for you. Jared, either."

"I don't know," Eric said. "None of this feels right. I mean we don't know how the chemo and the radiation will work; maybe it'll be good. And I feel bad about Carlson. He *is* the vice president. The people voted for him. Maybe it shouldn't be any of us. No one voted for us."

"No one voted for Tucker," Junior said. "They voted for Daddy and Tucker was along for the ride. And the only reason he was on the ticket was to stroke that old fuck, Murdoch."

Ivanka said, "He can't be happy about this. Murdoch, I mean."

"Fuck Murdoch," Junior said, "this is family now."

Eric said, "Can we stop talking about who's going to be president? Can you believe this is what we're talking about when Daddy is sick with cancer and it spread, y'know, all over. It's probably...." He wanted to avoid the word "fatal." "It's probably... real serious."

"You know he's thinking about...." Junior stopped. "Death," like "fatal," was not a word that came easily to a Trump, unless it involved someone with a different surname. "So, Eric, can you get Daddy to take a call from me?"

"*You*? Why you?" Ivanka demanded.

There was a clicking on the call; one click, then another, then a third. Some agency was using faulty equipment to tap the call.

"Hear that? That come from one of you?" Ivanka asked.

"No, not me," Eric said.

"Me, either. Must be…," Junior began. "Who the hell knows who it is?" None of them knew

*

It was the Russians; of course, the Russians. They felt no need to cover their tracks in the GSA. Their spying was tolerated by the administration, so they relied on obsolete Soviet-era equipment and reserved their most sophisticated gear for the other North American republics.

The moment the call ended, artificial intelligence software on a SVR computer in the Russian embassy in Palm Beach began translating their spoken English words into a Russian word-processing file. The full printed translation was on Vladimir Putin's desk in the Kremlin 45 minutes later — about fifteen minutes after Putin had received a Russian-language print-out of Walter Cholmondeley's BBC report.

After he read the two documents, Putin joked to an aide that perhaps the Russian Federation could save a lot of money by shutting down the SVR and the GRU and getting all of its intelligence from the BBC, because it was faster and more factual.

Nothing in the call or the Cholmondeley story told Putin anything he didn't already know. In fact, he had far more detailed knowledge than the BBC report because he, Vladimir Vladimirovich Putin, retired KGB spymaster, had been running his own personal intelligence-gathering operation against the GSA and had recruited for it a well-placed asset: the republic's president, Donald J. Trump.

CHAPTER TWO

If Putin likes Donald Trump, I consider that an asset, not a liability because we have a horrible relationship with Russia. — Donald J. Trump

The Kremlin, Moscow, Russian Federation

Vladimir Vladimirovich Putin never read any of the studies that proved society had lesser expectations for short men; he did not need to, he lived them. From early childhood Vladimir Vladimirovich, an instinctive translator of looks and body language, saw how people reacted to his size. Always the smallest boy in class, sometimes the smallest pupil, boy or girl, he read diminished expectations in the faces of teachers and fellow students. He saw it even in the face of the diminutive hall sweeper, Lev Borisovich, who was, himself, the object of much teasing by the students, all of whom — except Little Vlad — surpassed the sweeper's height by age 13.

The hall sweeper's plight did not inspire the young Putin to challenge those expectations; he needed no push; he was born a fighter. If teased, he taunted. If pushed, he punched. If punched, he picked up a stone and bashed his tormentor until he drew blood. Classmates learned to stop taunting, pushing and punching him; nothing brings a boy more respect than fear. He resolved to be feared.

Routinely, he vanquished low expectations, reduced them to rubble and stood triumphant on the pile. Napoleon, another short man at the head of a powerful country, crowned himself. Legend had it that Putin did the Frenchman one better by birthing himself: Vladimir Vladimirovich's mother was in labor for only minutes before he emerged, unaided by the midwife's helping hands, and drew his first breath on his own before anyone could slap his boney bottom. Even then he was eager to get on with it. That was the legend; there was no one alive who could refute it.

Putin grew, but was always short, although the term he preferred was "compact." He claimed to be 5' 7," but he gained that sub-stratospheric altitude with the aid of extremely well-designed lifting shoes custom-made in Italy. Standing barefoot, he was just under 5' 6."

Little Vladimir Vladimirovich was nothing if not competitive. How could he not be? His name ordained it. Vladi means "to rule" and miri means "great" or "famous." He had to be the fastest runner. He never was, but he acted as if he'd won every race. He had to be the best student. Again, he wasn't quite the one, but his academic self-confidence amounted to a best student's swagger. He completed every test minutes before everyone else — and let them know it by noisily tossing down his pencil or slamming shut his examination booklet and stage-whispering a triumphant: "Zakonchennyy!" — Finished! To give the appearance of finishing first, there were times when he didn't finish at all. He monitored the examination room and theatrically stopped as soon as he saw others reviewing their workbooks.

He was a small man running a big country, the biggest country in the world in land mass. When he met international counterparts, he always worked into the earliest moments of their conversation a fact that told them that, compact as the man was, they were dealing with a nation that was vast. "Did you know Russia spans 11 time zones, more than any other nation in the world?" he would ask visitors. "Did you know that Russia has the world's largest reserves of helium?" was another Putin ice-breaker. "Did you know Russia has the world's largest reserves of natural gas?" was a third. Everyone seemed to know that one, so he retired it.

Putin was ready with those three and many more the first time he met the then-President of the then-United States, Donald Trump. He used only one of his icebreakers before realizing that the American president needed no impressing; he had come to the meeting impressed, predisposed to falling into awe of Putin, if not falling in love with him.

It was 2017 at a one-on-one sidebar at the G20 in Hamburg. Only Russia, Putin let Trump know, had launch vehicles capable of bringing America's astronauts to the International Space Station, only Russia had the means to bring crews back as well. NASA had to buy seats to and from the space station from the Roscosmos, the Russian space agency. "We can charge anything we want to charge," Putin boasted. "Of course, we would never strand your people up there." Trump took that not as the implicit threat it was meant to be, but as a promise of a round-trip ticket for American astronauts. He all but batted his eyes and sighed at Putin.

Before the meeting, Putin had read the briefing papers GRU and SVR prepared for him. From them he'd learned that it would be extremely unlikely that Trump would bother reading the comparable briefing papers CIA gave him, so from the start the American president would be on the back foot. Putin was starting their race five meters ahead.

Putin knew Trump would walk into the room, size him up — literally — and think himself at an advantage because he was bigger. Putin was fully prepared for that. In fact, he had gotten an actor with Trump's exact dimensions, 6' 3", 244 pounds, had him made up with orange-tint foundation and a blonde fright wig and rehearsed the meeting. He recorded the rehearsal on video and kept rehearsing it until he was satisfied that the television images of that first handshake did not have him looking up at the American president but, rather, looking straight across at him. To accomplish that, Putin had fixed on the dimple at the bottom of the knot in the actor's necktie. When they did meet face-to-face, Putin discovered that Trump, like himself, lied about his height and was claiming an inch to an inch-and-a-half that simply didn't exist. Putin was looking at the American's orange chin, not at the necktie dimple.

The instant Trump walked into the room, Putin told himself, "Act fast Vladimir Vladimirovich, this zhirnaya svin'ya — fat pig — is digging his grave with a fork and spoon." So he saved all his ice-breakers about Russia's vast size for another time and greeted Trump in English, speaking slowly and with an exaggerated accent so it would appear he was less fluent than he actually was: "My brother, Donald, Meesta Prazident. So good to finally meet een person."

Trump's face lit up like a child scanning his presents under the Christmas tree. "My brother;" a brilliant suggestion from an SVR psychiatrist who told Vladimir Vladimirovich that Trump wanted nothing more than to be an American Putin. The psychiatrist was right; Putin had Trump eating out of his hand with "my brother." But he was wrong in one respect: he said Trump wanted to be *an* American Putin; he wanted to be *Putin*. He wanted to be the one who'd led the James Bond spy life. He wanted to be the one with the unencumbered cash flow and the numbered Swiss bank account and the gymnast girlfriend who could contort her body in unimaginable ways. He wanted to be the guy who could order his enemies killed with the nod of his head.

Putin had recruited the highest-level asset in the history of espionage without using bribery, ideology or kompromat; he'd done it by calling Trump "my brother."

Putin had played the spy game when it was a world-class, existential competition. As a lieutenant colonel in the KGB's foreign service during the final years of the Soviet Union, he had run dozens of assets out of East Berlin, becoming one of the agency's top operators. For him, there had been no thrill greater than being the first to get an intelligence report from an asset, judge its credibility and utility and then report it up the chain of command where a decision was made about whether it was actionable.

Today, he, himself, was atop of that chain of command: he decided if intelligence was actionable and what action to take. He kept his hand in the espionage game, running his single asset. Now there were no back-alley meetings and safehouses; agent and asset communicated over an always-open secure hotline.

Trump, code named poleznyy — useful, short for useful idiot — and Putin, who called himself khozyain — master — even exchanged their supposedly confidential Google calendars. Putin's was fiction, not a single entry in it was true. Putin knew his asset; knew Trump would not check the fake calendar, so Vladimir Vladimirovich tolerated the team of SVR jokesters tasked with creating his calendar when they manufactured a daily schedule for the president that would have been a challenge for three younger and healthier men to accomplish in a single day.

According to the fake calendar, Putin rose at six, jogged five kilometers before showering, had a massage every other day, ate breakfast while taking a meeting (Monday, Wednesday, Friday — defense council. Tuesday, Thursday, Saturday — economic council) and was in his office by half past seven. Trump, notorious for his disaffection for all exercise save golf — and that played riding in a golf cart — never questioned how Putin managed to pack three hours' worth of activity into 90 minutes every morning. At the office, the Putin of the fictitious calendar devoted ten minutes every morning to personally pinning medals for various levels of courage and martial brilliance on returning Ukrainian war heroes, amputees and strategists. (Medal-worthy Ukrainian War strategists was the best joke in the calendar and, fortunately for the jokesters, both Putin and Trump missed it completely.) Calendar Putin held three more meetings before lunch, dined with business leaders from different sectors of the economy and then plunged into an afternoon normally marked by five or six hour-long meetings. Dinner was always at the residence with a Russian scientist, academic, medical expert or some other brain-expanding intellectual the real Putin would have found insufferable for a five-minute chance encounter, much less a 90-minute one-on-one meal. Those dinners with top-flight brainiacs were supposed to turn

Trump green with intellectual envy. They had the reverse effect; he was happy he did not have to do the equivalent with domestic smartypants types.

Most evenings, Calendar Putin was off to a cultural or sporting event, including fictional concerts given by visiting American, Canadian and Western European artists who were in fact boycotting Moscow because of the Ukraine war. Real Putin usually appreciated the humor, but he did force them to make a single change one week: Calendar Putin would not be attending the Pussy Riot concert in the Cathedral of Christ the Savior. In the first place, given Pussy Riot's notoriety, even Trump might smell a rat. In the second place, half of Pussy Riot was in jail and the other half was on the lam in Western Europe, making Putin-bashing appearance on television. Trump, as a TV news addict, might see one of those bitches as he switched through the channels looking for reports about himself. And in the third place, Putin detested Pussy Riot and did not want their brand associated with his.

If Calendar Putin's days were as cluttered as a hoarder's closet, Trump's was the opposite: wide open space. They were so sparse and the listings so trivial they appeared fraudulent. But they were his actual calendar; Trump liked to keep his days lightly scheduled so there was ample time for schmoozing with friends on the phone and rage posting on social media. Each day did begin with 90 full minutes set aside for hair and makeup. There was also a daily hour scheduled for signing photos for donors (simple signature $500; inscription with donor's name $1,500; inscription with name and famous Trump quote like "The carnage stops now!" $2,500). There were machines that could do that sort of thing, but Trump felt it was a con job not to have his real signature on them. Putin could not understand why that was the one con at which Trump drew a red line.

Trump called their secure telephone connection the President-to-President Hotline. Putin called it the Telefon agenta k ob'yektu — the Agent-to-Asset Phone. The instruments on both presidential desks were identical: single line white phones with a flat circular LED light instead of a keypad. No dialing necessary; the line was always active. One party picked up his receiver, the light flashed on the other president's phone.

*

Four months ago, the phone on Putin's desk lit up. Putin had been in conference with two generals who had been briefing him on how this time for sure two companies of special forces were going to parachute into Kiev and get that punk Ukrainian Zhyd, Zelensky, and cook his goose with nerve gas. Just as soon as they figured out where he slept at night. Putin was about to tell them that if he ever saw a plot that stupid in a movie, he would walk out of the theater. Trump's call saved him from having to do that. "Tovarishchi, give me the room," Putin said. "Tovarish" -- comrade -- had survived the fall of the Soviet Union only in Russia's military services. As a former KGB officer, Putin used it with his generals.

"Mister President, Excellency, my brother," Putin said when he lifted the handset. "Are you well?"

"Donald. It's Donald. I thought we were Donald and Vlad on this line."

"I like that 'Excellency.' Very good... good... the word you use? Branding? Very good branding." Putin knew it was branding; he was toying with his asset. "I'm assuming you invent that?" Stroke an asset; keep him happy. With a rich guy like Trump, building his ego was more effective than building his bank account; it saved the Russian Federation money, too.

"I did, Vlad. I did. I needed to call you just now. I learned something you should know. Can you talk for a couple of minutes? If not now, you can call me later or I can call you. Whatever's best for you."
Putin detected an unusual constriction in Trump's voice; something was amiss.

"Go ahead. We're alone this end. I make no notes, no recording," Putin lied; their calls were automatically recorded the moment he lifted the receiver from the cradle. He assumed, incorrectly, the same was true on the GSA side.

"Well, I got myself into the clusterfuck of clusterfucks," Trump said.

Putin tried to remember if a clusterfuck was an actual sexual position, a sexual situation or just a figure of speech.

"What happen, my brother?"

The second time he called Trump "my brother" on the call, the American teared up; he was overcome that Putin considered him an equal, he nearly wept.

"I got it, Vlad. I got the cancer. They fucked up and I got cancer."

They? Were the Americans working on some sort of biological warfare program that we don't know about. Who was "they?" And how did "they" infect Trump with cancer?

Putin asked: "Where? Where the cancer is? What stage the cancer is? Who is this 'they' that fuck up?"

"The fucking doctors! It's their fucking fault. They did this."

Vladimir Putin knew a thing or two about cancer, being a survivor of the disease, himself. And if he knew anything, it was that doctors — fucking or not — did not have the ability to give anyone the disease.

In Putin's case, the cancer was a perfectly kept secret: A team of Swiss doctors had been flown to St. Petersburg to perform the surgery on an Army base. The story that was leaked had it that the Swiss were there, working in secrecy to protect the privacy of their important patient who was a three- or four-star general whose dick had been shot off in Ukraine. There was a protracted surgery during which the Swiss team were supposedly reattaching the appendage, which had somehow been rescued intact from the battlefield. What they were really doing was removing a meter and a quarter of Vladimir Putin's cancer-ridden colon as well as his rectum. Meanwhile, to provide plausible cover, a Putin double visited the front in Ukraine and was shown on video encouraging his troops to rob, rape and murder more Ukrainians. After the surgery the world never again saw Putin posing shirtless for photographers. Who wants to see a photo of a shit-stuffed colostomy bag strapped to their president's belly?

Trump was on a grievance roll: "They coulda insisted I get that fucking needle biopsy. But no. They just give in when Trump says no. Come on, I like a good argument much as the next guy, right? They need to give as good as they get with Trump to get his attention."

Am I talking to Trump or to someone else about Trump, Putin wondered.

"When I said no, they should of said, 'Fuck you, and fuck your no, Excellency.' That's what they shouldda said. But did they? Fuck, no! That's what you do, you say, 'Excellency, you gotta take the test. Your age, your background, your blood work, your PSA through the roof. It's fucking mandatory, Excellency.'

"Yes, mandatory," Putin said.

"I would of reacted okay if they said it was 'mandatory.' I mean, mandatory; that means there's no other option. You are *mandated* to take the needle biopsy. That's their job, the doctors, convincing the patient. I heard you piss blood after the needle biopsy. So maybe I'm squeamish about that. Extra squeamish. I admit it. Why wouldn't I be? You're pissing blood into the toilet. I don't wanna see blood coming outta my dick. No guy does."

"Of course not. No one want that," Putin said.

"So you're a doctor, it's your job to say to me, 'You gotta do it, sir. You just gotta. There's no way around it. Maybe you piss blood but that doesn't hurt. It's just it looks bad.' Or you tell me, 'Sit when you pee like a girl, Excellency, and keep your eyes closed until after you flush. You won't even see it.' You think they did that? You think they fought for me to have that needle biopsy? No. Not at all."

"Doctors!" Putin said dismissively.

In fact, he had great respect for doctors. He'd never had one assassinated; just sent to prison or penal colonies. It was important to Putin that doctors be respected.

Trump's word geyser continued, undiminished: "I'm not even the president when I have an elevated PSA. *Before* the election. They see the elevated PSA, they don't force me? I say, 'No thanks. I got a presidential campaign to run.' Instead of saying 'mandatory,' they say, 'Okay, sir. You run your campaign, we'll take your blood in six month and see how the PSA is then.' That's not what they should of said. They should of said, 'You want to die? You'll die you don't check this out. You're afraid of pissing blood? How about being afraid of being dead and never pissing again?' Gotta tell you, Vlad, they wound up doing it, the biopsy, but doing it what? Yesterday, they did it. Which is what, a year, maybe more than a year, late. Too late. Yeah, a year and a half too late."

Putin was having trouble following the timeline.

Trump made it more difficult: "Back then, what, a year, a year and a half ago, two years, something like that, six months after the first one. Or was it the second one. I dunno."

What first or second one? Was a noun coming? There was not: "But the PSA's high six months later, and now the U.S.

is coming apart and I gotta negotiate the new republics and all. But at that time they don't say, 'You negotiate, you're signing your death warrant?' No, they say, 'Please, sir, you gotta take care of this.' I say, 'I will, I will, but first I gotta take care of the part of the country loves me.' They love me, too, the doctors, so they say, 'Okay. We'll look again in six months.' Maybe they said two months but then I blew them off for the other thing — you remember that?"

What was he talking about now? Putin was beginning to doubt his English comprehension skills.

"You and me, we were communicating through that third party. You know when we were communicating through the guy. The guy in New York, sometimes. Remember that time?"

That gave Putin a handle on the timeline. How could he forget? "The guy," was Rudy Giuliani. And Giuliani had called him all the time, day and night, alone and with people around him. He called drunk and he called sober, but mostly drunk. He called to show off that he could get Putin on the line when he had nothing to say and he called when he did have something to say, but he said it in such confusing language it was hard to follow. Rudy was so annoying Putin considered having him killed.

"We didn't have this line yet," Trump said, "Hell, we didn't have the four republics yet. Anyway, I blow them off for the biopsy and do they make a big stink and *force* me? No. So that's their fault, not mine. I'm not a doctor. I don't know what I'm risking. That's their job to tell me. That's what they gotta say, 'Take this needle biopsy now or die.' But doctors, they don't like to say the word 'die,' do they? Do Russian doctors ever say die?"

"All the time," Putin said. "That's all they ever say."

"Well *my* fucking doctors here, my doctors, they won't say it to a guy's been president and is about to be president again. No one's willing to say die to scare the president. So another, another, what, six months goes by. Maybe they tried again after two months, but I'm busy as hell, you know? I never worked as hard running the fucking country as I got to work breaking it up into usable republics. Anyway, what I have to tell you is I got the needle biopsy yesterday, the results today and the cancer's gone beyond the prostrate."

"Prostate," Putin corrected.

"Yeah. Right. I do that sometimes. Everybody does."

Not Putin; the Russian and English words for prostrate and prostate were pronounced identically; Putin never mixed them up.

"Anyhow, they wanted to open me up, the doctors, take the thing out, and I told them hell no. You treat this thing with the chemistry set or radiation or whatever they do, but there's no opening up Donald J. Trump. No blood, my friends. I'm not going under the knife. No putting me out for a couple hours while Tucker Carlson runs the country.

"Meanwhile, I'm pissing blood since they did the needle biopsy. They were right about that, looks ugly as hell, but it doesn't hurt to piss. Not that there's no pain; I feel like I got beaten up from the inside between my legs there, but nothing the pills can't handle. I'll tell you one thing, Vlad, I die from this fucking cancer, it's their fucking fault, the doctors. They should of insisted. They should of overrode me back then. Overridden? I don't know. Anyway, I'm not taking the blame for this. It was their job to convince me."

The verbal firehose ran out; Trump was quiet. Putin's top concern was replacing the most valuable asset in the history of espionage.

Whatever else the relationship between agent and asset, there was always a psychiatric component, with the asset as patient. For the asset who spies for the money — the bribed source — the agent sits for hours listening to their financial woes. For that type, no payment is adequate, no amount large enough to cover their ever-expanding expenses. If you recruit them through ideology, you must listen to their endless Talmudic scholarship about your shared political or religious faith. If you recruit them through kompromat, it's their endless recitation of grievance at having been compromised. Agents should have a diploma — maybe several diplomas — hanging on the wall when they debrief an asset.

Putin did his best to imitate a psychiatrist: "So, Donald, what you feel about this? What you think is next?"

"This is shit," Trump said.

Not what Putin had asked. He tried another approach, "What we need do? What I can do? You want me to send best cancer specialists from Switzerland? From here; from Russia? Very discreet, these doctors. How I can help, my brother?"

Putin knew what he could do to help the Russian Federation and he acted on it without waiting for Trump's reply: "One thought, while you consider, my brother. And that is this: it would be prudent you think who should be next in presidency, in event…." He left the event unnamed, knowing Trump did not like to contemplate his own death.

"What? What are you talking about? I don't get to appoint my successor; it's in the constitution."

Putin said, "My suggestion your successor — just my opinion—successor should be named 'Trump,' not 'Carlson.'

Trump said, "We can't have a president whose first name rhymes with 'fucker,' can we? But how do I do that? Does the constitution give me that right?"

Why would the president of the Great States of America ask the president of the Russian Federation if the GSA constitution gave him the right to change his successor? Because the Russian president was more familiar with that constitution than the GSA president was. In fact, Vladimir Vladimirovich Putin had supplied the GSA with its constitution so he knew exactly how Trump could change the order of succession.

At Putin's direction, a team of Russian lawyers — experts on American law, customs, history and the speeches of Donald Trump — had written the constitution for the Great States of America; it was a codification of authoritarian rule.

Rather than risk hackers intercepting the document by sending it to Trump via email — which Trump did not use, anyway — the SVR delivered it physically, on a thumb drive. The drive was handed to Rudy Giuliani in New York. At the time, Giuliani was free on $5 million bail while appealing his Georgia conviction for election tampering. Rudy was holding court in the King Cole Bar at the St. Regis Hotel when the SVR courier, Henrietta Krajewski, found him.

Henrietta was a middle-aged flight attendant for LOT, the Polish Airline, who picked up extra money running errands in New York and Warsaw for the Russians. She reported to her handler that she lured Giuliani away from a table packed with his cronies, brought him to the bar and gave him the thumb drive, which he pocketed. Then he propositioned her, suggesting he get a room for "a quickie." She declined.

Putin thought Giuliani's behavior unprofessional; who volunteers to be caught in a honeytrap? Why does Donald put up with that p'yanitsa — drunkard?

The p'yanitsa flew to Palm Beach and turned the thumb drive over to Trump, who got someone with a computer to print out Putin's constitution. The editing and ratification process was singular. While the constitutional process in the other three republics began with a convention of state lawmakers and governors reading, analyzing and adapting the 1787 United States Constitution, the process in the GSA was different.

For one thing, the self-designated president of the republic was chairman of the constitutional convention. For another, he never actually read the document. Rather, he had Putin's constitution read aloud to him, first by Newt Gingrich — on the theory that a former University of West Georgia history professor might add some insights and perspective. Trump quickly tired of Gingrich's annoying nasal voice and brought in as his replacement Kait Parker, a weather reporter for the local Fox station, WFLX. She had scant understanding of what she was reading, but she did have long, flowing honey-blonde hair, great legs and a bosom Trump longed to fondle.

As Kait read the constitution, Trump made comments and suggestions. A team of lawyers and paralegals made notes. The team included partners-in-election lawsuits Rudy

Giuliani and Sidney Powell as well as a host of Fox News legal analysts and two justices of the former United States Supreme Court, Brett Kavanaugh and Clarence Thomas.

The legal team incorporated their notes of Trump's comments into a revised draft of the constitution which Kait read to him. This time around he made specific word changes, which is why the GSA constitution contains the words "great," "perfect" and "beautiful" multiple times.

At the end of the process there was a PowerPoint presentation to show Trump the final product. There were only 15 slides in the deck but that was ten more than he customarily sat through. To keep him attentive, the lawyers hired pretty student dancers from the A. W. Dreyfoos School of the Arts in West Palm Beach, vetting them to insure they were 18 or older. The girls read five slides each, switching from the blonde to the brunette to the redhead. They wore short skirts, high heels and low-cut tops. Their recitation skills were not on a par with their allure, but Trump appeared satisfied with the performance, and so the Putin constitution, as amended by Trump, was presented for ratification to the delegates Trump had selected for the Great States of America's constitutional convention.

The convention met for only four hours, most of that time being devoted to an invocation by Franklin Graham, a calling of the roll and a two-hour, 22-minute Trump speech.

The constitution was unanimously ratified without debate or discussion.

Vladimir Vladimirovich Putin read a Russian translation of the final document with a satisfied smirk; nothing of substance had been changed. It was like the old Soviet days when Moscow supplied constitutions and laws to captive Eastern European countries. But this satellite nation was on the continent of North America and and was composed of 26 states – more than any of the other American republics.

◆ ◆ ◆

Wow! Fox News is really pushing the Democrats and the Democrat agenda. Gets worse every single day. — Donald J. Trump

Newscorp Headquarters, 1211 Avenue Of The Americas, New York, Atlantic States Of America

The Proprietor was a voracious reader of newspapers. And not merely the front pages. He learned a lot by skimming the adverts, reading the features, considering the analytical columns and consuming the sport pages.

In the old days, there was always an untidy pile of newspapers on the table in his conference room and he would spend every spare minute leafing through them, silently critiquing headlines, raging at contrarian opinion columns and diving deep into political and business stories. To him, they were the same thing; every political story had an impact on business and every business story had an impact on politics.

Challenging and vanquishing stereotypes about the elderly, Murdoch was unafraid of digital media and used it to cast his reading net wider than ever. He spent an inordinate amount of each day on his iPad scrolling through a vast number of newspaper websites, his own and those of rivals. It was on one of those rival outlets, the online "Times of Israel," that he read this headline:

"Israeli Doctor Claims to 'Reverse' Aging With Pure Oxygen Treatment Study."

Murdoch clicked on the story:

"Sixty-three people aged 65-plus, took MRI scans and tested their cognitive abilities. Dr. Shai Efrati then gave some of them a 60-day course of treatment during which they spent two-hour stints in a pressurized chamber five times a week, breathing pure oxygen for some of the time. At the end of the experiment, those who didn't go in the hyperbaric chamber had similar MRI results as they did at the start, and similar cognitive ability. But Efrati reported a significant difference on those who received the oxygen therapy — and found the improvements held in tests six months later."

Shai Efrati turned down Murdoch's lucrative offer to leave his post at Tel Aviv University and become a Newscorp executive and personal doctor to a single patient. But it was easy enough to find a locally based physician to replicate Efrati's hyperbaric oxygen therapy regime on an exclusive basis. And, just in case ethnicity had anything remotely to do with the outcome, The Proprietor's people made sure the domestically sourced doctor was an Israeli-born Jew. One never knows.

Murdoch was at his desk, inhaling pressurized oxygen from a mask while simultaneously watching Fox News and skimming The Sun, his largest-circulation UK newspaper. Judy Travers, the only one of his three assistants permitted to communicate directly with him, buzzed the intercom. She had been instructed not to interrupt during his two hours of hyperbaric oxygen therapy, so it had to be extraordinarily important. He tapped the intercom.

"Yes?" All that emerged from the thick silicone mask was a hiss: "Ssssss."

"Mr. Murdoch? Sir?"

He removed the mask and spoke, "Yes, Judy?"

Although she was an American, Judy used British rules of pluralization: "BBC are reporting President Trump has prostate cancer and I've had calls for you from Peterson, and…."

The Proprietor interrupted her roll call of News Corp executives. He growled: "Why am I hearing about this now for the first time?" The growl became a shout: "How the hell did the Beeb beat us on this story? Where is my son?"

Travers had been with The Proprietor a long time: from the tail end of the second of his four marriages through the entirely of his fourth. She had been his conduit to the outside world through a thousand political battles as well. She knew not to take his occasional outbursts personally. In fifteen minutes, he'd realize he had been uncivil, and he would apologize. And add a $1,500 bonus to her weekly paycheck.

"Peterson and Winsome say they can't confirm it. Both say it may not be accurate. They don't know how BBC got the story." No article; another Britishism. "Nobody seems to know. I'm holding both their calls if you want to speak with them. And your son is on his boat. In Australia." He knew full well where his son was; he asked only because he was annoyed.

"Let's conference this at the highest editorial level," The Proprietor said, "get London in on the call, too. This is embarrassing. Godawful embarrassing!"

"Yes, Mr. Murdoch."

The Proprietor, energized and angry, said, "I talked to that clown just last week and he did a 25-minute monologue and never gave a hint! This from a chap who can't keep a secret if his life depended on it. Which in this case it may. Unless, of course, the story's not true. And I talked to that little shit, Miller, just yesterday. Nothing from him; not a word, not a hint. Maybe he doesn't know, although I doubt that very much. What they don't tell him, he snoops out for himself."

"Yes, Mr. Murdoch. Right away."

"Oh, and if he isn't too busy on his surfboard, get *him* in on the call. In 30 minutes, okay?"

That would give him time to finish the oxygen therapy and be as cognitively sound as possible for the call. He snapped the mask back in place just as Fox News interrupted regular programming with the "Breaking News" banner that was so overused no one paid it any attention. An anchor reported on the BBC scoop. It mortified Murdoch to see the hated BBC logo on Fox News. Trump let me be scooped by BBC? Is he playing a game? What could it be? Why BBC?

He removed the hyperbaric oxygen mask and buzzed Judy: "One more thing."

"Yes, Mr. Murdoch."

"Find that BBC Reporter who broke the story. I want to hire him. The chap is very good. Very good. Let's get him.

"You said the story might not be true," Judy reminded him.

He growled: "What's that got to do with anything?"

Then, as an afterthought, he decided he had the singular best source on the story on autodial. He punched a button; the call was answered on the first ring. Without waiting for a greeting, The Proprietor said, "Murdoch here, Rosalind. Need to talk to him."

Trump was on the line in seconds: "Yeah, Rupert?"

Trump usually responded with alacrity. And why should he not; he owed The Proprietor much. The old man's support cost Trump nothing more than pretending to be attentive during an occasional phone call. His most effective propaganda outlet was free, unlike earlier authoritarians who had to pay good money to publish their own newspapers or run their own radio or TV stations. Fox News was Trump's free Völkischer Beobachter or Pravda while earning The Proprietor billions. The biggest drawback in having an independent propaganda operation: when Hitler or Stalin were upset with any content in their media properties, they could sack, imprison or kill the offending publisher, editor or writer. Trump could do nothing but rant on social media about apostasy.

"You've seen the BBC story. I need to know if it's true," Murdoch said. There was a snappish chill in his voice; he was angry.

"First you report it on Fox and *then* you want to know if it's true? Isn't that backwards? And since when are you a reporter, Rupert?"

To the Proprietor, this was typical of Trump, a master of bad temper, the holder of a black belt in grievance. Patiently, as if to a child, he explained, "We reported that BBC reported it. We also said we could not confirm it. That's our job, report big stories, attribute them to the original media and try to confirm them. If the story is untrue, we will report that BBC went with a false story. So, is it?"

Trump was aspiring to high dudgeon; The Proprietor had been condescending to him; it rankled. He decided to make the old man work for his story: "Is it what?"

True?"

"Whaddaya think?"

"I think it would be best if you answer the question with an answer rather than with another question."

"Yes, but whaddaya think? How could you keep something like that secret? How could I do that?"

"You're answering questions with questions."

"No, no. Answer me. How could I keep something like that secret?"

"It's clearly not secret now, if it's true," Murdoch said. "BBC reported it. So it is true?"

Tiring of the game, Trump defaulted to mendacity: "Of course it's not true. It's made up. It's fake news. It's the BBC and they always make shit up. Especially about *me*. You, of all people, know. You compete against them."

"I do know them," The Proprietor said. "And I do compete against them." What he did not add was: I know them to be scrupulously careful to check facts before broadcasting them, especially with a huge story like this one.

"Wasn't it the BBC that had the pedophile hosting a kid's program or something like that?" Trump asked.

"That was Jimmy Savile and it was well over 20 years ago. Besides that had almost nothing to do with BBC News," Murdoch said.

"So you're gonna defend them, the BBC? Is that it?"

"That's off-point," Murdoch said.

"I already told you, Rupert, it's fake news. I'm as healthy as a horse."

Murdoch suspected Trump was lying. Given the man's track record, it was almost certain he was lying. He took the president's denial and swift pivot to attack the BBC as proof Trump was lying. Rather than make an accusation, he asked: "So will you release your medical records to us for a story in the Wall Street Journal and on Fox News? Will you give us an exclusive interview?"

"First you were a reporter, now you're booking guests on Fox News?"

"Will you give the Journal and Fox News an interview?"

Trump had no intention of giving anyone an interview, but he lied again, "Of course I will. As soon as you can figure out how a very edited version of the interview doesn't end up in the Washington Post or the failing New York Times and make me look bad. Guarantee me that and you've got your interview.

The "failing" New York Times was a Trump favorite; he deployed "failing" as if it was part of the paper's name. The Proprietor would welcome comparable "failure." The Times had recently surpassed 12 million paid subscribers to its digital editions. The Wall Street Journal's comparable figure was slightly more than three million.

"You can give the lie to this by releasing current medical records," Murdoch said, knowing neither his nor anyone else's media outlets would ever see Trump's real medical records. The best he could hope for was a mendacious cover letter from the Mar-a-Lago physician and a pile of fake test results. The letter would attest to the demonstrably alternative fact that the president was hale and hearty, and likely was the healthiest political figure in the four republics.

There was nothing to be gained by getting confrontational with Trump, so Murdoch gracefully exited the conversation.

The pair had bickered futilely since 2022 when The Wall Street Journal and the NY Post ran editorials telling Trump to move on from his fixation with his 2020 election defeat by Joe Biden. At the same time, Fox News pinched off Trump's political IV drip of live interviews and its slavish wall-to-wall live coverage of his rallies.

When the FBI served a search warrant on Mar-a-Lago and hauled away a large cache of government documents, Fox News repeatedly interviewed Trump's former attorney general, Bill Barr, who set the viewers straight on just who might have committed a crime by hoarding the files.

For the most part ignoring The Proprietor's outlets, Trump had plugged away on his national Stop the Steal grievance tour, generating local and statewide coverage wherever he went and raising hundreds of millions of barely scrutinized dollars. Murdoch suspected that Trump and/or the Trump Enterprises were the chief beneficiaries of that fund-raising, but he declined to unleash the Wall Street Journal's best investigative reporters on the story, lest he need Trump one day.

That day came after Trump won multiple primaries in 2024 against a platoon of Republican hopefuls. Murdoch, a reader of writing on walls as well as writing in newspapers, promptly restored the old, mutually advantageous relationship. But it was like the remarriage of a couple who had divorced acrimoniously. Resentment smoldered; old slights were remembered, nourished and exaggerated. There was no bliss in the relationship, just practical interactions. They were a couple once more, but cold realism replaced the warmth of political kinship. Each recognized the flaws in the other, and they could not forget or forgive them. The greatest of those flaws: the transactional motivation for their "remarriage" that each ascribed to the other without recognizing it in himself. Trump saw Murdoch's embrace as a ratings ploy. Murdoch saw Trump's reciprocal and tepid hug as part of his game plan to keep Fox News viewers in his camp. It worked for both. To The Proprietor Trump was stupid, lazy and mentally unstable. But useful. Trump thought Murdoch frail, senile and a bad businessman. But useful.

Murdoch was convinced Trump had metastatic cancer and likely was not long for this world. But he would not have his outlets reporting a hunch, even even if it was his hunch. He needed confirmation. And for confirmation, he needed reliable and informed sources, the sort of sources Walter Cholmondeley had.

◆ ◆ ◆

Despite the constant negative press, covfefe. — Donald J. Trump

Palm Beach International Airport, West Palm Beach, Florida, Great States Of America

"Mr. ….er, Mr. Chol-delay?"

The woman holding his UK passport took another look at his name and tried again: "Chol-o-modly?"

He pronounced it correctly for her, adding, "Exactly as it's spelled."

"Of course." She reddened. He took no pleasure in it; the comedic effect of Americans struggling to pronounce his name had worn as thin as the seat of a bus driver's trousers.

"Your ticket," she said.

"Thank you."

"Security is right through there. You've got an hour before your flight boards. "

"I need to sit down before I go through," he said. "I hurt my knee."

He had not hurt his knee; a WORM had hurt his knee; hurt it with a single vicious cosh blow. It was the same knee he'd skinned when he fell going up the step. That's all it took: a knee-skinning and a single blow. He'd betrayed his five sources immediately, to the disappointment of the cosh-wielding WORM.

Cholmondeley was mortified at himself. Centuries of British soldiers and spies had endured fingernail pullings, genital mutilation, hours of beatings, anesthesia-free extraction of vital organs, hangings, rackings and cuttings and kept their secrets.

Mel Gibson, who wasn't even British, endured all of that in the last reel of "Braveheart" and all he gave them was "FREEEEEEDOOOOMMMMMM!"

But for Cholmondelay, a single cosh whack was all it took.

He justified his cowardice by convincing himself the WORMs probably knew his sources before they asked the question. But then, why bother kidnapping him if they already knew; why not just round up the five and whisk them away?

He rose from the bench made his way toward the security checkpoint, limping more than the ache warranted. He had been declared persona non grata and was being deported. Like a criminal! At least that was the story from the WORMs who interrogated him. He thought they might be making it up; they gave him no paperwork, no deportation order. A one-way ticket was waiting at the airport. Destination: Washington, capital of the Atlantic States of America.

"Don't come back, Chumpley," a WORM said. "You're not welcome here."

"My gear. My clothing, office equipment, laptop."

"We're gonna pack it up and send it to you. You email the Mar-a-Lago press office and tell them where to send your shit. It'll get there."

The other WORM chimed in: "Not just you, neither. No more BBC reporters in the GSA. Any of 'em that's here got twenty-four hours to leave."

Again, no paperwork, no declaration, no official order. He had no idea if this was policy or a couple of WORMs improvising policy.

As he queued up for the security check, his phone buzzed. The caller ID indicated New York; the caller's name was "Unlisted." It might be one of his betrayed sources calling on a burner phone; he answered.

Unlisted identified himself: "Murdoch, here." The Australian accent was authentic, but if it was Murdoch, the caller ID would have said that, would it not?

"And I'm Father Christmas," Cholmondeley said. He rang off.

Unlisted/Murdoch called back. Cholmondeley did not answer. He'd had more than enough nonsense for one day.

He wanted no more. In two-and-a-half hours he would be safe in Washington, in a country where journalists weren't rounded up and tortured for their sources.

His phone buzzed again. Cholmondeley answered, "Persistent bugger, aren't you?" He hung up yet again on the most powerful media mogul in the world.

Once through security, Cholmondeley phoned the news desk in London. A young-sounding woman, answered.

"Cholmondeley, here." He rather liked Fake Murdoch's telephone style.

"Oh, they want to talk to you. *He* wants to talk to you?"

"They? He?"

"The gaffer. We're being kicked out of GSA. Have they told you?"

"They did more than tell me; they kidnapped me, they beat me up and then they drove me to the airport, handed me a ticket and declared me PNG which may or may not be official since I've seen no paperwork whatsoever. So, yes, I know, but as I say, I've seen nothing that makes it official."

"Kidnapped? You were kidnapped? That's a good story. can you file something on it now?"

"From the airport? No, not right now. Being deported, you know."

"So you can't file something? You don't have to write anything; we can have someone interview you."

"Too dangerous; still in GSA. They may be spying on me."

He surveyed his fellow travelers; a few of them struck him as candidates for GSA spies; not that he would know what a spy looked like.

"Where are they sending you? Can you file on the kidnapping and torture from there."

"To Washington. And I never said torture. I said they beat me up. More like they roughed me up."

"Which Washington? The state? Or… the other state?"

This was a more difficult question to answer than it once had been. The District of Columbia — that little enclave carved into the malarial swampland between Maryland and Virginia and designated the capital city of the United States — was now the State of Washington in the Atlantic States of America. But the westernmost republic, The Pacific States of America, also had a Washington State. Coming up in the next round of voting in November, residents of the Atlantic States of America's Washington would be offered a chance to change the state name to

Capitolia, which would differentiate it from the Pacific States of America's Washington State. But that vote was three months off and no sure thing.

"The eastern one," Cholmondeley said, "It's a cheaper flight and you know what a tightwad he is."

"Not his money, is it?"

"I suspect he sees it as his money. Tight as they come, don't you know? Unless it's being spent on him or at one of his properties."

"You're well-rid of that place. Although, you have to admit, being deported from Florida to Washington sounds a bit strange."

He said, "George Orwell would piss himself laughing."

"Who?"

Where do they find these people?

*

In the months to come, GSA's efforts to jam BBC broadcasts and to block its internet and streaming sites proved beyond the capabilities of the GSA's recently constituted Digital Cybersecurity Agency. While BBC reporters and crews were absent from the country, its reports were not because

GSADCA was as inept an agency as existed in the Great States of America, a country where governmental ineptitude was the norm. GSADCA was an at-war-with-itself amalgam of Ivy League marketing types, internet conmen and basement-dwelling computer hackers. The Ivy Leaguers were skilled at creating Facebook political ads, the conmen were experts in identity theft and the hackers were a slovenly lot who played internet games or traded cryptocurrencies, earning and losing fortunes as high as $1,500. The agency was headed by its cabinet-level director, Mike Lindell, the TV and internet pillow and bedding pitchman. Lindell claimed The Christ, Jesus himself, had saved him from compulsive gambling and crack cocaine addictions and destined him to run cybersecurity in a nation headed by The Trump, Donald J., himself. One look at the My Pillow home page would have convinced The Christ, or anyone else, that Lindell was unqualified for the job. But no one involved in vetting him bothered to look. The Trump wanted the My Pillow Guy and Trump always got what he wanted.

◆ ◆ ◆

Nobody's ever been treated badly like me. Although they do say Abraham Lincoln was treated really badly. — Donald J. Trump

The 45/1 Office, Mar-A-Lago, Palm Beach, Florida, Great States Of America

Rosalind Baskin had been Trump's personal assistant for so long they both thought of her as his secretary, because when she went to work for him, that's what the job was called. She stood in the doorway trying to keep them out of the 45/1 Office. "You don't want to go in there just now. You just don't…" Adding sotto voce: "Foul mood."

"Default mood," said the Secretary of Defense, "and he's got every right to it. You been fucked the way he's been fucked; you get to be in a foul mood."

Michael Flynn was not exactly in a peachy mood, himself. He had raced over to Mar-a-Lago as soon as he saw the Fox News report on the BBC scoop about The Boss's prostate cancer. Flynn commandeered the first vehicle he saw when he exited his office, so he arrived at the Mar-a-Lago security gate in in an up-armored Humvee mounted with a .50 caliber machine gun. He had ordered the driver — a Spc/5 daunted into speechlessness by encountering the secretary — into the passenger seat and took the wheel himself, driving the top-heavy Humvee at tire-melting speed.

Although the .50 caliber was not manned, or even loaded, its presence set off a wild scramble among the WORMs around the Mar-a-Lago perimeter and things were touch-and-go for several minutes — a frightening time for Flynn, who knew just how piss poor WORM training was. But then a couple of WORM NCOs recognized Flynn, and ordered a stand-down.

As he drove onto the property, some of the WORMs threw him salutes of varying degrees of sloppiness which he did not return because he'd be damned if he would violate saluting protocol by snapping one off while wearing civvies. If presidents wanted to pretend they were in uniform and return a salute, that was the prerogative of a C-I-C, but not this former soldier.

Standing next to that creepy little chief of staff — who was all a-flutter, don't ya know — Flynn got his agitation under control and acted the model of composed decorum: "You know, Rosalind, I'm a calming presence for him."

Miller shot him a sideways glance. If the boss was on the verge of a snit, Flynn would push him over. If he was in a snit, Flynn would fan it up to a rage. If he was in a rage, Flynn would boost it to volcanic level and find more lava for him to spill. To Miller, Flynn was no calming influence; he was an inflaming influence. Flynn was bat shit crazy and when he was around Trump, the crazy became contagious.

"We gotta see him. Well, I gotta see him," Miller said.

Who the hell kept the president's chief of staff in the hall? He was supposed to be the presidential gatekeeper, not some secretary. OK, personal assistant.

"What *you*? It's *we*," Flynn protested. "I didn't come all the way over here from the Pentagon to cool my heels in a waiting room."

Flynn did not like Miller. He did not Miller's kind in general and this particular example of that kind was particularly vexing. Especially since his office was so close to The Boss's office.

As if to justify Flynn's vexation, Miller corrected him: "It's not the Pentagon. *They* got the Pentagon. We got the West Palm Beach National Guard armory. Or you got that."

"It's a helluva lot more than a fucking armory, Chief, and you goddamn know it."

Inside the office, Trump shouted, "Who the fuck is out there making all that noise? Can't hear myself think for all that fucking shouting out there."

There had been no shouting until now; Rosalind turned and called into the office, "It's the Chief and the Secretary of Defense. They want to see you."

"I *need* to see him," Miller corrected. "Mike *wants* to see him."

"I *need* to see him as much as you do," Flynn protested.

"No, you *want* to see him, and I *need* to see him."

Trump bellowed: "Well what the fuck are they waiting for? Get their asses in here."

They walked through the wide door together, hurrying to be first to enter the presidential presence. It was a tie. Both stopped and radar-swept the 45/1 Office.

The room, built to Trump's orders, was round — going the White House's Oval Office one better. It looked as if a tornado had been confined within its curved walls. There were papers on the floor, on the chairs, on the mantlepiece. There was broken crockery. The 11th-Century icon Vladimir Putin had sent the president as an inauguration present had been thrown across the room, hit the far wall and came apart, leaving five fragments on the floor. The bust of Winston Churchill he'd had copied from the one in the White House had also been thrown, although it weighed 16 pounds, so it had only just cleared the desk. It appeared undamaged. Trump had taken the fireplace poker and played stickball with everything else that had been on his desk. The wild swinging left jagged scars on the desktop. There were shards and puddles where the water pitcher and glasses had been on the coffee table. The two multiline phones had been yanked from their cords and thrown against the wall. The white single-line phone was the only one still on the president's desk.

Trump stood behind the desk; navy blue suit, white shirt, red tie extending thee inches below his belt line. His shoulders were rounded, and he was tilting forward. The rage tornado had taken its toll on him, he was out of breath.

Why are these clowns here? Look at Flynn; he looks like he's going to cry. A fucking general crying. And Miller. Looks like a midget. Assholes, the both of them. Why doesn't Miller get hair plugs; cover up that shiny dome? Dopey-looking. Nice suit though.

"What?" Trump roared. "What?"

"Bad day, Excellency?" Flynn asked.

"*Bad* day? How about the *worst* day? You saw that fake news story those English fuckers made up about me? How's that for a bad day; lying fuckers. I got Rupert Fucking Murdoch calling me directly, asking me if it's true. Rupert Murdoch! But first he reports it on Fox News. He's letting the BBC tell everyone I'm going to die."

"Yes, boss. I don't think they quite reported exactly that" Miller said. He had learned to preface a correction of Trump with the word "Yes."

"It came over like Fox reported it! *Fox* is reporting I'm dying? *Fox?*"

That old fucker's trying to fuck me over again. Fucks me over in 2020. Arizona call; I won Arizona. No question. I remember even if nobody else does. Then that 'move on' remark. Who's he think he is? "Trump's gotta move on." Leaked. Leaked by who? By him. Fuck that; move on. Then his fucking Wall Street

Journal editorial; and the Post, too. I'm not moving on. "I didn't know they were going to print that, Donald." He says to me. Yeah, sure, you didn't. Like those guys don't take a shit without asking his permission first. Now this. What's his game? Tucker Carlson? Wants to see Carlson president. Have a puppet president. Well, fuck that; Donald Trump is president. And Donald Trump is nobody's puppet. Nobody controls Donald Trump!

"They said that the BBC reported you had prostate cancer and that Fox couldn't confirm it," Miller said.

"*That's* reporting it," Trump said. "That's as good as confirming it. They need to get out there and say it's fake. Because it is. It's a fucking lie and we gotta fight it with the truth."

"We'll go on the air and tell the people it's not true," Miller said. He was one of the few people who knew the story was true. "Anita's team is working on it now."

Flynn, eager to undermine Miller, asked, "You think she can handle that? It's pretty heavy lifting."

Trump answered for Miller: "Of course she can handle it. That's her job and the story's bullshit. Not true. Not true at all. It's a fucking lie. A dirty lie. A Democrat lie. Fake news. Make sure she gets that out there; a Democrat lie. What I wanna know is, how'd that limey get the story."

General Flynn reported for duty: "I can have him picked up. The reporter. We'll interrogate him. Once we know who gave him the story, we can take care of them. I'll have that reporter in custody in 20 minutes, Excellency."

Miller pricked Flynn's balloon: "WORMs already did that, General. Under my direction. I interrogated him myself. He spilled and we've already detained his sources. There were five of them."

Flynn was flustered: "What authority do you have to…."

Trump interrupted: "I gave him the authority. I told him to pick the guy up and find his sources and arrest them. Detain if you want to use pansy words." He asked Miller: "Your guys beat the shit outta him? Did they draw blood? Waterboard? I hope he doesn't have two teeth left in his mouth. Fucking BBC; what kind of government lets its media report fake stuff like that."

"Let's just say I got the names of his sources. They're in custody or will be very soon. They're not going anywhere," Miller said. "Now how about this: we go full court press to show that you're not sick. A rally a night for a week. Speeches. Play golf tomorrow. Take a ride on a speedboat."

"No speedboats. People get killed riding in fucking speedboats." The real reason Trump hated speedboats was what the wind did to his hair.

"Okay, Excellency, no speedboat."

"How's Tucker taking it?," Flynn asked. "He's not in line anymore. He's gotta be upset."

"Fuck him," Trump said. "Who cares how he's taking it? No one cares, except Rupert. 'Sides, you can't have a president whose first name rhymes with fucker."

The line had worked on Putin, so he used it again. They did not find it amusing.

Flynn was smarting. *He* was supposed to take care of national security issues, not Miller. Miller was smirking, having out-maneuvered a general. To Flynn that smug smirk was a challenge; one that he would eventually take up. Just you wait, Miller. Enjoy your minutes of victory, because that's about how long it's going to be, minutes.

"Can you *take care* of that reporter?" Trump asked Flynn.

"No problem, Excellency."

Miller, radiating smug, corrected him: "Actually, there is a problem. We declared him persona non grata and kicked him out of the country. He's likely midair to Washington right now."

"Who gave you that kind of authority? And which Washington?" Flynn demanded.

Miller said, "You do know killing reporters from allied countries is a bad idea, don't you?"

Trump exploded: "Enough! Enough with the fucking reporter. I changed my mind. Don't take care of him. Something happens to the guy, the reporter, it looks like he's getting taken out for telling the truth; at least that's the story the lamestream media will tell. So leave him alone and bury his bullshit story. Just get this fake cancer thing under control. It's fake news and we're gonna prove it's fake news. It *is* fake news. A BBC lie. You" — he pointed at Miller — "call Murdoch and say in so many words that the cancer story is a bullshit story; that it's not true. I talked to him, but I played mind games with him so maybe he didn't believe me."

"On it, boss." Trump cocked his head. "On it, Excellency."

"Then let's show what a lie it is; I wanna be everywhere: rallies, TV, parades, golf courses. But no fucking speedboats. Get it going. Now! And *you...*" — directed at Flynn — "...put on a big military parade. Miami Beach. Down Collins Avenue. The whole thing. Jets flying over, troops, tanks, artillery. The whole she-bang. Me in a reviewing stand. Make it happen. Make sure the viewing stand's enclosed and air-conditioned; I'm not spending 40 minutes, an hour, sweating on camera like Nixon. Make it happen. Just make sure there aren't any wounded guys in the parade. That won't look good for me. That Bastille Day parade I went to with Macron; they had guys in wheelchairs, guys on crutches. You know, wounded guys. That looked bad. It *was* bad; bad for Macron. I don't want that in my parade. Coordinate you two, but I want it happening ASAP! And don't say no. Don't you dare fucking say no. I'm tired of hearing no. I won't hear no. I want yes-men. If you can't say yes, don't say anything!"

"Yes, Excellency," Miller and Flynn chorused.

Miller noticed the flashing white phone on Trump's desk; he knew Putin was on the other end of the line. "Excellency, the white phone is flashing."

"Fuck *him*. He can wait," Trump said. Nonetheless, he ushered them out of the wreckage of his office and picked up the phone.

"Vlad, can't talk right now," he said.

"Call me when you can, my brother, I think there are things we can do for each other that will be very helpful."

"Okay. I'll call you soon."

Let him cool his Ruskie heels. I'll call when I'm good and ready. Helpful? He wants to be helpful. Bullshit. Only I can help myself here. I don't need Putin to wipe this story off the face of the earth.

In the anteroom, Flynn — who was standing far too close for Miller's comfort — asked, "What's that flashing phone line, Steve? It that Murdoch?"

"Party headquarters," Miller lied. He changed the subject: "We have our marching orders. Let's put this lie to rest."

◆ ◆ ◆

But they ask me, "Is Putin smart?" Yes, Putin was smart. — Donald J. Trump

The Office Of The President, The Kremlin, Moscow, Russian Federation

After Trump put him off, Putin used one of the multiline phones on his desk to call Stephen Miller.

"I can't talk now," Miller said, meaning there were others in the room with him.

"Is important," Putin said. "Is about your BBC problem."

"I'll clear my office." Miller did not mute his phone, so Putin heard him asking Mike Flynn to leave.

Mike Flynn, what a *sumasshedshiy* — lunatic. He is going to get them into trouble, maybe even a war, with his conspiracies. Someone should tell Trump.

"Dobroye utro," Miller said when he came back on the line. "And good morning to you," Putin said.

Who was Miller to try to speak Russian? What was he? The grandson, maybe great-grandson, of Belarusian Zhyds and he's speaking Russian? Trying to connect with your family heritage? Your ancestors, they never knew a word of Russian. Maybe they could haggle a little in Belarusian, maybe not. Zyhds spoke Yiddish, back then, not Russian. You, my friend, don't speak Russian and shouldn't pretend to. He said none of this.

"I can help with BBC problem, you can help me for something, too. Something I need. When he can talk, I need you tell him what I can do for him and what he can do me. Or he calls me himself and we discuss."

"Did you just try to call him? I was in his office, saw the phone flashing," Miller said.

Why ask when you know? Such an American thing to do; ask a needless question. "He too busy to talk, will call back, but I tell you what I want to talk about and you tell him, so no surprises when we do talk."

"I think we've got the BBC problem in hand," Miller said. "We kicked the reporter out of the country; he's probably in Washington by now.

"Vitch Vashington?" Putin said. He was capable of pronouncing Ws, but Americans seemed to like it when Russians substituted the V sound.

"The closest one, the Atlantic States Washington. We closed down their office, the BBC; we're kicking out any other BBC reporters we find."

"That not taking care of problem, my friend," Putin said. "*Ve* take care of our fake news problems."

Miller knew exactly how Putin took care of errant Russian journalists. Premature and suspicious deaths of Russian news reporters and editors had been running about one a year since Putin took power in 2000. After the invasion of Ukraine in 2022, the death toll among them quadroupled to four a year. Dissident Russian journalists died of a variety of causes, most frequently a bullet to the back of the head during a mugging in which no wallets, watches or jewelry were taken. There had been "accidental" poisonings with chemicals; drug overdoses among journalists who had never used drugs, and multiple accidental falls down stairs and out windows. A few Russian journalists had committed suicide -- or "suicide" --without leaving eplanatory notes.

Insofar as Miller knew, Putin's agents had "taken care of" no foreign journalists either within Russia's borders or beyond.

"We don't do that here," Miller said.

"Maybe think again your policy?"

"Wouldn't do us any good; they can cover us from the other republics."

"There aren't accidents in other republics? Violent muggings? Suicides? Do people fall in Atlantic States of America?"

"We're handling it by saying it's fake. The story's untrue. We're holding a briefing with his doctor then we're putting him out on the circuit to show it's not true. Putting Trump out there. Everywhere."

"Ah, correct misinformation? I have people can help with that," Putin said and he outlined three steps he would have the FSB, the GRU and the Internet Research Agency take. The last was a massive disinformation campaign to prove Trump was well and the story about his cancer was fake news disseminated by Ukrainian disinformation specialists

"I can see where the Ukraine angle serves your interests," Miller said.

"Serves yours more than Russia's," Putin said. "Now, the quid pro quo, as you say in English."

Miller did not point out that it was a Latin phrase.

"And that would be what, exactly?" he asked.

"An installation."

"What kind of installation? Where?"

"Get map, I wait. Map of Texas."

Miller used Google maps to call up a Texas map on his desktop computer.

"Look at area 200 kilometers west of Austin and about 400 kilometers north northwest of San Antonio," Putin said. "Is called Fort Worth Basin. In basin, there is no oil and gas, no oil and gas worth drilling. Very little. No reserves worth effort. That's where new company begins a play. Just a little drilling. Very little; it hasn't been productive area in past."

"I don't understand," Miller said. "You have the world's largest gas and oil reserves. Why drill here in an area where you know it's not going to be productive?"

"Listen," Putin said. "I explain you…."

And he did.

When Putin finished, Miller said, "I can't make that happen. And I'm not sure he's going to be willing to make that happen."

"Tell him. We will see."

Putin's ask was outrageous, impossible, impractical, historic. It was beyond reason, but it was Putin's best and possibly last chance. Trump might be dying so it was time to make the biggest demands on his asset. As he had learned in the KGB academy and saw first-hand while in active service in East Germany: there is no leveraging concessions from a corpse.

Putin knew Miller would report to Trump and Trump would wait at least two hours, if not two days, before picking up the hotline. Trump would imagine he was keeping Putin from attending to the business of governing, showing the Russian who was boss. A childish ploy. They both knew who the boss was, and he did not live in a private club in Florida, was not protected by mob of undisciplined hooligans and was not served by a government of cronies, toadies and profiteers. Well, Putin admitted to himself, they *did* have in common the government filled with cronies, toadies and profiteers. Both men knew that in the Putin-Trump relationship, Putin, was the boss.

Putin knew exactly what would happen next: the GSA president would make it sound as if he could not grant the request. Then he would negotiate around the edges, trying to cut back on the demand. And finally, he would negotiate himself into agreement.

Neither man had read "The Art of the Deal," although Trump was credited with having written it. No matter: Putin was the dealmaker. Putin had all the leverage, and

Trump knew that; knew Putin was the boss. Knew that a quick telephone call and a drop-off to a news outlet anywhere in the West was all it would take for Putin to set in motion the presidency of Tucker Carlson. Or Eric Trump, if the father stopped dithering and finally got to work on the dynasty plan.

"You not named Eric yet," Putin had said in a recent conversation. "He's legacy. He carries on your name."

"He's dumber than dirt," Trump answered.

Putin refrained from asking why dumber-than-dirt Eric was in charge of all of the Trump family businesses. Instead, he feigned empathy, "Not dumb, my brother, he's unsophisticated. I help him. I will help him."

Putin preferred Eric: he had no leverage with Carlson other than their shared distaste for democracy. Carlson worshiped authoritarian power; Putin had it. But the Russian knew that attitudes change, opinions evolve; his ideological sway over Carlson was iffy, undependable. With Eric Trump, Putin had more leverage, leverage in the form of spreadsheets, memos, bank records, emails and other documents. It was not as good as Putin's leverage over the father, so now was the time to use that leverage.

◆ ◆ ◆

Frederick Douglass is an example of somebody who's done an amazing job and is being recognized more and more, I notice. — Donald J. Trump

Mar-A-Lago Press Briefing Room, Palm Beach, Florida, Great States Of America

Anita Palacio's journalism credentials were skimpy: a 28-month stint as a weather girl on Telemiami, the Spanish-language cable station, and 12-weeks of employment at Fox News, where she was a decorative but mostly silent roundtable participant on "The Five." She owed her job as presidential press secretary to the fact that she was a beautiful, educated, Latina, a true-believing member of Trump's cult of personality and she reminded Stephen Miller of Rosarita Gonzalez, who had inadvertently shown him her breasts when they were in middle school.

Casting about for some diversity tokens to add to the administration's roster of mostly-white, mostly-male, mostly-older appointees, Miller saw Anita on "The Five" while it was playing silently on one of the eight TV monitors in his office. He turned up the audio, but she said nothing while he watched. Nonetheless, Anita's appearance triggered his unrequited lust for Rosarita, so he told the Secretary of Education and Information, the former Congresswoman Marjorie Taylor Greene, to hire Palacio as the Mar-a-Lago press secretary.

Greene, who felt her remit concerned the "Information" aspect of her agency more than the "Education" aspect, resisted the chief of staff's order; she didn't need or want any "Mexicans" in her department. Miller prevailed by telling Greene that Anita was Cuban-American. He had no idea if that was true, having decided to hire her based solely on the stirring in his crotch she inspired. A quick after-the-fact Google search proved he had unwittingly told the truth; she was a second-generation Floridian of Cuban extraction, her grandparents fled Cuba shortly after the Castro regime took over the island 1959.

Miller's timing turned out to be fortuitous for Palacio: Greene offered her the job only two days before Fox News was going to fire her. The pink slip had not gone out, so Palacio remained a loyal Fox alumna and gave its correspondents fawning and regular attention at briefings, always calling on them first and allowing them multiple follow-up questions.

Greene and Palacio quickly came to metaphorical blows. Anita saw her job as making the president look good; Greene, who intended to make a run for the GSA presidency when Trump's two six-year terms ended, saw the job as making Greene look good. Palacio appealed directly to Miller who acted decisively, removing the Mar-a-Lago communications shop from Greene's portfolio and placing it under the Office of the President, where it should have been in the first place. Greene moved on after the loss of Palacio, focusing her energy on her pet project: developing a mandatory Eugenics curriculum for all GSA public schools.

In the old days when there had been one republic and its capital was Washington, DC, routine on-camera, on-the-record White House press briefings began at 2:00

pm, giving TV networks plenty of time to cut stories for their evening newscasts. That schedule still prevailed at the other three republics. But at Mar-a-Lago, a 2:00 pm briefing would conflict with the press briefing room's primary purpose: serving food. The Mar-a-Lago Tearoom had been designated the briefing center, but Trump refused to staunch the restaurant's revenue flow, so he dictated that briefings be held only when necessary, not daily. He also dictated that when they were held, they were to be scheduled early enough for the Tearoom to open for paying luncheon guests. That meant clearing the media personnel, equipment and seating from the room no later than 11:45, although 11:30 was considered much better. So Mar-a-Lago press briefings began no later than 8:30 in the morning, an hour that held scant appeal to reporters and Mar-a-Lago communications staffers alike. The reporters did not like their early-rising schedule and the staffers did not like the fact that there were usually no developments to brief about that early, especially since the chief executive rarely made it to the 45/1 office much before 11each morning.

Fifty-two yawning, gritty-eyed reporters squirmed restively in their uncomfortable chairs. At the back of the room, still and video photographers fidgeted and, for the tenth time, rechecked their white balances, apertures, and ISO settings. It was 8:50, twenty minutes past the start time for the day's briefing.

"The Beast," as Anita Palacio called the collective media, was hungry and had to be fed. Its appetite had been whetted by the BBC reporting the president had metastatic prostate cancer and it wanted to dig into that meaty subject with knives, forks and bare teeth, despite the three lengthy refutations Palacio had emailed to all credentialed media.

Ordinarily tame and polite, the A-credentialed members of the media — the ones admitted to the actual briefing — were hostile this morning and the late start was only exacerbating their fury. Anita could not begin until the presidential physician arrived and he was late. That was unusual for him, so she assumed he'd been summoned to the chief of staff's office, or maybe even the 45/1 Office for last-minute tweaks to his report.

The briefing room was a beehive, abuzz with annoying animated conversation. If something didn't happen soon, the bees go into a stinging frenzy, so she stepped to the lectern to beg for patience. Before she could say a word, she met an unharmonious chorus of angry questions:

"Does the president have cancer?"

Why have there been no briefings for two days?"

"What's Trump's prognosis?"

"Is Trump dying?"

"We need to see his medical reports, he owes it to the nation."

"When was the cancer diagnosed and why weren't we told immediately?"

"What sort of treatment is he receiving?"

"Will he have surgery?"

"Where has the cancer spread?"

"Can we have the president personally brief us?"

"Will he make a prime-time statement to the nation?"

"Can you make Tucker Carlson and Eric Trump available?"

"What about the Constitution and the line of succession?"

If climate change is a hoax, why are you building a seawall to protect Mar-a-Lago?"

"Where is the First Lady? Why haven't we seen her in three weeks?"

That last question was based on an incorrect premise; no one had seen Melania Trump for *five* weeks. No one knew the whereabouts of the former FLOTUS and current FLOGS.

Anita held up a hand, but the tide would not turn back; questions kept coming. She held up both hands, a gesture meant to quiet them, but they took it as a surrender and they shouted the same questions, louder, more urgently.

"Please. Please. Can we take these one at a time? Can I make an announcement?" No one seemed to hear. She shook her head and stepped back from the lectern.

When she turned her back on them, the door behind the podium opened and the presidential physician strode in. The doctor had been a full colonel in the United States Air Force back when there had been a United States. He retired in December 2022, a little less than two years before the 2024 election. He moved to Palm Beach and joined a thriving group practice that was seeking a well-qualified African American internist for its roster. One of the other physicians in the group, the radiologist, Dr. Marvin Kugler, was a member of the Mar-a-Lago club and recommended his African American colleague for the role of presidential physician.

"It'll be good to have a Black doctor," he had told Trump. "And this guy's a top physician."

"Is he your doctor, Kugler?" Trump asked.

"Yes, Excellency, he's my internist. My primary care guy."

"Right! A colored doctor." Trump said, "That'll be a good look for me; could even get me the Black vote."

Trump ordered that the retired colonel be hired without interviewing or even meeting him.

After the internist was hired, Chief of Staff Miller ran some checks him and found nothing to indicate Trump had made a bad choice; in fact, he uncovered a key piece of positive information: the colonel had been a registered Republican most of his adult life.

The doctor walked with military bearing: back straight, shoulders squared, eyes front. He was a tall man with a shaved head and a well-trimmed salt-and-pepper goatee. He was wearing a white lab coat and a stethoscope was draped around his neck like a stole. His name was embroidered above his heart, Frederick Douglass, M.D. He was named for the 19th century social reformer who escaped slavery and moved north to become an abolitionist, author, orator and editor. The physician's family name was Douglas, with one s, but his father had added the second s as an homage to the abolitionist original.

"Thank God you're here," Anita said, "They are out of control."

"Sorry. Couldn't be helped. Miller and The Boss had changes to make. And then someone had to fix the grammar because…." He did not finish.

"Let me have the statement, we'll make copies and put it online," Anita said. Douglass gave her four sheets of duplex-printed paper covered in 11-point, single spaced type.

"Is there an executive summary? A soundbite version?"

"No. Just this."

"Damnit. If you don't give The Beast a soundbite, it finds one on its own and it's never good for us when it does that."

"There wasn't time. We were running late as it is and the restaurant manager was bugging Miller because he needs the room to set up lunch."

Anita escorted Dr. Douglass to the lectern and The Beast quieted.

"You all know the president's personal physician, Dr. Frederick Douglass," she said. "He's got a statement to read about the president's excellent health."

She stepped aside and Dr. Douglass tilted the gooseneck microphone up a notch. He got as far as "Good," in his "Good Morning," and The Beast erupted:

"Does the president have cancer?"

"Why have there been no briefings for two days?"

"What's Trump's prognosis?"

"Is Trump dying?"

"We need to see his medical reports, he owes it to the nation."

"When was the cancer diagnosed and why weren't we told immediately?"

"What sort of treatment is he receiving?"

"Will he have surgery?"

"Where has the cancer spread?"

"Can we have the president personally brief us?"

"Will he make a prime-time statement to the people?"

"Can you make Tucker Carlson and Eric Trump available?"

"What about the Constitution and the line of succession?"

"If climate change is a hoax, why are your building a seawall to protect Mar-a-Lago?"

"Where is the First Lady? Why haven't we seen her in three weeks?"

The well-worn "Breaking News!!!" banners began flashing on the cable news networks within five minutes. The earliest stories reported that Dr. Frederick Douglass, the president's personal physician, denied that Trump had cancer and proclaimed him to be in "extraordinary health and condition — not just for a man of his age, but even for a man 15 years younger." The take-away soundbite that ran over and over in the first hours of coverage was Dr. Douglass saying, "I only hope I'm as healthy at age 60 as President Trump is now at 80." Fox News did a hard cut immediately after Douglass said, "eighty." CNN and MSNBC let the clip run a little longer, so their audiences heard the laughter that statement drew from The Beast.

Later in the day, newspapers, networks and wire services had medical experts examine the eight-page report released by Dr. Douglass. Most experts thought the test results strained credulity for a man of Trump's age, weight, and eating and exercise habits — too much of the former and virtually none of the latter.

Others medical experts characterized the results as "unlikely," "clearly false," "virtually impossible," and in one memorable case, "a big fat lie." The urologists consulted by news outlets were particularly suspicious of the 0.40 prostate-specific antigen (PSA) score reported by Douglass. Other doctors found Trump's reported weight

(244 pounds), blood pressure (125/55) and pulse rate (55) highly suspicious as well.

Fox News featured interviews with none of the doubting doctors, but with Frederick Douglass himself. He was interviewed live on two of its prime time shows that evening and on "Fox and Friends" the next morning. On each program he repeated: "I only hope I'm as healthy at age 60 as President Trump is now at 80." Stephen Miller had written that and handed it to Douglass minutes before the press briefing.

"But I'm sixty-three!" Douglass protested.

"Yeah, but it's a great quote so no one's going to call you on it," Miller said. He was right; no one did.

◆ ◆ ◆

I have opposition like nobody has. And that's okay. I've had that all my life. I've always had it. And this has been -- my whole life has been like this. --Donald J. Trump

Situation Room, The White House, Washington, Atlantic States Of America

Senior staff and two cabinet secretaries from each of the three republics not headed by a president named Trump worked quickly to set up the virtual summit. It was arranged in under two hours. And now they were meeting via secure video link: Gavin Newsom, the tall, elegant president of the Pacific States of America, the billionaire president of the Central States of America, J.B. Pritzker, and the president of the Atlantic States of America, Jon Stewart.

Stewart kicked it off: "We all know the problem; we've heard the recording. What do we do about it? I think we're all agreed this can't happen. It's like the Cuban Missile Crisis but there are no missiles, yet. We can't have a Russian missile base in Trumplandia."

Stewart had coined "Trumplandia" instantly and reflexively upon the dissolution of the United States of America. The sardonic name had gained wide traction in the other three republics as well as in EU nations and the United Kingdom. On more than one occasion, the PM of the UK and the Uachtarán of Ireland had slipped and used Trumplandia in conversations with politicians and diplomats, but none of them had ever been recorded saying it. On the other hand, the president of Ukraine, like Stewart a former comedian, was particularly fond of the sobriquet and used it in public speeches, interviews and on other occasions when cameras were recording and microphones were open. But then, among world leaders, Volodymyr Zelenskyy was unique in having achieved the stature of a Churchill built upon a foundation of a Benny Hill.

As Stewart observed on more than one occasion: "Zelenskyy could stand in the middle of Fifth Avenue and tell a killer joke and he won't lose supporters."

Pritzker: "Call them out on this. Putin and Trump. They can't get away with this. We call them out on it."

Stewart: "Call them out? What are we, in middle school?"

Newsom: "This could be the end of Trump. His base isn't going to stand for this. Texas isn't going to stand for it."

Stewart: "Where have I heard that before, the end of Trump? He's had his political obituary written a thousand times and he's still around. He's the Freddy Kruger of politics. You can't kill him. When he was president of the U.S. the axis of adults in his administration couldn't contain or control him. Now there are no adults even trying, insofar as we know."

Pritzker: "He may be dying now. literally. That cancer's spread. That's the story."

Stewart: "I'm suspicious. We've got no confirmation from intelligence. He might have put out that story himself. For sympathy, or for who knows what purpose? He lies all the time, even when it's not to his advantage. He lies for the sport of it. He could be lying about this. But if it was a lie, why would Miller and Putin be discussing how Putin can debunk the story? That conversation points to it being true. It's the quid Putin wants that we need to be concerned about. We've got the Texas Missile Crisis on our hands."

There was some cross talk, then Pritzker said "Seems to me we have two issues here: Trump's cancer, if it exists, and Putin's missile bases in Texas. If that exists. Maybe this whole thing was a charade to get us to buy in."

Stewart: "We know they're talking, Putin and Trump. We haven't been able to compromise the line, but it exists. So why was Putin calling Miller? He must have known NSA would hear it. Hard to fathom Putin talking Russian missiles in Texas over an insecure phone line?"

Pritzker: "If we shine some daylight on this, it'll go away, I think."

Newsom: "I think we need to have someone talk to that BBC guy. That's the first thing. Do you think Miller will talk to us? He can't want Russian missiles in Texas."

Stewart: "Not so sure about that, about Miller. But the BBC guy; that's an idea. Why don't we find him, see just how solid the cancer story is."

Pritzker: "Yeah, reach out to the BBC guy. How the hell do you say his name?"

Stewart: "Chumley."

Pritzker: "Then why don't they spell it that way?"

Stewart: "They're British, they can't help themselves. Like the 'u' in color and pronouncing c-l-e-r-k 'clark.'"

Pritzker: "Favorite is another one — an unpronounced 'u.'"

Stewart: "Enough! What do we do about Putin's missile base in Texas? We can't very well bomb it." He paused. "Can we?"

Pritzker: "Sabotage it? Send in Navy Seals?"

Stewart: "They're probably all MAGA. I wouldn't count on them any more than we count on the Secret Service to supply security anymore; he's co-opted them all, Trump."

Newsom: "Go public with it. Pritzker's right. Shine a light. We've got Putin talking about it with Trump."

Stewart: "Wrong. We've got Putin talking about it with Miller, the Yiddishe Quisling. That's the recording NSA made. As far as we know Trump hasn't talked to Putin about it. We don't know. Yet."

Pritzker: "Trump can't keep his mouth shut; he'll confirm it to someone somewhere on one of the lines we have tapped. Then we go public with it. Not even his cult is going to go along with Russian missiles in Texas."

Stewart: "I'm more pessimistic about that than you are. I don't know that Trump won't be able to convince his base that Russian missiles aimed at the three republics aren't the greatest thing since Ben and Jerry invented Cherry Garcia ice cream."

Newsom: "Okay. Here's a plan. Find that BBC guy. Play the Putin-Miller recording for him; give him the story. Or, if and when Trump does call one of his cronies and we record it, play that tape for him. Let the BBC run with it. If that doesn't work, we rattle the saber. But let's start that way."

Stewart: "And now for your moment of Zen...."

◆ ◆ ◆

I know words. I have the best words. — Donald J. Trump

Internet Research Agency, St. Petersburg, Russian Federation

Sofia Ivanova's trade was dictated by genetics more than by her surname, Pushkina — the feminine version of Pushkin. She was no relation to Russia's most celebrated poet, Alexander Sergeyevich Pushkin; but like Alexander Sergeyevich, Sofia Ivanova was a writer, a writer of impactful, attention-commanding fiction. Sofia Ivanova Pushkina was Q.

Conspiracy creation ran in the family blood. In 1901 her great-great grandfather, Ivan Ivanovich Pushkin, employed by Okhrana — the Tsar's Department for Protecting the

Public Security and Order — wove together the strands of several far-fetched written and whispered conspiracy theories to create "The Protocols of the Elders of Zion." His pamphlet was the perfect document to motivate the pogroms the Tsar needed to take care of two problems at once: Jewish restiveness in the Pale of Settlement and unwanted public attention to financial hard times and famine.

Succeeding generations of Pushkins worked for Tsars, commissars and oligarchs, spinning webs of invented conspiracy in the service of the state, the ruler and expansive enterprises. Sofia Ivanova's father, Ivan Borisovich Pushkin, had made the transition from propagandizing for commissars to spinning advantageous lies for oligarchs, a more lucrative position in the misinformation industry.

Until she went to work for an informal branch of the Putin regime, none of Sofia Ivanova's ancestors had the impact of the patriarch's — whose creation helped inspire the Nazi's attempted destruction of European Jewery in World War II.

When Pushkina joined the Internet Research Agency in 2014, she brought the family's trade into the digital age and her impact was immediate and global: her skill in conflating an unauthorized email server in Hillary Clinton's home with mundane emails purloined by Russian intelligence operatives from the Democratic National Committee likely got Donald Trump elected president of the United States in 2016.

On first glance, Sofia Ivanova Pushkina was the ideal IRA employee: she had a master's degree from George Washington University, she spoke fluent idiomatic, American English and she was a fast writer with a lively imagination and sardonic wit. Despite that, as a woman — a tall, fashion-model beautiful woman — she was not taken seriously at first by her male bosses. Her first three years at the IRA were spent creating divisive and mostly silly Twitter and Facebook posts for fictitious right-wing American groups. She also expended an exhausting amount of energy hiding the fact that she was an active and promiscuous lesbian. Thanks to her cover-up skills, none of her colleagues suspected that she spent her nights clubbing and barhopping with the sort of people who were never trusted in vengefully straight Russia.

The IRA's informal motto was Razbit Ameerika -- Smash America. Colleagues greeted her in the halls by cheerfully calling it out: "Razbit Ameerka, Sofia Ivanova!" She returned the greeting with heartfelt energy. She despised Americans; to know them was to hate them.

Q was a masterstroke of Razbit Ameerika. She told colleagues she must have dreamt it, because it was a wholly formed idea when she awoke one morning, nauseous and hung-over. The vodka-fueled idea was this: create an oracle who would spin wild conspiracies inspiring chaos by uniting denizens of the darkest recesses of violent American extremism. Her first instinct was to call him

Z. But then, Stepan Arkadyevich Oblonsky, the youngest member her team suggested Q.

Oblonsky had been born in Brooklyn and grew up in the Russian and Ukrainian immigrant enclave of Brighton Beach. His family returned to the motherland when he was 11. He was a peculiar man, quiet and shy, who spoke Russian with an American accent. He had studied to become a monk but lost his calling and quit. He retained his scholarly monkish demeanor, still had his monk's long and unruly beard, and he spoke in an aspirant whisper. His posture bespoke someone who spent his days bent over a Bible although in Stepan Arkadyevich's case, he spent his days bent over a Latin alphabet keyboard, turning out English-language dezinformatsiya.

"Q is a letter common to the Latin and Cyrillic alphabets," he told his teammates. "But, more importantly Q is the name of the missing gospels."

"What missing gospels?" Pushkina asked. "There are missing gospels? I never heard of missing gospels."
No one else had heard of missing gospels.

"You see," Oblonsky said, "the Gospels of Matthew, Mark, and Luke were written well after the death of the Savior. So, the writers were writing about what they had not witnessed. Mark was written first and has the least amount of material, so the others must have had another source: and that source — the missing gospel — is called Q."

"Or Matthew and Luke could have just concocted the material," Sophia Ivanova said.

"No. That's not possible."

Sophia Ivanova failed to see how that was not possible, since she was the head of a team paid to manufacture stories every day.

Oblonsky, who she feared might don a monk's cassock right there in the office, continued: "You see, the concept of The Christ — not the name, Jesus Christ, but the title — The Christ, is based on the Old Testament concept of the Messiah. That Old Testament Messiah, or The Christ, is the one who will lead the Hebrews to redemption. In the New Testament, The Christ is the physical manifestation of God; He is God's son and physical manifestation all in one body. So Q, who is named for the missing gospel, can preach that The Trump is personification of God's will; the Lord's orders for humankind physically manifested…."

Pushkina took the fact that a bolt of lightning had not torn through the window and struck Oblonsky dead as a sure sign there was no God. She, and the rest of the team, also stopped listening to his theological droning. She did, however, like the idea of The Trump, the embodiment of God's will. She stopped Stepan Arkadyevich mid-sentence and thanked him for enlightening them.

"But there is more," he protested.

"Of course there is," she said. "And we will hear it at another time, Brother Oblonsky."

In the years to come, she was surprised that none of the many American Evangelical ministers who embraced Qanon took Q to task for promoting the concept of The Trump.

Her boss thought the whole Q idea was crazy. "No one will believe that, Pushkina," Alexi Kirillovich Vronsky told her.

When she told him about the theological background for the concept, he made the sign of the cross twice and told her, "No! This is sacrilege."

Pushkina had no idea Vronsky was religious. She persisted, "Let me try it."

"No. Go back to your Twitter accounts."

"But...."

"Pushkina! Do your job. This thing, this Q thing, isn't your job. This conspiracy; no one, not even Americans, would believe."

"I'm telling you; I know. They will. I know Americans."

"Four lunatics will believe. Probably four Ukrainian lunatics in Brooklyn. That's who you'll reach."

"No. American are *deti* — children — they believe everything and anything if you tell them enough times. And if it's written, they believe it the first time."

"No, Puskina. It's a very simple word, no. It means no."

She did it anyway. She invented a cabal of Satanic and cannibalistic American elites who were operating a global child sex trafficking ring in a vast conspiracy designed to undermine the presidency of Donald Trump. How a global sex trafficking ring would undermine a presidency she left unexplained. In a nod to her great-great grandfather's favorite target, the ring was financed by George Soros, a rich Hungarian-born American Jew, who donated a lot of money to shoring up democracies in Eastern Europe and still more money to Democratic candidates and causes. In Q's telling, Soros was aided by the Rothschilds, Europe's favorite scapegoats. The Rothschilds are a family of Zhyds so rich that in centuries past they had loaned prodigious sums of money to finance the wars waged by European monarchs. The family was so widespread in Europe there had been times when Rothschild money had financed both sides of a war.

In Q's telling, only The Trump, God's will incarnate, could save America from the scourge of the elitist and globalist child sex-trafficking ring. And Donald Trump was The Trump; he had been anointed by the Creator to do His bidding, express His will and save His creation.

Drawing on her years at George Washington University, when she had often gotten take-out pizza from Comet Ping Pong Pizzeria, she made that modest neighborhood restaurant the central headquarters of the child trafficking ring. In the basement of Comet Ping Pong – she was unsure that the basement even existed -- she invented cages filled with abused children, who lived in their own filth, were starved nearly to death and were uncaged only when some prominent Democrat showed up to molest them. The whole thing was so improbable, unlikely and incredible that it caught on at once.

A gun-packing North Carolinian, motivated by Sofia Ivanova's Q, drove to Washington and fired a shot inside the pizzeria in an effort to free the captive children. He was arrested, pled guilty and was sentenced to four years in prison. No caged children were found in the place. This was taken by Q as proof positive that the conspiracy existed, and the police were in on it.

"I told you no," a grinning Vronsky said after that incident. "You did it anyway. What did you learn? That you should never listen to me."

A week later, Alexei Kirillovich Vronsky was gone and Sofia Ivanova Pushkina was running the section of the IRA devoted to American disinformation. She assigned the most talented staff writers to the QAnon project and made Q a top priority.

"Don't hold back," she told them. "The more bizarre, the better. Americans will believe anything if it is written or on social media. Anything."

"Anything" was strained, even for Sofia Ivanova, when her team came up with the story that John F. Kennedy Jr., had faked his death to avoid becoming a victim of the elite Democratic cabal, had been hiding in Pittsburgh for 20 years posing as a man who looked nothing like him, and would emerge in public on the anniversary of his father's assassination at Dealey Plaza in Dallas where he would embrace Trump's lie that the 2020 election had been stolen from him. She hesitated, but eventually said, "Let's put it out just for laughs."

And she and her colleagues got their laughs when several hundred Americans showed up on November second, twenty days before the assassination anniversary. And they laughed again when three thousand showed up on the actual anniversary. Looking at news footage of the crowds holding up Trump/Kennedy 2024 signs and flags, Sofia Ivanova told herself, she had been right: Americans will believe anything and everything.

Now there was a new task. "There is a story from the BBC. Fake news," she was telling her team. "It reports President Trump has prostate cancer and this cancer is very serious.

The cancer has spread, the story says. We need to counter it, to create another narrative, a true narrative. Also, let us see if we can find something to discredit the BBC man who reported the story. His name is…" she hesitated. The name was written out in Latin letters on the page before her. She silently sounded it out; it made no sense. "Chom-delay. Chol-mon-delay." It did not sound right to her. Whatever happened to Smith or Jones or Watson — which she pronounced "Vatson"?

"Impossible name," she admitted. "Let's just use his first name. Valta he is called. Can we find anything to destroy him. Is he queer? Does he like little girls? Little boys? Sheep? Does he cheat on his wife? Is he a public wanker? What is it about him we can find? But that's the secondary mission. The first mission: we need to create medical records that are obvious fakes — in English but with lots of mistakes. Make them look like they came from another country, not the Great States, but Ukraine. We write fake medical records in Ukrainian and translate them word-by-word into English, publish both so everyone knows it came from Ukraine and is fake. So that's the job: make it look like Ukrainian dezinformatsiya that Trump has cancer to discredit the BBC report and discredit the BBC reporter. And third, distribute legitimate-looking medical exam record showing Trump is okay. That comes from Mar-a-Lago press office."

Oblonsky, the lapsed theologian, raised his hand: "So does he have cancer? Is the story true? The BBC is very reliable, usually."

"For our purposes, it doesn't matter," Sofia Ivanova said. "For our purposes this is fake news. Dezinformatsiya. So much dezinformatsiya out there nowadays. No one knows what to believe anymore."

Her team nodded and smiled.

CHAPTER THREE

My attorney general will restore the integrity of the Department of Justice which has been severely questioned. — Donald J. Trump

Department Of Law And Order Headquarters, West Palm Beach, Florida, Great States Of America

To more accurately reflect its purpose and values, Trump changed the name of his new nation's chief top law-enforcement agency from the Department of Justice to the Department of Law and Order, which was abbreviated DLO. The DLO was headquartered in the repurposed anchor store of a closed shopping mall in West Palm Beach. Walter Cholmondeley had been working on a story about how that site was chosen before he was exiled.

What he had discovered was this: like the other republics that succeeded the United States, the Great States of America had an agency called the General Services Administration, or GSA. In each country, as in the predecessor nation, the

GSA was the government's landlord and administrative agency, building, buying or leasing buildings and offices for other government departments.

To head the GSA's GSA — a bit of alphabet soup chaos that Trump enjoyed — the president selected his 2016 presidential campaign manager, Paul Manafort. Manafort's history included consulting services for Ukraine's former Russian-puppet authoritarian president, conviction on eight counts of tax and bank fraud and guilty pleas to witness tampering and conspiracy to defraud the United States. In most nations, that felony record would have rendered a person ineligible to run a Metro change booth, much less a government agency charged with billions in expenditures. But Trump felt his 2020 pardon of Manafort restored his old pal's bona fides, so Manafort got the job.

Manafort used eminent domain to take over the failed West Palm Beach shopping mall anchored by a long-shuttered J.C. Penney store. GSA paid the property's owner, Shining Star Realty, a 40 percent over-market settlement for the parcel and buildings. Cholmondeley had gotten that far in the story, and knew there was more, but he'd hit a wall and sources had dried up. Had he been able to continue, he would have learned that Shining Star Reality was a Trump family enterprise.

After DLO took possession of the mall, GSA's GSA paid $23 million to refurbish the Penney building. Nine million of that was spent on renovations, the remainder went to "overhead," "executive compensation" and "profit" for Bacciagalupe Construction, a previously unknown firm based in a post office box in the Bahamas and jointly owned by Trump Enterprises and Paul Manafort.

The $9 million had turned 225,000 square feet of retail space into a rat's nest of cramped offices, oversized bullpens and tiny cubicles. The air conditioning was hit-and-miss, the lighting ranged from dim to retina-damaging bright and the plumbing had been installed so haphazardly half the bathrooms were frequently out of service and the other half prone to Biblical-caliber flooding.

The best feature of DLO headquarters was the abundant parking; the mall developer had created hundreds of extra parking spaces to accommodate a ten-screen multiplex theater that was never built. In fact, by actual count, there were six-and-a-half spaces for every DLO employee.

Five black Suburbans rolled up to the parking stalls closest to the rear of the building and nosed into their reserved stalls. The first two and last two slots were marked "Reserved AG Security." The middle stall had only a "Reserved" sign, as if the identity of the Suburban's passenger was an impossible-to-guess secret.

There were four WORMs in each of the security vehicles. They hustled out and formed a corridor of black uniforms between the AG's Suburban and a pedestrian door. Once he was satisfied with the corridor, the WORM riding shotgun in the AG's vehicle emerged and opened a rear door. The driver remained behind the wheel, motor running, transmission in reverse, ready to race back and smash into any would-be assassin who came up behind the Suburban to take a shot at Attorney General Sidney Powell.

The driver surveyed the dashboard screen. No assassin lurked in the backup camera's field of view. "Okay," he said, and AG Powell climbed down out of the Suburban, carrying a slim briefcase and an open can of Dr. Pepper. She paused, tilted back her head and in one long gulp drained the can. She belched silently and handed the empty can to the nearest WORM

"Be sure that gets recycled," she said.

"Yes, ma'am." He stuffed the can into a pocket of his fatigue pants.

Powell was taller than some of her WORMs bodyguards, so walking the corridor they formed left her vulnerable to a sniper's headshot. She was indifferent to the danger and walked slowly, preceded by a WORM who hustled ahead, hoping to pick up her pace. Nothing was going to rush Powell. She strolled through the door he held open and into what had once been the loading dock of the Penney store. Now it was filled with chain link holding cages and interrogation rooms. The area reeked of sweat, urine and feces. The holding cages had only galvanized buckets for sanitation.

The Assistant Attorney General for the Criminal Division was waiting for her.

She said, "Good morning, Andrew."

"Good morning, Sidney."

She tolerated the familiarity from him and only from him because his name was Giuliani, Andrew Giuliani.

Andrew was the son of Rudy Giuliani, her partner in the effort to undermine American democracy by overturning the 2020 election. The older Giuliani had been convicted by a Georgia jury of election interference in early 2024 and was out on bail, appealing the conviction and his five-year prison term when the United States split into the four republics. The GSA constitution gave the president pardon power over convictions in the republic's constituent states, an addition to the original Putin draft suggested by Giuliani himself. On his first day in office, Trump pardoned Giuliani.

Instead of prostrating himself before his benefactor, Giuliani's first act upon receiving his pardon was sending Trump Enterprises a $12 million bill for legal fees. Trump instructed Eric not to pay and told Giuliani he had a choice: relocate to a retirement community in Florida and keep his head down or be declared persona non grata in the GSA and be deported to the Atlantic States of America. Giuliani, who was ducking nearly a dozen multi-million-dollar lawsuits in the other republics, followed the example of Ponce de

Leon and moved to Florida, seeking immortality. Unlike Ponce, he relocated to The Villages where he mastered the operation of a golf cart and spent most of his days driving around the community's four golf courses, observing others playing the game.

Andrew Giuliani was a lumpy young man whose ill-fitting seersucker suit did nothing for his shambolic image. He had a deathly pale complexion and ginger hair. Despite his title, assistant *attorney* general, he was not a lawyer. To compensate for his inadequate education, Andrew had been assigned two criminal prosecutors as deputies.

Giuliani's deputies were more noteworthy for their loyalty to the Cult of Trump than for their prosecutorial successes. Their primary task, explaining the law to Giuliani, was hopeless. They were hampered by the same challenges faced by every legal professional in the GSA Department of Law and Order: a brand-new unfamiliar constitution that had materialized wholly-crafted from God-knew-where and a library's worth of new laws that had been handed to the country's Congress by the president and passed en masse by representatives who had neither the time nor the inclination to read them before voting.

The deputies' secondary task was identifying local and state prosecutors who were insufficiently tough on crime or were too tough on egregious police excesses. That was a lot easier; all they needed to do was read newspapers and listen to right-wing radio commentators. Once the straying prosecutors were identified, Andrew's deputies gave their names to Giuliani who wrote a monthly memo to Powell listing the laggards. Powell, in turn, gave the memo to the Mar-a-Lago office of Legal Counsel which then exercised the constitution's provision enabling the president to dismiss any state or local prosecutor he deemed insufficiently devoted to enforcement of Law and Order; or, given the administration's priorities: Order and Law.

To date, 73 local prosecutors and one state attorney general had been dismissed by Mar-a-Lago. Six of the disgraced prosecutors faced criminal charges themselves, accused of violating the GSA Prosecutorial Misconduct Act, a vague piece of legislation proposed off the top of his head by the president, written by his non-lawyer chief of staff, Stephen Miller, and passed by the obedient Congress without debate.

Laws passed without being read, debated or understood was just one of the serial tsunamis of problems facing the 6,500 legal professionals at DLO. They were groping in the dark. For many that was literal — if they worked in interior offices, they had to use their smartphone flashlights to illuminate the unfamiliar legal documents they consulted daily. The confusion was compounded by a judiciary filled with lawyers who appeared to have come to the president's attention when he saw their roadside billboards or TV commercials. The challenges to DLO lawyers were simply insurmountable. Those who had not resigned in the first six months represented bottom-of-the-barrel graduates from non-accredited law schools across the former United

States. In addition, job security was nonexistent in the GSA's DLO; no one, not lawyers, paralegals nor clerical staff, had civil service protection. That was because there was almost no civil service in the GSA; the constitution gave the president the power to determine which government jobs qualified for civil service protection. For Trump, very few did.

In his GSA inaugural address, Trump had boasted, "First thing, I'll fire those civil service bums. They are hogs at the public trough; lazy dogs who collect a paycheck for watching porn on the internet. I'm gonna replace them all with loyal people; people you could count on to watch out for *your* money and *my* money. It's in the constitution: *my* appointees will *serve*; they know if they don't serve, I'll fire their worthless asses."

When it came to worthless asses, Andrew Giuliani was on his third set of deputies, this one being not much better than the previous two. One of his deputies had been on the job for two days. The other was a hardened veteran of the office, having served two months. The veteran deputy always carried an undated but already-signed resignation letter so he could make his exit expeditiously when the moment arrived.

Attorney General Powell, whose license to practice law had been revoked by the Texas Bar Association years ago, considered Andrew Giuliani's lack of legal education and credentials a minor annoyance; she was loyal to the Giuliani name. She and Rudy were combat buddies, veterans of 62 unsuccessful lawsuits they had filed alleging nonexistent voter fraud in the 2020 election. Like Confederate soldiers bonding over their lost cause, Powell and Giuliani shared a romanticized view of their effort. She respected the former New York mayor's passion, bravado and his astounding capacity for Scotch whiskey. Since he had moved to The Villages, she had not been in touch with him, so she transferred her sense of camaraderie to the younger Giuliani. She had to admit, though, this apple had fallen far from the tree; he did not have his father's belly fire. At best he would be a plodding, invisible bureaucrat.

"You got the BBC guy's sources locked up?" Powell asked.

"Yup. We got them over there," Andrew said, inclining his head toward the cages.

"Not together, are they?" Powell asked.

"Well, we separated the woman out, but the men are in the same cage."

"You didn't put the woman near Liz Cheney, did you?"

"No," Andrew said. "She's kind of in isolation, Liz Cheney."

"Shitting in a bucket, like the others, is she, Liz?"

"I thought to give her a cell with a toilet," Giuliani said.

"Move her!" Powell was annoyed. "No coddling RINO traitors."

"Sure," Giuliani said.

He had no intention of following through; he would leave the former Wyoming congresswoman and daughter of a vice president where she was, in the relative comfort of a cell with a functioning toilet. He, too, was the child of a political celebrity; they had that in common. And there was more: Andrew Giuliani had unsuccessfully sought the GOP nomination to run for governor of New York in 2022. Cheney had had the temerity to seek the Republican presidential nomination in 2024. Like Giuliani, she had been defeated. He was crushed in a single primary, while Cheney suffered defeat after defeat in primaries while driving a wedge in the party. Still, they shared the bitter taste of rejection by voters, so he was not about to stick her in a cell with a galvanized bucket.

Early in his Great States of America presidency, Trump had Cheney taken into custody and there she remained while his DLO and Congress tried to figure out a criminal law they could pass that she could be retroactively charged with violating. It was called Pre-Legislative Detention and there was a substantial list of such detainees in GSA jails, prisons and holding pens awaiting the passage of laws they would be charged with violating.

In addition to her qualms about Cheney's detention conditions, Powell was not happy with the accommodations for Cholmondeley's male sources: "No good. The men who talked to the BBC guy need to be isolated from each other. Far enough apart that they can't communicate."

"What difference does it make?" Andrew asked.

We don't want them coordinating their stories," the attorney-general said.

"Who cares? Ralphie says we can try them in camera."

"Who's Ralphie?" Powell remembered no one named Ralphie.

"Ralphie Moss. My new deputy. He says they broke the Whistleblower Law and that permits in camera trials." He paused, looked confused. "But, Sidney, I thought we banned cameras from courtrooms unless we wanted them there for show trials, so how can you have an in camera trial?"

"In camera means in private," Powell said. "No cameras, no press, no public. But what Whistleblower Law is — what's his name…."

"Ralphie."

"What Whistleblower Law is Ralphie talking about? We don't have a Whistleblower Protection Law."

In the old country, the United States, the Whistleblower Law protected staff and civil servants from retaliation if they revealed wrongdoing in their agency. She was aware of no such law in the GSA.

Giuliani said, "Ralphie says it's a law that criminalizes and punishes guys who violate their government NDAs."

So, not a whistleblower protection law but a whistleblower punishment law. The fact there was such a law was news to Powell; she would have to research it further.

"What are the penalties?" she asked.

"I don't know, exactly. I'll ask Ralphie. But he says we can detain them as long as we like without counsel before we have to charge them. He says it's in the law; the government has the right to investigate the full extent of the damage done by violation of the NDAs before we got to bring charges, and we can hold the person of interest indefinitely while the investigation continues."

"Good; like that," Powell said. "Who, exactly, are they, these sources? How did they know that BBC creep? And why'd they come up with that cock and bull cancer story? Do we have any answers yet?"

"We don't know. They were interrogated but, y'know not enhanced; not enhanced interrogation. That's next. One of 'em worked in Stephen Miller's office — the woman. Very junior member of his staff; no idea why she made up this shit. Two are National Guard medical people — a male nurse assigned to Mar-a-Lago and a pathologist. The pathologist is… was at the veterans' hospital. The other two are…." he lowered his voice "are lifelong Republican staffers. We think the story started with them."

"RINOS," Powell said. "The National Guard, they can court martial their guys. But how is that possible that two Republicans fed that bullshit to the BBC?"

"I don't know. Maybe they are Antifa infiltrators. If that's the case, it goes way back. They were Young Republicans in college; active their whole lives in the party."
"The Boss is not going to like that," Powell said.

"So should we enhance interrogate all of 'em? The woman, too?" Giuliani did not like that; he had people willing to torture the woman, but he wasn't willing to order them to do it.

"All of them."

"Yes, ma'am. On it." He would order everyone but the woman to be subjected to waterboarding; there was no way he would be responsible for torturing a woman.

"I'd like to get our hands on that reporter, too. The BBC guy, Chalemay — or however you say it. He should be in a cage here, too. Miller, that dipshit, kicked him out of the country; sent him to Washington, I heard."

"Which Washington?"

"Jon Stewart's Washington; the close one. Miller had him in custody and just kicked him out instead of turning him over to us. And there's no way he's coming back here anytime; you can bet on that."

"We could stage a rendition," Giuliani offered.

"No we can't. No one here has the skills. They'll fuck it up and embarrass us."

◆ ◆ ◆

*The fake news media is not my enemy,
it is the enemy of the American People.* — Donald J. Trump

Newscorp Headquarters, 1211 Avenue Of The Americas, New York, Atlantic States Of America

"Here y'are, 1211 Sixth Avenue," the cab driver said.

"No, no, 1211 Avenue of the Americas," Cholmondeley said.

"Same thing," the cabbie said. "Sixth Avenue, Avenue of the Americas. It'sa same street."

That made as little sense to Cholmondeley as the urgent summons from The Proprietor to come to New York for a meeting. But the summons was accompanied by an offer of $10,000 cash to fly to New York and meet with the old press baron for no more than thirty minutes, so why not?

Cholmondeley was at a disadvantage; he still wore the rumpled and torn-at-the-knee suit he had been wearing when the WORMs kicked him out of the GSA yesterday. His "stuff," which they promised to send, had not arrived, so he bought a fresh shirt and underwear, but there had been no time to buy a new suit. He made-do with the damaged goods on his back.

The old gaffer's spot was posh in an incongruous way. Located on a high floor of a glass-and-steel New York office tower and accessed by a dedicated express lift, the outer office looked like something out of the stately homes of Wiltshire. The walls were paneled with dark rich wood, the cement floors had been covered with wide plank dark oak, and well-worn vintage Indian and Persian rugs were scattered in high-traffic areas. There were three PAs in the outer office. Cholmondeley decided they had been chosen for beauty and diversity; one was a Viking blonde, one a dark-eyed brunette of an indefinable dusky racial mixture and one was flame-haired and of obvious Celtic origin. The women looked as if they'd just stepped out of a Victoria's Secret catalog; they wore tight blouses, short skirts and had forced their feet into Jimmy Choos with stiletto heels. Cholmondeley wondered if they might be veterans of topless pin-ups featured on Page Three of The Sun, The Proprietor's most successful UK tabloid.

Judy Travers, the one Cholmondeley thought looked dusky, rose from her chair, balanced beautifully on her impossibly high heels and led him into Murdoch's office. She walked with such abundant swaying of her buttocks that he only noticed the wizened man behind the desk when she stepped to the side and out of his line of sight.

Without a word, The Proprietor motioned to a seat across the desk. When Cholmondeley seated himself, one hand awkwardly covering his torn trouser knee, the old man handed him a sealed envelope with "$10,000" written on it in spasmodic penmanship. The envelope felt too thin to contain that much money, but Cholmondeley thought it bad form to open and count it in front of him.

"As agreed. Your fee."

Murdoch's accent, familiar to Cholmondeley from innumerable BBC interviews, was so thick he sounded as if he'd just decamped an outback sheep station. Cholmondeley suspected that was an act; he knew that Murdoch, was a graduate of the University of Oxford's Worcester College and likely could sound as plummy as a BBC presenter.

"Thank you."

"Don't you want to count it?"

"No need. I trust you."

"You know what the Russians say? 'Doveryay no proveryay,' Trust but Verify."

"I thought Ronald Reagan said it," Cholmondeley said.

"Where do you think he got it from? Believe me, it's Russian. Russians love proverbs, so Reagan learned that one when he was negotiating with them. Rhymes in the original Russian, you see. Doveryay no proveryay. Open the envelope and verify the amount."

There were ten crisp $1,000 bills in the envelope. Cholmondeley had never seen a $1,000 bill before; he had no way of knowing if it was genuine legal tender. The president depicted on the bill was Grover Cleveland. Cholmondeley was unfamiliar with a President Cleveland. Murdoch appeared to read his mind.

"They are real," he said. "The government stopped printing them in 1946 and Nixon recalled them in 1969 because Treasury thought they were being used for money-laundering, which — of course — they were. But those still in circulation are legal tender and you can deposit them in any bank. Just be sure you don't deposit all of it at once; that would be a suspicious deposit and the bank will have to report it to Internal Revenue. They might freeze your account until they verified the legitimacy of the bills. You are best off putting it into two or three different banks."

Why would Murdoch have thousand-dollar bills if they were so burdensome to deposit? Cholmondeley had no way of knowing The Proprietor kept $2 million in crisp, barely circulated thousand-dollar bills in an office safe for transactions best conducted with no paper trail.

"Yes, thank you. I will be careful about that," Cholmondeley said, slipping the $10,000 back into the envelope. "May I ask why I am here?"

The Proprietor wasn't ready for that part of the conversation. Ever the colonial subject, eager for acceptance as an equal from citizens of the motherland, he wanted first to establish his Britishness.

"Do you see these walls?" Like the outer office where the three Victoria's Secrets escapees worked, these walls were paneled in dark wood. "Well, the residence of the Italian Ambassador in Washington has the actual walls of Sir Christopher Wren's study. The building — more Tudor than anything ever erected in Tudor England — went up in the 1920s when rich Americans were scavenging antiques, and other treasure from bankrupt Europe after the Great War. The fella who built the mansion was Col. Arthur O'Brien. He bought Sir Christopher Wren's study and shipped it to the United States and installed it in the mansion. Italy bought the building and grounds later, but they left the study as it was. I tried to buy the study from the Italians and install it here. They were having none of that, the

Italians. So, I had it exactly duplicated. For all intents and purposes, you are sitting in the room where Wren designed St. Paul's Cathedral."

"I see. Interesting," Cholmondeley said. It wasn't all that interesting, but he had ten thousand reasons to be polite.

The Proprietor, having established his connection to King and Country, moved on to business: "We tried to find your agent. These things are best discussed with a representative. Less emotional involvement."

"I have no agent."

"Yes, we learned that. Bottom line: you are a good reporter; I like to have good reporters working for me. I want you to sign up with us."

"Us? Fox News, us or The Sun us? The Wall Street Journal us? Times of London us?" Those were all the Murdoch properties Cholmondeley could come up with on the spur of the moment; he knew there were many more.

"All of them, everything we have. All media. That scoop on Trump's cancer; that was our kind of story. It should have appeared first across all our outlets, instead of on the Beeb."

"Thank you, but I am happy at the Beeb."

"They pay you like a peon."

"I'm adequately compensated," Cholmondeley said.

The Proprietor knew exactly how much money the BBC paid Cholmondeley. He also knew the journalist came from a middle-class family; his father was a physician with a modest group practice on contract to the National Health Service; that could not have been particularly lucrative. So: modest salary, no sizable inheritance in the future; no real financial independence.

"How would you like to earn a million pounds a year with a guaranteed contract of five years?"

"Tempting, but no thank you. I'm quite content where I am." It was more than merely tempting; it was a fortune to Cholmondeley.

"There won't be a BBC in five years," The Proprietor said. "We… Well, not we, but the Tory government are going to destroy it. They have had it in the works for five, six years now. First, eliminate the license fee. Next, prohibit the sale of product outside the UK. It will be gone in a flash. Very soon."

"Sabotage the BBC, will they?" Cholmondeley asked. "What follows, state broadcasting with full-time government propaganda?"

"The free market follows. Independent outlets reign. Unfettered journalism." He let that sink in, then added: "They will disband Ofcom, too, so the market will rule the roost."

Ofcom was the UK's communications industries regulator and had issued a number of unfavorable reports in the wake of egregious journalistic sins committed by The Proprietor's properties, which had included stalking political and entertainment figures, printing privacy-invading photos of royals and celebrities and hacking the voicemail of a murder victim. Ofcom was a target second only to the BBC for The Proprietor and his wholly owned political party.

"I suspect you find some of my outlets...." Murdoch searched for a word; he found it: "...unsavory, shall we say?"

"We shall say."

"Ah. So journalistic idealism, is it? Idealism is admirable. So is a million-pound paycheck."

"With all due respect, Mr. Murdoch," Cholmondeley said, feeling no respect at all, "I'm not for sale."

"Not even if I give you a total free hand? You determine what to cover, your copy is edited only for grammar, diction and the like. No editorial input from my editors. You even get to choose the venue in which it appears. Solely Times of London and the Wall Street Journal? Fine. Those and Fox News as well? Fine. Go on Fox and present another viewpoint? Fine. The New York Post and The Sun? Fine, too, although from what I can see, you are not particularly fond of that form of journalism. Tabloids do pay the bills, though."

"Why would you do that? No one else has a deal like that."

"Because I want your reporting in my organization."

"I may not be the journalist you think I am. People tell me things. They always have. Within ten or fifteen minutes of my meeting someone, they are sharing secrets with me. Better yet, they share other people's secrets with me. I'm a secrets bin and strangers throw confidential information in. I've never really had to work particularly hard for a story in my life."

"Let's cut the false modesty," The Proprietor said. "That cancer scoop was the biggest story so far this year. *You* got that story. And you didn't get it just because strangers walked up to you and began talking."

But that was exactly how Cholmondeley got the story; a woman from Stephen Miller's office walked up to him in the Mar-a-Lago press office, took his arm, steered him outside into the heat and humidity and spilled the beans. He did not know why she had done it nor why she had chosen him as the recipient of the story. After that, his challenge was tracking down additional sources to confirm the details. To do that he had used the shopworn but reliable trick of telling potential sources he already had the story and was seeking further details to make sure he had it right.

"A million-pound offer does not come along every day. Every year, for that matter," The Proprietor said.

"I might agree to do it for six months with an option for the other four-and-a-half years if it works out."

Murdoch put on a vaguely annoyed expression, although he was delighted with Cholmondeley's response. "Well, I suppose we can craft a deal that way if that's what you require." Mentally, he high fived himself.

"And would I work out of here, out of New York?"

"That could be your home base. Or Washington. The one on this coast. Where do you want to work?"

"I didn't say I agreed. But New York would work as home base," Cholmondeley said. "First thing, though, I'd like to do is go back to Palm Beach and finish up what I started. There's a DLO — Law and Order department — story I was onto. And other things are going to get really interesting there. I don't think Tucker Carlson is going to just roll over and play dead for Eric Trump, do you?"

"Finish up," sounded to The Proprietor as "check to see my sources aren't dead." He would rather Cholmondeley stay away from the clutches of Stephen Miller and Sidney Powell.

"You're persona non grata there," Murdoch said. "I don't think you'd be very welcome."

"Can't you fix that? I thought he answers to you. Does he not?"

"That's what people think, but he is more independent than that. He is not at my beck and call."

Murdoch did not want to risk losing Cholmondeley, so he set the hook: "As soon as the paperwork is complete and executed, you'll be on your way back there. We can set you up with false papers for that, but please, just fly in, fly out and don't linger."

"That sounds as if we can make it work."

The fish was securely on the line. The Proprietor reeled it in, pulled it over the gunwale and watched it flipping around in the bottom of the boat: "Perhaps you should get yourself a lawyer to advise you on our deal. I can't really make a recommendation for you; anyone I suggest would be tainted with the perception of conflict of interest.

"I'm sure I can find someone," Cholmondeley said.

The fish lay still. It had not been all that difficult to catch.

In the elevator, descending to the lobby and the avenue with two names, Cholmondeley realized that he and The Proprietor had not shaken hands, either upon meeting or on concluding their deal. Also, the old man had never risen to his feet. Cholmondeley wondered if Murdoch might be too infirm to stand up.

Two days later he learned the answer when a photograph was published in the New York Post showing The Proprietor with his new fiancé, standing side-by-side. The finacé, half a head taller than Murdoch, was the buttocks-swinging dusky brunette who had led him into the old man's office. Cholmondeley hoped she would not cause his death in flagrante delicto until after his lucrative deal was signed.

◆ ◆ ◆

It was one of the greatest parades I've ever seen. It was two hours on the button, and it was military might, and a tremendous thing. We're going to have to try to top it. — Donald J. Trump

Collins Avenue, Miami Beach, Florida, Great States Of America

In advance of the military review the Mar-a-Lago press shop put out a release calling it the "largest-ever" parade in GSA history. The claim was indisputable: as the first parade in GSA history, it had to be the largest.

The procession was scheduled to kick off at the respectable hour of 11 am. Two minutes before, a pair of Texas Air National Guard B-1 bombers and five Florida Air National Guard F-16s roared by at low altitude. After the fly-by troops and equipment streamed down Collins Avenue for two hours.

In the air-conditioned tented reviewing stand across the avenue from the Fontainebleau Hotel, President Trump, his son, Eric, and key members of his administration watched, pointed, applauded and chatted. The group included Secretary of Defense Flynn, inexplicably dressed in his old United States Army general's uniform, three stars on his epaulets and all his ribbons and badges arrayed on his chest. Also close-by were Attorney General Powell and Chief of Staff Miller.

Amid the regiments of Florida, Texas, Oklahoma and Alabama Army and Air National Guardsmen were mobile field artillery pieces, armored Humvees, M117 Guardian armored cars, Bradley Fighting Vehicles and macadam-churning Abrams M1A1tanks.

A large and boisterous crowd endured Miami Beach's 88-degree heat and 80 percent humidity to watch the parade. They cheered from time to time as units marched by. They were impressed with the GSA's military might.

Inside the viewing stand, only Flynn and the few Defense Department aides who had accompanied him knew how pathetic and outdated the equipment was. While the American Treaty Organization (ATO) joint-republic force had B-2 bombers, F-18 and F-35 fighters, mobile multiple missile launchers, computer-guided self-propelled Howitzers, Abrams M1A2 tanks and MRAP armored vehicles, none of the National Guard units in the individual republics had such advanced gear. The marching troops carried old M4 assault rifles, not the new-generation XM5 carried by some federal troops. In the GSA, only the WRM units had been issued XM5s.

The media covering the parade were relegated to bleachers erected across Collins Avenue. TV cameras concentrated on getting shots of Trump viewing the passing personnel and gear. Print and radio reporters kept looking for signs of ill health, seeking confirmation or refutation of the BBC story about his spreading cancer.

The reporters agreed that Trump appeared well and seemed to be having a grand time watching the parade, taking and returning salutes from passing regiments and chain-drinking Diet Coca-Colas served him with robotic precision by a white-jacketed waiter. They were too far to see the sweat pouring off him.

An hour into the parade Trump bellowed: "Make it cooler! I'm fucking melting here. Cooler, please. *Now!*"

The technicians operating 30-ton rental AC compressor switched on their 15-ton reserve unit and the circuits in the portable diesel generator exploded loudly, flashes of bright blue flame flew from the power cords accompanied by a cloud of acrid smoke.

"We're outta business," one of the technicians told the nearest WORM.

"You're gonna have one unhappy president," the WORM said.

There was 45 minutes more parade to go when the air conditioning blew up. After a few minutes of suffering in the increasing heat, Trump signaled he wanted to leave the tent. A detachment of WORMs surrounded him and led him to a Suburban. WORMs ran into Collins Avenue and blocked the marchers so the SUV could make a U-turn and deposit the president at the lobby door of the Fontainebleau. He waited in the vehicle as WORMs cleared the lobby. Clotting around Trump, WORMs escorted him to the elevator that serviced the presidential suite on the top floor.

Inside the dining room of the suite, he grabbed another Diet Coke and a Wendy's hamburger. He commandeered one of the bedrooms, took a quick shower and, sitting in front of the makeup table installed that morning, he relaxed as Madelyn Morton, his favorite makeup artist, touched him up.

"It was hot as hell out there. I sweated like a pig," he told her.

"Tent wasn't air-conditioned, Excellency?"

"Air conked out. That's one outfit's not getting paid for today. What assholes."

She replastered his face with Bronx Colors orange concealer, powdered his shiny spots and left. Alone before the mirror, Trump went to work with hairbrush and blowdryer to restore his hairdo. The hair at the back of his skull was long, reaching to the nape of his neck. He brushed and blew that long hair forward, covering the large bald spot that looked like a metastasizing monk's tonsure. He worked the hair forward until it fell over his eyes, like overly long and wide bangs. Then he brushed and blew the bangs up and toward the back, folding the longest hair back upon itself. He brushed and blew some longer strands to the sides, covering the tops of his ears and curving it back behind his neck. Then he lacquered it all in place with BTZ Frozen Stiff hairspray. A few minor adjustments with a comb and he was good to go. He put on a clean shirt, a fresh suit, tied his red tie so the blade hung down three inches below his belt buckle and chugged down another can of Diet Coke. He crushed the can, rose heavily from the chair and opened the door to the living room.

"Let's go to Texas," he said.

Staffers and WORMs stashed their smartphones and jumped to their feet. The WORMs surrounded him and brought him to a flight of stairs that led to the hotel's roof where his helicopter was waiting to fly him to Opa Locka Executive Field where GSA-1 — a freshly renovated ten-year-old Gulfstream B550 — was waiting to fly him to Arlington Municipal Airport in Texas.

◆ ◆ ◆

A very big part of the Anger we see today in our society is caused by the purposely false and inaccurate reporting of the Mainstream Media that I refer to as Fake News. It has gotten so bad and hateful that it is beyond description. Mainstream Media must clean up its act, FAST! — Donald J. Trump

AT&T Stadium, Arlington, Texas, Great States Of America

Cholmondeley carried a passport, press card and driver's license identifying him as George Lazenby. The name was a joke: George Lazenby was an Australian actor who had played James Bond in a single 007 movie in 1969, "On Her Majesty's Secret Service." The pseudonym came courtesy of an ancient British tabloid editor now assigned to the New York Post, who decided it would be funny to use a forgotten 007 actor's name. The joke was lost on Cholmondeley; he never heard of the 57-year-old film or its star.

Cholmondeley/Lazenby got to the domed stadium three hours before the rally was scheduled to start. He was unsurprised to find people already lined up in the brutal heat, patiently waiting to go through the metal detectors.

Cholmondeley/Lazenby presented himself at the doorway labeled "Media." He was wearing two laminated press credentials on a lanyard, one from The Wall Street Journal, the other from Fox News. He offered the Fox credential to a WORM who scanned its QR code and pointed him to the press section.

"Seating's assigned. Look for your name," the WORM said.

"Right-o," Cholmondeley/Lazenby said.

Hearing the accent, the WORM got suspicious, "I never seen you on Fox News. I never seen any English guys on Fox News."

"Australian. Lazenby's an Australian name."

"Oh, yeah. Okay."

Cholmondelay/Lazenby followed a tunnel that led to the Dallas Cowboys playing field. The stadium had been chilled to vegetable crisper temperature. There was no green pitch for games; the Matrix Turf had been rolled up and stored under the stands, leaving a bare concrete surface that was almost 400 feet long and 200 feet wide. The vast space had been divided into 20 sections, each containing 30 neat rows of metal folding chairs that were attached to each other with plastic gang couplers. At one end of stadium floor, where a goal post would have been, a towering stage had been erected. Atop it was a large white lectern. The lectern bore the seal of the President of the Great States of America — an eagle in a circle surrounded by 26 stars. At the opposite end of the stadium floor was a set of risers for still and video cameras. Downstage of that, in a section separated by movable metal bike rack fencing, was the media pen. There were about 100 folding metal chairs in the pen. On the back of each chair was a small piece of white tape with the name of a reporter and their media outlet written in black Sharpie. The seats reserved for The Proprietor's outlets were in the first row: two for Fox News, two for The Wall Street Journal, one for The Times of London (written here as "London Times"), three for the New York Post, one for The Sun ("London Sun"), one for the Australian, and two for Fox Business News; a total of 12 seats. All were empty for now.

Cholmondeley/Lazenby claimed the Fox News seat labeled "Fox News/Lazenby" and studied the stadium. He'd done his homework on Google and knew the stadium could accommodate 100,000 spectators in concert/rally configuration. Some early birds were already seated, jamming the five sections closest to the stage. The gang couplers kept the folding chairs less than two inches apart and the Trump acolytes already seated tended to corpulence, so there was a lot of unwanted pressing of flesh in front of the stage. He might work that into his Wall

Street Journal piece, but he would leave it out of his Fox News report.

Suspended 100 feet above the field was the biggest video screen Cholmondeley/Lazenby had ever seen. At 180 feet wide and 50 feet high, it was the biggest video screen anyone had ever seen; it was the largest video display in the world. Playing silently on it now was footage of Trump addressing various rallies, boarding helicopters, shaking hands with world leaders, triumphantly ripping off his black surgical mask after returning from the hospital following his near-fatal Covid case, playing golf and speaking before Congress. All the footage, Cholmondeley/Lazenby realized, was from his time running for or serving as president of the old United States. It spanned the period 2015 to 2021, beginning with his descent down the gold escalator in Trump Tower to deliver his candidacy announcement before a crowd of paid extras and ending with his infamous January 6th speech before his supporters invaded the Capitol. There was no video of his 2024 run, his assumption of the GSA presidency or anything that had happened since the dissolution of the United States.

Cholmondeley/Lazenby took his digital recorder, his reporter's notebook and his BIC pen and went looking for color for his Journal piece.

He approached a woman sitting in the first row. She was so close to the stage she would have to tilt her head uncomfortably to see Trump behind the lectern, if she could see him at all. She was white-haired, plump to the cusp of obese and overly made-up. Cholmondeley/Lazenby guessed her to be in her mid-seventies. Next to her sat a tiny man wearing an American Legion overseas cap with "Vietnam, 1969-70" embroidered on it. He looked even older.

"May I speak to you?" he asked the woman.

Startled, she snapped her head toward him. She was wide-eyed and wide-mouthed. Her lips struggled to get words out, but she finally asked: "Who're you?" in an accent he took to be Texan.

He held out his Fox News credential.

"Lazarus?" she asked. "Like in the Bible?"

What was the American problem with names? Cholmondeley was admittedly difficult, but Lazarus for Lazenby? Did they read past the first three letters?

"Nothing Biblical about it, ma'am, it's Lazenby,"

"You Fox people haven't been all that fair to him since that election was stolen back in 2020. Stole from us and you didn't do nothing for him," she said.

"His vice president, Mr. Carlson, was a Fox News…." he did not want to say "journalist," that was incorrect.

"A Fox News star."

"Still and all."

"I just started working there last week," Cholmondeley/Lazenby said. Maybe his short-term of employment would mitigate her perception that he was in some way responsible for what she perceived to be Fox News' hostility toward Trump.

"Where you from, again? You an immigrant? I don't remember English people on Fox News."

"Australia. Lazenby is a popular name in Australia. Just like Mr. Murdoch; I'm from Australia."

Would she know who Mr. Murdoch was?

"You'd expect an American network to give Americans jobs, not Austrians."

"Australians."

"Yeah, Australia. That's different. You sure you're not English?"

"No, ma'am." He grimaced as if he had bitten into a lemon. "Not English, we Australians aren't that fond of the English."

She was studying the press pass. "And how'd you say you say that name of yours?"

He was about to say, "Cholmondeley," but stopped himself. "Lazenby. Just the way it's spelled. So may I ask you a few questions?"

If you're Fox News, where's your camera guy?"

"He hasn't arrived yet. I'm just trying to get a sense of the audience. What they anticipate. Gathering some color I can use in my report."

"Color? What colors are you expecting, Mr. Lazarus?"

"I didn't mean that literally," he said. "I just want to — well, you know — take the temperature of the audience."

She seemed to take that literally, "Temperature? This some kinda Covid thing? Screening or something?"

Covid was a fighting word in the Great States of America; its citizens were defiant about the virus. The vaccination rate for the 26 states before dissolution had been just over 65 percent and the uptake rate for the annual boosters was under 40 percent. In the states forming the other republics it had been 82 percent compliance for the initial vaccinations and about 80 percent for the annual boosters. The GSA recorded 400,000 to 500,000 infections a year with a death toll approaching 3,500. The other republics combined had fewer than 200,000 total annual cases and a death toll of fewer than 1,000.

"No. Nothing to do with Covid. Not what I meant at all. I meant I wanted to gauge the mood of the audience."

"Shoulda said that, then." She cracked a smile, "I was fooling with you. I knew you weren't talking 'bout Covid. And I knew what you meant when you said color."

"May I ask you why you came out here this afternoon, why you got here so early?"

"Came out early to get a good seat. Came out to see him." She said the pronoun with such awe, Cholmondeley/Lazenby wrote it in all-caps in his notebook: HIM.

"And why come in person? Why not watch it on TV?"

"You can't be counted when you're watching on TV. You can't stand up and applaud HIM when you're watching on TV. I guess you can, but no one sees that and hears you. We, my husband and me, we want everyone to know we're here. For HIM."

"So you are a big supporter?"

"I wouldn't say big. We're not rich, Edgar and me," she nodded at the skinny man. He was paying no attention and appeared to be on the verge of falling asleep in his chair. His chin sank lower toward his chest and his eyelids drooped. "We send what we can, but the big supporters, that's them in the skyboxes." She pointed up to glassed-in boxes suspended from the top level. "That's where the big money folks are. They got their own air-conditioning in there and waiters bringing them food and such. Drinks, you know. That don't cost them anything to get in — like a ticket, but I heard they contribute something like $10,000 to get invited to them skyboxes. Guess if they pay that much, they ought to get food and drinks and waiters to wait on them."

She lowered her voice, "You want to know something? Some of them younger people you're gonna see brought in and put back behind the stage — you know where you can see them on TV when HE speaks — they actually pay them to come here. College kids, mostly. They like to get some younger people, and some color back there, too. Black people, 'spanics. We got a granddaughter at SMU, Southern Methodist, you know, even though we're not Methodists; we're Baptist, Southern Baptist. So she's not political or anything, like us. Her parents, either. But she's gonna be here. They pay her and her friends $50, I think, maybe seventy-five, for them to come. And free buses right from the campus to here. A good thing, I think. She'll learn something here. Fifty, seventy-five bucks and hearing the truth. That's what I would call a win-win. 'Course some of them college kids would come on their own. HE's got a lot of young support. Don't be fooled by what you read in the lamestream media about young people being against

Trump; he's got a lot of 'em." Cholmondeley/Lazenby was scribbling so fast his hand began to hurt.

"So what is it that makes you and your husband" — who was now snoring softly — "so supportive. What is it he says or does that keeps you so loyal you're here three hours before the rally's going to start?"

"You gotta ask that question, mister, then you don't know HIM. Ever seen Trump? Not on TV, but in person? Must have never done that because how can you even ask that if you seen HIM?" She thought for a moment. "You know what? he loves us so we love him."

"And can you tell me how you know he loves you?"

"Well, for one thing, he told us he loves us. For another, he hates *them*."

"And who would that be, who is 'them?'"

"Like you don't know. Them! The big shots. The smarty guys. The you-know-who with a chip on their shoulders. The Mexicans coming over the border, the A-rabs killing us. Those Iran people; guess they're A-rabs. But mostly the big shots; the money guys. The globalists."

"But wouldn't you call the people who paid $10,000 to be in the skyboxes 'money guys'? If they can afford that price for a rally?"

"That's different. They're different. That's a contribution, anyway. They're *our* money people; that's different. You sure you're from Fox News?"

"I'm sure." He held out his Fox press card.

"You don't sound like Fox News."

"But you have to admit that someone's got to be a 'money guy' to have $10,000 to contribute for a skybox invitation."

"I guess. Yeah. Well, they got food and all up there, drinks, too, so...."

CHAPTER FOUR

The press is now going, they're saying, "Oh but there's such violence." No violence. You know how many people have been hurt at our rallies? I think, like, basically none except maybe somebody got hit once. It's a love fest. These are love fests. And every once in a while somebody will stand up and they'll say something. It's a little disruption, but there's no violence. There's none whatsoever. — Donald J. Trump

AT&T Stadium, Arlington, Texas, Great States Of America

The motorcade consisted of 20 armored SUVs, 15 local police cars, 10 state police cars, 20 WORMs on motorcycles with sidecars, two ambulances and a communications Humvee. It left Arlington Municipal Airport with something less than military precision but got itself straightened out after a few fits and starts. The most direct route, 5.8 miles straight up S. Collins Street, was risky: there were too many intersections where security would be compromised. So, the motorcade convoyed north for under a mile, then turned east on Interstate 20, exiting after two and a half miles to go north on Texas Route 360 to Interstate 30, then west to South Collins and south to the stadium — a route that was twice as many miles but could be driven in less time because it was mostly freeways which the motorcade took at 80 miles per hour.

The route took the motorcade past the cloverleaf at Routes 360 and 303 where many of the Dallas and Fort Worth homeless had been settled in a tent city after they had been rounded up and bused out of the downtown areas. There were camping tents in various stages of repair all over the cloverleaf; they covered all the grass between the highways. Shirtless men of varying skin colors stood around talking and smoking. There were shabbily dressed women, too, and not a few bare-assed toddlers. Dogs roamed everywhere. In full view of the motorcade, one of them lifted a leg and peed on a tent.

"What the fuck is that?" Trump thundered. "A fucking homeless relocation center?"

Trump was tired and irritable. The stress of the overheated tent during the military review weighed on him. And this was going to be his third rally in four days. He was looking for an excuse to throw a tantrum. He wrinkled up his nose as if he could smell the camp inside the closed SUV.

"That fucking place stinks to high heavens. I bet it does. Gotta smell like shit. And piss. That's criminal. Criminal!

Someone's going to shoot film of that and report that's what Trump saw when he drove to his rally. They're gonna blame that on me. So get them the fuck outta there. Move them further out. I don't want the people driving by seeing that shit. Who told them to move them there? I wanted them out of the cities, out of the towns. Not at freeway offramps. Put 'em out where nobody sees 'em. What part of that didn't you guys understand? You put them there, that close to town, they'll just move back into the town. Or they'll walk down the streets and begin bothering people."

Stephen Miller, in the passenger seat behind the driver, quickly agreed, hoping to forestall the impending rage hurricane, "Yeah. That's bad. Real bad." Then he undid his mollifying: "But, that's a state matter, though. Kind of is Texas's responsibility."

The storm surge struck, "We fucking pay for it. We fucking reimburse the state for moving them. *Bull*shit, it's a state thing."

"I'll get on it first thing tomorrow."

"No. You get on it now. And while you're at it, here's a rule: No homeless camps within five miles of any home. *Any* home. None. Five miles. Make it ten. No homeless within ten miles of any home. Otherwise, GSA doesn't pay for it."

"Consider it done, Boss.... Excellency."

"If it's gonna cost more, tell me. Congress will pay for it with a supplemental. I don't want my people seeing those people."

"Done, Excellency."

"*Not yet*, it's not. Get it done. ASAP."

Trump was miffed at Miller; any excuse to tear him a new one would do. In writing the rally speech that Trump was going to ignore, Miller had used the word, "conversely." That had set Trump off on a tear during the flight from Florida: "Conversely? What's this conversely? Trump never uses the word 'conversely.'"

"Excellency, it means…."

"You think Trump's stupid; doesn't know what 'conversely' means?" When Trump referred to himself in the third person, the conversation was turning fraught.

"I was saying 'conversely' before you were born. Trump, he doesn't say 'conversely' in speeches. *They* don't know what the fuck it means, so you can't use it in a speech. Haven't you learned anything in all this time?"

"Sorry, Excellency."

"Don't be sorry. Just don't fuck up my speeches again."

My speeches, not Trump's speeches; Miller breathed easier. Still, The Boss was on edge, looking for more blame to hurl.

The motorcade arrived at AT&T Stadium forty-four minutes before the rally's scheduled start time. On the streets beyond the parking lot there were about 200 protestors holding up pro-abortion signs, pro-immigrant signs, Black Lives Matter signs. The local police kept them far from the parking lot entrances, but when the long line of black SUVs, police cars, motorcycles and ambulances was at its closest — less than a city block away — a dozen protestors turned and shook their signs in his direction.

"Fucking traitors," Trump muttered.

He saw two drones hovering over the demonstration; he didn't like that, they could be news drones shooting video.

"Is there some way we can clear out those rioters? They're rioting, right? They're doing property damage, right? I don't want that on the local news. Or the national news. Those look like TV drones, don't they?" No one answered. "Am I talking to myself here? Is there some way we can clear out those Antifa communists or whoever the fuck they are? I don't want them on TV tonight. Get the WORMs to shoot them in the legs or something like that. You don't have to kill them."

Miller answered, "The damage is likely done, Excellency. TV's already got their video of them. And you don't want

WORMs shooting anyone or clearing them out; that'll look worse. That'll become the story, not the rally. We want the rally to be the story."

Miller's answer was unsatisfactory: "Just shoot a few of them. Shoot a few of them in the legs. We got guys can do that, don't we? What the hell do we train the WORMs for if they can't shoot people in the legs?"

"If shooting starts, I don't think there's any way for them to just aim for the legs," Miller said. "You saw what happened when the WORMs started shooting in Oklahoma City."

"They didn't kill anybody in Oklahoma City, did they?" Trump said. "Steve, you don't know what you're talking about. You ever fire a gun?"

"No. Not really."

"What the fuck's 'not really' mean? Either you fired a gun or you never fired a gun. Which is it?"

"Never."

Trump said, "I have. I went to a military school, you know. I know about guns. The NRA, they love me. Nobody's ever been more pro-gun than me. I fired so many guns, you can't count how many guns I've shot."

"I wouldn't worry about these bums, if I were you. Every local station's taking the rally live. Fox News and Newsmax are covering it live across the country and around the world. There's lot of streaming platforms taking it live. No one's going to notice those assholes."

"You wouldn't worry if you were me? Well, you're not me. Never will be, either."

"Yes, Excellency."

"I wanna get rid of 'em, Antifa scum. They're dirtier than those homeless." Trump dialed his iPhone. "Mike? Mike? Where are you? ... Where?"

He turned to Miller, "Flynn's back in Palm Beach. I thought he was coming here with us. Why the fuck is he in Palm Beach?"

Miller shook his head; the plan had always been for Flynn to return to Palm Beach after the military review.

"Listen, Mike," Trump said, "you know those Predator drones the Texas Air National Guard's got?" Trump paused to listen. "OK, the Louisiana Air Guard's got 'em. Okay. Well, where are they located?" He paused. "I don't know exactly where that is. Can you get them over to the Dallas area fast? How fast? Do they carry missiles or guns or anything like that? Any offensive weapons. How about tear gas? Can you outfit 'em with tear gas?"

He listened. "Well, what the fuck use are they if you don't have the.... whattaya call it, ordinance?" He listened. "Intelligence? Well, I think it's pretty stupid, which is the opposite of intelligence. I want you to look into what it would take to get that ordinance for the drones. Wanna blow up some of these fuckers."

He listened again. "Oh for Christ's sake, Mike, don't tell me what I can't do. Tell me what I fucking *can* do."

The motorcade entered the parking lot, leaving behind the protestors. Trump took in the large crowd; *his* people patiently waiting their turn at the metal detectors.

"Wow, we must have two hunnred thousand out there."

"Yes, Excellency, a really great turnout. Probably biggest turnout in Texas history. But, actually, I don't think the stadium can hold quite that many people, two hundred thousand," Miller said.

"I say two hunnred thousand then it's two hunnred thousand. Who's gonna argue?"

"The media covering it might know; they could check it out...."

"The fake news media? Fuck 'em! What are they going to do? Count every person? That'll be the day! Two hunnred thousand, I say. Maybe two hunnred fifty thousand. Even better, two hunnred fifty thousand. Have them put that out."

"Of course, Excellency," Miller said. He had no intention of putting that out; it was too easily disproved.

More than two dozen vendors stood behind tables spaced throughout the parking lot, selling GSA tee-shirts and UNITE! baseball caps.

"Are those authorized? Is that our merch they're selling? It doesn't look like our merch. Close that shit down," he barked. "Confiscate that swag. They can't do that. All this shit is copyrighted."

The WORM riding shotgun got on his radio and gave some directions. By the time Trump's armored Suburban entered the stadium and deposited him near his dressing room, squads of WORMs were swarming the vendors, knocking over tables, seizing and pocketing their cash, phones and wallets and stuffing their merchandise into black plastic garbage bags. The vendors were flexcuffed with their hands behind their backs and herded onto school buses. Once the rally started, they were driven 20 miles to downtown Dallas and released on the street, broke, anonymous and incommunicado.

To get to the dressing room, Trump had to pass through a large green room crowded with VIP donors and hangers-on who were stuffing their faces with snacks, drinking sodas and talking loudly. They fell silent when Trump entered. Someone began applauding, so the others applauded, too. Momentarily energized by their adulation, Trump puffed out his belly, gave his two thumbs up sign and grinned broadly. He nodded as he made his way into the dressing room; he spoke to no one. Later, more than a few of them would lie to friends and family about Trump stopping to shake their hands and chat for a few moments.

He slammed shut the dressing room door and plopped heavily into the makeup chair. The adulation euphoria subsided; he was tired and achy. His stomach was gassy, and he felt acid rising in his esophagus. He opened a fresh can of Diet Coke and chugged a quarter of it in pursuit of a satisfying belch. Nothing. He took another long swig. Still nothing. He swallowed some air and forced a burp; it was hardly adequate. He looked at his reflection.

Not bad after that fucking parade and the heat and that fucking Gulfstream. Can't even stand up straight in it. Well, almost can't. Narrow, too. That's no way for a president to travel. It's no Air Force One, that's for sure. Turns a decent buck, though.

Trump Enterprises owned the Gulfstream and leased it to the GSA executive branch.

He looked at his notes. The full speech that Miller and his team had written was on a prompter and he'd see that on three screens affixed to the lectern, but Trump never simply read what had been written for him. Following a script word-for-word bored him, even when the words were red meat for his base. He liked to ad lib, to improvise, to feel what resonated with the crowd and go with that.

Gonna kill tonight. Absolutely kill.

But first he opened another Diet Coke and chugged. That produced a long, satisfying belch.

Rosalind Baskin, his secretary, opened the door a crack.

"Do you want do a meet and greet for the VIPs in the green room?"

"Not really, but I will. They know not to shake hands?"

"Of course."

The big-money donors had been warned against any physical contact with Trump; he did not shake hands, fist bump, high-five or slap backs; they were told to keep their hands to themselves. Smiling, nodding, talking were all okay; physical contact was not. Even though they had passed through metal detectors to get into the stadium, they had submitted to additional rough and thorough frisking by WORMs before entering the Green Room.

When Trump stepped into the green room, the VIPs began applauding again. Trump worked his way around the room, unsmiling, nodding at each of them and delivering a stream of babel:

"How ya doin'? How ya doin'? Good t'see ya. Hey, how are ya? Good t'see ya. Hey, how are ya? Thanks for coming; 'preciate it. 'Preciate ya support.

Nice t'see ya. Thanks. Thanks. Thank ya. 'Preciate it. Thank ya. How ya doin'? How ya doin'? Good t'see ya. Hey, how are ya? Thanks for comin'. 'preciate it. 'Preciate the support. How ya doin'? Thanks, thanks. Thank ya. 'Preciate it. Thank ya very much."

He worked his way to the door, turned and said, "Better get out there and get in those sky boxes. It's gonna be wild. You don't wanna miss it. Thank ya. Thanks for your support. We're gonna *do* this thing."

The VIPs applauded. Before they left the green room, a member of Trump's campaign team passed out pledge cards with boxes for additional contributions starting at $10,000. The next options were $25,000, $50,000, $100,000 and $250,000. There was also a check box next to a blank line for those who needed even more from the administration than a quarter million dollars could buy. Most of them used the blank line to pencil in amounts ranging from $10 to $100. The sponges had been wrung dry.

*

Cholmondeley/Lazenby had spoken to five early bird attendees. He has as much color as he needed; more than he needed since much of it was redundant. These people firmly believed that, despite his flaunted wealth, his unrelenting lies and his incomparable self-regard, Trump loved them, listened to them and needed financial help from them.

The bought-and-paid-for attendees filed in behind the lectern. No grey beards, no white hair in that crowd. Most of them were white, but there were some African Americans sporting "Black Lives Matter to Trump" and "AAs for Trump" tee shirts. The were, as well, a few dark complexed Latinos and one or two who looked as if they might be South Asian.

Two WORMs, walked out and inspected the lectern, getting down on their hands and knees to look at the flooring, touching virtually every inch of its surface with their gloved hands. Satisfied there were no bombs, mines or booby traps, they walked back to the wings.

Behind Cholmondeley/Lazenby, high on the risers, Fox had two cameras trained on the stage. A third camera was in the upper-level stands. The network was feeding the rally live to its primetime audience, as it had earlier fed live the military review in Miami Beach. A blonde woman he recognized took the seat next to him. She wore a sleeveless dress and the cold had raised goose bumps on her arms.

"Ann Bailey," she said. "Fox News."

He had seen her in Mar-a-Lago briefings; she was the Fox News GSA bureau chief. They had worked in the same building, but had never before met; A-credentialled journalists did not mingle with the B-credentialled.

He took her limp hand. "And I know who you are. We all do. I just don't know how to pronounce your name. Your *real* name. Don't worry; your secret is safe with us Fox folks." She forced an insincere smile; it looked like she had double the normal allotment of teeth.

Bailey was in her late twenties or early thirties but had the look and shape of the high school cheerleader she had once been. Her skirt was only slightly longer than a cheerleader's costume and the colors she sported, bright red and white, could have been those of a school. Instead of a cheerleader's white sneakers, she wore stiletto-heeled white patent leather shoes. In a way, she was still a cheerleader, but now, in the guise of news reports, she shook her pompoms and wiggled her butt for Team Trump.

Cholmondeley/Lazenby did not know if she was a true believer or just playing the career game. In either event, he found her work shallow, ill-informed and gullible. He also found her quite shag-worthy.

"You know," Ann Bailey leaned forward until her toothy mouth was brushing against his ear. "They were willing to go to a million and a half.

Pounds, not dollars. A million and a half to get you. I hear you settled for a million."

Settled? More money than any journalist was worth, and she considered that "settling?" A million and a half? He could be making fifty percent more than Murdoch was paying him? Maybe she was manipulating him; trying to make him feel badly because she was jealous. Who knew?

A Wall Street Journal reporter — looking appropriately Wall Street in suit, white shirt and striped tie — took the seat to the other side of him. Cholmondeley/Lazenby thrust out his hand to introduce himself.

"Oh, I know who you are," the Journal man said. Of course he did. All News Corp employees apparently knew who he was, how much he earned and how much more he might have been earning if he had been a better negotiator. There was nothing to be done about it but cash the checks and enjoy the wealth while it lasted. And have a run at Ann Bailey, who had crossed her legs, affording him a fetching view of her taut thigh.

The sound system, adjusted to accommodate the hearing loss suffered by the president's largely over-60 audience, began blasting the Tom Petty song "I Won't Back Down" at an average of 108 decibels. The shock wave of sound was a physical force and caused some of the younger people arrayed behind the lectern to recoil. Seniors lucky enough to be wearing hearing aids pulled them from their ears and stuffed them into pockets and purses.

The song played twice, an act of Trumpian defiance. As far back as 2020, lawyers for Petty's estate sent the Trump campaign, the Trump Organization and the Republican National Committee cease and desist letters that read: "Trump is in no way authorized to use this song to further a campaign that leaves too many Americans and common sense behind. Both the late Tom Petty and his family firmly stand against racism and discrimination of any kind. Tom Petty would never want a song of his used for a campaign of hate. He liked to bring people together." Trump continued to use the song. Petty's family filed civil suits, Trump's lawyers refused to address them, and a series of judges gave the Petty estate default awards ranging from a low of $400,000 to a high of $3 million. Trump, his campaign, his supporters, his businesses and the RNC had not forked over a single dollar. Trump did not back down and continued to use the song at every rally.

Eric Trump bounded on stage, positioned himself behind the lectern, suffered scattered boos from Tucker Carlson fans and shouted into the microphone, "Are you ready?" His mouth was so close and his volume so loud, his words came out distorted and the audience heard a painful buzz that sounded like, "Rrrrrr eddy."

As one, they got to their feet, some jumping up, others struggling to rise. They screamed, "YES!"

"Americans, I present the one true president, my father, the most important man in my life and in yours, Donald J. Trump!"

All everyone heard was "Zzzzzzzzzzz Pxxxdent, zzzzther zzzzzztant zzzzzzzzzzzzzzz Trumzzzz!"

It didn't matter, the crowd went wild and "I Won't Back Down" began playing even louder.

In the Self-Realization Fellowship Lake Shrine, 1,439 miles to the west, just a few short blocks from the Pacific Ocean, Tom Petty spun in his grave.

Trump emerged from the wings, his hands balled into fists, rocking to the music. He awkwardly bopped his way to the lectern. The crowd, already wild, went wilder. On their feet, save for the wheelchair-bound, they were clapping, foot-stamping, hooting and cheering. The president forced the slightest of smiles — more smirk than smile — and shook his head to calm them down while waving his right hand in a "come on," gesture to rile them up.

Looka 'em. Look. They love me. This is love. Fucking love. They're mine! I got 'em. If I told 'em to set themselves on fire, they'd be asking me where the matches are.

Still smirking, Trump tilted his head and pumped his fist. The cheering grew louder. It continued for another minute, began a diminuendo and Trump pumped his fist to bring the volume back up again. He waited. And waited.

Trump pumped his fist a third time and brought the sitters to their feet. The applause and cheering grew louder. He let it go on for a minute. Then two. A few seconds into the third minute, he raised both hands, palms out and motioned for the crowd to quiet and sit.

"How about that? You love me!" he said. "You love me. And I love you!" They were on their feet again, stamping, cheering, applauding.

Huge. This is huge. Huge! I could keep 'em going an hour without opening my mouth.

He let it go on for another full minute, shaking his head in mock disbelief at their response. Then he began talking so quietly he couldn't be heard over the crowd noise. They quieted quickly. "Just saying I love you, too!" he shouted. And the cheering and applauding began anew.

After about 15 seconds, when their hands began hurting and voices were raw with shouting, they quieted without a signal from him. Some sat. Then more. Soon everyone was seated.

Cholmondeley/Lazenby glanced left and right. The audience was rapt, all eyes were on the lectern. They had their chins tilted up and their eyes were raised; there was a churchy aspect to their posture.

Trump basked in the adoration. He could not see the paid claque behind him where some smiled knowingly, some grimaced uncomfortably and others stared straight ahead, not visibly reacting.

When he had complete silence, he gripped the lectern with both hands, leaned in and said: "Do you miss your country? Our country? Do you miss the United States of America? Do you miss your favorite president being president of the United States of America? Well, I do! I miss it. And I'm telling you right here, right now, we're going to take it back. We're going to claim what's ours. We. Will. Be. Back!"

Everyone rose. In the media pen, Cholmondeley/Lazenby turned to the Ann Bailey, who had uncrossed her legs, eliminating any distraction from the lectern.

"Is it always like this?" he asked her. "The crowd going crazy like this?"

"Yeah, always."

When the cheering subsided, Trump paused dramatically. One second. Two. Three. Four.

Wait. Wait. Wait a little more. A little more. They're getting antsy. NOW!

"People are saying," said Trump, who always knew what people were saying. "They are saying that I alone can reunite the country. I alone can bring back the *United* States of America. But I can only do it with your help. You are the greatest supporters in the world. By the way you're also the smartest, the hardest working, and you pay taxes." He smirked; one of his mottos was, "Taxes are for Suckers."

"I know the fake leaders in the phony *republics*," — he loaded the word with sarcasm — "think it's impossible to re-create the country, to bring it back. Impossible to reunite the country? Well, I'm here to tell you that if an uneducated country lawyer like Abraham Lincoln — he never went to college, you know that? Lincoln never went to college. If he, Lincoln, could do it, someone smarter, richer and better educated — namely, me — can do it and do it even better. In fact, *only* I can do it."

No one was shocked he'd compared Abraham Lincoln unfavorably with himself. To the contrary, they were on their feet, cheering. Trump raised his hands to silence them; he was on a roll. Nothing he had said thus far was on the prompter; he could see the written script scrolling back and forth as the operator fought to find where he was in the speech. There was no finding the spot; he was free-associating and if he stopped the roll, or went to the script, he would lose momentum.

"Me? I'm a fighter. And I'm gonna fight to reunite the country. Reunite it under *me*! And I'm doing it for *you*."

More cheers. They were eating out of his hand, so he used the adoration to try to raise some money: "My people estimate each of you saves two thousand dollars a year by living in my Great States of America, the beautiful, most perfect country in the world, and not in the tax-and-spend *republics* where the government squeezes the life out of you with taxes, taxes and more taxes. And, believe you me, the smart people there don't pay their fair share. Or don't pay any taxes. I should know, I was one of them" That was greeted with laughter from a crowd filled with people who had no choice but to pay their taxes because they were withheld from their paychecks.

"Two thousand bucks. You're two thousand bucks ahead in *my* country. Two thousand. That's a sweet amount of money, don't ya know? And it's four thousand for a couple, filing jointly. So why not contribute some of that $2,000 to us and our campaign?"

Trump would not have to face the voters for nearly five years, but it was never too early to begin fund-raising.

"Ten percent sounds fair to me. Is it fair to you?" There was a decidedly reduced cheer. "Come on, folks, I'm rich but I can't do it myself. Your favorite president needs a little bit of your help. Consider it a tip for excellent service. What do you tip in a restaurant? Fifteen percent? Eighteen? Me, I tip 20 percent. For real good service, I tip 25 percent!" Actually, Trump tipped erratically. Sometimes he didn't tip at all. At other times, he would hand a $50 bill to a valet who brought him a Diet Coke.

"Are you real generous, like me? Then make it twenty percent? But all I'm asking is ten percent. Not even a restaurant size tip. And it's not ten percent of what you're spending, like a tip in a restaurant. It's ten percent of what *I'm* giving you. So think of it as getting eighteen hunnerd dollars a year from me. You're gonna be eighteen hunnerd bucks ahead of where you would be if you lived in those other three *republics*. Or if you still lived in the United States of America. You can buy a lot with eighteen hunnred dollars. And you get that from me every year. Year-in-year-out, I'm giving you two grand and all I'm asking back is a $200 contribution to the campaign. Ten percent of the two grand I send you every year. Four grand for a married couple, filing jointly, like I said. And, frankly, I'm sending you a lot more than that because of our high employment and low taxes and right-to-work laws. Hey, how about this: why not contribute to my campaign what would have been your union dues if we had the unions, which we don't, which is the best thing that ever happened to working people in the history of the world. We had unions, I bet that everyone's union dues would be a lot more than $200 a year. Much more money. Those unions suck the blood out of a working man. Believe me, I know. Back when I did 'The Apprentice,' the best reality show that was ever on TV; back then I had to join the union. AFTRA, it was called. You wouldn't believe how much money they took from me, AFTRA. For what?

Did they get me jobs and make me famous? No, I did that. Me. I did it."

The audience stood and briefly applauded the memory of that long-ago reality show. Some of them had seen it during its 13 years on NBC; many more had not.

"Like I say, I'm a fighter. You know even when I was a kid in elementary school, I was a fighter. In the second grade I gave a teacher a black eye. A music teacher. I punched him in the face because he didn't know anything about music. I knew more about music in the second grade than this guy did. But that didn't matter, he was a music teacher. Like all those teachers teaching your kids about stuff they don't know about. I almost got expelled for that, for punching my teacher. That's right, second grade. Almost expelled. How old are you in the second grade? Eight, nine? Whatever. What second grader does that? I'll tell you who, a fighter! At eight, nine, whatever I was, I was such a fighter. Now when I say I punched my teacher, you know a second grader can't punch so hard. And they didn't expel me. They treated me fair. And, you know, that was about the last time anyone's ever treated me fair!"

That got the laugh he wanted. "No, sir. Whoever got treated as bad as me? As bad as they treated me? Lincoln, maybe. Just maybe. But they impeached me twice, they cheated me out of my landslide victory in 2020. I won that by a landslide, and you know it. I was cheated."

The cult gave him a 15-second standing ovation for the election he had lost.

"I won that election, but they cheated, and Mike Pence let me down. He let all of us down, that Mike Pence." Trump screwed up his face when he said the name the second time, as if he had just been bushwhacked by the odor of a surreptitious fart.

The expression had been effective in the past; Trump's just-smelled-a-fart look every time he brought up Pence's name had ended the former vice president's political career.

In AT & T Stadium, the Mike Pence just-smelled-a-fart look was like throwing a switch. Instantly animated, the audience jumped to its feet and began chanting: "Hang Mike Pence, hang Mike Pence, hang Mike Pence." Even some of the younger and more diverse attendees standing behind Trump chanted, although it was clear they were more amused than angry. Trump stepped back from the lectern and watched with a little self-satisfied smile.

If Pence walked out on this stage right now, they'd rush up here and beat him to death. Maybe I should invite him to the next rally, the sanctimonious shit.

The chant got louder and spread further. Trump was smiling and nodding in time to the chant. "Hang Mike Pence, hang Mike Pence, hang Mike Pence, hang Mike Pence."

Trump raised a hand to stop the chant. It died down slowly, the crowd reluctant to relent.

"I guess Mike isn't the most popular guy in the world right now, right here. Good thing he's not here with us in the stadium, huh? Wouldn't be good for his health, would it?"

"Hang Mike Pence, hang Mike Pence, hang Mike Pence, hang Mike Pence...."

Trump let it go on until he sensed the volume was weakening and he raised his hand to turn it off.

"That's water under the dam. I won, but Mike didn't do the right thing. And that caused January Sixth. Mike Pence caused that by not doing the right thing, by not ratifying my landslide win. By putting an illegitimate president in office. And then they had the nerve to investigate *me*! To try and charge *me*! I was the one that won. I won and they stole it from me and then they investigated *me*? That's like getting mugged and having a cop arrest you for giving your wallet to a thug crook. Investigate me? Charge me? How dare they investigate and try to charge the victim?

"They broke into my beautiful home in Florida. Mar-a-Lago. The FBI raided it. Carrying guns, threatening my people. Good thing I wasn't there. I was at my place in New Jersey, but if I had been there...." He let them imagine what he would have done to stop 14 FBI special agents from executing a valid search warrant. Whatever they imagined, they loved, because in a beat they were again standing and cheering loudly.

"And you know what? You know who signed that search warrant? A judge I appointed. That's right, I appointed that clown. I give him a job for life and that's the way he repays me? *My* judge and he double crosses me. How's that for loyalty?"

The cult thought that was not much for loyalty, they booed.

"That judge; he's in jail now. Not jail, really, detention. He's in detention. He was disloyal and now he's paying for it. He should have thought down the road before signing that search warrant. He's in detention and he's going to be charged and tried. The Great States of America is a nation of laws, not a nation of men, like the United States of America was. A nation of laws, not a nation of men. And women; we don't want to forget the women. I love the women. The women know I love them. Love them."

Women, some with tears in their eyes, rose and applauded.

"Beautiful. Beautiful. Aren't my women beautiful? The beautiful women in my country know -- and the men know, too -- they know my country does not believe in locking people up without charges. But we also don't believe in letting dangerous thugs and disloyal traitors free on the streets. That's why we have pre-legislative detention in the Great States of America. So we can lock up those thugs and traitors while we pass the laws we'll charge them with. Then we'll try them for it and sentence them for breaking the laws. It's my concept. I call it retroactive justice and of the four *republics*, only the Great States of America has it. But believe you me when I reunite the *United* States of America, we're gonna have it everywhere. *Everywhere.* And the first thugs we're gonna lock up under it are Jon Steward, J.D. Pritzker, Gavin Newsom and their boss, George Sorros. The first! You mark my words." He had mispronounced Stewart's name intentionally; Trump always called him "Steward."

The audience was up, chanting, "Lock them up! Lock them up! Lock them up...."

There was no official tally of people currently in pre-legislative detention. It had started small — with some Democratic politicians in Florida, Texas and Georgia —and had grown steadily. Informal estimates, more guesstimates than estimates, put the number of those jailed for breaking laws which did not yet exist at 6,000. It was a challenge for the GSA's unicameral Congress to pass the laws fast enough to accommodate the detainees, since most of congresspersons were novice politicians who had come up through the ranks as party apparatchiks, low-level government functionaries and militia officers.

Trump went back to the injustices done to him: "That search by the FBI thugs working for that disloyal judge, that didn't stop me. You know what they did? They went through the First Lady's underwear drawer looking for stuff. As if I would hide anything there. As if she'd let me."

He paused for the laugh. It was tepid.

"Anyone knows Melania, knows she wouldn't let me anywhere near her… her stuff."

Another laugh, heartier.

"Almost said 'underwear,'"

A third laugh, heartier still.

"I mean who wouldn't want to…."

Laugh.

"Never mind; where I'm going with this, I'm going to get into trouble."

Final laugh; the best one.

"Despite the crooked FBI, I won again in '24 and what did they do? They broke up the country so I couldn't be president of the whole country. Just president of the states that love me. They broke the country! Our country! Now was that fair?"

The switched-on audience roared, "NO!"

They were on their feet; some were waving fists in the air. "NO! NO! NO! NO!"

Cholmondeley/Lazenby saw that some of the young and more diverse crowd behind Trump were working hard to suppress laughter. That couldn't look good for Trump on TV; they were amused while the audio track thundered angry "No. No. No."

Trump quieted the cult. He enjoyed controlling them, switching their emotions on and off. He stretched his hands out to his sides, almost as if he were positioning himself for crucifixion, but he was unable to raise his arms to shoulder level, so he looked more like a swept-wing airplane than a would-be martyr.

"You know, I'm the first man since Franklin D. Roosevelt to win the presidency three times. I won it in 2016 and I got to serve four years. Four years when life was better for every single one of you and you know that."

They interrupted with wild applause but remained seated.

"Four years when the Mexicans rapists and drug dealers and murderers and Islamofascist Arab terrorists were afraid to come across the border or fly into our country because they knew what would happen to them if they did. Four years when criminal thugs didn't go around the streets shooting and robbing people. And that's because I had unchained the cops. That's right, before me, the cops were chained up by Democrat regulation. By budget cuts. By Obama. Barack *Hussein* Obama. Who was our most pro-thug president ever. He was pro-thug, you know."

Boos filled the stadium.

"Obama defunded the cops. He handcuffed the cops."

"Thug Obama, thug Obama, thug Obama, thug Obama," began the chant. It morphed to, "Fuck Obama, fuck Obama, fuck Obama, fuck Obama."

Trump beamed appreciatively, nodding to the rhythm of the chant. When it began to lose steam, he raised his hand to stop it.

"I unchained them, the police. I *funded* the cops. I *supported* the police like no leader ever supported the police before or after. And crooks and thugs? When they go to *my* jails in *my* country they *pay* for their accommodations. It's right in the law. In the law we wrote. Convicts pay $250 a day for their rooms and $75 a day for their food. They can't afford it; they shouldn't do the crime. We send them a bill. Honest to God, we bill them for their cells. They can't pay it, we go after them for the money after they're out. Garnish their wages, if they can get jobs. And until they're paid up, they can't vote, can't get welfare, can't get food stamps, can't get medical care, can't get drivers licenses, can't even get a library card" — he pronounced it liberry — "not that thugs spend a lot of time reading.

"That's how we treat criminals here in the GSA. And that's because I unchained the police. Not so much the corrupt FBI, but the *real* police. The cops you see every day. I was the first and the only true law and order president. And you see it in the GSA, don't you?

"In my constitution, I got rid of The Fifth. You know, the Fifth Amendment where you didn't have to say a word if you are guilty and didn't want to admit it. You know who pleads The Fifth? I'll tell you who: the mob. Mobbed-up gangsters take The Fifth. And murderers and rapists and drug dealers. They all took The Fifth back in the day, back in the USA with Obama's constitution. He favored thugs and criminals over the rest of us."

Trump, himself, had pled the Fifth Amendment 440 times during a single deposition in a civil case in New York. The audience seemed unaware of that irony.

"But not in our country; not in the GSA. We said, 'If you're innocent, why are you taking the Fifth Amendment?' So we got rid of that. No Fifth for crooks and killers. And the police turned loose on coddled thugs, Obama's boys. Obama's coddled killers."

Boos for the coddled thugs.

"Ask any cop, ask my cops; they'll tell you. They'll tell you how pro-police I was when I was president of the whole country. And all of you know how pro-police I am here in the GSA. Ask any cop. Ask the cops in the other *republics* if I'm not more pro-cop than any president, ever.

"I unleashed the prosecutors on the drug dealers, too. You know that. You know that. Countries that give the death penalty to drug dealers don't have drug problems. The Philippines. Singapore. Pakistan. Saudi Arabia. In Saudi Arabia they cut the heads off of drug dealers in a stadium like this one. How many drug dealers do you think they have now in Saudi Arabia? Well, none. Because they had their heads cut off in a stadium. Well, *our* country doesn't have a drug problem. Not anymore. Because drug dealers know they'll get the death penalty. I already executed 24 of them. Hanged 'em publicly."

Publicly was an exaggeration; a small number of officials and journalists had been invited to the executions. Trump avoided the executions; he worried he might puke if he saw one.

"Twenty-four! Think about how many more people their drugs would of killed if I had let them off the hook the way they do in those drugged-up *republics*. *California!* The druggiest state anywhere. So, twenty-four of those scumbags dead, another ten gonna be tried real soon. And they'll get the death penalty, too, if I have anything to say about it. And I have a lot to say about it, I'll tell you that.

"Drug dealers, they're heading north or west to the other *republics* because that's where they get coddled; that's where the DAs let them off the hook, maybe even buy drugs off them.

"Our DAs don't do that. They prosecute the scum and the thugs and the Antifa traitors. They better or I'll fire their asses and put *them* in jail and they know that. If you're a prosecutor in my country, you *prosecute*. And if you don't, you get out of town 'cause I'll fire your ass. I tell the district attorneys if we don't have safety, we don't have freedom. I hold my prosecutors accountable in the GSA. We've got a prosecutor accountability law and if prosecutors don't prosecute, *they* get prosecuted. In fact, I've already prosecuted over a hunnred local prosecutors and two crime-coddling state attorney generals. And about half of them are in prison already! And there's more to come."

In fact, 73 local prosecutors and one state attorney general had been dismissed under the Prosecutorial Misconduct Act and six of those faced criminal charges. Three of them had fled to other republics and three others were out on bail, awaiting trial.

"We need an all-out effort to defeat violent crime and strongly defeat it. And be tough. And be nasty and be mean if we have to. And that includes the scumbag criminal defense lawyers. They're the ones getting murderers off. I did something about that, too. I made criminal defense lawyers criminals. I mean, they were always criminals, but me, I made it so they could be *charged* for their crimes. You give aid and comfort and defense to thugs, killers and rapists and drug dealers, you're gonna face criminal charges yourself. I'm gonna lock you up." He paused, then shouted, "Law 'n order!"

The audience roared: "Law 'n Order, Law 'n Order, Law 'n Order, Law 'n Order, Law 'n Order."

When the chant lost energy, he said, "In my years in the USA, China knew what was good for it. Because I told China what was good for it and it behaved."

He pronounced the country's name "Jiner."

"Before I was president, you read so much about Jiner, you read how great they are. How smart. We have great brain power right here in this country. Maybe not so much in that *California*, but here we do. There, they've all got their brains scrambled on pot. Cocaine, too. But we got greater brains than Jiner ever had or ever will have right here in my country, the GSA. When I was president back in the USA, they respected us, Jiner; they respected *me*. They didn't screw with me, I had their number, Jiner. And they didn't screw with our great companies and industries. I put them in their place; there was nothing they could do. I looked him in the eye, man-to-man and told him what was what, Xi, their president. He's a smart guy, Xi, but I'm smarter. It got so bad for them, they attacked the whole world with

Covid. That's right, Covid, the Jiner virus. Jiner gave us Covid. They tried to fight us with their virus. Took it right out of a lab and infected the whole world. That's what Jiner did. Only I beat Covid. I had the vaccine before you knew it."

No response. The cult was dubious about vaccines. He quickly moved off the subject.

"You look at North Korea, too." He pronounced it as if there were spelled KO-re-or." "I had a fantastic relationship with North KO-re-or. I had that Kim eating out of my hand. Nobody even talked to him before me. But I had him respecting us. Respecting me. Respect 'cause we had good chemistry, great chemistry. Perfect chemistry, me and Kim. All he wanted was to do something great with his little country, his beautiful litte country. And it *is* beautiful, take my word for it. I been there.

"Kim, he wanted to make his country great. I gotta say, though, and I saw this with my own eyes, when Kim speaks his people sit up at attention. I want my people to do the same. And you do, so thank you."

That opened the floodgates; applause and cheers poured out. When it began to diminish, he held up a hand, silenced it.

"And NATO? What about NATO? I forced NATO to shape up. And believe you me it wasn't easy. Especially with the Germans. They didn't want to pay their fair share. The richest country in Europe. The richest. They make some of the best cars in the world. Before, I had one of them, a Mercedes. What a great car that was. I loved driving it. I don't drive any more. I miss that. But Germany, they wouldn't pay their NATO dues, the Germans, so what good was it they made Mercedes cars?

"Now I understand them, the Germans. You know my grandfather, he was German. But he came here. From Germany. So I know; Germans are stubborn. Stubborn as hell. That's where I get it, I guess, my stubbornness. From the German side; from my father's side of the family."

He paused. Was he expecting applause because his grandfather emigrated from Germany? It did not come.

"And what about Putin? They were all afraid of Putin. Not me. We had four years when Putin didn't invade his neighbors. Stayed out of The Ukraine. How many people are dead there because I was cheated in 2020? I could of stopped that. I knew how to talk to Putin. I still know how to talk to him. When I talk, he listens. You didn't see him invading anyone because he knew me and knew I meant business. Knew I was as tough as he was. Tougher. Think of how much better off the people of The Ukraine would be if Mike Pence had done the right thing. I'd of put Putin in his place, alright."

He paused for effect. There was no response. There was nothing to be gained by demonizing Putin; the right wing had taken Moscow's side in the Ukraine war and they were rooting for the Russian dictator to crush democratic Ukraine.

"The foreign leaders, they all loved me. The Queen of England, may she rest in peace. I had such a great relationship with the Queen, and we were laughing and having fun. And her people said she hasn't had so much fun in 25 years. Then I got criticized for it because they said we were having too much fun. I feel I knew her so well and she certainly knew me very well, but we have a very good relationship with the United Kingdom, with England. No one ever saw her laughing so much. The Queen and me, we were talking all evening. That's how close we were, the Queen and Trump. And you know what? They didn't invite me to her funeral. How is that for disrespect? She loved me and they didn't invite me to her funeral. That's disrespect."

Cholmondeley/Lazenby wasn't much of a royalist, but he respected the late Queen and knew that the best that could be said about her relationship with Trump was that she showed astonishing aplomb and tolerance in the face of his preening, strutting and posturing. Elizabeth was the best-paid woman in the world, and she earned every pound and penny in June, 2019 when she put up with the loud and vulgar American. At the time she had made a significant but subtle statement by wearing in Trump's presence a little agate flower pin that had been given to her by Barack Obama.

Trump continued: "We had peace for my whole four years. We had four years of the best economy the country's ever had. *My* economy! The best. Ever. We had four years of making America great again!"

He had thrown the master switch. They were all charged up, on their feet, screaming and applauding. Those with the stamina and ability were stomping. He let them exhaust themselves; when the adoration began its diminuendo, he continued.

"Four years. Four years. Four years when everybody made money. You made money. I made money. Everybody made money. And I'm smart about money. I have a lot of money, and that proves how smart I am about money. You know how much money I have? I have nine billion dollars. Nine billion! That's a better mark of intelligence than those IQ tests. How much money does Joe Biden have? Are you kidding? I looked it up. Joe Biden, he's got maybe nine million. Obama? He's got close to two hundred million. I didn't know you could make that much money looting appliance stores in riots, but if you're Obama, I guess you can." That led to laughter and applause. "The rest of them? They got nothing compared to me. I got nine billion dollars. What's that John Steward in the Atlantic States got? Maybe a million, maybe two. And that Newsom in California — sorry, I meant Pacific States — he's got nothing. Maybe a couple of million. J. D. Pritzker in the Central States, he's got some money, but he inherited it, not like me. He's got maybe a billion. And the way he spends money — especially on food by the look of him — he'll be bankrupt in a couple of years. Bankrupt!"

Cholmondeley/Lazenby wondered if he was the only person in the stadium who appreciated the irony of Trump, who had managed to bankrupt a couple of gambling casinos, accusing Pritzker, a billionaire rival, with being on the verge of bankruptcy.

"So everybody knows that I'm real smart about money; I know money. And I financed my own elections. I didn't use a dime of anybody else's money. When I won reelection in 2020, and you know I won in 2020. I won in such a damned landslide; there's never been a landslide like I won in. No doubt about it. No doubt. I won that election. Fair and square, I won it. They all knew that. You knew that. Everyone knew I won. But there was so much fraud, so much cheating. Switching votes. Votes coming in in suitcases when they needed them. Immigrants voting. All Democrat votes. You know I bet half the Democrat total was fake votes: immigrants, dead people, people voting twice. And you know who did all that cheating? You know where it happened, don't you? And in spite of that cheating.... well, you know what happened."

Applause. The "Hang Mike Pence" chant began anew. Trump stepped back from the microphone and let it go on for nearly a full minute.

"Well, we tried, didn't we? We tried to make him do the right thing. Who knew Mike Pence was a RINO? That he was a Never-Trumper? The guy spent four years kissing my ass, he was so anxious to prove he was loyal. He wanted me to pat him on the head so bad. Four years I worked with that guy as my Vice President and he pretended — yes, he was *pretending* — that he was loyal to me until the end when it really counted. He sure as hell conned me, and I'm not easy to con. But Mike Pence, he conned me. When it came time to deliver, he double-crossed me, Mike Pence. He double-crossed *you!*"

"Hang Mike Pence, Hang Mike Pence, Hang Mike Pence, Hang Mike Pence."

Cholomdeley/Lazenby turned to Ann Bailey and said, "Don't you think that after six years he ought to come up with some fresh grievances?"

Her blank look and automatic nod indicated she had not heard him, had not understood him or didn't give a damn about the freshness of Trump's grievances.

Overhead, on the giant TV screen, Trump loomed over the stadium two hundred times life size.

He circled back to his unresolved grievance: "I understand why you want to hang Mike. I know, I know. But if I say that I'm gonna get criticized for encouraging violence. But what the hell, I get criticized for that anyway, even if I don't say it, so I'll say it: I understand your feeling and why you want to hang Mike Pence. He double-crossed you, he double-crossed me. And he got away with it. He got away with it. He paid no price for that double-cross."

The stadium was filled with boos. The "Hang Mike Pence" chant started in one section, but quickly died out.

"Okay, so Mike Pence and a bunch of Democrat judges — and even some judges I appointed, let's be fair about that; some of them were *my* judges — screwed me out of my landslide win. No loyalty. No loyalty at all. I give them a job for their whole life and that's how they repay me? That's how they show their loyalty? You know what, they are worse than the Democrat judges. The Democrat judges you know what to expect. They cheated me, my judges. *My* judges. You know that; I know that. Everyone knows that. I was cheated. Cheated. If I could, I'd throw every one of them in jail, where traitors belong."

A chorus of boos, then "Lock them up. Lock them up. Lock them up. Lock them up."

"Lock them up. Right? Lock them up. Traitors, that's what they are. Disloyal traitors. You're right. We were all cheated. And look what happened. Putin went to war in The Ukraine, the economy went to hell, the pandemic got worse. A million of you died. A million! More than a million now. That wouldn't of happened if I'd been in the White House and you know it. Everybody knows it. I got Covid. I had the Jiner flu. It didn't kill me. Jiner tried to kill me with their virus, but I beat it. I beat it and then I got cheated. I was robbed. *You* were robbed."

A lesser wave of boos. Were they getting tired of this hoary grievance? Were they on to the con game he'd been playing since November 4th, 2020?

Trump looked surprised; the tepid reaction told him to move on. But that was tough for him; what had started as a cynical manipulation of his supporters had become a belief for him; he had conned himself. Despite having been told by his advisors, lawyers, campaign aides and most of the mass media that he had lost, Trump believed he had won the 2020 election. Reluctantly, he took his cue from the audience, he moved on to his next grievance.

"So what happens in 2024? I win again. I win and you know I win. I beat that little New Jersey punk comedian. Comedian? I never thought he was funny, did you?"

The audience responded with boos.

"New Jersey! Can you imagine a president from New Jersey? What, the 'Jersey Shore?' president? Can you imagine that? Snookie or The Situation in the White House, as president? The whole world would be laughing at us, a president from 'The Jersey Shore.'"

Behind him, the young faces reflected confusion; none of them knew what "The Jersey Shore" was.

"I beat him fair and square, that guy who thinks he's funny but is so unfunny, that Jon Steward. There never was a unfunnier comedian. Maybe that shrimp in The Ukraine. He isn't funny, either. What is he, Zelenskyy? A dwarf? I never saw a president so short. Maybe Jon Steward; he's a dwarf, too. But I won that election and what did they do? They broke the country up. To keep me out of the White House, they made their four *republics*. Well, guess what? Mar-a-Lago is nicer than the White House any day of the week. Much classier. Less crowded, too. But I'll tell ya; I'd make the sacrifice and live in the White House if the country was whole again. I'd do that because it's part of the job and I do my job. I serve you when I'm president. You don't see me off on a golf course when I'm president. I'm shoulder to the wheel, nose to the grindstone. I'm serious about the job, not like that Obama who played golf all the time at country clubs where he wasn't really welcome, but they let him in because what are you gonna do when the president shows up at the course with his clubs and the Secret Service? You gonna turn away the president? I didn't think so."

The audience didn't react to his outrage about Obama's golfing habits.

"They busted up the country, my country, your country. Those sore losers, they destroyed it, my country. Our country. Formed The American Union. Like the European Union, only here. The AU and the EU. They made that. Four countries out of what was one. Okay, so Canada and Mexico, too, in the AU. They copied the failed European Union which doesn't work and never has worked. Boy, the English were smart to get out of that mess. And this American Union. Is it working? Is it working for you here in Texas? Is it working in Florida? Is it working anywhere in the GSA?"

They were on their feet with new energy, chanting: "GSA, GSA, GSA, GSA, GSA."

He raised a hand and cut it short. "No. No. It needs to be USA. Not GSA, USA." He hit the "U" hard and brought his palm down on the lectern. "USA!"

Given its script, the audience began chanting "USA, USA, USA, USA!"

"They had their Brexit, the English. Maybe we need to have our Grexit — the Great States leaving the American Union. Grexit first, then re-unite the country. Like those other three are *republics*. My ass, they're *republics*. They're *people's* republics, is what they are. Like Russia was in the Soviet Union back when they were failing. Some of you don't remember that, but I remember that. These *republics*, they are run by Democrat dictators."

Fresh boos for the new grievance.

"Cheated again. We were cheated again. Think about the people in Pennsylvania and Virginia and Arizona and Wisconsin that never voted to be in one of those Democrat people's *republics*. They wanted *me* to be president; they voted for *me*, they're *my* people. I was cheated and they were cheated. At least you here in the GSA weren't cheated. You got me, right? You got *me*!"

A standing ovation. It went on for a minute-and-a-half.

"Okay, so what do we do? We reunify the country. We become the *United* States of America again. And let me tell you something: We're gonna use the GSA constitution, my beautiful constitution, the constitution I wrote, the constitution we all love. It's a perfect constitution. Perfect. We're gonna use it for the new *United* States of America. The smartest lawyers helped me write it, our constitution, our beautiful constitution; that's why it's perfect. The best minds from the best law schools. Harvard. Yale. Chicago. Sanford." He meant Stanford. The audience knew no better.

"The best. The best. None better. The greatest lawyers, my lawyers working with me, your favorite president, to write my constitution. Most of them, my lawyers, worked for free. Pro bono, like they say."

Cholomondeley/Lazenby wondered if the lawyers had worked pro bono because Trump, true to form, simply ignored their bills. From what he knew, Trump took pro bono — short for pro bono publico — to mean pro bono praesidis.

"The perfect constitution. A beautiful constitution. Such an improvement over the old constitution. You wouldn't believe how much better it is. You know why? No birthright citizenship: no one comes to the GSA to drop a baby and get automatic citizenship. No more anchor babies. And we also ended asylum-seeking. No more bullshit illegal immigrants claiming they are seeking asylum. No asylum in the Great States of America. Stay where you are or go someplace else. You rapists and murderers and drug addicts and transgenders aren't welcome in *my* country. Our country. And religious freedom; freedom from having the government regulate your religion, tell you when and where you can pray, tell you who you gotta do business with.

"Government isn't a religion, but you can't have government *without* religion. Government shouldn't regulate religion; religion should regulate government."

Cholmondeley/Lazenby was surprised that line did not elicit cheers. Was the base less fervent about wearing out the knees of their trousers than he had been led to believe? He knew Trump saw the inside of religious edifices only for weddings, funerals and when it was otherwise totally unavoidable.

"And we put *guns* into the Constitution. Your guns. Your freedom to own guns to use for your self-defense. A man's home is his castle and he's entitled to protect that castle with whatever arms he cares to buy. Women, too. And you need to protect your person, too. From thugs. You need to be free to carry those guns anywhere and everywhere. So I put that right in the constitution. Did you know the old USA constitution never used the word 'gun' and the words 'self-defense?' Never. Not once can you read 'gun' or 'self-defense' in there. I fixed that. It's right in the constitution now — your right to own guns and use them for self-defense. Right there. Those exact words. No one's taking your guns away in the Great States of America. And they won't take your guns away in the Re-United States of America!"

Trump was all in on gun ownership and gun-carrying, as long as the gun owners didn't tote them in proximity to him. No one in the audience was carrying a gun. Now. The WORMs monitoring the magnetometers at the stadium entrance required anyone packing to check their firearms. They found that one in five of the rally-goers carried a gun.

The cheering was dying so Trump killed it off by stepping toward the microphone and speaking, "Those two — your guns and your religion — aren't in some amendment. What's an amendment? It's like an afterthought. No, those things are baked right into the body my GSA constitution. Which, like I say, will be the USA constitution when I reunite the country. That's right. You get to keep your guns. You get to keep your Bibles. Obama, he wanted to take both away from you. And abortion? Well, THAT you don't get to keep. And you don't want it, right?"

They were on their feet roaring approval.

"So it's right there in the constitution, not waiting for judges or for laws. No abortion, right in the constitution. It's absolute, too. Absolutely no abortion. Right there. In the constitution, not in some amendment. Life? That begins at conception. Spelled out in my constitution, where it says just that. You kill a fetus; you've committed a federal crime. You've committed murder. Our constitution tells you whose country this is. We don't call it the constitution of the *Great* States of America for nothing. It's the *Great* States because we have a *great* constitution. My constitution is probably the greatest legal document ever written. Not probably. It is the greatest legal document ever written. And that's going to be the Constitution of the *United* States of America when I bring the country back together."

They cheered the prospective reunification of the United States of America under Trump.

He cut it short: "I don't know, maybe we should keep the *Great* States name for the whole country. Why not? I'm going to make the whole thing great just like I made the Great States of America great. Just like I made America great again when I was president of the whole thing before the Democrats and the RINOs like Mike Pence cheated me out of my country."

He paused for applause, but there was only a smattering. The audience was through litigating 2020.

"Okay, I gotta talk about how we're going to unite the country, how we're gonna have all 50 states back in the Great States of America. How we're gonna absorb the babykiller states, only they won't be killing any more babies when we're back together and I'm president."

Many leaned forward, eager to be let in on the secret of reunification.

"You know how we're going to do that, unite the country? We're gonna call their bluff. We're gonna force their hand. We're gonna challenge them. And you know I'll do it. Not by a war. We had a civil war once when Lincoln was president, and it was terrible. I don't know why Lincoln gets so much credit for being a great president. What'd he ever do? He had a war. Okay, he freed the slaves, but the dead in the Civil War, that was a lot more people than the slaves he freed. If he had *prevented* the Civil War, that would be one thing. But he didn't do that. When I was president, we didn't have any wars. You know why? War is bad for business and what's bad for business is bad for Americans. We saw that back then in Lincoln's time; the Civil War was bad for business. And bad for the people that got killed. A lotta people got killed. Thousands. Hunnreds of thousand. Maybe a million, I don't know. And a lotta people will be killed if we have a civil war now. Well, we don't need to have a civil war because I'm the best negotiator that ever lived.

I can make any deal. *Any* deal. I'll make the deal to bring the country back together. And they're gonna see why it's important to re-form the union. I'm not threatening here, but they're dying with all their crime and the homeless and the transgender athletes in the wrong locker room and the wrong toilet and the wrong shower. Yes, shower! And all that other LG— whatever that alphabet soup bullshit is. Who knows what it is; it keeps changing. And what about the immigrants — who are some of the worst criminals. You know that. And you know who they are; where they come from.

"The lying media's gonna say I'm threatening violence. Well, I'm not threatening violence. I specifically said there was gonna be no civil war. Civil war; terrible. I don't have to threaten violence. I don't have to use it, either. They already have violence, those failed *republics*. We don't have to invade the democrat *republics*. Their crime and poverty and homeless and immigrants and communism are tearing them apart. I alone can fix that. I alone can bring the country together. I alone can end the carnage. And you know that! The Supreme Court said the country could break up; it did. But I say it can come back together. But only I can make that happen."

The applause was more sustained.

As a reporter in the BBC's Washington Bureau, Cholmondeley had covered the Supreme Court decision that made it legal for the United States to break into four separate republics. It came amid a flurry of SCOTUS decisions overturning earlier rulings. First there had been the ruling overturning Roe. Then these precedents fell to the fury of the far-right justices: Obergefell, which had guaranteed same-sex couples the right to marry; Griswold, which guaranteed access to contraception; Loving, which permitted interracial marriage; Brown, which had ruled segregated schools illegal; Sullivan, which had buttressed press freedom, and, finally, Texas v. White.

Texas v. White was an 1869 decision that made a state's secession from the Union unconstitutional and declared the Union "perpetual." The irony of the SCOTUS ruling overturning Texas v White was obvious; by permitting the union to be broken up, the Supreme Court justices eliminated their jobs, because each of the newly formed republics created their own court system and the nationwide court on which they served was no more.

The vote in the Texas v. White reversal was 5-4, with the decision written by the most dependable overthrower of established court precedent, Justice Samuel Alito. He got out his inkwell filled it with vitriol, dipped his razor blade into it and carved his decision on the bare back of the country.

He asserted the Union was "totally voluntarily and dissolvable at any time by any state for any reason." Alito wrote, "Had the Confederate States of America been free to secede, the Civil War would not have been waged. Six hundred thousand lives would have been spared."

In a separate concurring opinion, Justice Thomas speculated that slavery would have eventually ended naturally, a victim of "a flawed business model that required the owners of human chattel to supply food, housing and other benefits far beyond the useful working lives of their employees."

Commentators from the far left to well past the right side midpoint of the spectrum went wild with the word "employees," pointing out that Thomas was himself descended from slaves and that he grew up in a family that spoke Gullah, a patois developed by slaves mixing English and several African tribal languages. Slaves used Gullah to prevent their "employers" from eavesdropping on conversations.

When the applause for Trump reuniting the United States diminished, he moved on to the elephant in the room: "Lemmie talk about the big fake news story out there. I bet some of you came out tonight just to see if it was true. See if I was sick. Do I look sick? Do I sound sick? Do I?"

The cult roared, "*No!*"

"That story. That cancer story, it came from the BBC. You know what that is, the BBC? It's the *British* Broadcasting Company. *British*! To you and me that's England. Where do they come off reporting on us, the English? Why don't they stick to reporting on themselves? The royal family — bunch of losers they are now the Queen, my friend, is gone. Report on their health. I'm ten years — maybe more — older than that king they got, but I'll bet ten thousand dollars — make that a hunnred thousand—that I'm healthier than that old fart of a king they got.

"So some English guy on the BBC, he makes up this story about me. Totally false. Forgive my French, but total bullshit. Bullshit!"

That invitation was irresistible. The audience was on its feet chanting, "Bullshit! Bullshit! Bullshit! Bullshit!" Trump was enjoying himself. He joined the chant: "Bullshit! Bullshit! Bullshit! Bullshit!"

In the press pen, Cholmondeley/Lazenby shrank down in his chair. All his News Corp colleagues knew who he was. If one of them ratted him out, he would face grievous bodily harm, if not death, at the hands of a furious crowd of red-faced, spittle-spraying Trump cultists. He glanced over at Ann Bailey. She was making notes on the pad balanced on her thigh, disinterested in provoking his murder by identifying him to the crowd.

Trump continued: "That story, that I caught cancer, that's what the bullshit is. Fake news. The fakest news. Do I look like I have cancer?" He threw his arms wide and tried to puff out his chest but puffed out his belly instead.

"Huh? Do I look sick to you? This morning I'm in Miami at a military parade. Tonight, I'm here with, what, two hunnred thousand of you. Would two hundred thousand of you turn out for a sick guy?"

The audience roared, "NOOOO."

"I am probably the healthiest president of any of the *republics*, I gotta tell you. That Newsom guy in California — sorry, in the Pacific States? He's a cokehead; a drug addict. His brain's so fogged with pot he can't think straight. That fatso in the Central States? J. B. Pritzker? J.B.? What, he can't afford a first name? Anyways, you just take one look at that fat slob, you know he's got diabetes and heart problems and who knows what else? High blood pressure. He's got high blood pressure; you can tell by looking at him. Me? I got the best blood pressure. A hunnred twenny over sixty. How about that?"

They cheered his fictitious blood pressure.

"And that Jon Steward shrimp in Washington? The dwarf president? A midget? I know you're not supposed to say those words anymore, but what else do you call a dwarf? Anyway, you just know he's sick, too. Not to mention that he's crazy. I never met a comedian wasn't crazy and this guy's no different, except maybe he's crazier than the others. And not anywhere near as funny. You want funny, you listen to Dennis Miller. Now that guy's funny. Not to mention he supports Donald Trump. That Jon Steward, not funny at all. People are saying he's diabetic, too, Jon Steward. Wouldn't surprise me. They keep it secret, though. You just look at him, you know. I learned a lot about medicine when I was defeating Covid, the Jiner virus. I can tell you by looking at that Jon Steward, he's unhealthy. And you know, dontcha, that's not even his real name."

He got kissing distance from the microphone and stage whispered, "His real name is Jon Leibowitz. Jon Steward Leibowitz. And lemmie talk about that for a minute, about Jon Steward Leibowitz and the others who don't recognize that when I was president of the United States, I did more for Israel — their country — than any president before me. The Evangelicals, they appreciated what I did for Israel. They are better friends of Israel than the Jews here. The Israelis, they appreciated it. They were so grateful, and I was so popular there, I could of been elected prime minister there. But the Jewish people, especially the Jewish people here, they didn't recognize what I did for their country. They voted against me, most of 'em. Against me, the best friend Israel ever had. The Jewish people who lived in the United States, the ones living here and in the other *republics*, they don't love Israel enough. Does that make sense? Any Jewish people that don't or didn't vote for Donald J. Trump, that didn't make sense, did it? I was their country's best president ever. Better than FDR. Better than even Reagan. Well, they better get their act together, the Jewish people, before it's too late. I tell you that."

That prompted a new chant: "Jews will not replace us. Jews will not replace us. Jews will not replace us."

Trump grinned. He turned to the wings to see how Stephen Miller was reacting.

Standing there smirking, Miller. Or is he smiling? What the hell's he smiling at? He's not pissed? They're shouting about HIM. Eric, he looks pissed. Upset, at least. Miller oughta look down next time he's at a urinal and see the hem some rabbi stitched in his dick. He's the one should be pissed off. Fuck it, I should be pissed. Got three Jewish grandkids, for Christ's sake. Allen Weisselberg. Took a bullet for the organization. For me. A Jew. How about Roy Cohn, my man? My lawyer? My spirit guide, Roy Cohn.

He held up a hand, quieting them.

"That's not nice, be nice." he said. His sly smile said it was perfectly alright with him.

"About this fake news cancer story. It's the kind of thing our enemies do, spread fake news. I said it before and I'll say it again, the fake news is the enemy of the people. You out there," he pointed to the risers and the penned media section. "Aren't you enemies of the people? Enemies of *my* people?"

The boos got louder. Many of the crowd had turned around and were facing the media.

"Oh, shit," Ann Bailey said, "he's going to turn them loose on us."

She held high her microphone with its Fox News logo, like a vampire's prey holding up a crucifix. Cholmondeley/

Lazenby had nothing that obvious to identify him as a serf in The Proprietor's fields. Small print on his credentials gave his affiliations as Fox News and the Wall Street Journal; hardly equivalent to a crucifix or Fox News microphone flag for warding off danger.

He half rose from his seat. "Maybe we should get out of here," he said. The Wall Street Journal reporter was on his feet, he had peeled off his suit jacket and was unknotting his tie, readying himself to blend in with the crowd if they attacked.

"Don't hurt them," Trump commanded. "They are your enemies, *my* enemies. But we need to be nice to them. Nicer than they are to us." He said it with heavy sarcasm, so it sent the exact opposite message. "Besides, you don't want them running home crying to mommy, these enemies of the people."

A folding chair sailed through the air and landed in the pen, striking two reporters who dropped from their seats. It was followed by another and then a third. There was shouting behind Cholomondeley/Lazenby as the flying chairs found upraised arms, shoulders and — in one case — an upturned face. More chairs flew as audience members figured out how to unsnap the plastic gang couplers, freeing their seats from their neighbors' seats. The chairs were aimed at the crews on the risers, not at the reporters in the pen, but most of them fell short.

"Fox News. Fox News. Fox News," Ann Bailey was shouting, waving her microphone. "Fox News."

"They can't hear you," Cholmondeley/Lazenby said.

"Fox News. We're on your side. Fox News."

The Wall Street Journal reporter was gone. His suit jacket and tie lay crumbled on the floor. He had stepped into the crowd and was working his way toward an exit, occasionally turning around to shout for his colleagues' blood so he would not stand out.

"Stop. Stop." Trump shouted. He was in earnest now. He'd seen chairs strike cameramen and knock them off the risers. He'd seen other chairs crack skulls of the seated press. He could see blood. He turned to the wings and shouted, "Get this the fuck under control. Now!"

The microphone on the lectern picked that up and across the four republics and around the world, "Get this the fuck under control. Now," was broadcast live.

A dozen WORMs emerged from the wings. More entered from the rear of the stadium. One of them aimed his XM5 at the dome and emptied the 30-round clip into it. That stopped everyone in their tracks. Rally-goers reached for their handguns, only to realize that weapons had been checked at the entrances. They were unarmed, except for their folding chairs. But none of those sailed toward the media now.

"I understand," Trump said. "I understand. But you can't just kill them. We gotta have trials, first. Charges. Prove treason. We have a constitution. You can't just kill them. So let's go back to our seats. We got a lot to cover here."

The crowd turned away from the media pen and the risers, but instead of taking their seats, they began queueing for the exits. It was slow going. Several audience members had been struck by chairs that fell short of the media pen; there were bloodied elderly people sprawled on the cement floor.

In the media pen, most of the injuries were minor: cuts, bruises, scrapes. A handful were serious. One reporter who had been hit full on the head lay unconscious on the floor, a thin trickle of blood dripping from an ear. There was more blood from broken noses, and superficial head wounds.

An older reporter had a compound fracture of his right forearm, the bone poking through his skin just below his elbow and blood was pulsing from the wound; an artery pierced, if not severed. A couple of technicians were trying to create a tourniquet for his arm using a necktie, but it wasn't working.

WORMs swarmed the area. There were no medics among them and they had received no first-aid training. Not knowing what to do, they did what came naturally to them, they shouted: "Shut the fuck up. Get the fuck out. Shut the fuck up. Shut the fuck up. Shut up."

The uninjured photographers and videographers had recorded the chair barrage and now recorded the aftermath. Behind the lectern, Trump saw them and shouted, "Confiscate the cameras. Grab the cameras. Don't let them take pictures or movies. Get the cameras." That went out live across the four republics and the world, too.

The WORMs began seizing cameras, so photographers shot stills and video with their phones. The WORMs tried to confiscate those. When photographers resisted the WORMs began swinging their rifle butts at cameras, phones and the men and women who were using them. Some of the journalists were live streaming from their phones. On the risers, several network cameramen, above the reach of WORMs kept shooting, zooming in for close-ups of individual confrontations. WORMs clambered up the risers to get at them.

A WORM at Cholmondeley/Lazenby's elbow emptied a magazine into the stadium dome, bringing down a rain of black particles. The sound deafened Cholmondeley. He stuck his Fox News credential in the WORM's face and, in the best Southern accent he could summon, shouted, "Fox News. We're on your side. We're with you. Help us out here."

The WORM stared at the laminated card; no reaction. Was he illiterate? Cholmondeley/Lazenby pulled the microphone out of Ann Bailey's hand and showed the WORM the Fox News logo. *That* he recognized: "Follow me, sir, ma'am."

Cholmondeley/Lazenby grabbed Ann Bailey's hand and pulled her after him; they followed the WORM. He looked back, stopped and stared Bailey up and down. "She's with me. She's Fox News, too," he forgot about his Southern Accent and spoke in BBC English. It didn't matter. The WORM pushed his way through the crowd, shouting, "Clear a path. Clear a path. Clear a fucking path here. WORM coming through. Clear a path." He roughly shoved people out of the way, sending several to the concrete. He hustled Cholmondeley/Lazenby and Ann Bailey out to the parking lot where people were scattering in every direction. The WORM said, "There you go, sir, ma'am. You two have yourself a nice day, y'hear?" He turned and bulled his way back into the stadium.

*

In a foul mood, Trump lumbered off the platform, fists clenched, red-faced and scowling. He muttered to no one in particular, "This is a fucking disaster. The media'll have a field day. Gonna make it look like my fault. Those people are so fucking literal; they're like fucking children."

He looked for someone to berate.

Eric was upset. He looked like he might cry. But Miller! He stood there, right in front of Trump, smirking as if he were in on a secret no one else knew. "This is your fucking fault, Stephen," Trump shouted. "It was your fucking speech that set them off."

Trump had not read a word Miller had written for him, nevertheless the riot was Miller's fault. Trump took one more step, invading Miller's personal space, he was so close Miller could feel the heat coming off him.

Trump opened his mouth to say more and passed out. He did not crumple to the floor, but fell face first, spinning slightly so he missed Miller. His left elbow and knee absorbed the impact of his full weight. And there he lay, while Miller, aides and WORMs stared at him and did nothing for a very long moment. Then, bedlam.

◆ ◆ ◆

Show me someone without an ego, and I'll show you a loser. — Donald J. Trump

AT&T Stadium, Arlington, Texas, Great States Of America

Fat Jimmy Gibbons. That's what they called him when he was seven and that's what they called him at 55. Everyone called him Fat Jimmy Gibbons except his mother, his father and the nuns who taught at Our Lady of Perpetual Help Catholic Academy in Brooklyn. The nuns may not have said it, but they thought it; he could tell. His other cruel nicknames included "Fatso," "Humpty Dumpty" and "Rollo," but Fat Jimmy Gibbons — his most noticeable characteristic prefacing his full name — was the one that prevailed.

Through OLPH, Bishop Loughlin Memorial High School and the semester-and-a-half he spent at Fordham, he was Fat Jimmy Gibbons.

Fat Jimmy Gibbons was bitten by the acting bug while still at OLPH. After school one day, he was sitting on the carpeted floor in his parent's Flatbush apartment watching TV, eating pretzels from a bag, and drinking a 12-ounce Pepsi from the bottle. On screen was a 20-year-old old black and white Western, "The Adventures of Wild Bill Hickok." It starred a lean, handsome actor named Guy Madison, who thundered across the screen on a bold stallion named Buckshot. It was Madison/Hickok's sidekick, Jingles, lumbering along behind Wild Bill, who caught Jimmy's attention and inspired his career choice. Jingles was too large in height and girth for his horse, Joker. He called out in a voice that was both high and raspy, "Hey, Wild Bill, wait for me!" The actor playing Jingles was Andy Divine and Fat Jimmy Gibbons thought, "If Jingles can be on TV, so can I." Sitting there on the pretzel crumb-strewn carpet, a thespian was born.

TV, movies and the stage always have roles for character actors of all sizes, shapes and types. The several acting guilds are filled with little-known but successful character actors who work regularly and earn a decent living. Fat Jimmy Gibbons problem with finding that sort of success was his unshakable "deze, dem and doze" Brooklyn accent and the fact that he could not deliver lines as simple as, "Hello, how are you?" with any degree of credibility.

Fat Jimmy Gibbons moved to Los Angeles and found work only as a silent extra, occupying seats in cinematic and television jury boxes, theaters, restaurants and bars. Occasionally — for comic effect — he appeared shirtless on a beach, sunning himself on a towel a bit too small to contain his mass.

Then, in 2015, Donald Trump happened. Trump, who claimed to be 6' 3" and weigh 244 pounds, needed a body double. Fat Jimmy Gibbons was 6' 1" and weighed 260 pounds, yet he was chosen. His "audition" consisted of trying on one of Trump's suits. It fit perfectly; he was hired on the spot, and he had been on the Trump campaign payroll ever since.

Like Trump, Fat Jimmy Gibbons had a large head, a short neck and hands too small for his bulk. Fat Jimmy Gibbons was the large guy with the shaved head who was sometimes seen in the presidential entourage with a garment bag slung over his shoulder. His was a career of standing by, waiting for the moment when he would be needed to slip into a men's room stall, don the suit he was carrying, affix the wig that mirrored the presidential coiffure and lumber forth in imitation of Trump.

Presidential stand-in moments were rare because Trump liked to be out where his public could see and adore him up close.

Once, when Trump was president of the U.S., Fat Jimmy Gibbons had gone golfing in the president's stead so Trump could slip off and do something Gibbons could only guess at. Fat Jimmy Gibbons was far better coordinated than the president and played the game with a skill Trump lacked. After that outing, he told to never again play a round, only to dress in Trump's golf wardrobe and be photographed from the distance piloting a golf cart.

In the 2020 campaign he was sometimes tasked with energetically jumping from an armored SUV, briskly walking a few steps across the tarmac and sprinting up the dozen red carpeted steps to Air Force One. In the 2024 campaign, he did the same stair clamber to a campaign-chartered jet. He easily exhibited more vigor than the candidate who was 24 years older.

During Trump's speech AT & T Stadium, Fat Jimmy Gibbons sat in the back seat of a motorcade SUV in the parking lot, watching the TV screen embedded in the back of the driver's seat. He'd seen the chaotic end to the rally and assumed that the vehicles would be making a hasty departure as soon as Trump's Suburban exited the stadium's interior.

There was a rap on the glass and the back door opened.

"We need you," a WORM said in a voice that was just above a whisper and tight with urgency. "Grab the suit bag; follow me."

Fat Jimmy Gibbons did as he was told.

The WORM, holding his assault rifle across his chest, jogged toward an open pedestrian door, with Jimmy only two steps behind him, moving fast for a big man.

As he jogged, Jingles' cry, "Hey, Wild Bill, wait for me!" flitted through his mind, but he kept his mouth shut; no one would know the reference.

Inside the stadium, he found himself on a loading dock far from the stands and playing field. He was startled to see an unconscious Trump prone on a Gurney. The president's suit jacket and shirt had been cut off; their remains littered the floor. He was wearing his suit pants, but the belt was undone, and the fly was open. An oxygen mask covered his face, and an IV drip was in his left arm. Dr. Douglass, who accompanied Trump everywhere, was bent over him. There was also a male nurse in green scrubs at the doctor's elbow, following Douglass' commands.

Stephen Miller stepped forward. "You've seen none of this. Get that? You have seen nothing."

Fat Jimmy Gibbons nodded.

"Say it!" Miller hissed. "You've seen none of this."

"I seen nuttin," Fat Jimmy Gibbons said. "Nuttin."

Eric Trump was standing behind Miller; he looked frightened, his eyes darted from his prone father to the doctor and back again. He had a phone to his ear and was whispering into it.

Miller turned, grabbed the phone and snapped, "Not now. No phone calls. This does not get out."

Miller ended the call.

"Who the hell were you talking to?"

"My wife?" Eric's reply sound like a question.

"Don't you know who you were talking to? Was it your wife or...."

"No, no. My wife."

"Can't do that," Miller said. "No one can know."

"But...." Eric reached for the phone.

"How much did you tell her? How much?"

"Not this," Eric said, jutting his chin toward the Gurney.

"Keep it that way," Miller said. He dropped Eric's phone into his suit jacket pocket. "No one hears about this. No one. This didn't happen."

Miller turned to Fat Jimmy Gibbons. "Well? Why are you standing there? Don't just stand there. Get into wardrobe?"

"Here? In fronna everyone?"

"Yes, here," Miller snapped. "Get in the suit and hairpiece now!"

"What're ya gonna do wit'...."

"Not your business. Suit up. Now! Make it quick. People are going to wonder why it's taking so long for us to leave the building, for the motorcade to leave. Come on, man."

Eric turned to look at his prone father, then turned back to Miller. He was angry, "What are you doing? You can't take my phone away. Give me back my phone. Someone's got to call Tucker and tell him the president's unconscious. We have to...."

"Are you crazy, Eric? Don't you want to be president? We can't tell Carlson anything. We can't tell anyone anything."

"No, I do not want to be president and…."

"Just shut up, Eric, and do what I tell you." Miller turned back to Fat Jimmy Gibbons, "You, why aren't you getting dressed?"

A WORM held up the garment bag and Fat Jimmy Gibbons frantically yanked items of clothing from it. "I'm goin' fastas I could."

He indicated Trump, "He hurt? Shot? Wha' happened?"

"Not your business. It's under control. I'm in charge. I have a plan. Go faster, goddamnit."

The large metal vehicle door clanked open, and the motorcade's ambulance pulled in. Extracting Trump from the stadium and the parking lot was easy because there were multiple ambulances pulling in and out of the structure and the parking lot, taking the chair- and rifle butt-wounded to hospitals. The presidential ambulance could join them until it cleared the parking lot, then peel off and head for Arlington Municipal Airport where GSA-1 was waiting with engines idling.

Placing secrecy over security, Miller dictated that the ambulance be unaccompanied by WORM SUVs, police cars, motorcycles or any other vehicles. The only security measures he put in effect was to order a WORM to ride shotgun in the ambulance passenger compartment and three WORMs to squeeze into the back with Dr. Douglass, the nurse and the unconscious president.

After the ambulance had cleared the parking lot, Fat Jimmy Gibbons, in full Trump regalia, surrounded by a cluster of WORMs, exited the stadium, walked a few yards to an armored Suburban, waved to the rally-goers who happened to spot him and climbed into the vehicle. The full motorcade, lights flashing and sirens screaming, scrambled for Arlington Municipal.

At the airport, news cameras were kept at a distance when Fat Jimmy Gibbons exited the Suburban, walked up GSA-1's short flight of stairs, turned to wave and give the Trump double thumbs-up sign. He disappeared into the plane's interior and the hatch closed behind him.

Multiple elements of Miller's plan were dependent on WORMs, who he knew were not the world's greatest band of high-achieving independent thinkers. However, nothing went wrong. Miller, simultaneously the plan's architect and principal skeptic, was surprised at how well it worked.

*

For the next week, while the real President Trump was hidden from public view, Fat Jimmy Gibbons was his doppelgänger on golf carts, in motorcades, boarding helicopters and riding in speedboats, all venues where even the longest lens would yield only a high pixilated image of him. It was the highlight of his theatrical career. And no more than a dozen people ever knew about it.

CHAPTER FIVE

You know, it really doesn't matter what the media writes as long as you've got a young and beautiful piece of ass. — Donald J. Trump

Hotel Crescent Court, Dallas, Texas, Great States Of America

Ann Bailey, grateful enough to Cholmondeley for engineering their escape from AT & T Stadium, accompanied him to the Fairmont for a drink in the lobby bar, but she was not sufficiently grateful to follow him to his suite for a thank-you leg-over.

After the drink – which he put on his room tab – she took a taxi to the more modest Marriott where Fox had booked her.

Cholmondeley had a second whiskey at the bar before retiring to his room. He opened his laptop and had begun transcribing his notes when there was a knock on the door. Through the peephole he saw two men in suits. One of them held a credential which he could not read. He opened the door for a better look.

"Mr. Chol-mundie," the credential-waver said, "I'm Fred Adamo of the Central Intelligence Agency. And this is my colleague Ben Harris with the Federal Bureau of Investigation."

"Lazenby," he said. The Wall Street Journal and Fox News credentials were still around his neck. He held them up so the men could read them.

"We're not GSA. We're ATO — American Treaty Organization. Look at the credential, please," Adamo said.

Cholmondeley read Adamo's credential with more care; it was issued by ATO, the joint defense organization that protected all four republics.

Adamo took Cholmondeley's nod as a signal to continue: "We know who you are, Mr. Chol-mundie. "Nothing to worry about from us."

"It's 'Chumley.' Aren't you more than a bit outside your jurisdiction? I thought CIA was forbidden to do domestic operations."

"Mr. Cholmondeley — sorry, won't make that mistake again. It's not really an operation, sir," Adamo said. "It's more a courtesy call."

He was tall, narrow-shouldered and looked too young to be CIA. He had a weak chin and his eyes were set too close together. Altogether not a very intimidating type. His suit was ill-fitting, and his shirt collar was an inch too big for this thin neck. A casting director would have sent him packing in favor of a square-jawed muscle-bound type.

The other one, Harris, from the FBI, looked like his father's accountant, round, balding, glasses perched on a tiny nose whose wide flaring nostrils sprouted a forest of jet-black hair.

"May I see your ID, too?"

"Of course, sir." When Harris reached into his suit jacket for the wallet with his badge and FBI ID card, Cholmondeley caught a glimpse of the Sig Sauer tucked in his armpit holster. Harris instantly became far more authoritative than his father's accountant.

Adamo said, "Mr. Cholmondeley, we have a very big, very important story to share with you. But we need you to come to Washington with us because we can only give you the story there. But before we do we need a guarantee that under no circumstance will you reveal the source of the story."

"I'm not finished with my reporting here. And I can't give you any sort of a guarantee of confidentiality without knowing more. A lot would depend on the nature of the material. And its veracity."

Harris, the FBI agent, said, "The material is legitimate; there's hard evidence. We'll give it to you. Just not here in the GSA."

Adamo added an inducement: "It's the transcript of an audio recording of an intercepted telephone call. The call is between two extremely high-level persons in two different governments, whom I can't identify here but can identify in Washington. We'll also give you a digital file with the full conversation in MP3 format."

"Surely it can wait until I'm finished writing my stories here. Did you see what happened at Trump's rally? Did you see the violence? I have work to do here. And I need to know more before I can guarantee you confidentiality."

Adamo played another card, this one a lie: "Intelligence intercepts indicate the GSA knows you're in the country. It'd be best if you come with us now. We have a charter waiting. You stay here, you may be putting yourself in danger."

Harris added, "The people that sent us were very impressed with how you protected your sources in that report you did on Trump's cancer and the political results of that."

"Yes, yes," Cholmondeley said. How could a spook and a spy-catcher *not* know he had given up his sources at the first blow from a WORM's cosh? If they didn't know, they weren't very good at their game. If they did know, they were lying to him, and that made everything else they said suspect.

Adamo said, "We're not journalists, but what we are talking about is as big a story as the cancer story, maybe even bigger."

Cholmondeley did not believe that. "A bigger story? That was an extraordinary story with many sources. I find it difficult to imagine a bigger story than that."

Adamo shifted his weight from leg to leg, undecided how much to give away. "Sir," he said, "this *is* as big a story or a bigger story. We can't tell you more than that unless you come with us to Washington. And we need one more thing: a guarantee that the story will reach the public."

If it's as big as you say it is, I can't see any problem with that."

"Well, to be frank about it," Adamo, the CIA man, said, "at the time you broke the cancer story, you were working for the BBC. Now you're working for Rupert Murdoch. The people that sent us were one-hundred percent confident that if you were still working at the BBC and you got this story, the BBC would run it. But with the Murdochs it's...."

Harris filled the gap: "News Corp supports Trump and his administration. Our people are less than confident that the powers-that-be at his outlets will run this story."

"I can't guarantee that," Cholmondeley said. "Especially since I have no idea what the story is."

"The story involves national security," Harris said.

"Potentially the most serious breach of national security in a very long time."

"I am sure that News Corp's political orientation would never lead it to jeopardize national security," Cholmondeley said. Even as he said it he began to doubt it. Might The Proprietor risk security to serve his political goals?

Adamo said, "We can't tell you how or when, but they have done just that on at least one occasion in the past; put national security second to loyalty to Trump."

"Oh, bollocks they have. You sound like you're working for the White House press office, not the CIA and FBI."

Cholmondeley was surprised at his own passion; had he been co-opted by a million-pound paycheck? In point of fact, he was by no means sure The Proprietor would put journalism ahead of politics.

"Sorry you see it that way," Adamo said.

Cholmondeley doubled down: "That *is* the way I see it. And I still have no idea if this story is as big as you say."

"I can give you a parallel," Adamo said. "A historical parallel. This story is as big as the Cuba Missile Crisis. You know about the Cuba Missile Crisis? It happened in 1962?"

Cholmondeley knew; he knew that the Soviets shipped missiles to Cuba to set up a base there and that the United States blockaded the island. He knew that the Soviets in Washington chose an ABC News correspondent, John Scali, to be their conduit to the White House and he wound up being the communications back-channel between the governments.

The U.S. and the Soviets prohibited Scali from reporting what he knew, and eventually he was scooped on the story.

"I'm not going to be your John Scali here. I'm not playing go-between for you," Cholmondeley said. "Especially if I can't report it."

The ATO emissaries had no idea who Scali was, but they did know that they wanted Cholmondeley reporting the story.

"No, no. That's not the case. Our people, the people that sent us, they want you reporting the story. That's the whole point," Adamo said. "They want the story out."

Cholmondeley took a blind stab: "So what you're saying is the Russians — or maybe the Chinese — are going to put missiles close-by? Is that what you're saying?"

Neither agent gave anything away verbally, but their faces told him he'd hit the nail squarely on its head.

"If you'll come with us, sir, you'll have everything right after we get to Washington," Harris said.

In his head, Cholmondeley was already packing: laptop and power cord = attaché case; underwear and socks in top dresser drawer = suitcase; toiletries, still in dopp kit in bathroom = suitcase; shirts and second suit in closet = suitcase; second pair of shoes, floor of closet = suitcase; notes, recorder, Bics = attaché case.

"Okay. I'll go with you. Let me see the evidence, hear the recording or recordings. I'll call Murdoch, himself. You may not think it, but he's a journalist first and last. Above all else, he thinks of himself a newspaperman. If it's valid, he'll print it, broadcast it and promote it. I'm sure of that," Cholmondeley said, unsure of any of it.

Adamo and Harris were dangling red meat, but Cholmondeley did not know if the old lion was still hungry.

♦ ♦ ♦

The Intelligence people seem to be extremely passive and naive. — Donald J. Trump

Small Homes Industry Trade Association Headquarters, Washington, Atlantic States Of America

It was not until the graphics department created the logo for the Small Homes Industry Trade Association that anyone at the CIA realized the acronym for the fictional trade organization was SHITA. By that time, it was too late; the lease for the 2,250 square-foot office had been signed, the name had been posted on the lobby directory and furniture had been moved in; SHITA it was and SHITA it would remain.

The graphic artists came up with a work-around for using the acronym on the circular logo — they spelled out the full name, not even abbreviating "association," and they printed it in near-agate type around the outer edge of the circle. Within the circle they created a stylized image of a small house with trees and a mountain in the background. They did all they could to focus attention away from the name.

SHITA was one of 12 small offices the agency maintained in downtown Washington for meetings best conducted away from headquarters in Langley. Each office had been rented by a fictional company, trade association or attorney. They were in seedy buildings with vintage elevators, grimy lobbies, inadequate air-conditioning and scant on-site parking. The Company liked the anonymity of buildings that catered to nuisance lawsuit attorneys; one-client, one-publicist PR agencies, and marginal lobbyists. These were under-the-radar commercial structures where agents could meet with assets without arousing suspicion, where an occasional congressional staffer could slip in unnoticed and receive a classified briefing and where stories could be leaked to dependable journalists who would protect The Company by keeping their source confidential.

SHITA's suite consisted of three small offices and a conference room. The offices were furnished with well-worn desks and chairs and empty file cabinets. The carpeting was shabby, the doors squeaked. The table and chairs in the conference room were similarly modest, but there was an impressive array of the latest screens, speakers, phones and other electronics stashed in the credenza against one wall.

Adamo and Harris had accompaniedCholmondeley on the chartered jet from Texas to Reagan National Airport.

A Suburban was waiting for them at the private aviation terminal. It took them downtown and the agents dropped Cholmondeley in front of the seedy building, after giving him the suite number. It was after midnight; the entire capital seemed to be sleeping. The lobby of the building was especially creepy, like something out of a film noir.

"Do you want me to call you when it ends?" Cholmondeley asked.

"No need," Adamo said. "We'll be waiting right here. We'll know when the meeting ends."

Of course they would know; they were CIA and FBI.

The office was on the fifth floor, at the end of a long hallway, far from the elevator.

There was a small reception area where a very large man with a shaved head sat behind a desk. He wore an ill-fitting suit that Cholmondeley noticed bulged under his left armpit. What Cholmondeley could not see was a short barrel Tavor 7 bullpup assault rifle at his feet. The Tavor had a 25-round clip with a 26th round in the chamber. The safety was off and the weapon was switched to fully automatic mode — ready for a confined space firefight. In the top drawer of the desk were two smoke grenades.

"Mr. Cholmondeley," said the large man man, "welcome to Small Homes."

"Thank you. And you are?"

"Immaterial," the large man said.

Cholmondeley asked Immaterial if he would be doing the briefing.

"No, I'm just security," he said.

A thin middle-aged woman in a dark suit stepped into the reception area. "Mr. Chum-deley, won't you follow me? I'm Della Moss and I've been assigned to brief you."

Della Moss was not the movie version of a CIA agent; she looked as if she would last five seconds in a hand-to-hand struggle. If she was packing a shooter, it did not show under her suit.

"Ms Moss. Are you permitted to tell me your role at CIA?"

"No. Not in any detail. And please make that is the last time you mention the name of my employer."

"Sorry."

"No need to apologize. Adamo should have explained the rules of the game. It's Small Homes when you are referring to it here. As to me, I can only tell you that I'm qualified in cyber intelligence; I'm not a spy. No rough stuff, shoot-outs, exfiltrations, nothing like that."

Obviously.

In the conference room she first played a video recording of Putin giving an interview in Russian. Then she printed out a voiceprint that looked very much like an EKG readout. "That's Putin," she said.

Next, she played a video of an interview Stephen Miller had given to Fox News and she printed out his voiceprint. She placed the two voiceprints on the table, side-by-side.

Following that, she played the phone call between Miller and Putin during which the Russian, speaking accented but otherwise very good English, volunteered to help give the lie to Cholmondeley's BBC cancer story in return for GSA giving him permission to install a missile base in Texas. She placed the voiceprints from the phone call next to the earlier voiceprints and said they conclusively proved that the phone call was between Putin and Miller.

Cholmondeley nodded and said, "I'm not at all qualified to evaluate this voiceprint material; I have no training in that. Also, I had no idea Putin spoke English. Certainly no idea he spoke English as well as the Russian man on that phone call."

"Yes, we've known for years that Mr. Putin is fluent in English. German and French as well. He also speaks a considerable amount of Belarus and a bit of Polish. Quite accomplished in languages."

"I think we — and by that I mean News Corp — will want to confirm the authenticity of the recording — actually the accuracy of the voiceprint material — with our own or with independent voiceprint experts. I don't know that we employ any voiceprint experts in the company."

She nodded. "We — and by that I mean Small Homes — understand. The vetting process must be done with portions of the phone call that do not involve the missile base, we don't want that getting out prematurely and I'm sure you don't want that, either. To help you with that we'll give you two audio files: one that contains most of the conversation, but nothing about the missile base request. The other will be the full phone call. We're insisting that for verification purposes you use only the edited version. You'll also have a full transcript of the whole phone call, as well as the audio file. And if you'd like to verify the transcript, I can play the call over again for you while you follow it in the transcript."

"Yes. I think that's a good idea," he said.

When Cholmondeley finished verifying the transcript, Della Moss gave him a USB thumb drive. "The full transcript is on here as a PDF. There are also two audio files. One is the full phone call; it's labeled 'Full.' The other has been edited to take out the references to the missile base; it's labeled 'Partial.' Partial is for the voiceprint expert you hire. There is also a video file on the thumb drive. It's satellite and drone footage of a Russian engineering crew surveying the site in Texas. You can tell it's not a typical engineering survey; there are 15 people, 12 men and three women. But only the women and five men appear to be doing the survey; the others are heavily armed and are posted all around the location perimeter to keep away intruders. The 15 arrived on four different flights from four different European cities.

Passenger manifests indicate they all began their travels in Moscow. The manifests are also here on the thumb drive in PDF format — some of that's in Cyrillic--Russian, in fact -- but there are translations supplied. But before I hand this over...."

"I'll call him now," Cholmondeley said.

Cholmondeley phoned the 24-hour news desk at Fox News. They would know where The Proprietor was. Not in New York, it turned out; Murdoch was on his honeymoon at a location that was not registered with the desk.

Cholmondeley had Murdoch's private mobile number and The Proprietor had told him, "Call me anytime, day or night, if you have something as big as the cancer story. Anytime."

Cholmondeley dialed the number. On the third ring, the phone was answered, but The Proprietor did not immediately speak. Cholmondeley worried he'd interrupted a Viagra-fueled conjugal moment. But then he heard chewing, swallowing, the slightest slurping of a beverage and, finally, The Proprietor's gruff voice and Outback accent, "Murdoch here, Cholmondeley. What's up?"

Cholmondeley squelched the rude joke that came to mind and said, "Mr. Murdoch, you told me to call anytime."

"Yes, yes. It's okay. Just having a bit of breakfast."

Cholmondeley looked at his watch: 3:25 a.m. in the Eastern time zone. Where might it be breakfast time? Likely the U.K. or Europe.

"Mr. Murdoch, sorry to disturb your breakfast, but this is bigger than the cancer story. I've heard conclusive proof of this in Mr. Putin's own voice."

"*Mister* Putin? When'd you get so formal?"

"Sorry. BBC habit" Cholmondeley said. "But that's not relevant, sir. I have proof that the Russians...."

◆ ◆ ◆

Every one of these doctors said, "How do you know so much about this?" Maybe I have a natural ability. — Donald J. Trump

Veterans Affairs Medical Center, West Palm Beach, Florida, Great States Of America

The media were set up in a pen and on risers far from the entrance. To get video or photos of the president, they had to zoom in as far as their lenses would go. The reporters assumed the distance was to ensure Trump would not have to answer questions about the chair-throwing at the AT & T Stadium in Arlington two days earlier; even the most robustly shouted question would not be heard across all that distance and over the din of the motorcade's running engines.

The world's media was reduced to silently recording the arrival of Fat Jimmy Gibbons, wearing a blue presidential suit and his Trump wig. Anita Palacio told them the president was visiting the hospital for his annual physical. And Fat Jimmy Gibbons gave it his theatrical all so they would have something to show that evening, hopping enthusiastically from the armored Suburban, turning and waving vigorously to the far-away cameras and barreling though the door to the hospital with the sort of enthusiasm he might muster if he were bellying up to the refrigerator case at a Baskin-Robbins store.

At the same time, an armored ambulance pulled into the garage of Kugler Imaging Center in North Palm Beath. It was accompanied by a protective convoy of four WORM-filled SUVs and six WORMS on motorcycles. Trump refused a wheelchair and walked the six yards from the parking garage to the elevator lobby. His gait was slow but steady. He looked pale and his messy hair was hidden under a red Great Again! baseball cap.

The imaging center was owned by Dr. Marvin Kugler, the Mar-a-Lago club member who had recommended Dr. Frederick Douglass to Trump. Kugler was a devoted Trump acolyte so could be depended on to keep things secret. To further protect the president's privacy, Kugler had closed the center and given the staff the day off. Assisted by a single trusted technician, Kugler would run all the tests and do all the diagnoses himself. The patient's name on all the imaging files and diagnostic records would be Gibbons, F. James.

While Trump was poked, probed, punctured, MRIed, CT-scanned and X-rayed at Kugler, the real Gibbons, F. James sat in a private room in the veterans medical center with six WORMs, the president's favorite makeup artist, Madelyn Morton, and Stephen Miller. The room had snacks, soft drinks and a makeup table so MM could touch him up if need be. Morton fussed about, patting a bit of powder on Fat Jimmy Gibbons' shiny forehead — although no camera would be close enough to see the shine – and adjusting his wig ever-so-slightly. After that, there was nothing to do but snack and wait until the real president was spirited out of Kugler and back to Mar-a-Lago. Miller turned on the TV. Like all TV sets in all official buildings in the Great States of America, the default station was Fox News.

Fox coverage of the "disruption" at Trump's Texas rally was skimpy on video and AWOL on the casualty count. The news anchors and reporters called it a minor "altercation" or "confrontation." Ann Bailey, the Mar-a-Lago bureau chief, had overcome her contemporaneous feelings of panic and appeared on multiple broadcasts explaining only a few chairs were thrown, no one was hurt, and she did not feel the least bit threatened. She claimed she had made an orderly exit, escorted by red-hatted Trump supporters who were concerned for her safety. The Fox opinion anchors found a nefarious conspiracy at play; they reported that agents of the other three republics plus Antifa freelancers had infiltrated the stadium and began the assault to tar the image of Trump and his supporters.

When he turned on the TV, Miller expected to see Ann Bailey once more recounting her exit under the protection of Trump supporters or, even better, attention moving on to something distracting like a report of a tornado destroying a mobile home park in Tennessee or Arkansas. Instead, he saw a split screen image. On the left was his own face. On the right, the face of Vladimir Putin. The disembodied voice had the rich, plummy tones and careful enunciation of a BBC presenter. It was unmistakably the voice of Walter Cholmondeley.

"... and that conversation, intercepted and recorded, has been obtained by Fox News," Cholmondeley said. "Here are excerpts. The first voice you will hear is Vladimir Putin, not a translator. Apparently, Mr. Putin's English is excellent and he does not need a translator, even when discussing something as delicate as placing nuclear-armed missiles in the State of Texas. The other voice is Stephan Miller, the Mar-a-Lago chief of staff."

"What the fuck!" Miller screamed. "What the fucking fuck!"

Fat Jimmy Gibbons, Madilyn Morton and the WORMs stared at him.

"They can't do that. That's our network. They can't...."

The audio track switched to a scratchy recording. The text of the dialog was superimposed over the photos of Miller and Putin:

Putin: "Now, the quid pro quo, as you say in English."

Miller: "And that would be, what, exactly?"

Putin: "An installation."

Miller: "An installation? What kind of installation? Where?"

Putin: "Get map. Look at the area 200 kilometers west of Austin and about 400 kilometers north northwest of San Antonio."

On-screen, a map of Texas appeared. The map zoomed in on the area Putin had described.

"It's called Fort Worth Basin," Putin said. "There is no oil and gas exploration there. That's where new company begins a play. Just modest drilling because it hasn't been productive area in past."

Miller: "I don't understand. You have the world's largest gas and oil reserves. Why drill here? It makes no sense."

Putin: "Listen, I explain. Drilling is cover. We build underground base for Sarmat missiles. Aimed at rival republics."

Miller: "What is a Sarmat missile?"

Putin said, "Is called RS-28 in NATO and ATO. Each one have 12 warheads. Nuclear payload or conventional high-explosive. Ninety thousand kilograms."

"We don't use kilograms, we use pounds, or tons."

"One hundred tons, maybe. American tons," Putin said.

"And how many do you want to put in Texas?"

Putin said, "Only ten."

"That's 120 warheads?"

"Yes. Should be enough for the purpose."

"I don't think he'll like this," Miller said.

"He will. I convince him to like this. I am sure that after we speak, he will like this; he will do this. For me."

"I don't think that's going to happen," Miller said.

"You tell him to call; we talk; it happens."

Cholmondeley was on camera now: "To summarize, the Russian president, Vladimir Putin, telephoned Donald Trump's chief of staff, Stephen Miller. In that phone call, they discussed debunking a report that President Trump has metastatic prostate cancer. The cancer story was reported by me and aired by BBC radio, my employer at the time. The Mar-a-Lago press office has denied the cancer story and issued a medical report from the president's physician, Dr. Frederick Douglass. That report has been widely regarded with suspicion.

"In the phone call we just heard between Mr. Miller and President Putin, Mr. Putin offered to use his powerful network of internet trolls to debunk the cancer story and as a reward, as a quid pro quo, Putin asked for a missile base in Texas, where his nuclear-armed rockets could threaten the Atlantic, Pacific and Central States of America."

Miller was pacing the room, muttering, "Shit, shit, shit, shit, shit."

Cholmondeley was in a two-shot with the Fox anchor, Brian Weatherly, who said, "So, Walter, *have* the missiles gone in, in Texas? Has GSA permitted it; has Putin followed through?" His tone was challenging. "You're not reporting that the missiles have been installed, are you?"

"No missiles have gone in yet, according to my sources, but Russian teams have been on the ground, surveying the area; we have video of that. So this has certainly gone beyond the discussion and negotiation stages."

As he spoke the screen showed drone footage of the Russian team surveying the area in Texas.

"Chief of Staff Miller did not have the authority to sign off on something like that, so the decision was up to the GSA president, Mr. Trump. My sources don't know what, if anything President Trump has discussed or negotiated with Mr. Putin, but the fact that we have video of Russians on the ground indicates the plan is not dead and may be advancing."

"We just call him Putin," Weatherly said. "What I'm unpacking from all this is there are no Russian missiles in Texas right now; nothing pointed at the three republics and that Putin only *wants* to put them there. It's obvious President Trump denied him that quid pro quo, since there are no Russian missiles anywhere in North America."

Cholmondeley was annoyed: "No, that's not *quite* what I am saying. We can't say Mr. Trump denied Mr. Putin, sorry, Putin. You cannot remove the context here, which is what you're trying to do by concentrating solely on the Russian demand. What I am saying, first, is that President Trump is in the advanced stages of metastatic prostate cancer. He may well be dying…."

"Fox News has not been able to confirm that, and Mar-a-Lago's press office denies it. Moreover, we've just seen him do three rallies and a parade in four days; not the sort of thing you see from someone who's at death's door."

"Then why has he appointed his son, Eric, as his successor, despite Eric not being Vice President," Cholmondeley asked. "Secondly, the very performances you cite show an effort — I believe it's fair to say an extreme effort — to distract from and disprove the cancer story, *my* cancer story. That parade and three rallies in four days — putting Trump out there for the cameras repeatedly — that's meant to prove he's healthy. Third, Mr. Putin — sorry — Putin offered aid debunking the cancer story. If the story were not true, why would Miller need Putin to help debunk it? Clearly from the phone call, both Putin and Mr. Miller -- is he a mister? — are tacitly acknowledging the story is true. And, finally, I am reporting that Putin — in return for helping knock down the cancer story — is seeking a base in Texas for one of Russia's most powerful offensive weapons and that if he gets that base, Russia becomes an immediate and mortal threat to all four republics, even to his ally, the Great States of America. *That* is what I'm saying. That's also what the recording we just heard is saying."

"And I'm saying Fox News has been unable to confirm any of it."

"You have *me* reporting it and *I* work at Fox News, so how can you say Fox News is unable to confirm it? Moreover, you, yourself, heard the recording of the call between Miller and Putin. We just *played* it on the air!"

"That's just it; it's only audio. How do we know that's really Chief of Staff Miller and Putin? No one's ever heard Putin speak English. The word is he can't speak that much English. We have no way of knowing...."

Miller watched Weatherly loyally trying to spin the story, but he was muttering, "Shit, shit, shit, shit" because he knew the story had escaped the cage, gone feral and there was no capturing it and putting it back; it had torn the hinges off the cage door.

Fox News was going to be embarrassed by Weatherly's dogged challenge to his colleague. Miller was going to be embarrassed by the recording. Trump, on the other hand, lying in an MRI tube at Kugler Imaging and unaware what was going on, would not be embarrassed; nothing embarrassed him.

And Putin, Miller guessed, would be delighted because the world would know how much power he wielded in the GSA. Miller wondered whether it might not have been Putin who leaked the recording.

From the makeup chair, Fat Jimmy Gibbons asked, "Whadda want me t'do?"

"For now, just shut up and let me think," Miller said. "There has got to be a way out of this."

He feared the way out would afford him a fine view of the undercarriage of a bus.

◆ ◆ ◆

I have never seen a thin person drinking Diet Coke. — Donald J. Trump

Executive Office Suite, Mar-A-Lago, Palm Beach, Florida, Great States Of America

"Do I work here? Am I a part of the team? Haven't I been loyal to The Boss like no one else? And you didn't trust me enough to tell me? You *lied* to me!"

Anita Palacio was angry. And shocked. For weeks she had been glibly lying to The Beast without knowing she was lying. She was perfectly okay with the lying; it was part of the job. But she resented her omission from the truth loop.

The chief of staff, Dr. Douglass, even the president, himself, had misled her. No, it was worse: they lied to her. The lies meant they did not trust her with the truth. Did they not know that she had to be in on the facts so she could aid them in wording the lie? She was skilled at tweaking untruths so they gained maximum credibility.

Palacio felt the way she had as a weather reporter at Telemiami, when they left her out of editorial meetings. Even when hurricanes threatened, she was often omitted from the sessions. She had something to add but her contribution was unwelcome.

"You know, I feel... I don't know. Betrayed. I feel like you don't trust me."

"We trust you. I trust you. The Boss trusts you. Dr. Douglass trusts you."

There were three of them in Miller's office, but only Anita had been kept in the dark about Trump's cancer.

Douglass said, "Don't feel bad about it, Anita. If you had known you would have been suspected of being a source for that BBC story."

"You knew," she said. "Were you suspected?"

"You bet he was," Miller said.

"They gave me a lie detector test the same day the cancer story broke, didn't they, Steve?" Miller nodded. Douglass added, "Wasn't me."

"Oh, I know that; I know it wasn't you," Anita said. "They got the five people who gave him the story. They're holding them somewhere until they can charge them."

Douglass looked surprised; Miller, seeing an opportunity to assuage her, said, "See, Anita, you're in on some stuff that Frederick isn't."

"Well, this is all water under the bridge," Douglass said. "The cancer is in remission now." He held up the file folder that had been resting on his lap.

Miller said, "Let's talk briefing. We have a dilemma here and we need to resolve it."

Anita raised a dubious eyebrow. A dilemma? How about multiple dilemmas? The cancer dilemma, the missile base dilemma and any other possible dilemmas they had chosen not to tell her about.

"Which dilemma," she asked. She hoped Miller would hear her sarcasm.

He pretended to have missed it: "About the cancer thing."

The cancer thing dilemma: Trump's disease was in remission. The radiation treatments had succeeded in stopping the spread, and the bone cancer showed signs of retreat. This was the conclusion from the many tests at Kugler Imaging, plus abundant bloodwork. ("Leave some for me, will ya?" Trump had snapped at the phlebotomist when she went to fill the sixth sample tube," I gotta have some to live, you know.")

The cancer's containment and retreat were positive developments that Anita could not share with the media because announcing the remission would expose their earlier lie that Trump did not have cancer.

Douglass said, "Just as well we don't say anything about remission. They are going interview oncologists who're gonna say cancer in remission is still cancer; it can come back at any time."

"So you'd still have to call him a cancer victim or patient?" Miller asked.

"I don't like victim it's a layman's term. The cancer is in remission. But the disease is still there. His PSA is down to 5.3, which is progress."

Anita said, "We told them it was zero point four. The fact is none of the reporters believed it, especially the men, who know about that stuff. They gave me a hard time about it."

"The radiation treatment worked; did its job," Miller said. "But we can't talk about that, either."

"He had radiation treatment? When did he go to the hospital? I knew nothing about it."

"We installed a radiation machine here, in the basement, an accelerator," Miller said.

"A linear accelerator," Dr. Douglass said.

"And, of course, no one ever told me."

Miller turned to Dr Douglass, "If it's in remission, why did he pass out?"

"He passed out?" Anita was close to shouting, "Why didn't I know about that, either?"

"He passed out after the Dallas rally," Miller said. "Off stage. No one saw it. And you weren't told so you wouldn't have to lie to the media."

"I lie to the media every day; that's my job, for Christ's sake. And if no one saw it, the media would not be asking about it, would they?"

Douglass said, "They — we — wanted it closely held to avoid leaks."

"If it got printed or broadcast that he passed out, the cancer story would become credible," Miller said.

Anita said, "If it wasn't the cancer, why did he pass out after the rally?"

"Dehydration," Douglass said. "He was totally dehydrated."

"Still, he was out playing golf and riding in a speedboat the day after the Dallas rally, " Anita said.

"That wasn't the Boss, that was Gibbons, his body double," Miller said.

"The president has a body double? Why am I just now learning this? Who is it? Is he someone around here?"

Miller said, "The fewer who know, the less likely it is to leak. Now you know."

"What else don't I know about? Is there more? What about the Russian missile bases in Texas? The conversation you had with Putin. That's true, too, isn't it? Despite what we said, despite the statement we issued in your name."

They had put out a statement attributed to Miller saying it was fake news; Miller claimed to have never spoken with Putin on the phone. A statement from GSA intelligence claimed Putin didn't speak English and the video of the Russian survey team was fake; clearly shot using a drone in a region of Arizona in the Pacific States of America. The phone call, Miller said in the release, was voice actors reading a script. The voiceprints were fake. It was a plot by unnamed deep state actors, likely in the Pacific States of America, to tarnish Trump. On social media, Trump unleashed a Niagara of accusations and insults, his primary targets were PSA president Gavin Newsom, Mike

Bloomberg, George Soros and PSA Vice President Adam Schiff.

"Then that *was* you on the phone with Putin. And that *was* Putin," Anita said.

"I can't answer that," Miller said.

"You just did, Steve. You know what? I quit. I hereby tender my resignation."

"You can't quit, Anita; there's a briefing coming up…" Miller looked at his watch "… right now. Fact, it should have started five minutes ago. Brief The Beast, then we'll talk about your resignation. Which I'm going to refuse. Your story — our story — there's no cancer and never has been; there are no Russian missile bases and never will be. I had no conversation with Putin and never will have one."

The door opened and five WORMs rushed in, stomped behind the desk and hauled Miller to his feet.

"You can't…."

One of the WORMs cut him off, "Shut the fuck up, asshole!" He made sure his order was followed by stuffing a rag in Miller's mouth. The WORMs lifted Miller and carried him from the office, they were scrupulous about roughing him up as they hauled him out of the room.

Anita and Douglass followed the violence and were looking at the empty doorway when Trump stepped into the door frame. "Whadda ya waiting for, honey?" He asked. "Go brief the schmucks. Make it good, too."

She did not move; she stared at him.

"Hey, girlie, you hearing me? Time to get off your pretty ass and do your thing. Dr. Fred, you stay here; I wanna talk to you about this remission thing."

*

When Anita stepped up to the lectern in the briefing room, The Beast was especially restive because she was late. It roared:

"Are the Russians putting missiles into Texas?"

"Did the president give the Russians permission to put missiles in Texas?"

"What are the Russians doing in Texas?"

"How did Fox News get the Russian missiles story? Was it from Mar-a-Lago?"

"Does the president have cancer?"

"Why have there been no briefings for five days?"

"What's Trump's prognosis?"

"Is Trump dying?"

"We need to see his medical reports, he owes it to the nation."

"When was the cancer diagnosed and why weren't we told immediately?"

"What sort of treatment is he receiving?"

"Will he have surgery?"

"Where has the cancer spread?"

"Can we have the president personally brief us?"

"Will he make a prime-time statement to the people?"

"Can you make Tucker Carlson and Eric Trump available?"

"What about the Constitution and the line of succession?"

"If climate change is a hoax, why are you building a seawall to protect Mar-a-Lago?"

"Where is the First Lady? Why haven't we seen her in three weeks?"

Anita looked The Beast in its many eyes and lied valiantly. The Beast was having none of it. As soon as she answered an individual question, The Beast erupted once more:

"Are the Russians putting missiles into Texas?"

"Did the president give the Russians permission to put missiles in Texas?"

"What are the Russians doing in Texas?"

"How did Fox News get the Russian missiles story? Was it from Mar-a-Lago?"

"Does the president have cancer?"

"Why have there been no briefings for eight days?"

"What's Trump's prognosis?"

"Is Trump dying?"

"We need to see his medical reports, he owes it to the nation."

"When was the cancer diagnosed and why weren't we told immediately?"

"What sort of treatment is he receiving?"

"Will he have surgery?"

"Where has the cancer spread?"

"Can we have the president personally brief us?"

"Will he make a prime-time statement to the people?"

"Can you make Tucker Carlson and Eric Trump available?"

"What about the Constitution and the line of succession?"

"If climate change is a hoax, why are your building a seawall to protect Mar-a-Lago?"

"Where is the First Lady? Why haven't we seen her in three weeks?"

CHAPTER SIX

Putin is a nicer person than I am. — Donald J. Trump

The 45/1 Office, Mar-A-Lago, Palm Beach, Florida, Great States Of America

"Why did you talk that thing with our friend? Why take that risk, Vladimir?"

"You was not available, my brother. I call you first, but you say you can't talk then. I had very best people ready to do biggest internet campaign for you. They would have destroyed BBC cancer story. I had best team in St. Petersburg to work on it."

"That thing's fake news. Now. It's gone. Cured. I beat it."

Putin knew "our friend" was Miller and "that thing" referred in the first instance to his missile bases in Texas and in the second case to Trump's cancer. He also knew that cancer in remission is not cancer cured, but he said only: "Very good. Very good."

"Now that the story broke, we gotta cool it on it, the thing. Cool it on it for now. Not do anything about it, the stuff, you know. For now. Gotta delay," Trump said.

Putin was annoyed at Trump's vague talk; never using nouns when a pronoun would do. He talked ganglord style, avoiding incriminating words like "missile," "Texas," "base" and "cancer."

Putin imposed no such restrictions upon himself; he called a spade a spade and a missile a missile: "I disagree. We take advantage of momentum. Military engineers returned to Moscow. Military planners and architects working now. Is good progress, why slow it? We can have missiles in Texas in two months, three if we have trouble with building and drilling. Or supply chain problem."

He then used an analogy Trump would appreciate: "Not to go forward is like pulling out of pussy too soon before you come. You don't do that. I don't do that. We don't do that."

Trump did not want to talk about the strategic version of coitus interruptus; he turned to his favorite topic, his personal grievances: "I can't believe the thing broke on the old guy's network. I can't believe he did that to me, the old guy. And, did you see, it was the same fucking reporter? The BBC guy? He's working for the old guy now. Only possible reason the old guy hired him was to piss me off. Send me a message. Well, I got the message; I'm pissed. Good and pissed. They get no more exclusive interviews with Donald Trump; I tell you that."

"About missile base, my brother...."

"You gotta say that, huh? Well, fuck that. I've been double crossed by that old fuck so much it's a triple cross by now..."

Putin's voice did not betray his vexation, "We must talk about starting work on missile silos, other infrastructure."

"Fuck that. And I dunno what you're talking about. I don't know a thing about that thing. We need to focus on getting the old fucker back for that."

Putin had not written the agent's playbook, but he had memorized it: Listen to the asset; empathize with him; assuage his grievances, cater to his concerns. Then bring him back to the mission at hand. He gave up the missile base fight — for the moment.

"This English reporter," Putin said, "this.... how you say his name?"

"I don't know. It's nothing like the way it's spelled. Chump-lee, or something like that."

"He cost you a lot, this Chump-lee."

"Tell me about it. I've got his sources where we want them and they're going on trial as soon as we get a law passed that they broke. I don't know what's taking Sidney and her gang so long to write it. Hell, time it's taken, I could of written a law and got it passed. I should of signed that law two weeks ago."

"My brother, you need my lawyers to write law for you? We are very good here with journalism laws. In Russia we punish disagreeable journalists. One television presenter we send to penal colony fifteen years for her bad comment about special operation. Not holiday camps, women penal colonies. Those shlyukhi from the Pussy Riot know that. One goes away married with kid, comes back a dyke. Maybe all of them."

"People tell me that you're also pretty good at taking care of the thing for longer than that. That's what I hear from people," Trump said.

He didn't know the specifics, but Trump was aware significant numbers of "disagreeable" Russian journalists and editors had been murdered, committed "suicide" or died prematurely of "natural" causes. Most were shot dead in muggings gone wrong, but one was blown up in a stairwell of her apartment building, another was flung from a window and one was garroted with his own belt. The last was ruled a suicide.

"If you want, we find and take care of him, we have methods," Putin said.

"Well, *I* can't do anything about our not-so-good friend. He's in New York or Washington. They tell me our not-so-good friend was here for my Dallas rally. Used fake ID. You can bet the old man did that for him, got him the ID, got him into the country. The old bastard's been on a campaign to do nothing but fuck me over since 2020. He puts our not-so-good friend right in the same stadium with me and I never knew it. Slipped in and out without our finding him. And him a criminal, a wanted criminal. If we'd of known we'd of arrested him, too. He'd be in a cage like a dog. Which is what he is."

"A dog never do what Chump-lee do to you, my brother. Never."

Putin owned three large dogs and did not understand why Trump equated those totally loyal animals with anything negative.

"Fuck that guy, our not-so-good friend. He's a fucking dog. And we'll arrest him next time he's here. He'll be back. This is where the news is, so he'll be back. And we'll arrest him, try him and lock him the fuck up."

Drawing on his considerable experience handling disagreeable journalists, Putin said, "You don't want him in trial. No court. That gives him stage to speak. You want him shut up, not speaking."

"Twenty years in a GSA prison for high treason will shut our not-so-good friend up. I just can't believe the balls on that guy; showing up here at *my* rally."

"Still, you don't want trial, Donald. You don't want trial."

"The nerve of him; coming to my rally. He wrote a piece for the Wall Street Journal about it. And they ran it in the London Times, not that I give a shit about that. Why should I care what they read in England?"

"Is that rally where you pass out? How you feeling now, my brother?" Putin was letting Trump know he had intelligence sources deep within the administration. The message was received: the only people who knew about Trump's fainting spell were Eric, Stephen Miller, his WORM bodyguard, his makeup artist and the big fat guy who looked nothing like him but somehow passed for him on tarmacs and golf courses. Putin had tapped into one or more of them. Trump was simultaneously impressed by and pissed off at Putin's network.

Trump did not probe; he knew Putin would never reveal a source.

"I never passed out. And even if I had passed out that would of had nothing to do with the thing, you know. The thing's gone. I beat it. Just like I beat Covid. I was dried out; dehydration, they said. No matter how cold they make those stadiums, I sweat like a pig. I was dehydrated. It wasn't the thing. But I never passed out; I got a little dizzy, is all."

Putin, under no restraints, named the thing, "Of course, not cancer." He sounded unconvinced.

"No, really. Really. Dehydration."

Was Putin taking his protestations as proof? Trump knew he should dial it back, but he incapable of that. He was a grievance roll. "When I had the Covid… remember? When I was president and got Covid, I wanted to step out in front of the microphones and tear open my shirt and have a Superman shirt underneath. I may do that now; now that I beat the thing."

"You can't do that, my brother. If you do that, you admit you had cancer, which you deny many times. You can't get cured of disease you never had."

"Shit, you're right."

"I can help you with this Chump-lee, but only if you want. Or you do it. They don't go around with bodyguards, reporters. Or we can talk about old man, if you feel he turns on you."

"Tempting; very tempting. The one -- the not-so-good friend, not the other one, the old guy. Leave that one be. He's an old man anyways. How long's he got?"

"This Chump-lee, we look into him; into kompromat; destroy his reputation. Nothing there. Not a pedik — you say faggot — even though he's English. A lot of that, pedik, with the English."

"The gays I don't mind so much," Trump said. "It's the ones lop off their dicks or dress up in women's clothes that get me. We got gays here, but not so many trans. They know they're not welcome in my country, in the GSA, the trans. Those other republics; they're like magnets for 'em, though. Trans, gays and lezzies all over the place. Especially New York and California. Here, not so much because we're religious."

Trump religious? Putin stifled a chuckle. "We have none in Russia, the gays. A few, almost none. The gays we have, we take care of so they don't do it more, the gay thing."

"We took care of that trans shit in the constitution," Trump boasted, forgetting that Putin had supplied the draft GSA constitution and knew it contained nothing about transgender people.

"Easy to eliminate, Chump-lee, "Putin said. "Could look like car accident. A disease; natural cause. Think about it. Is easy. We do it all time."

"I will think about it," Trump lied, "I'll think real hard about it." He had no intention of taking Putin up on the offer and putting himself further in the Russian's debt.

"Now, how he gets story, Chump-lee? Is clear to me Miller telephone was not secure. But he tells me it was secure. So NSA or some other agency listen in and record and the recording they gave to Chump-lee. That's only way it could happen. Unless…."

"Unless what?"

"Unless *Miller* records the call and gives to the NSA or CIA or someone in Atlantic States. Or Miller gives to Chump-lee direct."

"Steve would never," Trump said. "He's loyal."

"He so loyal you arrest him yesterday?"

Putin knew that?

"No. No, no arrest. We put him in protective custody because of the thing." Trump said. "He's always loyal to us. I should of said he's always *been* loyal. Inna past. Now, maybe…." His voice trailed off.

Putin had planted a row of doubt seeds, now he covered them with soil: "Only Miller and me on telephone call. Then Chump-lee has tape of call and puts it on Fox news. Only

Miller and few others see you faint after rally. But I know about that. You surprised I know. How I know?"

"Wasn't fainting. I was dehydrated and that made me a little dizzy. But, Vlad, are you telling me…."

"Not telling, Donald, *asking*. Who is on telephone discussing missiles with me? Who is there when you faint? I mean when you get dizzy?"

"Can't be."

"If can't be, then is not," Putin said. "But then why you arrest him if can't be?"

The doubt seeds were germinating.

Trump changed the subject: "Good thing I don't have the thing anymore; Eric doesn't wana be president."

Putin seemed to have intelligence on that, too: "I know. I have been told. They tell me that."

◆ ◆ ◆

Putin has no respect for our president whatsoever. — Donald J. Trump

Internet Research Agency, St. Petersburg, Russian Federation

Sofia Pushkina was not easily intimidated. A lesbian in a gay-intolerant, male-dominated society did not rise to a position of authority and responsibility by giving in to bullies. Yet now, the phone to her ear, her mouth agape, she was intimidated to the point of mute surrender. On the other end of the line was the unmistakable voice of Vladimir Vladimirovich Putin, president of the Russian Federation, a man whose every utterance held the authority of holy writ — or at least of binding law. Putin could have her fired, arrested, disappeared — in other words, killed — with a casual remark to a sycophantic subordinate.

"Grazhdanka Sofia Ivanova," Putin said. "Razbit Ameerika!"

The president knew the agency's informal slogan? But how? Did he know everything? Everything, including her sexual proclivities?

"I want to thank you myself for your past efforts on behalf of the motherland with regard to our American…" and here the most powerful man in Russia paused and considered. "Our American *friend*." The way he said "friend" indicated that he really meant "former friend" or "ex-friend." Putin had found a way to render a noun in the past tense.

"I understand that you deserve credit for that work, although — as you can imagine — others in the agency have tried to take that credit. Success has many parents; failure is an orphan."

Putin had rendered the expression meaningless by finding many parents for his catastrophic war against Ukraine. All manner of Russian generals and defense ministry officials had been branded as parents of the disaster. None of them were named Putin.

Sofia Ivanova Pushkina wondered if Putin knew he was paraphrasing Mussolini's fascist son-in-law when he used the parents/orphan expression. It would be impolitic to enlighten him; she remained silent.

"Are you there, Sofia Ivanova?" he asked.

"Yes, Sudar Putin," she said. She used an obsolete word for "Mister" as a sign of respect.

"Sudar? Please, no Sudar. Even Gospodin is unnecessary for a patriotic woman like yourself, who has served so well. Feel free to call me Vladimir Vladimirovich."

She could not bring herself to use the president's first name and patronymic; Putin inspired a mixture of awe and fear in the citizens of Russia. For Sofia Ivanova it was primarily fear. Like most Russians, she loved — no *loved* — Putin. *Loved* him because he wielded fearsome power. Russia today was Oceania in "Nineteen Eighty-Four," a nation of Winston Smiths who had been trained, disciplined, intimidated or tortured into *loving* Big Brother. A propagandist by trade, she was immune to dezinformatsiya, but her work had not inoculated her against fear.

Putin now sounded impatient, "Devochka, have you lost your tongue?"

Devochka — girl — was meant to be an insult. She took it that way.

"I am sorry President Putin. I was tongue-tied. I've never spoken to anyone… anyone of such rank before. Forgive me."

"Oh, I am just a man, like others," he said, believing not a word of it.

Just a man? In that case, she detested him. In her experience men were loud, dismissive, insulting bullies. They were often drunk and always sexually predatory. Even on her evenings out, dressed in dykey leather with henna tattoos on her neck, some hooligan would make a pass at her or put his hands on her ass. Thinking of Putin as a man like others turned the fear, awe and *love* into disgust, disrespect and disaffection.

She became all business: "Is there something further you wish from me and my department, President Putin?"

"Yes. Our American *friend*…" again, past tensing a noun "is becoming our American burden. He needs to learn his lesson. He lied to us; he told us he had cancer then he told us he was not suffering cancer. Our intelligence services have confirmed it: he is ill. And not just physically. Our FSB psychiatrists diagnosed him a narcissist. He has narcissistic personality disorder. This is a mental condition."

"I am familiar with it," she said. She did not add that she had seen it first-hand with her own father, a man who was self-confidently convinced of his own importance while constantly in need of attention and admiration to confirm that importance. Ivan Petrovich Pushkin's fragile self-esteem was masked by posturing self-confidence. His empathy for his wife, daughter and son — as well as his underlings at work — was non-existent. And he exploded with rage at what he perceived to be the slightest criticism. Pushkina knew Donald Trump as well as if he had been her own father; in a way, he had been her father.

"Something will happen. Something very dramatic will happen. Our *friend* will suspect us as the source of his troubles. But I want you and your people ready to do two things: First, you will be ready to make it look like the Ukrainian terrorists did the dramatic thing. Second, I want Q to give his followers a new direction; a totally new direction."

"Of course. We can do what you need. Q is always at your disposal President Putin."

"Please; Vladimir Vladimirovich. Razbit Ameerika!"

She felt free to use his first name and patronymic now; after all, he, himself, had told her he was only a man, and the man was asking a favor of her. She said: "Razbit Ameerika, Vladimir Vladimirovich."

◆ ◆ ◆

I was mugged by the media. — Donald J. Trump

Beaverhead Ranch, Southwest Montana, Great States Of America

It is not easy to spirit a vice president out of the country without being noticed, so when Tucker Carlson called The Proprietor and said he urgently needed to meet, Murdoch suggested that Carlson fly to The Proprietor's most remote property in the GSA, his 340,000-acre Montana spread. Murdoch bought the working cattle ranch in 2021 for $280 million, the largest land transaction in Montana history. The Proprietor felt more at home in urban settings, so he rarely visited the place.

The Vice President's office announced Carlson was taking a long weekend to tour Yellowstone Park, like all the former United States National Parks, a facility jointly owned, managed and operated by the four republics.

After the vice-presidential Gulfstream landed at Big Sky Airport, it was a simple maneuver for three Suburbans to peel off from the rear of Carlson's Yellowstone-bound motorcade and head west. The area was thinly populated, and traffic was sparse; no one noticed the three armored SUVs barreling toward The Proprietor's ranch.

"Well? You wanted to meet." Murdoch said, not bothering to rise from his chair nor to exchange pleasantries. Straight to business, Carlson liked that about the old man.

They were in his ranchhouse office, a modest room with chinked log walls, a replica antique oak desk, and five TV screens mounted on the wall. Some tooled leather chairs and a couch as well as a Navaho carpet completed the furnishings. Carlson thought the attempt at rustic atmosphere Disneyesque.

The TV screens flickered with the silent video feeds of the three major all-news networks and the two all-business networks. The Proprietor owned two of the five and the screens on which his outlets played were significantly larger than the other three screens.

"You wanted to meet, Mr. Vice President."

Carlson heard a hint of frost in Murdoch's voice. Was it his imagination or was it the influence of The Proprietor's new mixed-race bride. *They* — no need to identify them further — didn't like Tucker Carlson. Well, no matter, he didn't like *them*. He'd made his fame and no small fortune expressing his distaste for *them*. Doubtless, as one of *them*, the latest Bride of Murdoch was not a Tucker Carlson fan. Moreover, she had the ear — as well as other body parts — of The Proprietor, which could give her great influence. Carlson knew there was no talk more persuasive than pillow talk.

In his Fox News career, Carlson's stock-in-trade was public whining about any effort to enhance or protect the civil rights of nonwhite Americans — which he said inevitably diminished the civil rights of white Americans because such enhancement or protection inevitably came at their expense. His worldview denied that American racism existed, even as he did his professional best to fan its flames. Opportunity was a zero-sum game; not an asset all could share, but a prize to be won by the chosen at the expense of the unchosen. This was no cynical act by Carlson; he truly believed in the superiority of the race he privately called Aryan.

He was convinced that other, lesser, races were trying to replace Aryans. They were coming for Aryan jobs, wives, neighborhoods, wallets and kids. His critics dismissively called it "replacement theory," but there was nothing theoretical about it to Tucker Carlson: *they* were trying to replace him and those like him.

Look no further than Judy Travers replacing The Proprietor's previous wife, Jerry Hall. Carlson wondered at the The Proprietor's spousal choices: two white women followed by a Chinese — Wendi Deng — followed by Jerry Hall, in turn followed by… by what? Carlson could not begin to guess at what appeared to him to be the swill of races and ethnicities that resulted in the beautiful but clearly non-Aryan Judy Travers.

Carlson understood why The Proprietor thought it advantageous to have at least one of his secretaries be black, or Latina, or South Asian, or Judy Travers. Even banging her was understandable; she was beautiful and sexy. But marrying her? That was a too much for Carlson.

Travers, whose skin color now resembled charcoal in Carlson's imagination, was nowhere in evidence. He assumed she had not made the trip with The Proprietor, which was all to the good. He could count on getting his message across to Murdoch and having him contemplate it for a considerable time before the Nubian temptress launched a counterargument. Not that Carlson had any idea what a Nubian was. But he was certain they were dark-skinned and originated from somewhere in Africa.

"Boss," Carlson said. "I want to be president. This Eric Trump president-select business is unconstitutional. We are a nation of laws, not a nation of men."

The old man nodded, but his expression told Carlson he did not give a shit about a nation of laws nor about a nation of men.

Carlson turned over his final card: "If I'm president, you know that I'll be looking out for our mutual interests. I think Trump is sick. I believe that BBC story about the cancer. I've heard a rumor that he passed out after that Dallas rally...."

"Tell me more about that? We had that well-staffed. In fact, the reporter who broke the cancer story was there, Walter Cholmondeley."

"The BBC guy?"

"I hired him. How did you miss it? He broke the Putin-Miller missile base story on Fox."

"That was the same guy?"

"Don't you watch Fox News anymore?"

"I read a summary. Wasn't it Weatherly who broke the phone call with Putin?"

"No. It was Cholmondeley. Weatherly debriefed him and got into an argument with him about the story. He got a talking-to for that."

"Who, Cholmondeley?"

"No, Weatherly."

"There was no argument mentioned in the summary."

"You need better summaries. Better yet, watch Fox News. Read the Wall Street Journal. You may find out that he's had Stephen Miller arrested."

"Miller, I knew about. The Boss called me up and told me right after it was done. The rest of the stuff, I just read a summary of the Fox story."

"Summaries!" Murdoch said. He was dismissive of summaries but what was the stock-in-trade of his media outlets if not a steady stream of summaries?

"This is why the vice presidency is a shit job," Carlson said. "The job, it's like being an understudy or a stand-by announcer. Maybe you shuffle papers and cut ribbons and make speeches, but you're really just waiting for some guy to die. But, still, the people of the GSA elected *me* to be the vice president, to be *first* in the line of succession. Not Trump's son. So we have to do something about that."

"We, huh? How do I fit in? Isn't this your row to hoe?" As he spoke, Murdoch shifted uneasily in his chair. Carlson had arrived early and deprived him of the opportunity to take a pre-meeting hyperbaric oxygen treatment. He was not sure he was at his cognitive best.

"Yes, it's my responsibility. In part, it's mine. But it's a media responsibility, too. I was democratically — small d, of course — elected vice president. If you believe in democracy, then you should be concerned that Trump is trying to do something against the constitution."

Carlson's embrace of democracy seemed highly transactional to The Proprietor. But he had been highly transactional, himself; willing to bargain away some of democracy's more nuanced advantages in return for commercial advantage.

Carlson continued, "Trump ignores you — us — he bad-mouths you in private. He probably bad-mouths me, too. I'm sure he does. But you know me, boss. Your input would be very important to me."

"Trump always takes my calls," The Proprietor lied. "But, I am not fond of the idea of Eric as president of anything — even his family's business. I think he's a lightweight."

"You'll help me, then? Preserve the constitution?"

"You mean preserve the part of the constitution that pertains to the line of succession? I'll see what I can do."

The Proprietor suspected there was very little he could do now, since Trump had not formally made Eric his successor nor had he admitted he had cancer.

"That's all I can ask for," Carlson said.

"Yes, it is."

When Carlson left the house, he discovered Judy Travers Murdoch standing next to his Suburban, chatting with his WORM detail, all of whom were reciprocating her friendly manner with varying degrees of barely-disguised lust. It amused Carlson, who knew them all to be white supremacists, bigots, racists and replacement theory adherents. He, himself, gave her an appreciative head-to-toe.

"Mrs. Murdoch," he said, and extended his open hand.

"Judy. You've known me too long for missus."

She took his hand, a soft handshake, very feminine. He tightened his grip, very macho. She matched him, squeezing his knuckles together. She won; he pulled back. What had he ever done to her? His long-running record of blowing racist dog whistles? She couldn't take that personally; he had always been very friendly to her.

"Hope to see you again very soon," she said. "Maybe you can stay for dinner next time." The frown and knit brow told him she meant not a word of that.

"Yes, that would be nice," he said. She'd likely poison him if he stayed for dinner.

He climbed into the back seat and the door closed behind him. There was a bulky satellite phone on the seat. How did that get there? Did *she* put it there? He sniffed the air, to see if she had left behind a hint of perfume. The only scent was the leather of the seats.

The satphone chirped. Carlson was alone in the back seat, so he answered.

"Tucker, my friend, my ally, how are you?" The voice had a heavy Eastern European accent. Carlson thought he recognized it but could not be sure.

"To whom am I speaking?"

"Whom? I never know when to use that and when to use who. But my English, it's good enough, correct? It is your friend Viktor."

Viktor Orbán, the authoritarian ruler of Hungary was Tucker Carlson's role model for the perfect leader of a nation besieged by lesser races, religions and nationalities. An authoritarian Christian nationalist, unapologetic in his bigotry, Orbán had managed to so alienate other member states of the European Union they had voted unanimously to expel Hungary. In ten years. If Orbán didn't reform his authoritarian ways, which he had no intention of doing.

"Viktor, how are you. Did you have someone leave this satphone for me?"

"No, not me. Someone with more talent for that sort of thing arranged that. He just asked me to introduce you. So I am introducing you and leaving the call, my friend. Here is Vladimir Vladimirovich Putin, President of the Russian Federation."

"*What?*"

"Here is Putin, President of Russian Federation," a different, heavily accented voice said. "Are you alone in vehicle? Viktor forgets to ask."

Questions swirled. Whose phone was this? Who had left it in his vehicle? Was it Judy Travers? Was it a WORM? The first voice sounded like Orbán, but was this really Putin? If not Putin, who was it? Was this some sort of trap? Was Murdoch behind this? What was his game? Was it Trump setting him up? Did Putin even speak English? Was the phone secure?

"I'm going to hang up now. I'm not playing your game," Carlson said. "Besides, Putin doesn't speak English."

"And this you know how?" Putin asked.

"Well...."

"Shall I tell you what Trump and I discuss in Helsinki and prove who I am?" Carlson considered this for a moment, then said: "Mr. President, what did you want to talk about?"

MINE!

◆ ◆ ◆

The problem is not that Putin is smart, which of course he's smart, but the real problem is that our leaders are dumb. — Donald J. Trump

The 45/1 Office, Mar-A-Lago, Palm Beach, Florida, Great States Of America

There was no computer in the presidential office because Trump was a willful digital semi-literate. The only modern device he used was the iPhone with which he posted rants to Truth Media. So, Michael Flynn, his new chief of staff, brought a Toshiba laptop into the 45/1 office to play the recording of Tucker Carlson's conversation with Vladimir Putin.

When they finished listening, Trump's face was contorted with anger; his hands were balled into fists. He took it out on the messenger: "What the fuck, Mike. How could *you* let that happen? How could you let that happen?"

"Me, Excellency? I didn't let it happen, I sure didn't make it happen; I only recorded it. I reported it to you. What? Would you rather not know?"

"I can't believe Tucker. I can't believe Putin. Why the fuck did you let them talk?"

"How could I have stopped them? What was I supposed to do about it, since I couldn't know in advance? I had no way.

How could I stop them from talking? How was I to do that, Excellency? I didn't slip the satphone into the VP's car. I didn't make the call. Tucker didn't, either; they called him. All I did was monitor the bug I had planted in Carlson's vehicle."

That was a lie; his predecessor, Stephen Miller, had ordered the Vice-Presidential SUV bugged. Flynn gambled that Miller had done it on the sly and not informed Trump. He was right.

"Yeah. Good idea, bugging Carlson"

Flynn said, "Without that bug, *my* bug, those two would be plotting behind your back, sir.... Excellency. My bug got us the whole conversation."

"They *are* plotting behind my back. The disloyal fucks. The fucking losers! Putin! Tucker! Can you believe those fucking guys? Who do they think they are?" He answered his own question: "Putin, he's supposed to be my friend. My brother, he calls me. Carlson, he's *my* vice president, Goddamnit. I did Rupert a favor and made that whiny wuss what he is today. And Putin, too. I made him the most powerful leader in Europe. The most powerful leader Russia's ever had."

Were they alive and in attendance, Stalin, Lenin, Catherine the Great and Peter the Great might disagree.

"Can't trust the Russians; never could," Flynn said. "You've got a disloyal vice president, Excellency. Corrupted by the Russians."

"Carlson's fighting a lost cause. He's not gonna be president. I beat the cancer. I'm cured. Next campaign, I pick a different vice president. Who knows, Mike, maybe it would be good to have a military man as a VP candidate."

"Well...."

"Carlson's fucking disloyal. And Putin, too. After all I did for him. I'm gonna whip them like dogs."

Dog-whipping Putin was off the table and Trump knew it. The Russian was secure in the Kremlin, where he slept in an underground bunker and was surrounded by a regiment of bodyguards whose proficiency and training made the WORMs look like a troop of cub scouts. Carlson, on the other hand was one phone call away from a detention cell.

In the recording, Putin said he was disappointed Trump wanted to "cool it" on the missile bases in Texas. Carlson, without promising to permit the bases, commiserated.

"He does that," Carlson said. "Doesn't always keep his word."

Putin then asked, point-blank what Carlson's policy toward the bases would be if he were president. Carlson responded coyly.

"President Trump is healthy. I don't think that's a decision I'm going to have to make. Besides, he's designated Eric as his successor."

Putin said it was a violation of the GSA constitution to take the vice president out of the line of succession. He said Carlson could prevail in court. He said Eric Trump did not want to be president and the Trump children who would jump at the chance, Junior and Ivanka, were so far removed from the seat of power they had no way of seeking the job.

Still, the president is healthy, Carlson told the Russian.

Putin said, "Cancer story BBC reports is true. He has prostate cancer. It spread; now he has bone cancer. In remission right now from radiation treatment. That stopped cancer but remission cancer can come back in two years, three years, five years. Who's to say when cancer returns."

Trump asked Flynn to replay that portion of the recording.

"Okay, stop. Stop the tape. Y'hear that? First, he's saying to Carlson that the fake news about cancer is true. And then he's threatening me, Putin. Y'hear, he's threatening me? He's threatening me and Carlson's letting him. I can't have a vice president like that. We have to get rid of him."

"As in get *rid* of him get rid of him, or…?"

Flynn was unsure of the mob boss code Trump used. As a former Army general, he was accustomed to unambiguous orders, not hazy "get rid of" language.

"Of course, like you said, *get rid of him*," Trump said.

"I didn't say it, you said it, Excellency."

"You just did."

"Sir… sorry, Excellency, I was just quoting you. To be clear, do you mean *kill* the vice president?"

"I never said that. Did you hear me say that? Did I ever say the K word? You never heard me say that word. Oh, and we gotta figure a way to take care of Putin, too."

"If you do mean killing, I don't think there's any way to take care of Putin," Flynn said.

"Why the fuck not? He's been disloyal to me, too."

"Don't know how we do that."

Trump had an inspiration: "I know. I'll ask Putin to kill that BBC reporter. The guy, Chump-lee is here — or in the Atlantic States, at least. He's working for Rupert. And when Putin kills him, we release the tape of the call,"

"Excellency, we can't do that. *You'll* be on the tape asking Putin to take out Cholmondeley, so we'll never be able to release the tape."

Trump had not thought that through. "Right! Shit! Okay, *you* ask Putin to do it."

"Then it will be my voice on the recording."

Trump saw merit in that: "Well, that's okay, then. Nobody knows what you sound like. Also, depending on what Putin says, we may be able to edit the tape."

"I'm uncomfortable with that, Excellency. You can't trust Putin; he could record the call. If we let out an edited version, there's nothing stopping him from putting out the whole call."

"Then we call it fake news. Say it never happened."

"If the reporter is dead then it sure looks like it *did* happen," Flynn said. "Can't really trust Putin, like I said. I bet he's the one who put out that call with Stephen Miller."

"No," Trump said, "Putin told me he doesn't record our calls. He wouldn't record a call with the chief of staff, either."

Flynn stopped himself short of saying, "Sure, trust Putin, Excellency. Who could be more trustworthy than Putin?" Instead, he said, "You really can't rule it out, Excellency. Putin might be the one put out that call with Miller."

"Why would he do that? It was no good for him, either. But *you* gotta be glad whoever put it out. Now you're sitting here in Mar-a-Lago instead of some old armory drawing arrows on a map. Chief of staff instead of secretary of defense."

"Those aren't just arrows, Excellency. You give me eight brigades and I'll have California cut in half in two, three months."

Trump had the two or three months, but not the brigades. "You're my chief of staff now, Mike. Put those plans on the shelf. We're going to reunify the country without firing a shot. Except for a little militia guerrilla action by our guys. our friends. No invasions. Putin showed us how stupid invasions are. He's bogged down forever in The Ukraine, and he could of had the whole country if he'd just worked it politically. I'm way smarter than Putin."

Flynn nodded, unconvinced, but all he said was, "They've dropped the "the," it's just Ukraine nowadays."

Flynn asked himself if a President Tucker Carlson might find him the eight brigades he needed. Maybe. It might be a possibility. Trump had proven his bark worse than his bite; he was a physical coward. Carlson? Who knew? It was probably worth protecting the vice president for the moment; they could always dispense with him down the road by leaking his conversation with Putin. Mike Flynn set about convincing Trump to spare Carlson — for now.

"Excellency, you may not want to move on Carlson right away. You have great leverage with him, you have the recording of him plotting with Putin behind your back. It's the kind of thing that'll keep Tucker loyal forever."

"Yeah, but there's got to be some price for disloyalty."

"I'm from Rhode Island, Excellency. I grew up mostly with Italian kids. It's like the Italians say, 'Revenge is a dish best served cold.'"

"Yeah, I heard they say that. And no one knows more about revenge than them."

◆ ◆ ◆

I think Viagra is wonderful if you need it, if you have medical issues, if you've had surgery. I've just never needed it. Frankly, I wouldn't mind if there were an anti-Viagra, something with the opposite effect. I'm not bragging. I'm just lucky. I don't need it. — Donald J. Trump

Hilton Midtown, 1335 Avenue Of The Americas, New York, Atlantic States of America

The Proprietor had arranged for Walter Cholmondeley to move into a two-bedroom suite at the Hilton Midtown until found something more permanent.

The Hilton is a large and busy commercial hotel with mediocre restaurants on three levels, dozens of meeting rooms and a steady and annoying flow of businesspeople in and out of the lobby at all hours of the day. The hordes on the basement level, ground floor and mezzanine reminded Cholmondeley of nothing so much as a railroad station in India — except at the Hilton the crowd was better dressed and, being mostly Americans, a lot louder.

It was in his suite at the Hilton that his pursuit of Ann Bailey culminated in below-average shag during lunch hour. Their first kiss revealed to him that Ann fumigated her lungs with tobacco; she tasted like an ashtray — or the way he imagined an ash tray tasted – never having done that experiment. It went downhill from there. Her silicon-enhanced breasts produced the reverse of their intended effect, her repeated requests to "watch the hair," were off-putting, and when she started talking about Trump in bed, Cholmondeley realized their first leg over was their last leg over.

Gentleman that he was, he completed his carnal duty. She, on the other hand, failed to do his self-esteem the courtesy of faking an organism. The instant the deed was done, she was out of bed and pulling on her clothing, not bothering to come up with even the feeblest excuse for her rapid departure. Slam, bam, thank you, man; without the thank you, man.

He was not sure she said goodbye on her way out the door. Cholmondeley followed her ten minutes later.

A steady rain fell, and he turned up the collar of his Burberry and hurried along Avenue of the Americas, sticking close to the soaring walls of the skyscrapers as if they offered some shelter from the rain.

"Valta Chummy," a woman's voice called out. He turned to face a handsome middle-aged woman wearing dark blue raincoat and carrying a large umbrella with the words "LOT Polish Airlines" printed on it.

"Cholmondeley," he said. "Do I know you? Have we met?"

"No. Ve nevah meet. But I know who you are and I hev somethin' for you for your television." She pronounced it "talafishion."

She pulled a padded envelope from her purse and handed it to him.

"What's this? Who are you? Where's this come from?"

Henrietta Krajewski, the SVR courier, said, "My name don't matter. You vill figure out who send dis. You vill see. Don't open here; open in office, you vill see."

She turned and walked briskly to the curb where a black Lincoln Navigator had been waiting for her. She climbed in the back seat and the car eased into the chocked traffic and sat there.

Cholmondeley opened the envelope. There was a stack of documents typed in Cyrillic letters and a thumb drive. Cholmondeley looked up; the Lincoln had advanced a single car length and stopped, gridlocked. He ran to it through the rain and rapped on the right rear window. It slid open crack.

"Who is this from?"

"I tol' you; you vill know and it vill make good story for talafishion."

"I can't accept unsourced material."

"Read papers, look at wideo. You vill see. You vill understand."

"I can't read Russian, if that's what it is."

"I tell you not open envelope here on strit. You don' listen. Not jus' Russian. Some een Ukrainian, too."
"That's neither here nor there, I can't use this if I don't know the source. I don't know your name or your connection to this."

"My name? Don't metter. It's Henrietta Krajewski. I am just delivery gerl. I could be giffing you fake name. You don't know."

"Delivery girl for whom?"

"You know who ess Volodymyr Zelenskyy?"

A space opened in the next lane and the Lincoln's driver lurched into it. Traffic loosened a little and the SUV lumbered north four car lengths. Cholmondeley did not follow it into the middle of the street.

*

In his office he laid out the contents of the envelope. The documents were printed on A4 paper, not American letter-sized paper; that likely meant they were brought to New York already printed. That was not very good spycraft; papers were harder to hide than a thumb drive.

They appeared to be in Russian, despite Henrietta Krajewski identifying the Ukrainian president as their source; he recognized the word Россия — Rossiya — in the address blocks of some of them. One had a Санкт-Петербург address, which he took to be St. Petersburg. The other had a Moscow address; he recognized the word Москва.

The thumb drive was a standard Chinese-made SanDisk Cruzer Glide with a 256-gigabyte capacity. He hesitated to insert it into his laptop's USB port; it might be a Trojan horse, bearing a virus that could take down the whole News Corp computer system. He called IT and asked for someone to collect and vet the thumb drive. Then he called the news desk and asked where he could find a reliable and discreet Russian-speaker to translate the documents.

*

It took the remainder of that day and the next full day before IT tested the SanDisk Cruzer, certified it was virus-free and returned it. They reported there were ten PDF files and five video files on the thumb drive. By that time a translator had been found, vetted, and signed a confidentiality agreement. The translator said eight of the nine documents were in Russian, one was in Ukrainian. They had to find and vet another translator for the Ukrainian document. It turned out to be a cover letter, explaining that the Russian-language contents had been purloined by Ukrainian agents in the Russian Federation and were being delivered to News Corp for publication.

The Russian-language documents were two laboratory reports and sworn and notarized affidavits from seven individuals. The video files were the output of four separate cameras secreted in walls and fixtures of a suite in the Moscow Ritz-Carlton. A fifth video file was a six-minute edited version that combined the output of the four cameras. The visible matching time code on the four cameras indicated the edited video was a faithful, real-time version of what had transpired.

Cholmondeley, The Proprietor, Peterson from Fox News, Winsome from the Post and Robinson from the Wall Street

Journal and four News Corp lawyers watched the videos in Murdoch's office.

The edited video began with an introduction that had been recorded at another time: three woman, two blondes and a brunette were standing shoulder-to-shoulder in front of a pale blue flat. They were of approximately equal height, young and beautiful in a near-anorexic fashion model way. They were framed from head to waist. They wore dark blouses of different colors, unbuttoned sufficiently to prove the absence of brassieres. Each wore an identical Slavonic cross on a chain long enough for the third, slanted crossbar to be pressed between the inner curves of their breasts. Their makeup was minimal. The brunette was on the left, the blondes were next to each other, center and right.

The brunette spoke in a husky voice, her English heavily accented: "Vat you vill see ess true wideo of event vif my frients chere and me dot heppen vif Donald J. Trump een Ritz-Carlton Hotel, Moskva, de night ef nine Novemba, two tousant tirteen, so help me Godt." And here a slender hand reached up and touched the cross between her breasts, pulling the fabric of her blouse a little further apart and affording a view of a few more millimeters of very white flesh.

The video cut to the clandestine cameras. First there was a wide-angle shot from a camera placed inside the suite, aimed at the front door. The door opened and a younger, grinning Donald Trump stepped in, his arm around the brunette. They were followed by the blondes. The quartet exploded into the room, the women laughing and gesturing, even doing some dance steps to imagined music. The audio was indistinct: just laughter and four people talking at once, the three women in Russian, Trump in English.

The women dropped their fur jackets immediately upon entering. Trump was wearing a long, dark overcoat, a blue suit and yellow tie. He kept his coat on. Under their jackets the women wore glittery minidresses of different shades. They looked as if they'd just stepped out of a disco.

The riotous quartet moved off camera to the right and the video cut to another wide-angle view from a camera that appeared to have been planted above the headboard of a huge bed. It might have been in the frame of a picture centered above the bed.

The door burst opened and the quartet danced into the bedroom. Trump now dropped his overcoat to the floor. One of the blondes picked it up, brushed it with her hand, took it to the closet and hung it up, speaking what they took to be Russian all the while. She seemed to be admonishing him for tossing his coat so carelessly.

The other women were already shedding their clothing; a quick procedure because neither wore undergarments. The coat-hanging blonde shed her dress, too. All three kept their spike-heeled shoes on. Their casually tossed minidresses littered the floor.

The brunette pushed Trump into an overstuffed chair facing the foot of the bed, knelt in front of him and began untying his shoes.

The point of view cut to a wide-angle camera implanted in the ceiling. The brunette was working on Trump's shoes. The blondes kicked off their high heels, climbed on the bed and began jumping up and down like kids at play.

The brunette was saying something to Trump and in response, he tried to struggle out of his suit jacket. She helped him, then pulled down his tie and opened his collar. The audio wasn't clear; individual words were hard to distinguish. She was speaking a mixture of English and Russian, and he was talking at the same time. The bed-bouncing blondes were also speaking and laughing, turning the soundtrack into bilingual babble.

The blondes stopped bouncing on the bed, embraced and kissed with a passion that was phony even in a wide-angle overhead shot. The brunette had Trump's belt open, zipped down his fly and stuck an exploratory hand into his pants. She found what she was looking for and exclaimed VOT! — Russian for Here *it* is! That was the first clear word on the audio track. Her head blocked the camera from seeing the *it* she had discovered.

The video cut to the fourth camera which was planted somewhere to the right of the armchair — in a wall-mounted TV set perhaps — it started wide and began to zoom in on

Trump and the brunette. She was holding *it* in her right hand, inches from her face. She said loudly, "Ya delayu tebe minet." A subtitle on the screen helpfully translated: "I give blowjob."

She did.

The video cut to the wide-angle camera above the headboard. The two blondes were performing unconvincing oral sex on each other on the bed in the foreground and the brunette was going down on Trump in the background. This camera began to zoom past the stagey girl-on-girl activity on the bed settling on a closer view of the brunette's bobbing head.

The video went back to the profile shot. The brunette's head snapped back and she exclaimed, "Uzhe!" Helpful subtitle: "Already!" The brunette spat into the palm of her left hand and closed her fist.

It was obvious to the viewers in The Proprietor's office she was preserving a specimen.

The camera above the headboard was back on its wide shot and the two blonds were up now, half squatting as they peed on the bed. In the background Trump was applauding while the brunette appeared to be busy wiping her left hand with a handkerchief, carefully folding it and stuffing it into her tiny purse before turning to Trump and stuffing *it* back in his pants.

The video ended as it began, with the three women in front of the blue flat. The brunette said, "I yam proud for vhat I did ven I vas young gerl for my country. Ve do vhat ve must. De semple I take from Meesta Trump I gif to laboratory in Moskva and laboratory in St. Petersburg for DNA to prove not imposta but real Meesta Trump. Laboratory prove just dot. Both of dem prove same. Ess Meesta Trump you see vatch girlie show and get mouth sex. I swear."

And again, her slender hand found the Slavonic cross in its fleshy nest.

The Russian-language translator had produced English versions of DNA reports from a Moscow lab and from a St. Petersburg lab attesting that the DNA from a semen sample delivered to them less than 24 hours after the purported scene in the hotel suite exactly matched the DNA from a hair sample taken from a hairbrush owned by Donald J. Trump.

Also translated: seven sworn affidavits from four women and three men. The woman were a maid at the Moscow Ritz-Carlton, who swore she had collected hairs from a hairbrush used by Trump, and the three prostitutes, attesting that what was seen on the video was real. The men were two camera technicians and a video editor. The technicians swore they had remotely operated the two cameras that had zoomed in on the action. They attested to the veracity of the video. The editor's deposition swore that he had neither added nor subtracted content and that the visible time code in the edited piece identically matched the time code on the recording cameras.

The Ukrainian-language document was an attestation that agents of the Ukrainian government had obtained the videos and documents from sources in Russia and were presenting them to News Corp in the interest of transparency.

No one in the room believed for a minute that the material came from anywhere but Russia.

The Proprietor said, "Recommendations? Anyone?"

For a pregnant moment none of the eight other men in his office had anything to say. Cholmondeley looked around, saw one of the lawyers start to open his mouth and jumped in before the attorney could tell The Proprietor why he couldn't use the material.

"We have no choice but to run something," Cholmondeley said.

All eyes were on The Proprietor. When he nodded in assent, the others fell all over themselves seconding Cholmondeley's recommendation. Even the lawyers were on board having seen their client's preference.

Seb Winsome, the Post editor, was a veteran of 30 years of British tabloids. In the past he had hacked phones, bribed witnesses, blackmailed others and used threats of physical violence to get stories. If anyone knew how to handle and promote sleaze, it was Seb.

"First, I say if this came from Ukraine, I will kiss your ass in front of St. Patrick's Cathedral before midday Mass on Easter Sunday. This has Vladimir Putin written all over it. Next, I say we can't *not* go with it. I mean we've all seen video of the bloke getting his knob slobbered. He's the fucking president of a country! How can we not report it?"

"I expected you would say that," The Proprietor said. "pretty much in those very words. Anyone else?"

Cholmondeley, so bold when he was cutting off a lawyer's anticipated objection, now raised a tentative hand, as if he were in class seeking recognition from the teacher. Murdoch nodded at him.

"If we don't use it, they will leak it to someone who will. And I agree it has Putin's fingerprints all over it. Question is why did he turn on Trump? Did it have to do with that missiles-in-Texas story?"

"We'll likely never know," The Proprietor said.

Peterson, a Fox News vice president who owed his more-than-comfortable lifestyle to catering to Trump's cult of personality, said, "It *is* Trump, you know. We've got so much invested in him. We better be careful...."

Seb Winsome cut him off, "Oh fuck him. He's held us hostage long enough. And it's not as if he didn't bring this on himself. You don't see those girls pointing a gun to his head, do you?"

The Proprietor had a gleeful smirk on his lips. His ancient eyes seemed to twinkle. "I think I hear a consensus. Do I hear a consensus?"

"May I say something, Mr. Murdoch?" It was Cholmondeley again; this time without the raised hand asking permission. "However we do this story, it is an indecent incident that we have to handle with decency. Obviously, we can't show the knob job or the girls taking a slash. But we must tell the story. So we either freeze the frame before the nasty bits are exposed or put some sort of blur over them. I think the bobbing head would be in very bad taste for TV. Pardon the pun, it was unintended. For print we run screen grabs with nasty bits blacked out. And I'd like to volunteer to write all versions. It is my story, after all."

"Your story in that someone handed it to you on the street," Seb said.

"Yes," Cholmondeley said, "People tell me things. They just come up to me and tell me things. It's the secret of my success."

"Goes without saying, Cholmondeley writes it, reports it on air, too." The Proprietor said. "It's your story in all outlets. You'll obviously have to write different versions: one for the Journal and the Times of London, a different one for The Post and The Sun. And I want you reporting it on camera on Fox News."

He turned to Peterson: "Assign your best producer and your best video editor to this piece. And I don't want a repetition of one of your trained seals challenging Mr. Cholmondeley. If any of your anchors has an objection to our reporting the story, I don't want them sharing the screen with Mr. C. They're free to express their reservations later, but I will not have them challenging his reporting, even if he is falsely modest about it and says people just tell him things. We know better. Everyone in this room knows the story is true; we've all seen the man having his dick sucked by a Russian whore. We also know to just short of a certainty that it did not come from Ukraine and the Ukrainian letter is a false flag. Cholmondeley, work that in; we're not Putin's messengers here. There is no doubt that this happened."

He paused to let that sink in. "Jesus, when is Donald Trump going to stop embarrassing his friends, let alone the whole country?"

Murdoch waited for one of them to supply a date. No one did, "Well, that's it, then. Peterson, understand that I will brook no challenging of the facts here. Is that clear?"

Peterson joined the chorus of "Yeses."

"Good. Cholmondeley, get going. I want this in the first edition of every paper and on Fox News in prime time. That means you've very little time to make the UK papers, so write those stories first. The Times story will work for the Wall Street Journal with just a bit of editing. The Sun story should work for The Post, just make it shorter for The Post. Write the two print stories first and then concentrate on the Fox piece. This breaks tonight on Fox News and is in every edition of every paper tomorrow."

"Don't we need to ask Mar-a-Lago for comment before we publish and broadcast?" It was one of the lawyers. "You *are* publishing in the Times of London and the Wall Street Journal. Highly respectable papers. It's their practice to never publish without first seeking comment from all participants."

"Hell, no," The Proprietor said. "I'm not giving him a chance to get out in front of this story."

Peterson tried one more time: "How does this make us look? We've backed him to the hilt since he started winning primaries in 2015. And now we're showing video and stills of him getting head in Moscow? How does that make us look?"

"Like journalists," Murdoch said.

He turned to Cholmondeley. "Well, Walter, get going. The UK papers are off stone in two and a half hours. Less than that; not even two and a half. Fox News needs the story in four."

"On it," Cholmondeley said.

When he got back to his desk, his iPhone buzzed. It was a text message from The Proprietor: "Did not want to say front of others. Giving U £25K bonus for this scoop. Many thanx." Murdoch added two thumbs-up emojis.

◆ ◆ ◆

I'm also honored to have the greatest temperament that anybody has. — Donald J. Trump

The 45/1 Office, Mar-A-Lago, Palm Beach, Florida, Great States Of America

There was nothing on the presidential desk; no papers, no pens, no Diet Cokes, no telephones -- not even the white Putin ring-down phone with the LED light where the keypad should have been.

In a blind fury, Trump had thrown everything to the floor. Behind the desk, he had emptied the bookshelves flinging books, trophies, mementos, bric-a-brac and framed photos everywhere. The coffee table between the two couches was on its side, victim of a violent kick. Food stains from a thrown lunch marked the walls; plate shards littered the floor beneath them.

Trump had pulled the portrait of Andrew Jackson astride a rearing horse from the wall and punched Old Hickory's face, leaving a five-inch tear in the canvas.

A fire burned in the metal waste basket alongside the desk and Trump was feeding it crumpled balls of paper.

The smoke detector went off as Mike Flynn ran into the office.

Trump acted surprised to see him, "What the fuck! Why the fuck are you here?"

Flynn did not answer. He strode up to the desk, lifted the burning trash basket and ran it into the president's private bathroom. He dumped the flaming paper into the sink and opened the faucets, extinguishing the flames. The bathroom filled with smoke. Flynn emerged, coughing, shaking his burned hands.

Trump screamed so Flynn would hear him over the wailing fire alarm: "Why the fuck are you here? Who said you could come into my office uninvited?"

"I'm your chief of staff, Excellency," Flynn shouted back. "And Rosalind called me. Said you were tearing up your office. She didn't say you were burning the place down, too"

Flynn crossed to the French doors and opened them. A warm, damp breeze blew in, rustling the papers littering the floor.

Somewhere in the building, a technician silenced the alarm. Trump moved beyond his arson rage to its source: "They ran it. HE ran it. That stinking Aussie bastard cocksucker antique fucker double-crossed me. He ran the story in all his papers. Fox News, for Christ's sake, ran the video. Some of it. They ran me getting blown. Blown! Who'd of thought they would run a blowjob on TV? Blocked out the girls' tits and my joint, but you knew what was happening. I'm gonna kill him. And that limey bastard reporter, Chump-lee, too."

"I saw," Flynn said. Of course he saw. Everyone in the GSA government had seen. By executive order, every TV set in every government office was tuned to Fox News 24 hours a day, seven days a week. Even though the channel played with the sound turned down or off in most locations, no one needed the narration or ambient audio to know what they were looking at. If there had been any doubt, a succession of lower-third chyrons spelled it out: "Trump in Moscow, 2013." "Trump With Moscow Prostitutes." "Russian Hooker and Trump, 2013." "Moscow Lez Show for Trump." "Trump, Hookers in Moscow Romp." And lower right on all these: "Breaking Fox News Exclusive!"

"It fucking happened in *2013*, how is that *breaking* news?" Trump's voice climbed an octave as he found another grievance. "That's not *news*. That's not *breaking*. It happened 15 years ago. Before I was even a candidate, much less a president. Breaking news is *new* news. Isn't that the definition of breaking news? Doesn't everybody know that? This was 15 fucking years ago, so it can't be *breaking* news."

"Thirteen years ago," Flynn said. "Not fifteen; thirteen. Just deny it, Excellency. Deny it all. Say the video's phony. Say it's an actor. Or it's CGI."

"A CGI gets a blowjob?" Trump had no idea that CGI stood for computer-generated imagery.

"Why not? You told them to ignore what they were seeing on TV before. Tell 'em to ignore it; fake news."

"It *is* fake news. It was thirteen years ago. So that's not new. Something's gotta be *new* to be news. And especially *breaking* news." Trump warmed to Flynn's suggestions. "Besides, that's not me. The whole video is fake. Those girls; they're CGIs. The guy in the chair, he's a CGI."

Flynn said, "Excellency, it's me, your chief of staff. I'm on your side here. Don't bother trying to convince me, just deny it to *them*, boss. They'll believe you; they always do."

"This is different, Mike, don't you see? I tell 'em to ignore the failing New York Times or crooked CNN, sure, they're all in for that. The Bezos Washington Post. Any one of them. They listen to me. But this is *Fox*. Fox, for Chrissakes.

This is the one they watch. This is the one supported me for so long."

He seemed to have forgotten how Murdoch had briefly turned on him in 2022, calling on him to "move on" while he was on his stolen election fantasy tour.

"Fox, Mike, *Fox*. *My* Fox. My people believe it when it's on Fox. How to I tell them not to believe Fox?"

"Excellency, it's just not the same Fox it once was. Tell them that. Tell them the old man, he's senile or something. I mean, look what he married. I don't know what she is, but the base, they gotta be freaking out about her. The kid, Murdoch's kid. Lavin, Latvin — is that his name? He's the one running the operation, not the old man. Say he's a Democrat or a commie. Say *he*, the kid, hired that BBC guy. Right? Go on the offensive; the best defense is an offense. George Washington, himself, said that."

"I thought it was Vince Lombardi."

"Probably was, but Washington said it first. You gotta attack, attack, attack. Go after them. Go after the Democrat son."

"That's the other son," Trump said. "The one with all the causes. He even raised money for Biden in '22, that one."

"No matter," Flynn said. "Go after Lavin, or Latvin, whatever he's called. Go after the BBC guy."

"He's a Fox guy now."

"Doesn't metter," Flynn said. "He's British, isn't he? Not an American. Your people, they'll believe you before they believe their eyes and they sure as shooting shit will believe you before they believe some British guy. Attack Fox for faking the video and the story. Call it fake. CGI. And then, while you're at it, throw Tucker under the bus. Put him in the crosshairs. Only reason Fox attacked you is to promote Carlson."

"Are you seeing what I'm seeing? I'm seeing light at the end of this fucking tunnel."

"Yessir, Excellency. Here's the way to handle the whole mess: First, have Anita and her crew put out a denial that that's you in the Fox story. Have her say it's actors. Or CGI. We gotta make up our minds on that; it's one or the other, can't be both. Okay you've created doubt about the Fox story, about the BJ and the bed-pissing. Good. Now, two, we supply them with a reason why anyone would do that. For that we put it on Carlson. Release the audio of Carlson and Putin. Now it looks like Putin's serving Carlson's interest in framing you with the fake hooker tape. I mean, where else could it have come from if not from Putin and the Ruskies?"

"The Ukraine?" Trump asked.

"Forget Ukraine. It's Putin."

"Putin," Trump said. "Putin and Murdoch both double-crossing me."

"Of course. Putin's fucking with you and Carlson's gonna pay him back, give him what we kept Miller from giving him: the missile bases in Texas. See? Putin and Carlson, in cahoots. It was Putin released the video to discredit you and put Carlson in Mar-a-Lago. By this time, no one's paying attention to the blowjob and the pissing hookers anymore. Now all they can think of is Carlson's treason. See the logic here? Putin wants missiles in Texas. Miller would have given him the missiles, so you fired Miller."

"Fired? I had him fucking arrested. Locked up!"

"Exactly, Excellency. Then Putin goes to Carlson with the same missile plan. For it to work, Carlson's got to replace you. So, Carlson and Putin, they enlist Murdoch. The old man's too soft in the brain to know he's being used. The son, Lavin, he's a red, so he's on board with the plan. You got them all."

"Yes. We got them all," Trump said.

"We arrest who we can," Flynn said. "No problem laying our hands on Carlson — here's right here in the GSA. We can pick him up in a minute. Hell, I can have his WORM detail arrest him right now. Murdoch, well, that's tougher; he's in the Atlantic States most of the time. He's got that ranch in Montana, so if he ever goes there, we grab him up. The son, who the hell knows where he is. And Putin, he's another matter. He's in Moscow; we can't get to him."

Flynn liked Carlson; the commentator had always had the general's six. And there was the possibility that if Carlson somehow became president, he might supply Flynn the eight brigades he needed to invade the Pacific States. But he needed a scapegoat now and Carlson was the closest plausible candidate.

"Where's my Putin phone? I gotta talk to him. He's the one started this fucking clusterfuck. Rupert and that BBC guy didn't find that video on their own. Putin's the one gave it to them. Where'd I throw that fucking phone?"

That was the first Flynn knew of the Trump-Putin hotline. "Is it the white one from your desk? I think I saw it over by the door," he pointed.

"That's the one."

Flynn retrieved the phone. The plastic plug had been torn off when Trump pulled the phone out of the wall. The plug on the handset cord was also damaged.

"We'll get that repaired," Flynn said. "Don't worry, I'll have you guys talking in no time. Maybe I should be in here with you when you talk to him. Help out a little. I know the fucker; met him, you know."

"Changed my mind," Trump said. "Putin fucked with me; now I get to fuck with him. Issue an alert. I'm done talking to that Russian double-crosser."

"An alert, Excellency? What kind of alert."

"Any kind. Just issue an alert. Who needs that fucking Putin? I don't need him. He needs me more than I need him. Just issue an alert!"

"An alert, yes, Excellency." Flynn came up with something because he had to: "How about a fake news alert?"

"Is there such a thing?" Trump asked.

"There is if we say there is," Flynn said. "We make it seem like we've been doing it all along. Ever since 2017."

"That's it. That's *it*! An emergency fake news alert. Get the communications office on it right away. Have Anita issue it in your name; it'll have more credibility. You're not on the video."

"Consider it done, Excellency."

"And arrest Carlson. Throw him in that lockup at the DLO. He's been disloyal. He's a traitor to me. And to my country."

When Flynn got back to his office, he picked up his desk phone to order Carlson's arrest. That's when an alert buzzed on his iPhone. He dug it from his pocket; the alert was from Q. Flynn dropped the desk phone and opened the Qanon app.

◆ ◆ ◆

*My whole life is about winning. I don't lose often.
I almost never lose. — Donald J. Trump*

The Internet Research Agency, St. Petersburg, Russian Federation

Four hours earlier, Sofia Ivanova Pushkina gave the finishing touches to her team's masterpiece. The concept was hers, but she had allowed the whole group to write the first draft. It was a racehorse designed by a committee — it looked like a camel.

After three rewrites by the team and one by her, she was happy with the result. She translated the English-language original into Russian and sent it to Vladimir Vladimirovitch as an encrypted attachment to an email.

An hour later, he was on the phone. "Sofia Ivanova, this is a masterpiece. Give me an hour, two. Two hours. I'll alert the security and intelligence services. Then have Q issue it."

"Thank you, Sudar Putin. On behalf of my department, I am honored."

"Sudar, again? Please, no archaic formality."

Two hours later, Q distributed this to the select few of his followers who had the Qanon app on their phones:

"The One True Trump, embodiment of God's will on earth, is dead. President Donald J. Trump of the Great States of America, former President of the United States of America, was murdered several weeks ago by a team of 'doctors' from The Ukraine who had been summoned to deal with a fictitious medical condition, metastatic prostate cancer.

"The BBC and other leftist Western media outlets reported that President Trump was afflicted with prostate cancer, but that was untrue, a fake story propagated by The Ukraine and its globalist elite allies.

"Fifth columnists within Mar-a-Lago, headed by the secret globalist, Stephen Miller, substituted fake Ukrainian medical reports for Trump's real examination results and the team of Ukrainian 'doctors' was called in to treat The Trump.

"The 'doctors' on the team were actually assassins and they killed our revered leader. Trump never had cancer or any other disease.

"Q sources in New York State report Mrs. Trump was not told of her beloved husband's death until a week after his life was taken. She is being held incommunicado by the globalists at a secure location in the Atlantic States.

"Quisling traitors in the Great States of America, in the secret employ of President Jon Stewart of the Atlantic States, have hired an actor, Sylvester Simmons, to play the role of Mr. Trump. It was Simmons who addressed the three rallies in four days recently and who attended the military parade on Collins Avenue in Miami Beach.

"Simmons, who at first had only a slight resemblance to the GSA president, had multiple plastic surgeries to enhance that resemblance. An accomplished mimic, Simmons mastered the tone and cadence of Trump's speaking style so well that even close staffers were fooled into thinking they are interacting with the real president. But the deception is proven by these photos of Trump's and the imposter's ear lobes. It is impossible to perform cosmetic surgery on ear lobes and the actor, Simmons, has ear lobes that are very different from Trump's. See the photos below."

Below that paragraph were photographs of two very differently shaped ear lobes, the one on the right purporting to be Trump's right ear, the one on the left was captioned as Simmons' right ear. In fact, they were photos taken of the ear lobes of two men in Sofia Ivanova's department. No one in the Internet Research Agency had any idea what Trump's ear lobes looked like, and they gambled that no one else would know, either.

The Q post continued: "Trump's body was cremated in order to prevent forensic examination which would prove the cause of death. His ashes were thrown into the Atlantic Ocean or were buried somewhere in Florida, possibly on the Mar-a-Lago grounds.

"Mr. Trump's children, especially son, Eric, who he had designated as his successor as president of the GSA, have not been told of his death but have also been kept away from the imposter, Simmons, because Simmons' handlers believe that the Trump children will spot the imposter.

"While Simmons and his masters work to undermine the Great States of America, those of us who cherish the memory of The Trump, must rise up and defeat Jon Stewart, J.D. Pritzker, the Nazi Ukraine president, Volodymyr Zelenskyy, and George Soros. They, and their bought-and-paid-for toady, Gavin Newsom are committed to undermining the independence of the GSA and turning it into a pedophilia playground."

*

Sofia's great-grandfather, Ivan Ivanovitch Pushkin, author of "The Protocols of the Elders of Zion," would have been proud of her. In her fiction four Zhyds and a useful idiot gentile had murdered Trump. Or, as Stepan Arkadyevich Oblonsky would have it, The Trump.

All that was missing from the Q post was the plotters drinking Trump's blood or using it to make matzoh. But even she would not go that far.

The last two paragraphs of "Q's" message read: "We are the armed people. And this is the moment we have been arming ourselves for. Now is the time to take action against Stewart, Pritzker, Newsom and all those so-called journalists and Democrat politicians who are determined to destroy the moral compass of our nation and subvert the GSA into becoming a corrupt, Godless puppet of the other republics.

"We cannot stand idly by and let the Atlantic States of America and the other "republics" destroy everything Trump created for us. The time for action is now! Lock and load; avenge The Trump, take down the fake."

◆ ◆ ◆

Throughout my life, my two greatest assets have been mental stability and being, like, really smart. — Donald J. Trump

45/1 Office, Mar-A-Lago, Palm Beach, Florida
Great States Of America

Rosalind found a single line phone in a janitorial room and brought it into the wreckage of the president's office.

Despite all his "Fuck Putins" to Flynn, Trump needed to talk to his brother.

Trump plugged the phone into the wall and lifted the handset. The line sounded open, but he heard no voice.

"Vladimir? You there? Vladimir?

Putin answered. "My brother, I was going to call you. Do you know Rivieria Beach Marina in West Palm Beach?"

"Never heard of it."

"Find it. Fast. And get there. Fast. Get to Riviera Beach Marina in West Palm Beach! Immediately! Boat is waiting for you there, black hull with red deck. Pier 6. Go now; you are in danger. Q turned on you. With video out on television and Q telling your followers to lock and load — those are words Q uses, lock and load — there is big danger, very big danger. Q people will be out for blood. Your blood, my brother."

Trump protested. And lied: "Wait. The video was fake. CGI. That wasn't me, that was a CGI. Imposters. Models. Actors. Porn actors. Cartoons. It wasn't me. You, of all people, know it wasn't me."

Putin, of all people, knew it *was* Trump. In 2013, he had set the kompromat campaign in motion, exactly as he had set a dozen similar plans in motion. He had personally viewed videos of twenty women before selecting the Trump honeytraps. If he was not the writer-director of the video, he was certainly its producer.

Putin continued, an unusual urgency in his voice: "Your supporter, Q, you lost him. Or her." Let Trump chew on that possibility, that Q was a woman!

"Q reports you died weeks ago. Killed by Ukrainians. Ukrainian doctors. He — or she — says imposter replaced you; imposter works for Jon Stewart. Is very dangerous for you now. Qanon people are armed; you know that better than anybody. They are loyal to Q and to Trump but if they thinking Trump is dead, this is very bad for you, my brother. For us is bad. This is dangerous. A lot of bodyguards, your WORM people, are Q people, too. Send the one you call Fat Jimmy Gibbons to your golf course to distract, then go to Marina. Pier 6."

How did Putin know about Fat Jimmy Gibbons? Trump had not told him he had a body double.

"Say nothing to no one. Bring documents we discuss to Marina. Two boxes you have still. Bring boxes. And come alone. No staff; no family."

"Of course," Trump lied; he had no intention of coming alone.

How to activate Fat Jimmy Gibbons? Miller had taken care of that in the past. "Rosalind," he shouted, "Do you know how to get that fat guy who plays me sometimes? Do you know how to get him to go somewhere?"

She stepped into the office. "I have a memo on it from Miller. I assume it's still operative," she said.
"Okay," Trump said. "Here's what I need...."

◆ ◆ ◆

This is what winning looks like! — Donald J. Trump

Executive Offices, Mar-A-Lago, Palm Beach, Florida, Great States Of America

There were more than a dozen Qanon true believers in the Mar-a-Lago executive offices. Throughout the upper ranks of the GSA there were perhaps a thousand more. But none of them was closer to Trump in physical propinquity than Michael Flynn, the chief of staff. Their offices were fifty-five paces apart — Flynn had silently counted the steps to secure accurate bragging rights.

Flynn's wholehearted embrace of Q's Niagara of "facts," and conspiracy theories, was inconceivable to those who had served with him in the Army, where his disciplined and analytic mind had earned him the three stars of a major general. Yet now he was enthralled by a fictitious conspiracist with insufficient imagination to manufacture more than a single letter for a name. Flynn was one of the handful of GSA leaders who had the Qanon VIP early-warning alert app on his iPhone. He read Q's revelation about Trump's death slowly; as he read, he muttered "Holy shit. Holy shit."

When he put down his iPhone, he asked himself how it could possibly be true. He had been talking to Trump — The Trump — minutes ago. The man was 55 steps away. He'd been with him on countless occasions; he saw him every day. How, he asked himself, could he have missed that ear lobe thing?

The man he served, The Trump, the embodiment of God's will, had been played by a substitute for weeks and he, Flynn, had not noticed. But now, suspicious events were coming to the fore. The incident at the Collins Avenue parade, when "Trump" left the tent because it got too hot? Trump would never retreat in the face of heat.

And the reports of "Trump" passing out from dehydration after the rally at AT & T Stadium? That rang false, too. Flynn had not been there, but how, he now asked himself, did a man who consumed 14 Diet Cokes a day get dehydrated? It was impossible. Clearly "Trump," the impostor, couldn't match the real Trump's soft-drink consumption.

Flynn reached for his desk phone, then decided, no, not that one. Not the official land line. *They* — whoever they were — might be monitoring it. In fact, *they* were certain to be monitoring it. He had probably ordered the monitoring himself, when Miller occupied the office, although he could not specifically remember doing it. They could be monitoring calls from his iPhone, too. He took the burner phone from his top drawer. This would be secure; he'd gotten it himself from a mobile phone store in a West Palm Beach mini-mall. His first call was to the armory. He lucked out; two companies of Florida Army National Guard Rangers were drilling at that moment. He ordered them to arm themselves and head for Mar-a-Lago. He ordered the commander of the unit to halt half a mile from the destination and call him for further instructions.

Then he called Tucker Carlson.

"Mr. Vice President, General Mike Flynn here." His former Army rank always impressed candy-ass civilians who had never served.

"What does *he* want?" Carlson was suspicious; Flynn would only call at Trump's behest.

Flynn played his best card, the truth as he knew it: "What he wants, Mr. Vice President, is for me to have you arrested for dealing with Putin. For that phone call with Putin." Flynn said.

Carlson played it cagey. "What phone call? I've never spoken to Putin in my life."

"You have and I've heard the conversation. And so has The Boss. Only it wasn't Trump that heard it."

"You're not making any sense, General."

See? Candy-ass civilians are always impressed with stars on shoulders. Flynn's basking in Carlson's respect lasted only a second; he realized he was beginning the story in the middle; Carlson was ignorant of the truth; the VP did not have Qanon's early-warning alert app.

"Let me bring you up to speed, sir. I think we've all been noticing that the president hasn't been acting like himself for a while. You know, he's irritable, impulsive, angry all the time."

To Carlson, that was Trump acting like himself. But he said nothing.

"Turns out, Trump died a month or so ago. Qanon just made it public, but my internal intelligence agents had worked this up about a week ago." Flynn was winging it; lying to ensure that Carlson would find him irreplaceable once he took over the presidency from Trump's stand-in.

Flynn continued: "We were hoping to handle this quietly, except now Q made it public and people all over the world will know soon."

Trump dead? This was news to Carlson. "You've been with him repeatedly. You see him every day, several times a day. You know he's not dead, Mike."

"The ear lobes, Mr. Vice President. You know from the ear lobes."

Carlson laughed.

"Not funny, Mr. Vice President. The president, President Trump, he died. Not of the cancer, that was fake news. Some people in the executive branch — Stephen Miller, according to Q, was one of 'em — they had Ukrainian doctors come in to take care of a medical problem, but they weren't doctors, they were medical assassins. They have those in Ukraine. Teams of them. Medical assassins. Very skilled. Ever since they killed Trump, Miller and those others, they've had an actor playing him. For quite a while now. He had me fooled until I looked at a photo of the real President Trump's ear lobes and compared them with the actor in the 45/1 Office."

"Ear lobes? Really? Ear lobes?"

"They can't do plastic surgery on ear lobes. The actor, he had all kinds of cosmetic surgery, but it's impossible to alter ear lobes. So last time I was in the 45/1 Office, which was a couple of minutes ago, I compared the guy wearing Trump's suit and impersonating Trump with the real Trump's ear lobes and that was enough for me."

Flynn was lying with enthusiastic abandon now: "I was working on an orderly transition: arrest the imposter, do the DNA testing thing, find out who he really is. I was going to involve you in all of it, since constitutionally you're the first in line to become president, no matter what he wants to do for his son. For Eric. Who, by the way, doesn't even want to be president."

Carlson had heard his share of conspiracy theories. As a Fox News personality, he had embraced and amplified more than a few of them himself. But what Flynn was talking about went beyond conspiracy theory into certifiable lunacy.

"You're calling to tell me Trump wanted me arrested, but it's not Trump and you were getting ready to do what, exactly…."

"It was a plot by the other republics, Mr. Vice President. Technically, I should be calling you Mr. President. Or Excellency, if you prefer that."

"I'm not the president."

"Actually, you are, even though you haven't been sworn in. The president dies, the Vice President immediately becomes the president. So you're Mr. President. Or Excellency, if you like that better."

"Mr. President will do."

"Remember that speech in Dallas where he said he would reunify the country? Well, that was the actor, and the other presidents – Stewart and the others – they control him. The actor gets the base to go along with reunification then the actor steps down and you've got Jon Stewart or that druggie in California as president of the Re-United States of America."

"And tell me again how you were going to stop this…."

"Mr. President, I was getting ready to arrest the imposter and see to it you didn't get arrested and that you get your rightful office. If you wanted to keep me on as chief, fine. If not, I realize you have your own people who are loyal to you and who you're loyal to, so I would help in the transition and go away, no hard feelings. Before I could act, it got out from Q. You should check out their report. It's everything intelligence agencies had discovered; totally accurate."

Carlson was having trouble believing any of it. He asked, "So what now? Now that it's out? You say Q reported it. You *do* know, of course, that many if not most of the WORMs follow Q? What if one or more of them takes the law into their own hands? How are you going to control them?"

"Sir, I've got two companies of Florida National Guard Rangers on their way here to take control of the situation. We'll disarm the WORMs and arrest the imposter. We'll take specimens and do DNA testing. We'll interrogate him and learn who else to arrest. The imposter is a fat guy in piss-poor physical condition; it won't take much to get him talking."

MINE!

None of this was plausible to Carlson, but he saw an opportunity: have mad Mike Flynn take out Trump and make way for the Carlson presidency.

"Maybe you should do something before the rangers get there," Carlson suggested.

"What? Arrest him myself? I might have to shoot my way into the 45/1 Office to get at him."

"But what if a WORM picks it up from Qanon and tries to take out the imposter before we've questioned him? It'll look like I staged a coup."

"You're right, Mr. Vice President. I mean Mr. President. I'll see what I can do."

"Yes. Arrest him. That's an order. Call me; keep me updated," Carlson said.

"You sit tight, Mr. President; I'll keep you posted, sir."

Flynn hung up, opened his bottom desk drawer and drew out his old Army-issue Colt .45 automatic. He slid out the magazine, checked to see it was a full load, then snapped it back in and chambered a round. He thumbed the safety off. Locked and loaded, Flynn was ready to avenge The Trump and take down the imposter, just as Q and President Carlson had ordered. If he had to, he would litter the hall with dead and wounded WORMs; if the imposter resisted, he would use force. Deadly force if necessary.

Gingerly, keeping his index finger away from the trigger, he nestled the gun into his pants at the small of his back. He hustled the 55 steps to the president's office. Strangely, there were no WORMs in the hallway. When he poked his head into the outer office, Rosalind said, "Golf."

"Golf? He was here five minutes ago," Quinn said. "When'd that happen? Was that on his schedule?"

"Spur of the moment. He's playing with Junior."

"*Donald* Junior? Since when is he on a golf-playing basis with Junior? Doesn't even talk to Junior."

"He just came up with it a minute, two minutes ago. Out of the blue."

From Q, Flynn knew that the imposter was steering clear of the Trump children. And the imposter must have known that Trump was on the outs with Junior ever since the eldest son had given that deposition to the January Sixth Select Committee. What was going on? Why would the imposter risk exposure by cozying up to an out-of-favor son?

"Son of a bitch!" Flynn shouted. "Junior's in on it."

Rosalind stared at him. "In on what?" she asked.

Flynn did not answer her. He saw it all: Junior was working with them, the fifth column. Doubtless, Kushner, Junior's brother-in-law was part of the cabal. Soros. The Rothchilds. Jon Stewart. Them! A fifth column in Mar-a-Lago and in the family. Of course!

"Chief?" Rosalind said. She was concerned; there was a mad caste to his face. "Chief?"

"They're all in on it," Flynn said. "All of them." He was working out how the pieces of the jigsaw fit together when his burner phone rang, interrupting his conspiracy fantasy.

"Flynn!"

"Sir, this is Captain Reynolds of the Florida National Guard, reporting for duty. You asked that we call when we were half a mile from Mar-a-Lago."

"Change of plan, Reynolds. Send one unarmed vehicle to Mar-a-Lago to pick me up and turn the rest of the convoy around. We're heading for The Boss's golf course in West Palm. Trump International. You know the place?"

"Yessir, I know the place, the golf course. Do we head over there directly or wait on you to join us."

"Wait for me," Flynn said. "Are you in the lead vehicle. Reynolds?"

"I am, sir."

"I'll ride with you. I want to be in the lead vehicle. Brief you as we go. I'll assume command. Any problem with that, Reynolds?"

"Nosir, no problems. Anything else I can do now while we're waiting on you?"

"Order your men to lock and load and be ready for action. I can't tell you any more about the mission except to say that we are going to make history today."

"Yessir!" Reynolds said. "History, sir."

◆ ◆ ◆

Can't you just shoot them? — Donald J. Trump

Trump International Golf Course, West Palm Beach, Florida, Great States Of America

Bewigged and made up to orange perfection, Fat Jimmy Gibbons emerged from the clubhouse and waved to the media pool 50 yards away. He wore too-tight tan slacks, tan-and-white spiked golf shoes and a white polo shirt.

Even with lenses zoomed out to their maximum, it was impossible to tell that the man waddling toward the armored Suburban wasn't President Trump. He waved again at the assembled media and gave them the Trump double thumbs-up sign. There was a WORM on either side of him and two more in the Suburban's front seat.

In front of the presidential SUV were four similar black Suburbans, behind it five more. The ambulance and the communications truck were stacked at the rear of the motorcade. Engines revved; the column of vehicles was ready for a fast exit.

It had been very last-minute. Fat Jimmy Gibbons had been in his windowless office in the basement, playing a computer game on his iPad when Rosalind phoned and instructed him to suit up in his Trump golf outfit and head out to Trump International in West Palm. Half an hour later, he was whiling away the time it would have taken Trump to play 9 quick holes and now he was heading toward the motorcade. He wondered where the real President Trump had gone. Attending to very serious business, no doubt.

As Fat Jimmy Gibbons climbed into the Suburban, Michael Flynn's convoy of Florida National Guard Rangers pulled up and the soldiers began piling out and running toward the motorcade, weapons at port arms. The WORMs, confused but ever ready to protect Trump, scrambled out of the motorcade vehicles, their weapons also at the ready.

A dozen news cameras were zooming in on the brewing confrontation. Still photographers broke from the media pen and ran toward the action.

That's when the presidential Suburban exploded. The bomb was attached to the vehicle's undercarriage.

The blast split the doors from the chassis and sent them flying to the sides where they brought down six WORMs.

The Rangers stopped and dropped to firing positions, but there was no enemy to shoot at, just dazed, wounded and bleeding WORMs.

The roof of the SUV had split open and orange flames roared skyward.

A chorus of screams rose from the media pen. WORMs were on the ground, writhing, wounded by shrapnel or severely burned.

One nervous guardsman began firing indiscriminately; others, unsure where the shooting was coming from, joined in. They brought down WORMs and some of the advancing photographers.

The Suburbans directly in front of and directly behind the destroyed presidential vehicle were aflame, the driver of the following vehicle pinned in the inferno by his seatbelt.

The driver of the lead vehicle managed to struggle out of the flames and was hit by lethal fire from the rangers.

The few WORMs who were left standing dropped their weapons and raised their hands in surrender.

Guard NCOs were shouting, "Cease fire! Cease fire!" But nervous guardsmen ignored the order and mowed down the surrendering WORMs.

Michael Flynn ran toward the flames, looking ridiculously out of place in his dark suit and red tie. His flopping Gucci loafers barely stayed on his feet. He had his Colt automatic in his hand.

"You're unner arrest," he shouted at the flaming Suburban. "Do not resist. You are unner arrest by the authority vested in me by Vice President Carlson. I mean President Carlson."

When he was close enough to feel the heat, he assumed a perfect two-handed shooter's stance, shouted "You are unner arrest," once more and emptied the clip into the flames.

The charred corpse of Fat Jimmy Gibbons did not respond.

The guardsmen stopped slaughtering WORMs; it was silent except for the sound of the fire and the screams of the burned and wounded.

Captain Reynolds ran up behind Flynn, his M-4 pointed at the chief of staff.

"Area secured. What now, sir? What do you want my men to do?"

Flynn turned from the flaming Suburban; he was sweating and breathing hard. He looked down the barrel of Reynolds' rifle. "Lower that weapon, soldier," he snarled.

Reynolds slung his M-4 over his shoulder. "Sorry, sir. First time in combat, sir."

"You only point a piece at someone if you're gonna shoot him."

"Yessir, I know that, sir. Sorry, sir. Anything else we can do, sir?"

Flynn spoke in a low voice: "Disarm the WORMs, get ambulances here for the wounded. Oh, and call President Carlson," he said. "Tell him to start planning his inauguration."

"Yessir!" Reynolds pulled an obsolete flip phone from one of his fatigue pockets.

"Excuse me, sir, would you happen to have a phone number for President Carlson?"

MINE!

◆ ◆ ◆

I play to people's fantasies. People may not always think big themselves, but they can still get very excited by those who do. That's why a little hyperbole never hurts. People want to believe that something is the biggest and the greatest and the most spectacular. I call it truthful hyperbole. It's an innocent form of exaggeration and a very effective form of promotion. — Donald J. Trump

Vice Presidential Residence And Office, Palm Beach, Florida, Great States Of America

Tucker Carlson unmuted the audio on the office TV. A full-screen billboard had appeared:

"AN OPINION

FROM FOX NEWS & NEWS CORP

SPECIAL CORRESPONDENT

WALTER CHOLMONDELEY."

Cholmondeley was on the Fox News set, an American flag graphic behind him — a visually-dissonant image once he started speaking in his rich, upper-class English voice: "Donald Trump is a liar. For Trump, lying is instinctive, reflexive, habitual. It is as natural as breathing and was just as vital to his life. The first book Trump is credited with having written is 'The Art of the Deal.' It should have been 'The Art of the Lie.'

"His statements, comments, observations, promises and exclamations are dependably untrue. Mendacity is the common currency of his human, business and political intercourse. He had built around himself a big, beautiful wall of lies.

"The Washington Post tried to keep score when he was President of the United States. They chronicled 30,500 demonstrable lies. That was a serious undercount because the newspaper was able to tally only Trump's public lies and not the falsehoods he told in private to his vice president, to his cabinet, to his staff, to his congressional allies, his political supporters, his donors and even his family members.

"He lied for political gain, financial profit because…."

Cholmondeley's microphone went dead mid-because and the screen filled with a "BREAKING NEWS" card.

There was dramatic music and Ann Bailey appeared on the screen, reporting from the golf course — the smoky wreckage of the presidential SUV in the frame behind her.

She was hyperventilating, but managed to announce that Donald J. Trump, President of the Great States of America, had been assassinated by a person or persons unknown who had planted a huge explosive device on the underside his armored vehicle. She was having trouble speaking.

MINE!

Her chin was quivering, and it appeared she was about to descend into hysterics.

Bailey struggled, caught her breath, got her mouth under control and continued: "Mr. Trump had come here to his golf course in West Palm Beach for a quick and unannounced round of golf. He had completed a shortened game — nine holes we were told — and had just climbed into the back of his Suburban SUV when a bomb exploded, instantly killing Mr. Trump and destroying the SUV.

"The resulting fire — which you can see is still smoldering behind me — was intense. Fox News cameraman Bobby Schwartz was rolling video at the time, and we have that for you now. A warning, this is a devastatingly large explosion and a man — not just any man, but the President of the GSA, Donald J. Trump — was killed in the blast and the subsequent fire. If you are sensitive or if there are children in the room with you, we urge you to take the proper precautions...."

Carlson's phone rang. "Yes?"

"Mr. President, Chief of Staff Flynn is calling."

"Put him on. Mike?"

"General Flynn, here, Mr. President, sir. Reporting on the assassination of the imposter. Someone — we have no idea who — blew up his vehicle."

"Yes, I know. It's on the news right now. On TV. What do we know about it? Was it a Q person?"

"Not much, Mr. President. we don't know much. My men and I got here to arrest him just as the IED blew. It was a huge bomb, sir. Big enough to take out a tank, I'd guess. Everyone's acting like it was the president got blown up. May I suggest, sir, we play along with that story. Say that it was Mr. Trump in the Suburban? It might be a lot simpler that way."

"I think you're right, Flynn. Thank you. But what's Q going to do about it? What's he going to say?"

"I dunno, Mr. President, but you can't have Q run your presidency, sir."

He'd been called "Mr. President" four times by two different people in the last two minutes; a man could get used to that.

◆ ◆ ◆

Sometimes by losing a battle you find a new way to win the war. — *Donald J. Trump*

Riviera Beach Marina, West Palm Beach, Florida, Great States Of America

Defying Putin, Trump had tried to bring along his eldest sons. Eric was out of the country, in New York, attending to Trump Enterprises business. Trump told him to stay there until he called in a few days. He explained nothing more; there was no telling who was listening. Eric would have to extract himself from North America soon and on his own, but that would be easier from The Atlantic States than from the GSA. In addition, Eric was safer in New York, where the weapons of choice for Trump's enemies were words and subpoenas, than he would be in Florida, where his friends-turned-enemies were armed with all manner of semi-automatic military-grade hardware.

Donald Jr was in Florida and was happy to hear from his father.

Lying with customary ease, Trump told Junior he had a new yacht that he wanted him to see and sail on. He said he was keeping it at the Riviera Beach City Marina so it wouldn't attract the attention of political enemies and spies from the other republics.

Junior drove himself to the Marina and as soon as he saw the boat, confirmed what he'd suspected: his father had lied to him. There was no yacht, just a getaway boat: a 60-foot-long open boat with a black hull and red-cushioned bench seating. Six outboard motors were attached to the stern transom. The boat had a windshield and short roof, but no cabin where Trump Senior could sequester to protect his hair from blowing in the wind.

Trump came clean with Junior: "It's not a yacht. It's a speedboat. I hate speedboats. I thought it was going to be a yacht, even a super yacht like those Russian guys, those oligarchs have. It's not mine, in any case. We're getting outta here. We're going to Cuba."

Before Junior could ask any questions, a WORM walked up to them, his XM-5 slung along across his belly because his were hands full; he held two orange life vests. "This one should fit you, Excellency." He handed a vest to Trump. On the inside collar it was marked XXX-Large. The WORM handed the other vest to Junior.

Trump struggled to get the vest on over his suit coat. Junior helped him.

"Can't close it," Trump muttered, as he pulled hard to close the vest over his belly.

"It's got straps that buckle, Daddy."

"Do yourself a favor and don't call me 'Daddy.' Makes you sound ten years old."

Trump snapped the straps closed. The life vest felt too tight.

"Dad, then. I'm not going to call you Excellency, you know."

"I never asked you to. 'Dad' is okay."

"Why are we going to Cuba?"

"Escaping. Everything's turned to shit. We're not staying in Cuba. We'll fly to Russia from there. Putin's sending a plane. It may already be there."

"Escaping from what? What turned to shit?"

"Don't you watch TV? Didn't you see the thing. About…. Never mind. The shitstorm turned to shit. We are escaping the shitstorm."

"I'm not going to Cuba, Dad, much less Russia."

"If you stay here, you're in danger. They'll come for you."

"Oh, bullshit. You're the president. No one's coming for you. Your people will stop them."

"I don't have people. Anymore. It's over. For now."

For the first time in his life, Junior saw his father crestfallen. Trump was no longer a puffed-up braggart, posturing aggressively and daring adversity to do its worst. This was a hollowed-out replica of his father. It stunned Junior. Was his own bravado equally vulnerable? Then, something more important than his bravado occurred to him:

"What about money? Are we leaving our money here? How will we get our money out, if we're in Russia?"

"It's already out. Eric's been transferring billions into a couple of Swiss banks. There's nothing to worry about on the money score."

"What about Eric? What about Ivanka and her family?"

"Eric's in New York. He'll join us when he can. He'll get away, no problem."

"Ivanka? Tiffany? Barron? Melania? There's more than just you and me, Dad."

"Melania and Barron are safe. Don't worry about them. They're real safe. Tiffany's in the Atlantic States, and she's on her own. She distanced from me, I distance from her. Ivanka and Jared? They're on their own, too. Jared, he knows what's what. The Saudis aren't gonna let anything happen to him. Got too much invested in him."

As they spoke, Trump waddled toward the boat, imaging he looked like an orange version of that Michelin guy made from tires, Beebop, or some such stupid name.

They were helped aboard by two WORMS. A small, elderly man dressed in what looked like a baggy U.S. Navy double-breasted dress blue officer's uniform, complete with white cap and gold scrambled egg markings on the visor greeted them. His uniform had no badges or patches, the brass buttons were mismatched and tarnished. The old guy was a fake officer in his very own fake navy.

"I'm Captain Kelly, your ride today, Excellency," he said.

"Ya know how to work this thing okay, Kelly?" Trump asked.

"Yessir, Excellency. She's my boat, a Cigarette Tirranna. I've made the Cuba run hundreds of times in her."

"Doing what? Nothing legal, am I right?" Trump winked at the old "captain."

"Smuggling out Cubans who don't want to live under Commies," "Captain" Kelly said.

"Good work," Trump said.

Although his political career had begun with a 2015 rant against illegal immigrants, Cubans fleeing their island were, to his mind, not immigrants. They were automatically legal entrants; they got a pass.

"Nice boat," Trump said. He hoped the compliment would motivate the "captain" to smooth the ride so he would not be hanging over the gunwales puking his guts into a fierce wind.

"So how long's it take? To get to Cuba?" Junior asked.

"An hour, hour and fifteen," "Captain" Kelly said. "She'll do 90 miles an hour. And don't worry. The Coast Guard, they got nothing this fast. Maybe a helicopter could catch us, but that's all. And to catch you they gotta be looking for you. And they won't be. Be dark before we get there, and they can't go after what they can't see."

Trump wondered how safe it was to be speeding across open ocean waters in the dark of night. He did not ask.

Trump glanced back at the stern. The six outboard motors were labeled Honda BF 250.

"You really oughtta be running this on American outboards, not rice-burners," he told the "captain." "You know what my bikers — and I have all the bikers — they love me, the bikers. You know what they say, the bikers, 'Better clap than ride jap.'"

"There are no outboard motors made on the American continent any more, Excellency. If there was, you'd see 'em there; I'd be using 'em. Give my left nut for six Evenrudes with this much power. But they stopped making 'em during Covid."

"Fucking Jiner," Trump said. "That's what's wrong with this country. Put me in charge of the whole thing and in a couple more years you wouldn't see a single Jap, German or Jinese car, outboard or TV in the country. We were on track to make America great again. Great."

"Dad?"

"Okay, okay. Let's get going." The "captain" turned a switch and the engines roared; they were so loud further conversation was impossible.

They had no luggage, but two WORMs hustled to load the only items they were taking with them: two banker boxes of classified documents that had been removed to his Bedminster golf club immediately before the 2022 FBI search warrant was executed at Mar-a-Lago. They were brought to Mar-a-Lago after the United States split up. They were his final bit of leverage with Putin; their price was luxurious sanctuary in Russia for the two Donalds and Eric, when he made his escape.

Trump's wife, Melania, and youngest son, Barron, were already there, living on an estate about 100 miles from Moscow. The property, once home to a noble Russian family, had been seized by the Bolsheviks, repurposed as a psychiatric clinic by the Soviets, then purchased and restored by an oligarch who was himself now deteriorating in a penal colony where Putin sent him after confiscating the place so he could host refugee VIPs there.

◆ ◆ ◆

Anyone who thinks my story is anywhere near over is sadly mistaken. — Donald J. Trump

Newscorp Headquarters, 1211 Avenue Of The Americas, New York, Atlantic States Of America

The Proprietor stared at the TV monitors playing silently on his credenza. All five had "Breaking News" banners across the bottom of the screen. All five had split screen images of anchors on the right and rolling video on the left. In the rolling video, a large man in golf clothes climbed into a black Suburban and the vehicle exploded; doors flew off, bringing down WORM bodyguards left and right; the roof split down the center; a fireball erupted.

When the Suburban settled down on its rims, the video repeated. Then repeated again. And again. Below the Breaking News banner, chyrons kept changing: "GSA's Trump Assassinated." "Car Bomb Kills Trump." "Trump Assassinated at Golf Resort." "Trump Blown Up, Killed." "Blast Kills Golfing Trump." "Assassination at Trump Golf Course." "SUV Blast Slays GSA's Trump." "Trump Dies in Vehicle Blast." "Bomb Takes Trump's Life."

Murdoch's intercom buzzed: "Tucker Carlson on the phone."

"Yes, Mr. President," The Proprietor said. "Or do I have to call you 'Your Excellecy?"

"Tucker will be fine, Boss. I'm in the vice-presidential office. Think it's a little unseemly to move into Mar-a-Lago just now."

"Will you be safe there; do you have bodyguards?"

With the GSA leadership under attack, The Proprietor was concerned about his investment.

"I've got a WORM contingent. They're loyal to me, I'm not worried about them. And Mike Flynn is coming over with some National Guard rangers. I'm okay. The Qanon bullshit didn't mention me at all. I'm good; safe."

"Mike Quinn? Don't trust him, Mr. President. He's a crackpot."

"I know, I know. But he's a useful crackpot at the moment. I'll get rid of him as soon as I can."

"If you need anything, Tuck... Mr. President. Feel free to call any time."

"I've called all five GSA Supreme Court justices. First one who responds and can get over here swears me in."

Unlike the other republics, where nine-member Supreme Courts were the rule, the GSA constitution stipulated a five-member supreme court, with justices appointed by the president. The five currently serving were former United States Supreme Court Justices: Clarence Thomas, Joseph Alito, Amy Comey Barrett, Brett Kavanaugh and Neil Gorsuch.

Carlson had called only four of them; he omitted Thomas. He thought the optics of being sworn in by a Black justice were bad; it would inspire ironic commentary from his critics and outrage from his fan base.

The Proprietor did not know that. He said, "Could be historic; you could be the first North American president sworn in by a Black justice or a female justice."

"Hoping Barrett gets back to me first," Carlson.

"Yes, that would be best," Murdoch said. "Fox News should cover it, no matter who it is."

"That's why I was calling. I'd like to offer the alma mater an exclusive on the swearing-in. There'll be a more formal inaugural ceremony, and everybody's got to be able to cover that. But for now…."

"I appreciate that, Mr. President. At the risk of appearing greedy, could we ask you a few questions when the swearing-in is over? Exclusive for Fox?"

"Of course, Boss. I'll sit for five minutes. But you've got to get someone here fast. Once a justice shows up, we're doing the oath. The country needs to have a sworn-in president as quickly as possible."

"Ann Bailey and her crew are at the golf course; I'll send them to your office. I'll send another crew, too. You want this covered by more than one camera, Mr. President, don't you?"

"Yes. Of course. Good. She's a good girl. I like her."

"She's badly shaken by the explosion, the assassination. She saw it. So please, understand."

"We're all shaken, Boss. I understand," Carlson said.

After he hung up, The Proprietor ordered Ann Bailey and two camera crews to the vice president's office. Then he called Walter Cholmondeley.

"I need you to write five to ten good, intelligent and probing questions for Tucker Carlson. We've got an exclusive for Fox with him right after he's sworn in. Think about the other properties, too. I want material for The Journal, The Post, The Times of London. But primary focus should be questions for Fox News."

"Am I doing this remotely? Am I going there? Where is he? Where is the swearing-in?"

"No, no, no. *You're* writing the questions. Ann Bailey's doing the interview. He's in his office in Palm Beach and he'll be sworn in as soon a justice gets there. He's giving us an exclusive on the swear-in and then he'll sit with Bailey for a few minutes. If I leave it to her, she'll ask him how it felt when he learned about the assassination, how it felt when he was sworn in as president, how it feels to have all this responsibility, how it feels to be the first Fox News veteran to become the president of a Republic. I don't give a flying fuck how Tucker Carlson feels about anything, but you and I know that's all that girl will ask him, so you write five or ten real questions, and we can just hope she asks them. I want to get something usable out of him."

"I think I should do the interview," Cholmondeley said.

The Proprietor got snippy, "Don't you go all prima donna on me. She's there and you're here. So just write the bloody questions for her."

Cholmondeley wrote the bloody questions. As a mischievous act of sabotage, the first question he wrote was, "How do you feel about becoming president because of President Trump's assassination."

It was the only one of Cholmondeley's ten questions the cheerleading slag asked.

◆ ◆ ◆

They say, "Trump said Putin's smart." I mean, he's taking over a country for two dollars' worth of sanctions. I'd say that's pretty smart. — Donald J. Trump

The Kremlin, Moscow, Russian Federation

Trump sat in the low ornate white and gilt armchair, leaning so far forward his shoulders were out beyond his knees. His hands were defensively clasped in front of his crotch — the classic CUPP position: Cover Up Private Parts. From what had seen in his high-speed tour, the Kremlin had more gilt paint and gold fittings than all Trump properties combined. Their unrestrained use would have caused an interior designer to smirk, but it made Trump jealous. Of course, Putin hadn't built the place, the way he, Trump, had built most of his signature properties. So the Kremlin reflected the taste and wealth of long-ago Russian aristocrats, commissars and autocrats much more than it did Putin's.

For fifteen minutes, he had been working his way through an extensive à la carte menu of grievances, boring Putin to a near-catatonic state.

Trump unburdened himself on the two elections he had not won, but claimed to have carried in landslides; about the animus he experienced at the hands of the media, Democrats, Blacks, Jews and academics; about greedy bankers who demanded he repay loans; about ungrateful women who had invited his advances and then accused him of abusing them; about Europeans, and about the ultimate turncoat, Q. For dessert, he selected the five state and federal criminal indictments handed down before the 2024 election:

"Those fuckers indicted me for crimes that didn't exist. The biggest coordinated witch hunt in the history of any country; in the history of the world. No one was ever indicted for more crimes they didn't commit than me. No one. They indicted me in Georgia. They indicted me in New York. They indicted me — the feds did — in Washington DC *and* in Florida *and* in Pennsylvania. And I never did any of it. Not a single crime. They never put me on trial. Never. If they had such strong cases, why didn't they put me on trial? Never went on trial. Never found guilty of a single thing. Never. And even if I would have been tried, I would have beat the raps. I didn't do it. And even if I'd been found guilty, do you think I would ever do a day of time? I would never, ever see the inside of a cell. And you know why? It's because I'm rich and rich guys, especially rich white guys — and I'm the richest white guy you'll ever meet, I can guarantee that — rich white guys don't go to prison. Not in America, they don't. The only time rich white guys go to prison is when they steal from other rich white guys. I never stole from any rich white guys. I never stole from poor white guys. I never stole from colored guys. I never stole. I was innocent and that's why they couldn't dare put me on trial.

"Now, Epstein, he was just stupid. What'd he do? Never stole anything. He would have gotten away with it, but he killed himself in jail. Maybe he killed himself; maybe he had help. Who knows. But he would have gotten off. What? Fucking a 17-and-a-half-year-old? *That's* a crime. Tell me about it; that's a crime. If she's legal in six months how is she not legal when he did it? Stupid law. But Jeff, he got depressed and hanged himself — unless someone did it for him. He would have beaten the case. Rich white guys don't go to prison...."

Putin knew exactly who Epstein was; a friend of Trump's who trafficked in underage girls and supplied them to his high-and-mighty friends. Epstein had been arrested and hanged himself while awaiting trial in a New York jail. The circumstances of his death were murky; a suicide under similar circumstances in Russia would not have been a suicide, so Putin suspected it was not one in America, either.

Putin was fed up listening to Trump's kvetching; he interrupted his guest: "In Russia, justice is blind, and we send rich — richest, even — to prison when they commit crime or take disloyal action. Plenty of millionaires — billionaires, even — in our prisons and in colonies."

He launched into what sounded like a televised address: "We Russians are last free and just generation of humanity. Where else you find such freedom? We are free from West's queer and transgenders. Their bad influence. Free from West's dissent and protest. Would we have windows broke, stores looted here? Never. We are free from that. Free."

Trump recalled windows broken, stores looted, fires set and government officials assassinated when Putin mobilized 300,000 "reservists" to fight in Ukraine in 2022. Determined to be a good guest, he said nothing.

"You know, my brother," Putin inclined his head toward Trump, "there are more homeless children in America than anywhere else in world? In entire world. That includes India and Africa. Afghanistan. More poverty in America than Afghanistan. We have records, we have data. We have analyzed data. On per-capita basis and on basis of absolute numbers, is true nowhere has poverty like America. Those are official statistics. Poverty on American continent is medieval. Like Europe in Dark Ages. Not even Somalia is as bad as republics of America."

Trump could not abide *his* republic being defamed alongside the others; he interrupted his host: "Not the GSA. We don't call it the Great States of America for nothing, you know. We live pretty good there. Pretty good. You won't find homeless in my country."

"Not because you put them in house," Putin said. "No, my brother, you arrest them and put them on bus and ship them to camps outside of towns or to nearest republic. You abandon them."

To Trump's discomfort, Putin was as well-informed about the homeless problem in the Great States of America as he was about everything else.

"Is Russian destiny to help America. Help it become what could be; should be. Help it be like Russia: free, Christian, straight, strong. Strong economy; strong military. Normal country raising children without gays and transgenders. In normal, classic way."

"You just described the Great States of America," Trump said. "And I can bring that sort of stability to the other republics. I can reunify the country. Mike Flynn, you know him; General Flynn, he has a plan. All he needs is eight brigades and air support."

For the first time since they had met, Putin laughed at Trump to his face.

"Eight brigades? Do you know how many men are in brigade? Five thousand, six thousand in combat brigade. He wants 40,000 soldiers? From me? I'm fighting war."

"No, no, no. Flynn can raise the troops in the GSA. He just needs air support and some heavy weapons; we don't have all we need. He'll take Arizona, Colorado and New Mexico, and then he'll invade California. He can talk you through it; he's got the specifics."

Putin laughed again. "No he won't. Does he think three republics will lie back and spread legs for him like prostitutka? They tear his eight brigades to shred. Air cover from the Russian Federation? I am in war. I need to deal with that Zhyd actor in Ukraine who don't know what is good for him and his country, not that Ukraine is country...."

Ukraine's stubborn and unrelenting resistance had badly damaged the unruly and undisciplined Russian military and cost the Russian Federation an acknowledged 100,000 casualties. If Russia acknowledged 100,000, it had suffered 300,000.

For years there had been a steady stream of zinc coffins out of Eastern Ukraine, a river of dead that branched out and reached every part of the Russia's vastness. Meanwhile, the Ukrainian president, the Zhyd comedic actor, had become the Winston Churchill of the 21st Century, praised and respected around the world for stopping the Russian bear in its tracks and for humiliating Putin.

"They had campaign of hatred against you, my brother. Even your ally, Q, turns against you. Maybe they reach him and buy him off. Maybe they kill him and put in imposter." Putin delivered that with a poker face; Trump had no clue that Q was a woman in the employ of his "brother," Vladimir Vladimirovich.

"You are fortunate you not get assassinated, Putin continued. "You see what happens to your double. Q has violent followers, we see that. This is bad scenario, there is history of political assassination in America: John Kennedy, Martin Luther King, attempts to kill Roosevelt, Reagan, Ford. Attempts to invade White House when you were there and when the chernyy, Obama, was there."

"Barack *Hussein* Obama," Trump said quickly. He wanted it on the record — or at least implanted in Putin's mind — that

Obama was a Muslim. Or at very least had a Muslim middle name. His Russian "brother" had had his own difficulties with Muslim dissidents, as had every Russian ruler since Ivan the Great in the 15th Century. Having a common foe was good bonding cement.

"I advise move on, my brother. Mr. Obama is no longer political opponent for you."

An FSB assassin, dressed in a formal waiter's livery, slipped into the room. He bowed slightly and spoke Russian to Putin. Putin asked him a question. The waiter responded with: "My proverili korobki, kotoryye prines etot tolstyy kloun. U nikh mnogo sekretnykh bumag. Nekotoryye iz nikh ustareli, no drugiye po-prezhnemu tsenny." Neither Trump nor Junior, who had been listening quietly, understood any Russian beyond Da, Nyet, and dobryy den, so they did not know the waiter had told Putin, "We have inspected the boxes this fat clown brought. They have a lot of secret papers. Some are outdated, but others are still valuable."

Nor did they understand Putin's response, "Khoroshiy. Idiot bol'she ne nuzhen. Sdelay eto," which meant, "Good. This idiot is no longer useful. Do it."

Putin turned to Trump: "He tell me that we have gotten several cases Diet Coke for you. We work around ridiculous sanctions to get it for you. Would you like one?"

"Sure would." Trump was pleased his host had had to pull strings, make an effort, take extraordinary steps to cater to him.

The FSB "waiter" stepped into the hall and retrieved an ornate serving cart on which there were half a dozen glasses one-third filled with ice cubes and a large glass bowl with more ice cubes and a dozen cans of Diet Coke. He wheeled the cart to Trump's left side and said, "Otkryt' duly vas banku, vase. prevoskhoditel'stvo?"

Putin translated: "He want to know if he should open the can or if you want do it, yourself. We know the American practice of opening a bottle or can in front of president. We do similar here."

"He can open it," Trump said.

The waiter understood that much English, maybe a lot more. Without waiting for Putin's translation, he pulled the tab and poured half the can's contents into a glass.

Secure because he'd heard the release of carbon dioxide when the can opened, Trump swallowed the glass of Diet Coke in one gulp. Instead of refilling Trump's glass from the open can, the waiter selected a fresh one from the bowl of ice. He popped the tab and poured.

"Bol'she l'da, prevoskhoditel'stvo?" the waiter asked.

Putin translated: "He want to know if you want more ice?"

"No, I'm okay. It's cold enough; this is enough ice."

"Yes," Putin said, "Enough ice."

The thallium, colorless and tasteless, was in the ice cubes, not in the cans of Cola.

It was not enough ice; Trump suffered through a sleepless night of unrelenting intestinal volcanism. A doctor was summoned to his suite shortly after 4 am. She was a stern, middle-aged woman named Marina Oskarova Korokovskya who had a medical degree but had never practiced medicine in the conventional manner. Instead, served her motherland as an FSB assassin, pharmaceutically dispatching persons inconvenient to Putin.

Even in extremis, Trump appraised her sexually and found her wanting, not his type. In shape and coloring she reminded him of one of his nemeses, Rosie O'Donnell.

Her English was more than adequate for her assignment. After a brief examination that involved no laying-on of hands, she said, "I giff you Prochlorperazine intravenous."

Instead, she injected him with the coup de grace — enough phenobarbital to kill a steer.

Minutes after Dr. Korokovskya confirmed the senior Trump was dead, another FSB assassin dispatched Junior with a single small caliber round to the back of his head. The shot made a terrible mess. The bedding, pillows and mattress had to be thrown out. As punishment for not garroting Junior, as he had been instructed, the assassin was reassigned to guard duty in a Siberian penal colony.

Before dawn, the cadavers of father and son were cremated and their ashes were dropped into a garbage receptacle on Tchaikovsky Street, not far from where the United States embassy had once been located. By 9 am they were in a garbage truck with 35 cubic meters of other rubbish, en route to the dump in the Aleksinsky Quarry, the scene a decade earlier of one of Russia's many environmental disasters. In the aftermath of the disaster, the area around the dump had been depopulated so there was no one to witness the solitary dump truck when it deposited its load of detritus.

EPILOG

Late in the afternoon of his swearing-in, President Tucker Carlson issued an executive order: all flags in the Great States of America were to be lowered to half-staff for 30 days in honor of the assassinated president. Government offices, except for law-enforcement agencies, were to be closed for the remainder of the week. Since it was a Thursday, this did not pose any undue hardship to the running the nation.

A state funeral for Trump would be held the following Saturday; meanwhile the charred remains of his body were to lie in state in a closed coffin in the lobby of Mar-a-Lago.

Florida Army National Guardsmen in dress uniforms stood at attention at the four corners of the white and gold leaf coffin. A steady stream of respectful visitors, nearly all of them white and elderly, some of them weeping, filed past for 16 hours a day paying their respects to Fat Jimmy Gibbons.

Visitors paid $15 per vehicle to park in the Mar-a-Lago lots, plus whatever tips they gave to the valet parkers. The club's restaurants remained open for breakfast, lunch and dinner and vendor carts set up in discreet corners of the lobby to sell mourners cold drinks, snacks and Trump memorabilia, including red "Make America Great Again" golf caps, tee shirts and coffee mugs with the late president's likeness on them and GSA flags with a ghostly image of Trump giving his thumbs up sign under the stars and bars. The viewing grossed Trump Enterprises $1,438,212.59.

*

Although invited to the funeral of their fellow president, Jon Stewart, J.D. Pritzker and Gavin Newsom declined to attend and sent their vice presidents instead, foiling Michael Flynn's plan to arrest or assassinate the three presidents and declare the country unified under President Carlson. Stewart, Pritzker and Newsom knew everything about Flynn's plan because Carlson had discussed it with Putin in a phone call over an unsecured line.

The vice presidents were permitted to travel unmolested, save for the boos and catcalls they endured from Trump acolytes when they entered and left the church where the memorial service was held.

The Trump funeral was full of pomp and ceremony. Rev. Franklin Graham delivered a fire-and-brimstone eulogy filled with innuendoes about the presidents of the three republics, assorted bankers and globalists who — everyone knew — were responsible for the car bomb that took The

Trump from his adoring followers. Q's revelation that Trump had died weeks earlier had been discredited by Q himself who reported it had been concocted by Ukrainian hackers who briefly took control of the one true Q's communications network.

The president's widow as well as his oldest and youngest sons were inexplicably absent from the funeral; no one knew where they were.

They were in Russia: Junior's ashes were in a plastic garbage bag under nine hundred kilos of trash in the Aleksinsky Quarry. Melania and Barron Trump were "guests of the citizens of the Russian Federation." In other words, under house arrest.

*

Javanka, Jared Kushner and Ivanka Trump, and their three children attended the funeral, as did Eric Trump and his family. The Kushner boys were persuaded to leave their yarmulkas home for the day out of respect for the Evangelical Christian funeral service and out of fear of what their grandfather's white supremacist cult followers would do if they saw such a Judaic display. As soon as the ceremony was over, Eric went to Mar-a-Lago, tallied the receipts, deposited them in a Swiss bank and caught a plane for New York, where the worst he faced were fraud charges, which were far less daunting than the murderous plotting of the GSA's executive branch.

The Javanka family removed itself even further. When the funeral ended, they drove directly to the Palm Beach airport and boarded a chartered jet that flew them to Israel, where they took up residence in a decidedly less-grand home. They hired ex-Mossad covert operators as a 24/7 security detail and never ventured out save in a convoy of armored vehicles. The security costs, upkeep on the home and loss of all their North American properties — confiscated for unpaid taxes or in satisfaction of civil fraud suits — led them to the brink of bankruptcy. Then Saudi Arabia demanded the return of its $2 billion investment in Jared's start-up hedge fund. Within two years of their having made Aliyah, they were reduced to life in a modest — for them — 1,000-square-meter four-bedroom apartment overlooking the beach in Tel Aviv.

*

Cholmondeley returned to the GSA a week after Amy Comey Barrett swore in Tucker Carlson, so he was on hand to cover the new president's formal inauguration four weeks later.

In his inauguration speech President Carlson pledged to continue the policies of his predecessor and role model, Donald Trump.

Even as Carlson spoke, National Guard soldiers in every state in the GSA were executing warrantless searches across the country. Their mission was to find and confiscate all weapons, whose possession was guaranteed all citizens by the constitution. Carlson had ordered the confiscation because he believed an unarmed restive citizenry was better than an armed restive citizenry.

Knowing Chief of Staff Mike Flynn would block that order, Carlson had Flynn arrested and detained the day before the Inauguration. Flynn was charged with involvement in the conspiracy to assassinate Trump.

*

As News Corp's Mar-a-Lago bureau chief Cholmondeley held a Class A credential and was given advance word on most GSA breaking stories. In his first big scoop, he reported that Eric Trump tried to triple the rent at Mar-a-Lago. President Carlson personally gave Cholmondeley the story as well as the follow-up: the GSA seized the property under its eminent domain laws. Carlson gave Cholmondeley a third-day angle on the story, too: the private club operation would end and all of Mar-a-Lago would be devoted to government offices and presidential living quarters.

Cholmondeley had an exclusive on the pre-Inauguration arrest and detention of Mike Flynn and was on hand with a Fox camera crew as the pajama-clad chief of staff was led out of his home at 2 am in handcuffs. He also exclusively covered the arrest and pre-legislative detention of Sidney Powell.

Cholmondeley wrote stories about Carlson's firing the rest of Trump's cabinet and the installation of new cabinet members. The fact that all the cabinet members were drawn from a list The Proprietor had submitted to Carlson was absent from his stories; no one shared that detail with him. He did write that all the new executive branch appointees were Fox News analysts, commentators or on-air personalities. That story failed to make air or print.

*

Carlson's new attorney general-designate was not a Fox News hireling, although he had been a regular presence on the network: Rudy Giuliani. Carlson rescued him from his golf cart in The Villages and installed him in DLO headquarters in the defunct J.C. Penney store.

Giuliani's first order as AG was to require all news reporting about the GSA government be submitted to DLO for content approval. The constitution Putin had written and Trump had altered did not guarantee freedom of the press, but it had no provision to permit the press to be censored, either. Giuliani and his son, Andrew, wrote a law authorizing Department of Law and Order censorship and submitted it on Mar-a-Lago letterhead to Congress for ratification. It passed unanimously without hearing, debate or revision.

When he saw the law, President Carlson was miffed Giuliani had not consulted him in advance but was pleased to have the power — which he wrested from the Department of Law and Order and assigned to the Mar-a-Lago press office.

*

The next morning, Cholmondeley went to his bank in West Palm Beach and wired the full amount in his account to his London bank. He took a taxi to the airport and bought a one-way first-class ticket to London. Enough! He'd had enough. He'd seen enough. He'd been paid enough. He was finished with this insane country. He hoped the BBC would welcome him home. It did.

*

Putin and Carlson had their first secure phone call the day after Cholmondeley returned to the safety and sanity of the BBC.

"About missile base in Texas," Putin said straightaway; not even a hello, how are you? Carlson was not surprised; charm was not Putin's strong suit.

"Not happening," Carlson said. The Proprietor thought that was a terrible idea; Carlson did, too.

"Oh? But Tucker, my brother, you made promise. You gave me word."

"My brother" cut no ice with Tucker Carlson: "Sorry but it can't happen."

"I have recording of conversation when we discuss it while Trump was president."

"Fake. It's fake and I'll have our intelligence and our law enforcement people *prove* it's fake."

"Very disappointing," Putin said.

"New regime, Mr. President."

"I prefer Excellency, like your Trump," Putin said.

"I know you do. If there's nothing else…."

"No," Putin said. "Nothing else."

*

Sofia Ivanova Pushkina recognized Putin's voice. "Pushkina," he said, "we have a problem that Q can solve."

"Of course, Vladimir Vladimirovich. Whatever you need."

"Q needs to convince Trump's cult that Tucker Carlson assassinated Trump, maybe he was in the Fifth Column Miller organized. Maybe he brought in the Ukrainian assassins who killed Trump. I don't know. Maybe his Ukrainians planted the bomb in the car. There are so many possibilities, thanks to you and your people. You can work it out?"

Anticipating Putin might sour on Carlson, she had laid the groundwork for such a campaign. It needed only slight revision and Putin's approval. She said in Russian and in English: "Ne problema. No problem."

###

APPENDIX

The Constitution of the Great States of America

Preamble:

We the People of the Great States of America, in order to form a perfect union, establish beautiful law and order, insure tranquil peace, provide for the common defense, promote life at every stage of development and secure the blessings of a God-loving Christian nation, do ordain and establish this Constitution for the Great States of America.

Article 1, The Presidency and Executive Branch

Article 1, Section 1

1. The executive Power shall be perfectly vested in a President of the Great States of America. He shall hold his office during the term of six years, and, together with the Vice President, chosen for the same term, be elected by a majority of votes cast (fifty percent [50%

+ 1 vote]) of those eligible and voting in the election. If no candidate for president, together with his choice of candidate for vice president, reaches a majority, the two candidates receiving the most votes shall face each other in a runoff election to be held no later than 60 days after the initial election. The candidate with the majority of votes cast (fifty percent [50% + 1 vote]) in the runoff shall be proclaimed President.

2. Election Day shall be the second Tuesday of the 11th month. Early voting is permitted in each state if authorized by the state legislature provided such voting begins no more than four weeks before the second Tuesday of the 11th month. Mail-in voting is prohibited except in circumstances of medical necessity, such necessity being validated by a signed and notarized attestation from a state-licensed physician or other, similarily-licensed health-care provider.

3. No person except a natural born citizen, or a citizen of one of the constituent states of the Great States of America at the time of the adoption of this beautiful constitution, shall be eligible for the office of President; neither shall any person be eligible for that office who shall not have attained the age of thirty-five years.

4. In case of a President's tragic death, unforeseeable resignation, or unexpected inability to discharge

the powers and duties of the presidential office perfectly, said powers shall devolve on the Vice President who shall serve to the end of the deceased, resigned or incapacitated President's term. In the event of the death, resignation, or inability to discharge the powers and duties of said office by both President and Vice President, said powers shall devolve on the Speaker of the Congress, who shall serve to the end of the former President and Vice President's term.

5. The president shall receive for his services, a beautiful compensation package, which may be increased but not diminished during the period for which he shall have been elected, and he may receive within that period other perfect emoluments from the Great States, from any of the beautiful individual states or from any foreign nation, domestic or foreign corporation, association or individual. He may also engage in commercial business as well as make investments in stocks, bonds, commodities and other financial instruments.

6. Before he enters on the execution of his office, he shall take the following oath or affirmation: "I do solemnly swear (or affirm) that I will faithfully execute the office of President of the Great States, and will to the best of my ability, preserve, protect and defend the Constitution of the Great States and serve the will of God."

Article 1, Section 2

1. The President shall be the Commander in Chief of the Army and Navy of the Great States of America, and of the beautiful National Guard of the several states and of private militias in the constituent states.

2. The President may require the opinion, in writing, of the principal officer in each of the executive departments, upon any subject relating to the duties of their respective offices.

3. The President shall have the power to introduce legislation to the Congress which, if ratified by a simple majority vote of the Congress (50% + 1 vote of those present and voting), shall become perfect binding law.

4. The President shall have the power to veto legislation passed by Congress; if such veto is exercised, the President shall have 30 days to introduce legislation bearing on the matter addressed in the vetoed legislation, which Congress must vote to accept or reject within 15 business days.

5. The President shall have the power to reverse decisions rendered by the Supreme Court when said decisions concern the constitutionality of legislation passed by Congress and signed by the President.

6. The President shall have sole power to dismiss or engage all cabinet department executives, who will serve at the President's pleasure.

7. The President shall have the power to dismiss for cause the governor, attorney general, secretary of state of any constituent state as well as officials in any state including, but not limited to judges, mayors, county executives, prosecutors, police chiefs, sheriffs, and justices of the peace within those states.

8. The President shall have the power to determine which levels, if any, of the federal workforce shall have civil service protections.

9. The President shall have power to make treaties, provided a simple majority of Congress (50% + 1 vote of those present and voting) ratify said treaty.

10. The President shall appoint ambassadors, other public ministers and consuls, judges of the supreme court and lesser courts, and all other officers of the Great States. He may seek advice and consent of the Congress in such appointments, but such advice and consent are not mandatory.

11. The President shall have power to fill all vacancies that may happen in the Congress, which

appointments shall expire at the end of the next session of Congress.

12. The President shall be the judge of the elections, returns and qualifications of members of Congress. He is authorized to compel the attendance of absent members of Congress, in such manner, and under such penalties as Congress may provide.

13. The President shall have the sole power to pardon and/or commute the prison sentence of and fines levied against any person convicted of a felony or misdemeanor by the Courts of the Great States of America. The President shall have the power to pardon and/or commute the prison sentences of and fines levied against any person convicted of a felony or misdemeanor by the Courts in any state of the Great States of America. The President shall have the power to override any pardon or relief of fines issued by any chief executive or governor of any constituent state for persons convicted of a felony or misdemeanor by a Court in said state.

14. It shall be a felony to defame, demean, libel, or slander the President of the Great States of America, the office of the President of the Great States of America, the Vice President of the Great States of America and any officials of the Great States

of America appointed by the President or Vice President of the Great States of America. Penalties for violation of this offense shall be enacted by the Congress.

15. The President may not be charged with a crime nor subject to civil lawsuit during his term in office.

16. The President may designate an official state religion and limit the number of adherents of other religions permitted to reside in the Great States of America. Should the number of adherents to an unofficial religion exceed the limit set by the President, the President may, at his sole discretion, deport however many such adherents he deems proper. Those being deported shall pay for travel from the Great States of America and their property and other tangible assets held within the Great States of America shall be forfeit to the Treasury of the Great States of America.

Article 1, Section 3

The President shall from time to time give to the Congress Information on the State of the Union and may adjourn Congress at any time he deems appropriate. Congress may not reassemble after such adjournment until the President summons it.

Article 1, Section 4

The Vice President and all civil officers of the Great States, shall be removed from office on impeachment for, and conviction of, treason, bribery, or other high crimes and misdemeanors. The President may not be impeached, charged or tried.

Article 2, The Legislative Branch

Article 2, Section 1

All legislative powers not assigned by the constitution to the President shall vested in a Congress of the Great States, which shall consist of a single chamber (Congress).

Article 2, Section 2

1. The Congress shall be composed of members chosen every fourth year by the people of the several states, and the representatives in each state shall have the qualifications requisite for election to the most numerous branch of the state legislature.

2. No person shall be a Congressperson who shall not have attained to the age of twenty-five years, and been an inhabitant of that state in which he shall be chosen.

3. Representation shall be apportioned equitably among the several states. The actual enumeration shall be made every ten years, in such manner as Congress shall by law direct. The number of Congresspersons shall not exceed one for every fifty thousand, but each State shall have at least one Congressperson. When vacancies happen in the representation from any state, the President is empowered to fill such vacancies, pursuant to Article 1, Section 2, Part 11.

4. The Congress shall chose their Speaker and other officers, subject to confirmation of those choices by the President.

5. Congress shall have sole power of impeachment for all federal offices, except the presidency.

Article 2, Section 3

1. The Times, Places and Manner of holding Elections for Congress, shall be prescribed in each state by the legislature thereof; but the Congress may at any time by Law make or alter such regulations.

2. The Congress shall assemble at least once in every year, such meeting to occur no later than the second Monday of every year.

Article 2, Section 4

1. A majority of members of Congress shall constitute a quorum to do business.

2. Congress may determine the rules of its proceedings, punish its members for disorderly behavior, and, with the concurrence of the President, expel a member.

3. Congress shall keep a journal of its proceedings, and from time to time publish the same, excepting such parts as may in their judgment or the judgment of the President require secrecy; and the votes of the members of Congress shall be entered in the Journal.

Article 2, Section 5

1. The Congresspersons shall receive a compensation for their services, to be ascertained by law, and paid out of the Treasury of the Great States. They shall in all cases, except treason, disloyalty, felony defamation of the Presidency or the sitting President and breach of the peace, be privileged from arrest during their attendance at the session of the Congress, and in going to and returning from the same. They shall be responsible under law for slander, libel, sedition and blasphemy contained in any speech or debate in

Congress and they may be questioned in any other place, court or legal forum for opinions expressed on the floor of Congress or elsewhere.

2. Representatives may, during the time for which they are elected, be appointed to any civil office under the authority of the Great States, which shall have been created, and may receive compensation for performance of said civil office.

Article 2, Section 6

1. All bills for raising revenue shall originate in the Executive Branch and be presented to Congress; but the Congress may propose or concur with amendments as on other bills.

2. Every bill which shall have passed the Congress, shall, before it become a law, be presented to the President of the United States; if he approve he shall sign it, but if he does not approve, he shall amend it or veto it.

Article 2, Section 7

1. The Congress shall have power to lay and collect taxes, duties, imposts and excises, to pay the debts and provide for the common defense and general welfare

of the Great States; but all duties, imposts and excises shall be uniform throughout the Great States;

2. To borrow money on the credit of the Great States;

3. To regulate commerce with foreign nations, and among the several states.

4. To coin money, stipulate the likeness of individuals on said coinage, regulate the value thereof, and fix the standard of weights and measures, but may not adopt the metric system;

5. To provide for the punishment of counterfeiting the securities and current coin of the Great States;

6. To establish post offices and post roads and determine whose likeness or image will appear on postage;

7. To promote the progress of science insofar as it encourages investment, jobs and economic expansion.

8. To promote useful arts, sciences and technologies, by securing for limited times to authors and inventors the exclusive right to their respective writings and discoveries;

9. To create tribunals inferior to the supreme court;

10. To raise and support armies;

11. To provide and maintain a navy;

12. To make rules for the government and regulation of the land and naval forces;

13. To provide funding and expertise for organizing and arming, the volunteer private militia;

14. To make all laws not initiated by the President which shall be necessary and proper for carrying into execution the foregoing powers, and all other powers vested by this constitution in the government of the Great States, or in any department or officer thereof.

15. The right to self-defense being basic to public safety, Congress shall make no law limiting or regulating the individual ownership, storing, handling, carrying or utilization of guns or other weapons, nor may any of the constituent states of the Great States make any such law. The right to ownership of firearms is inviolate and eternal.

Article 2, Section 8

1. Immigration being an economic, cultural and public safety emergency, Congress may vote to restrict any person or persons from any nation it designates from entering the Great States of America for whatsoever period it sees fit. Congress shall pass appropriate legislation to make unauthorized entry into the Great States a felony crime, punishable by not less than five nor more than 25 years imprisonment.

2. The privilege of the writ of habeas corpus shall not be suspended, unless, as determined by the President there is a case of rebellion or invasion or the public safety requires such suspension.

3. Persons may be held in detention pending passage of criminal legislation pertaining to their actions.

4. No tax or duty shall be laid on articles exported from any State.

5. No preference shall be given by any regulation of commerce or revenue to the ports of one state over those of another: nor shall vessels bound to, or from, one state, be obliged to enter, clear, or pay duties in another.

6. No money shall be drawn from the Treasury, but in consequence of appropriations made by law or made

by emergency stipulation by the President; and a regular statement and account of the receipts and expenditures of all public money shall be published from time to time.

7. No title of nobility shall be granted by the Great States: And no person except the President holding any office of profit or trust under them, shall, without the consent of the Congress, accept of any present, emolument, office, or title, of any kind whatever, from any president, prime minister, king, prince, or foreign nation.

Article 2, Section 10

1. No state shall enter into any treaty, alliance, or confederation; coin money; emit bills of credit; pass any bill of attainder, ex post facto law, or law impairing the obligation of contracts, or grant any title of nobility.

2. No state shall, without the consent of the Congress, lay any imposts or duties on imports or exports, except what may be absolutely necessary for executing its inspection laws: and the net produce of all duties and imposts, laid by any state on imports or exports, shall be for the use of the treasury of the Great States; and all such laws shall be subject to the revision and control of the Congress.

Article III, The Judiciary

Article 3, Section 1

The judicial power of the Great States, shall be vested in one Supreme Court, and in such inferior courts as the Congress may from time to time ordain and establish. The Supreme Court shall consist of five Justices. Appointment to the Supreme Court and to the inferior courts shall be upon nomination by the President. The judges, both Supreme and inferior courts, shall hold their offices during good behavior, and/or at the pleasure of the President, and shall, at stated times, receive for their services, a compensation, which shall not be diminished during their continuance in office.

Article 3, Section 2

1. The judicial Power shall extend to all cases, in law and equity, arising under this constitution, the laws of the Great States, and treaties made, or which shall be made, under their authority; to all cases affecting ambassadors, other public ministers and consuls; to all cases of admiralty and maritime jurisdiction; to controversies to which the Great States shall be a party; to controversies between two or more states; between citizens of different states, between citizens of the same state claiming lands under grants of different states, and between a state, or the citizens thereof, and foreign states, citizens or subjects.

2. In all cases affecting ambassadors, other public ministers and consuls, and those in which a state shall be party, the Supreme Court shall have original jurisdiction. In all the other cases before mentioned, the supreme court shall have appellate jurisdiction, both as to law and fact, with such exceptions, and under such regulations as the Congress shall make.

3. The Supreme Court shall not annul an act of Congress for violating this constitution. Only a presidential veto or a superseding Congressional law can void a law passed by Congress and signed by the President.

4. The trial of all crimes, except in cases of impeachment, shall be by jury; and such trial shall be held in the state where the said crimes shall have been committed; but when not committed within any state, the trial shall be at such place or places as the Congress may by law have directed.

Article 3, Section 3

1. Treason against the Great States of America shall consist only in levying war against it, issuing false and/or derogatory comments about it or its President; or in adhering to its enemies, giving them aid and comfort or violent demonstration against the established order. No person shall be convicted of treason unless on the testimony of one witness to the same overt act, or on confession in open court.

2. The Congress shall have power to declare the punishment of treason to include the forfeiture of the accused individuals' property and tangible assets.

Article IV States' Relations

Article 4, Section 1

Full faith and credit shall be given in each state to the public acts, records, and judicial proceedings of every other state. And the Congress may by general laws prescribe the manner in which such acts, records and proceedings shall be proved, and the effect thereof.

Article 4, Section 2

1. The citizens of each state shall be entitled to all privileges and immunities of citizens in the several states.

2. A person charged in any state with treason, felony, or other crime, who shall flee from justice, and be found in another state, shall on demand of the executive authority of the state from which he fled, be delivered up, to be removed to the state having jurisdiction of the crime.

3. In recognition of the concept that life begins at conception, no state shall permit the termination

of a pregnancy at any point in gestation following conception. No state may enact any laws permitting abortion for any reason, to include preserving the health or life of the pregnant person, eliminating possible suffering by an unviable fetus or avoiding birth defects.

4. A marriage is a religious and legal bond between a man and a woman. No other definition of marriage is recognized in the Great States of America and may not be recognized by any constituent state. Couples who do not meet this criterium whose unions are recognized as marriage in other nations, shall be considered co-habiting partners when traveling in or visiting the Great States of America and shall be subject to such co-habitation and sodomy laws as have been passed by the constituent states of the Great States of America.

Article 4, Section 3

1. New states may be admitted by the Congress into this union and states from other North American republics may apply for admittance to the Great States; but no new state shall be formed or erected within the jurisdiction of any other constituent state of the Great States of America. None of the original constituent states of the Great States of America may leave or apply to leave this union.

Article 4, Section 4

The Great States shall guarantee to every state in this union a republican form of government, and shall protect each of them against invasion; and on application of the legislature, or of the executive (when the legislature cannot be convened) against domestic violence.

Article V Mode of Amendment

Whenever two-thirds of the body shall deem it necessary, Congress shall propose amendments to this constitution, or, on the application of the legislatures of two thirds of the several states, shall call a convention for proposing amendments, which, in either case, shall be valid to all intents and purposes, as part of this constitution, when ratified by the legislatures of three fourths of the several states, or by conventions in three fourths thereof, as the one or the other mode of ratification may be proposed by the Congress.

Article VI Ratification of this Constitution

The ratification by the legislatures of the twenty-six states of the Great States of America, shall establish this constitution between the states so ratifying the same.

Done in convention by the perfect and unanimous consent of the states present the seventeenth day of September in the year of our Lord two thousand and twenty-five.

ABOUT THE AUTHOR

George Merlis

George Merlis was born in 1940 in Dothan, Alabama, the peanut capital of the world, to a family of tenant farmers/sharecroppers. His family lived the type of hardscrabble life that informs the work of so many American writers; his formative years marred by poverty, family abuse, alcoholism, drug addiction and petty crime.

Despite graduating at the bottom of his high school class, he was accepted at Yale with a full scholarship. He graduated with honors and attended the Iowa Writers' Workshop at the University of Iowa.

"Mine" is his second published novel and his sixth published book.

If you believe any of that, save for the book tally, you'll believe everything in this novel.

Printed in Great Britain
by Amazon